Mothering Sunday

Sara James

ORION

An Orion paperback

First published in Great Britain in 2021
by Orion Fiction
an imprint of The Orion Publishing Group Ltd
Carmelite House, 50 Victoria Embankment
London EC4Y 0DZ

An Hachette UK Company

1 3 5 7 9 10 8 6 4 2

A CIP catalogue record for this book is
available from the British Library.

ISBN (Mass Market Paperback) 978 1 3987 0409 1
ISBN (eBook) 978 1 3987 0410 7

Typeset by Born Group
Printed and bound in Great Britain by Clays Ltd, Elcograf S.p.A.

www.orionbooks.co.uk

Mothering Sunday

Sara James studied at St Martin's School of Art and went on to write for national papers and women's magazines. She also has an MA in creative writing from Sussex University. She is the director of bluepencilagency, an editorial consultancy working with both published and unpublished authors. She has four children and lives in London and Wiltshire.

'No daughter and mother ever live apart, no matter what the distance between them.'

Christie Watson, *Tiny Sunbirds, Far Away*.

For Joseph, Oliver, Freya and Sofia

Prologue

Mother's Day, 2019

Alexandra Abbott was late. She started to run towards the river, hugging pages of life drawings so that they crumpled and creased. Charcoal stained her hands, her camel coat, the pale blue mohair scarf a friend had gifted her, but there were more important things to worry about than sartorial scuffs. It was Mother's Day, her children had been arrested on a protest, *again*, and her mother, who was unbearably punctual always, was waiting at the Hayward Gallery, probably getting more agitated by the second.

'I can *do* your mother and I can *do* art but not both at the same time,' Rob had said that morning. 'Besides, I've got work to do.' Rob always had work to do but then they'd had the call announcing that Josh and Freya were being held at the police station. When Ally had called her mother to explain the reason for her grandchildren's absence, her mother had sounded relieved.

'Well, it's probably a good thing,' she'd said.

'How can it be a good thing? Our children have been arrested!'

'They won't charge them. At least they didn't last time,' her mother said. 'Shall we forget the exhibition?'

'How often do we get to see art together?'

Her mother sighed. 'You know it's not really my thing.'

'This was *your* idea, Mum!' Ally knew a visit to the gallery had been suggested for her sake but she could feel her day crumbling and was desperate to have some quality time with her mum.

And now she was late.

Circles of bubblegum blemished the pavement, a cyclist hummed past, a boat sounded its horn. London was bustling with a sense of purpose even though it was a weekend, the tall red buses chugging towards Waterloo Bridge, diesel fumes choking the air. This had always been her favourite London bridge; as a young girl she remembered running across it in that carefree manner that she'd lost somewhere along the line. She pulled the collar of her coat closed against a tunnel of wind, tucked her bobbed hair behind her ears and took a moment to take in the skyline: to her left the tall glass structures of the city pressed close to each other, a childish urgency about them as if toppling over each other, and to the right the Houses of Parliament and Big Ben, stately in comparison. As she walked across the bridge's wide girth, watching the river threading its way through London's centre like a lively worm, the force of it brimming against the concrete shoreline, she felt for an instant a youthful optimism, until she remembered Josh and Freya. They'd laid themselves down on Westminster Bridge in protest at the lack of political response to climate change. The two of them glued together with a whole load of other demonstrators, prone against a barrage of traffic. Her children behind bars, who would have thought it? Not once but twice. Extinction Rebellion had become a new religion in their house. What if this time they had to go to prison! Optimism and reality were incompatible Josh said. They were right – of course they were. Every young generation was right about the future because it belonged to them.

The thought forced Ally to march on, head down, the wind buffeting her towards Southbank. A part of her felt that she should be with Rob at the police station, but she rarely spent time with her mother and surely they didn't need both parents to fill in the various forms. Rob was always defensive on their behalf.

'It's not as if they're criminals,' he'd said. 'They care!' No doubt all four of them would be obliged to spread-eagle themselves against grubby concrete at the next protest, have their customary visit to the police station. Life had got so complicated.

Ahead of her was the Hayward Gallery, the cubist landmark unapologetic. In pink neon the exhibition was announced: The Americans. A retrospective. Josh said: 'How on earth could art be relevant against the tide of a dying planet?' but to Ally art was humanity's voice, it was an expression against whatever problems the world was facing.

She could see her mum by the entrance and a feeling of gratitude swept over her as she recognised her practical sturdy body patiently waiting, her short white hair wind-swept and her gloved hands clutching a holdall.

'You're late,' her mother said. Ally felt almost relieved to hear her predictable curt tone even though she was smiling.

'I can't help the fact the children have been arrested.'

Her mother rolled her eyes. 'What have you got there?'

'Happy Mother's Day.'

'What's this?'

'They're life drawings, Mum,' she said. 'My answer to a potentially empty nest.'

Her mother unrolled them and held them up. 'These are wonderful, Ally. Since when have you drawn nudes?'

'Started a class a couple of weeks ago.'

3

Ally always sensed disapproval when she showed her mother her art. Rob chastised her, said she was being oversensitive. But she had always felt apologetic for her interest. Her father had been a successful businessman, her mother had been his accountant and her brother taught physics in Perth. Art just wasn't part of the family identity and yet she had always been drawn to it.

'Well they're pretty good,' her mother said. 'I shall frame them and put them up in the bedroom.' Her mother's lips twitched into a smile. Maybe Rob was right, she'd been oversensitive. Her mother's approval meant a lot. She leaned forward and gave her mother a hug.

'Well, I'm glad you like them. Shall we go in?' She held out her arm and her mother smiled, her skin soft, her cheeks blushed by the crisp air.

They queued for the cloakroom. Her mother instructed the attendant to take great care of the drawings Ally had given her and even managed to persuade him to find an elastic band. Once inside, each of them gravitated to different paintings. Ally stood staring at a Rothko, over-whelmed by the awe-inspiring size of it. She turned to see her mother admiring a Pollock and felt instantly reassured to see she was at least enjoying herself. She walked up beside her, looped her hand inside her arm. The children – she must stop calling them that – will be fine, she thought.

'The gallery was a great idea, Mum. Thank you.'

'What about you? Your Mother's Day has certainly been eventful, if nothing else. Did you get a present or was saving the planet more important?

'They gave me a tree to plant to improve my footprint.' Her mother laughed.

'And Rob did his usual thing of presenting me with daffodil bulbs and some chocolates. Vegan chocolate this year.'

Her mother's face changed instantly, her jowls heavy. 'Why vegan?' she said.

'Let's not go there, Mum,' she said.

Her mother tutted. She was in that kind of mood.

Later, she found her standing in front of an expressionist painting. There was something so striking in the way a solitary red thickened blob ran down the canvas like a tear in a pool of blue, little rivulets of fine red spread like veins on a hand. She drew closer to see who the artist was and what it was called: *Loss*. 1963. Kitty Campbell. Not a name she was familiar with.

While she examined the large red blob, resisting the desire to reach out and touch it, her mother stared at her, that same frown deepening.

'Don't you like it?' Ally asked.

Her mother glanced at the painting. 'I suppose now is as good a time as any to tell you,' she said in her customary curt way that never failed to make Ally stand up straight. 'There's a reason I suggested this exhibition.' There was a worried glint in her eye. 'I should have told you long ago.'

'Told me what?'

'About Kitty Campbell.'

Ally felt the hairs on her arm stand up. 'Is she a friend of yours?'

'Ally, let's go and sit down.'

The gallery was getting busy, but then again it *was* Mothering Sunday. A Japanese couple were sitting on the end of the large leather bench. She and her mother went and sat on the other end. Ally waited while her mother rooted around in her bag and pulled out her handkerchief, dabbed her forehead with it before screwing it tightly into a balled fist.

'Ally, I should have told you this years ago,' she said again. 'There was a reason I didn't. When Antony was born everything was so . . .' she looked confused. 'Oh I just loved having the two of you. Life just took over, I suppose.'

'Mum, you're not making sense.' Ally reminded herself that her mother was old. Actually she looked much younger than a woman in her eighties and she'd happily hop on a plane to see Antony in Perth, stopping off at Singapore for a weekend's shopping. But this look was different. Ally realised in that instant she'd never seen her mother afraid before.

'It's not been easy, Ally. People make mistakes. I made a mistake and Kitty made one too.'

'Kitty Campbell?' Ally looked across at the painting, but the thickening group of heads and shuffling bodies meant she couldn't see a thing.

Her mother nodded. Ally's stomach knotted up but it wasn't just her mother's nerves, it was anxiety over what was going on at the police station. She looked at her mother, patted her arm. 'Tell me later, Mum. It's getting busy. Soon we won't be able to get a good view. And I'm worried about the kids, so we can't take all day.'

She stood up, picked out her phone and texted Rob to ask if there was any news. *Still here!* he replied. Ally felt overwhelmed with love for them all at the thought of them stuck in the police station while she was enjoying the gallery. She was proud of their moral compass even if it did mean they'd have a criminal record. Her mother saw her smile and she felt guilty then at having interrupted her mother's broken attempt to communicate something that was obviously important to her. She looked wounded and crumpled up on the bench. What on earth was her mother going on about? Could this be dementia? She didn't seem herself somehow, or was it Ally who wasn't feeling herself? These days – since the children were more independent – she'd felt it in waves. She didn't know who she was any more, although sometimes she wondered if she ever did know who she was. The human mind is a minefield, she thought.

She went up to the Basquiat, felt the distress screaming out of it, which she reasoned was possibly her own. The day was feeling muddied and she just wanted to resurrect that feeling of optimism she'd had on Waterloo Bridge. Should she have stayed with Rob and waited for the children? But Rob had been so insistent because he knew how she hated letting her mother down, and her mother was getting older and she knew the children would have hated the idea of their granny being alone.

It wasn't until they sat down to a cup of tea, both tired from absorbing all the art and chatter, and she saw her mother's dry lips twitching in anticipation, that the feeling of anxiety returned. Ally felt a desperate need to get going. It was all wrong, her not being there for Freya and Josh.

'Any news?' her mother asked.

Ally got out her phone. 'Nothing yet.'

She hoped her mother had forgotten the conversation about the artist, Kitty. She simply didn't have time for it. She felt a need to get everyone back home, eat some proper food, put on an old black-and-white movie and hunker down with her family.

'I can't leave without telling you,' her mother said.

'Telling me what?' Ally's heart sank. She was distracted by a small child who was tugging at her mother's sleeve so that it stretched over her fisted hand.

Her mum picked up the postcard she'd bought of Kitty Campbell's painting, her eyes filled with tears, wobbly and unsure. Ally could sense the emotion rising. She'd seen her mother cry over sentimental silly things, washing powder adverts or the John Lewis Christmas commercial but the only time she'd truly sensed the deep well of feeling inside her mother was on the day of her father's funeral, and even then she didn't break. The way her hand shook as she fingered the postcard worried her.

'This was painted the year you were born.'

'I saw that.'

'And you see the title: *Loss*. Well . . .' Her mum looked at her, a concentrated frown forming. 'That *loss* was you.' Her mother returned to the postcard. Ally felt herself tense up, as if anticipating a physical blow. Then her mother looked up. 'You see, Ally, Kitty Campbell is your mother, your biological mother.'

Ally felt as if she'd smacked right into a wall without seeing it first. She looked down at the postcard, suddenly transfixed by the little red dot. She felt her mother's hand around her wrist and understood in that moment something she'd always known or sensed.

'I'm sorry, Ally. I made a decision to tell you when the time was right, but the time was never right. But if you found out after I died, I'd never forgive myself.'

'Mum, don't say that.'

'Besides, I promised your father and I also promised Kitty. It's been on my mind for a very long time and it was your father's dying wish. I suppose I didn't want you to feel you were any different to Antony, to think you were less loved just because you were adopted. I'd read about children that felt abandoned or the odd one out and I didn't want that for you.' The words ran out of her. 'I've asked myself again and again why I didn't tell you before and I think I was scared you see. Scared you'd want her more than me.'

'Mum, stop!' Ally felt heavy. The need to belong, the feeling of wrongness she'd never quite understood suddenly made sense. The not fitting in, looking nothing like her parents or her brother, always feeling like an outsider to her own kin.

Her mother watched her with a childlike eagerness. Ally felt a wash of anger and wrapped her arms around herself. 'Isn't Antony adopted then?'

Her mother shook her head. 'I don't see you any differently.'

Ally turned away and looked out at the London skyline that had meant so much to her just a few hours earlier and now had no effect. She turned back to her mother and it was as if she didn't know her any more.

'I always thought I had Dad's nose and wished I had yours,' she said.

'A lot of children look nothing like their parents.'

'I know, but . . .'

'Do you remember a day on Brighton pier when you were young?'

Ally remembered the sea glistening, her mother's shoes. She'd fallen over in a funfair and remembered someone fussing over her, and how the music of the carousel whined on and on. It was her first memory, pretty much. 'I have a vague recollection. Why?'

'That was the day everything went too far.' She picked out her hanky from inside the sleeve of her cardigan, blew her nose, then looked again at Ally, her expression steadier for having offloaded. 'We never went back to Brighton for that very reason.'

Ally felt an odd sense of longing, a feeling she connected to that day. 'Does Kitty Campbell know you're telling me this now?'

Her mother shook her head, then nodded. 'She's waited a long time. It's my fault. Every now and again, she'd write and I'd ask for more time, but since your dad died I realise time's running out.'

'Don't say that, Mum.'

Her mother held her gaze, her eyes filled with pain. 'She's here, Ally. She's here in London. She called me last week and asked if she could see you.'

Ally looked around at the bustling energy of her surroundings and then back at the darkening skyline. She could see a faint reflection of herself like a phantom and then it disappeared and the outside appeared once again.

'You see she's desperate,' her mother said. 'And I feel it's my fault.'

'I need to go and help Rob. I don't like to leave him dealing with this on his own.' Ally leaned forward, reached out for her mother's hand, but her mother pulled it away.

'Are you listening?'

'I haven't had time to absorb it all, Mum. I need time. I . . . I . . .' But the words didn't come because she knew in that moment that some part of her wanted to meet this woman and at the same time she felt overwhelmed by a sense of rejection she didn't even understand, not from Kitty but from her mother who seemed suddenly willing to give her up. It seemed childish, but the feeling of oddness she'd grown up with, not understanding why she felt like the outsider was suddenly overwhelming. Right now she wanted her mum, the woman that was sitting opposite her, to be her real mum and for all of this to be a lie.

She had a sudden urge to be with her children.

'I have to go, Mum.' She hadn't finished her tea or even touched her cake.

'This doesn't change anything,' her mother said.

'How can it not?'

'I love you, Alexandra. We both loved you, but it was Kitty who had to make the sacrifice.'

Ally thought about the red splodge of paint, the thick texture of it, knobbly and rippled, and was aware of a lump forming in her throat. Odd, she thought, to empathise with a stranger.

Her mother took out an envelope from her handbag. 'I thought you'd want to see these. This is Kitty when she was young,' she said, tapping the envelope. 'With you. I took them on Brighton pier that day. There are others too.'

Ally was seized with a desire to look at the photographs but she knew that once she'd seen them it would be harder to ignore. She could just grasp a memory of a hand, of her head pulled towards an itchy cardigan, of a deep feeling of loss, yes 'loss', that was it. She felt herself redden with a shame that wasn't hers.

'I have to go. I need to think about this.'

'It can't wait.'

'Mum, you can't say that! Not after waiting a lifetime to tell me the truth. Can't you see how hard this is for me to take in. You're not my mother!'

'I didn't say that.' Her mouth trembled. 'I said I wasn't your biological mother.'

'Mum, I just can't handle this right now.'

Ally stood up quickly. The chair fell to the floor with a crash. Heads turned towards the commotion. She picked it up, unable to look at her mother. She wrapped her scarf around her neck, noticed the charcoal stains, but didn't bother to brush them away. She saw the exit and without another word hurried towards it, knocking over a pile of books on the way, knowing her mother would be ashamed of the spectacle. Never in her life had she cut her mother dead. She found herself bumping into people, unable to find a clear path. It wasn't until she was outside and had walked down to stare at the river that she allowed herself to cry.

She watched the tourist boats, the flock of people on the bank opposite, all of it blurred by tears, the slosh of the water sounding underneath her. Seagulls hovered and screeched above the Thames. She'd never seen seagulls this far inland before. She couldn't seem to collect her thoughts and then the memory returned of her suffocating inside a woman's embrace, the sea sparkling, the constant rush of the waves pushing onto the shore and a terrible feeling of sadness. Now she thought about it, the melancholy had never truly left her. Why had Kitty abandoned her? She remembered her own children at that age. She'd been so absorbed by their bodies, fearful that she might lose them. How could a mother just give her child away? She caught sight of the little girl who had pulled her mother's sleeve upstairs in the tea room. The girl was sucking her thumb, staring at her. Ally smiled, but the girl buried her face into her mother's legs. She must look a mess, she thought, her face all ruddy and flushed with emotion. Her mother would be in a similar state. She couldn't just leave her, there was so much more she needed to know. She turned and threaded her way back through the crowds to find her mother sitting with her hands in her lap, the cake uneaten. She was staring vacantly into the room and it clearly took her a while to register it was Ally walking towards her.

'Are you feeling any better?' her mother asked.

'I feel completely lost.'

'I know, dear. I know.'

'I need to know why she left me, Mum.'

Her mum pushed the envelope towards her. 'Many women had to give up their children at that time because they were unmarried, but Kitty's story was even more complicated.'

Ally wanted so desperately to see those photographs, but she was frightened. Her heart started to drum inside her chest, an odd feeling of prescience floating about her, or was it déjà vu? Ally slipped out the pictures with shaking hands, the well of anxiety growing. The restaurant was still buzzing and she was aware of the long queue of people waiting for tables.

'You looked a lot like her when you were that age, different colouring, but there were similarities,' her mother said, her voice trembling.

The photograph was black-and-white with cream crinkled edges: a snap taken of her on the pier with this woman, Kitty Campbell. The sea glistening in the background, the helter skelter a beacon behind them. Her own tight smile looked back at her now, stiffly holding Kitty Campbell's hand. It was true, Ally did look similar, but the resemblance between her and Freya was far more striking, and for some reason it was this small simple fact of genetics that made her cry in front of her mother.

'She looks like Freya.'

Her mother nodded, digging around in her handbag for a tissue which she handed to Ally. 'I'm so sorry, Ally,' she said.

'What about my biological father? I take it Dad's not . . .'

'No.' Her mother picked up her spoon, carved a well into the sugar bowl. 'That's the part of the story that's complicated.'

Ally sighed, a weight settling inside her. 'I have always felt like the odd one out and this explains why. My whole

13

life I've been thinking there was something wrong with me, that this feeling was self-indulgent and I was mad.'

Her mother reached across for her hand. 'Ally, your mother has been so desperate to see you.'

'You're my mother, Mum. You were there for me. She abandoned me, why would I want to meet her now?'

'Ally, you know well enough that motherhood is never that simple.'

Ally felt her phone vibrating in her pocket. Outside the sky was darkening, stained with orange street lamps. She plucked the phone out of her pocket. *We're out*, Rob said. *No charge.*

She felt a wave of appreciation for her mother's wisdom. She leaned forward and patted her arm. 'You were right; they didn't charge them.' But her mother didn't smile. Ally felt a weight descend, the memory in Brighton pushing for attention, a feeling of loss she didn't understand that had followed her about, through her childhood and into her adult years. She actually believed there was something wrong with her.

'In a way I've always known – often felt this sense of rejection and I need to know why. Why did she abandon me, Mum? I need to know.'

Her mother nodded.

'Do *you* want me to meet her?' Ally asked. That's when she saw the grief her mother had carried. The pain registered on her face.

'It's not up to me,' her mother said. 'Let me tell you the story. Then you can decide.'

PART ONE

—

April 1963

ONE

When she was anxious, Kitty Campbell dreamed of spiders, imagining them as big as a baby's fist, crawling up inside her nighty or striding across her pillow to climb into her mouth. It was April, not exactly spider season. While she waited for the doctor, she found herself scanning the room to see if there were any hidden in the corners, the thrum of the clinic about her, the tinkling of metal tools giving her the shivers. The doctor was due to take her stitches out and the memory of Alexandra's birth was already faint. Just the sight of her small bloodied body as they pulled her free remained imprinted.

Morning light leaked into the room, the neon inside the surgery brash in comparison. A member of staff bellowed out orders in the hallway. 'Please *do* get a move on.' The patter of footsteps followed, and then the shocking sound of someone retching. 'Fetch a bucket. Quickly!'

Kitty's legs were scissor wide, pools of sweat collected under her arms and the stiff hospital gown creased around her flaccid belly itched.

The nurse bent down, whispered into her ear. 'Sorry, the doctor's been delayed. Monday is always difficult.' She squeezed Kitty's hand. It was all it took to disarm Kitty, a gravelly saltiness collecting at the back of her throat. Alexandra had been born two weeks ago on Sunday. She had such little time left.

'Sister James hasn't taken Alexandra yet has she?' Her hand was clasped around the nurse's wrist. 'I was meant to have five minutes.'

The nurse smiled and placed Kitty's hand back on the bed. 'I've not been told the details. It's usually the mothers who take the babies over to the Crusade, isn't it?'

Kitty nodded, not wanting to explain how her own mother had intervened. How protocol wasn't something the Campbells adhered to.

The doctor arrived, hunched and weary, dragging with him whatever previous experience had left him harassed, entering through the swing doors so that the sound of them closing ricocheted through the clinic. The nurses fluttered into action as he held out his hands, disinterested as one of the women gloved them. Then, pushing his glasses back onto the bridge of his nose with his forearm, the doctor turned.

He didn't look at Kitty, not into her eyes anyway. His tongue slipped out of his mouth like a small wet grub. A thin film of sweat beaded on his top lip. *He might as well be tinkering with his train set*, she thought.

'Try to relax,' he said.

Kitty would have thought it funny in normal circumstances. Closing her eyes, she listened to rain falling. She pictured Alexandra in the row of bassinets, always quiet, her head tilted to one side, unaware that her mother was going to disappear and that her own life was in the hands of the gods. Months of Alexandra pressing Kitty's insides up then down and she hadn't been able to imagine this, hadn't understood the loss. Her brother, Tom, would get to keep his child, due any minute, might even be born already for all she knew. Her thoughts drifted to Henry and a hot summer's evening, a moment in the boat house, the moss that covered the stone steps, the gaping darkness of the lake below.

She tried to imagine Sister James handing Alexandra – her baby – over to someone else, reminding herself over and over that there was no choice. Her mother's parting words before leaving for Kenya, a mantra: 'It's for the best.' Her heart was thumping at the prospect of her daughter's absence. She could feel the throb of it like a big hollow drum.

The doctor stepped back, ripped off his gloves, dropped them into the bin.

'All done.'

Back in the dorm Kitty sat on the edge of the bed fingering the green eiderdown, touching her hair, brittle from the last spurt of lacquer. Angela, one of the girls in her dorm, had dropped by to say goodbye.

'You will write, won't you?' she said. Angela was two weeks overdue but was still expected to do her duties: cleaning, bottle washing, laundry. Kitty could see the pain in Angela's eyes, knew that her friend was feeling the loss of her own child that hadn't even been born yet.

'Oh, Kitty. It will get better, I promise.'

'Will it?' Kitty asked.

'They say it does.'

Kitty found herself wondering if the car would start and whether the starter handle was in the boot.

'You have five minutes,' Sister James said, fixing Kitty with her grey eyes. Nurse Wilmot was at her side holding Alexandra wrapped up in a hospital blanket. The sight of her fingers curling from underneath its frayed edges made Kitty's stomach clench.

'Angela, you're on bottle duty,' Sister James said.

Angela stooped to hug Kitty. 'I'm sure her new parents will love her, she's a beautiful girl.' She squeezed Kitty's hand. 'Good luck.' Angela smiled and then left, nodding at Sister James. Kitty would probably never see Angela again.

'You'll need to sign the final papers. Twice you've been asked to do so. Your mother won't be happy if she finds out you've failed to jump through the necessary hoops.'

'I'll do it straight after I've said my goodbyes, Sister.'

Sister James nodded. 'Well you won't be able to leave until you do.'

Nurse Wilmot handed Alexandra over.

'Thank you.'

Kitty dipped down to catch Alexandra's milky breath, closed her eyes, wanting the imprint, the memory of her daughter's face to stick. Normally it was the mother's duty to deliver the child to the offices of the Crusade a few streets across, but Kitty had been told that Sister James would be taking Alexandra to meet her new parents later that afternoon after they'd been in to sign the papers. This was obviously Kitty's mother's doing. Against that Kitty was powerless.

Her mother, Clarissa, had been to visit a week before Alexandra was born. Sister James had escorted them both into the office, all smiles and reverence. Clarissa had worn a sober grey suit, her hair neatly pinned into a pleat. Kitty could smell her mother's Chanel perfume and the faint trace of tobacco. Sister James left them alone sitting opposite each other with a tray of biscuits and a pot of coffee. Her mother poured them both a cup, adding cream afterwards.

'I'm off to Kenya next week. There's been a fire. Your father thinks it's arson. Poor Adamu has suffered severe burns. I need to show support to his wife and family. Your father can't handle this alone so Tom and I are accompanying him.'

'Tom is going? What about Anne?' Kitty couldn't believe that her mother was disappearing at a time like this. Tom's wife, Anne, was due to give birth as well.

'Anne's got a few weeks to go, which makes sense if you count back to their honeymoon.' This was a deliberate dig at Kitty's own pregnancy, a child conceived out of wedlock. Her mother was making a fuss mopping up a drop of coffee. Finally, she looked up and smiled.

'Anyway, I thought I'd better visit beforehand as it's unlikely I'll be able to get back in time to pick you up. You have the car of course.'

'Yes, thank you.'

'So, how are you feeling?' Clarissa asked.

Kitty knew there was no point in expressing her distress. 'The girls are making bets on a boy,' she said.

'Really,' Clarissa said. 'Well it hardly matters now does it?'

'Most people prefer a boy,' Kitty said.

Clarissa looked out of the window. 'Gosh, is that a chaffinch in the garden?'

Kitty bit her lip until it hurt.

'I do believe it is, and in London,' Clarissa said. She turned to face Kitty. 'I've asked Sister James for you to be released early. I think it will make it easier for you.'

'I can feel him kicking,' Kitty said.

'Kitty, you need to think what's best for the child. Isn't it enough that he or she is illegitimate, let alone the father running off with another woman. After all we've done for him. It isn't fair, not really. And what future could you offer the child? Your duty is to your family and this child.'

'Have you heard from Henry?'

'Henry has been offered a permanent job in America. I would have thought he'd told you about that. As I said, he's seeing someone in Boston, so I really wouldn't give him a second thought. He's not worth it.' Clarissa picked at an invisible fleck on her skirt. 'You haven't told him about the baby, have you?'

Kitty shook her head. The tears dropped into her lap. Her mother leaned forward and patted her knee. 'Kitty, sweet Kitty. You need to do what's best for everyone concerned. You know that, don't you?'

Kitty nodded.

'Good.' She sat back. 'Biscuit?' Clarissa handed the plate to Kitty. Kitty picked up a digestive.

Kitty looked up from her reverie, the memory of her mother's expression as she left that day sticking like sap. Sister James was walking away, the click of her heels precise against the tiled floor. Once at the doorway she turned. 'The taxi will be here in fifteen minutes. I'd put your coat on. You're not to keep the driver waiting.'

To Nurse Wilmot, Sister James said. 'Make sure you escort Miss Kitty to my office before she goes.'

'Yes, Sister.'

Kitty hadn't asked for a taxi, but she was expected to follow procedure. She'd tell the driver to take her to the end of the road where the Morris had been parked for several weeks.

The familiar infant cries echoed in the nursery across the way. Alexandra's eyelids fluttered, her head rolled to the side, searching for her mother's nipple.

A couple had been found: nice people, churchgoers. Kitty's mother Clarissa had stipulated right at the beginning that the process was to be over as quickly as possible. Kitty would not complete the regular eight weeks, and she should not be allowed to name the child. But secretly she had called her daughter Alexandra.

The nurse was retying her pinafore, tugging at the straps.

'Will you make sure Angela knows what to do on her next feed?'

'I'm off at two, but Angela is quite capable. She'll have to learn. As will her new mother.'

Kitty didn't want to contradict, say anything about a mother's instinct. She'd forgone that right. 'I do hope she takes it.'

'She'll take it if she's hungry enough.' The nurse gathered up the bed linen Kitty had carefully folded.

'Can we be alone?' Kitty ran the back of her hand across Alexandra's cheek.

Nurse Wilmot had the sheets hugged close to her chest. 'You know I can't do that,' she said, her voice softening.

'It's just that I have such a terrible headache after the doctor took out the stitches. I'd be very grateful if you fetched me an aspirin before I go,' Kitty said.

Nurse Wilmot shook her head, tut-tutting, a shadow of compassion in her eyes. 'I'll see what I can do, but Sister will be cross if the taxi is kept waiting.'

Kitty knew Nurse Wilmot would have to walk to the end of the corridor, climb two flights of stairs to the store cupboard, write it all down in the pharmaceutical log book. It would take her ten minutes at the very least. The taxi would have to wait. She took Alexandra to the window, showed her the big plane trees, the daffodils laced around the mossy protruding roots. Further into the back garden she could see the gardener stooped over the damp earth, his hands at work with a trowel. A woodpigeon cooed from the budding branches. London pulsated in the distance. It had stopped raining and there was enough blue sky to make a pair of sailor's trousers.

'You'll love the world,' she said, kissing Alexandra's cheek.

Outside, a young girl crossed the road wheeling a bicycle uphill. In the fresh light of spring, Kitty saw the possibility of living another life. The thought she might never see Alexandra again, know her as a girl, a young woman pushing a bicycle, throbbed like a physical ache. Holding Alexandra in one arm she pulled the window up a fraction. The smell of grass and foliage made her long to be out there, to take a paintbrush or a piece of charcoal and draw. She yanked the sash window up further so that the net curtains floated back across their faces. Dipping under the white veil she stuck her head out, wanting Alexandra to smell the sharp tang of spring. The drainpipe was ringing with the sound of dripping rainwater. Alexandra stirred, her eyes flickered open. The gardener was wheeling the laden barrow towards the shed, his body hunched inside a stained raincoat. It had been the most appalling winter – sixty-two days of snow so that even London came to a halt. People were ice-skating on the Heath and on the news she'd seen people actually walking on the Thames. Kitty and the girls had made snowmen but their playfulness waned after weeks and weeks of it. But now the garden was showing signs of life and colour.

She noticed a Rover drive through the gate and park. A man got out and ran round to let his wife out of the door. Something about the couple made her shiver. Supposing this was them. The woman climbed out of the car, adjusting her coat. She patted her hat into place before she took hold of her husband's arm with a stately gesture. She looked just like someone her mother would approve of. They walked towards the main building. Kitty didn't like the look of her at all.

The gate was still open, the ground just two feet below. A quick twist of her feet over the window ledge offered freedom. She checked the time. Seven minutes gone.

She looked at Alexandra, her face freckled with white pimples, her mouth perfect. Kitty ducked back inside and crossed the room. The clanging of a steel bucket as it dropped to the floor made her jump. She laid Alexandra on the bed, flicked open the safety catches of her suitcase. She picked up a notebook full of sketches she'd drawn of Alexandra sleeping, drawings of her hands, her lips, her ears – the pages crinkled with the weight of the lead on paper – and a Polaroid Angela had taken of her with Alexandra. She tucked them all in the folds of her clothes, took a deep breath, stuffed a spare napkin on top, along with a jar of Sudocrem and a safety pin, then popped the case outside onto the patch of grass underneath the window. Hooking her handbag in the crook of her arm she scooped Alexandra up and slipped one foot over the sill, hugging her daughter tight. Alexandra croaked. She could feel her short breaths of panic as she bent down to retrieve the suitcase.

'Hush, now. It's for the best.'

She was twenty-five yards from the front gate and in normal circumstances it would seem like no distance at all.

'Excuse me, miss,' the gardener cried out.

Kitty started to trot, careful to keep Alexandra concealed. Her shoes slopped about where they'd stretched in the last month of pregnancy. She couldn't seem to move her feet fast enough. The Morris was parked at the end of the road and she wished to God she'd had the foresight to find her keys first.

'Hello there!' the gardener shouted. 'You can't just jump out of the window. There's a door, you know!'

Twenty paces and she would be through the gate. A morsel of gravel from the driveway bit into the arch of her foot.

'Oi. Where do you think you're going?'

The taxi pulled into the driveway. Kitty scuttled past it. She had no idea where she was going to go.

25

TWO

Elisabeth Abbott made the fire so the parlour lost its chill. She folded the sheets of newspaper, tied them into a knot, poking the firelighters into the far reach of the grate, nestling pieces of coal until she'd made a neat mound. She struck the match, lit the paper, watched as it flickered before lifting the dead match to her nose to smell the ammonium phosphate. Then she unfolded another broadsheet, held it flat to the fireplace so the fire would draw.

Purley offered another wet Monday but she couldn't let that dampen her spirits. For the first time in months she was hopeful, perhaps because at the end of the week they were moving house. Much as she loved their two-up two-down, too much had happened there and she was ready for change. She could hear her husband Samuel bustling about upstairs. There was a purpose to his movements which she knew meant he had something to tell her. Probably the car dealership looked like a real possibility, or the grocer's was making a tidy profit. She knew it was doing better than the tea shop; well, they both knew the tea shop was just there to keep her busy.

They'd tried to conceive again – God knows the neighbours must have talked, the amount of trying that went on – but with no success. Since losing Johnny to influenza, Bet Abbott's body failed to embrace the possibility of new life. They strived to forget, but there was no forgetting the wanting as far as Sam was concerned.

26

She went into the kitchen to fetch a pot of tea, laying out a plate of cheese scones she'd baked that morning ready for the tea shop and lining a tray with linen. As she passed the stairs she called up.

'There's warm scones if you fancy.'

Sam didn't answer but she heard him step across the bedroom, knowing that he would brush down his trousers with a clothes brush before descending the stairs. The fire was raging, the room already warming up. Sam walked in, his eyes darting to the tray of scones before he sat down in the armchair opposite, straightening the antimacassar.

'You need to get yourself into the shop,' he said.

'I'm aware of the hour.'

She turned to face the fire. She'd grown fat and she was conscious of the fact that Sam didn't like it. He'd commented a couple of times at the tightness of her clothes. The knuckles on her fingers seemed unnaturally large, her ankles bloated. She saw the reflection of the flames dance in the window behind them and went to open it a crack to rid the room of its stuffy mothball smell.

'A lot of fuss over a cuppa,' Sam said.

'You've a hard day ahead of you.'

'I've only just had breakfast.'

'I've been thinking about what you said last night and . . .' She didn't know how to soften the blow. 'I'm not going to change my mind.'

Samuel leaned forward, put his hand on hers. 'We're not getting any younger, that's all.'

'We're not *that* old,' Bet said. But she knew in part he was right. She was twenty-eight but Sam was thirty-four. She'd looked at other mothers in the street and thought how young they looked; innocent faces that didn't bear the signs of loss that hers did.

'More importantly we'll be giving a nipper a home.'

'But the baby won't be ours. We can't replace Johnny, Sam.'

'I think it will make no difference once you've seen him.'

'Him?'

'I thought if we adopted a boy, it'd be easier.'

'Not a boy. I couldn't. Adoption isn't for me.'

Not being able to conceive another was difficult enough, but losing a child and watching friends' children of the same age grow up healthy was hard for both of them. Samuel often made excuses to avoid the company of friends with children, crossed the road if he saw a pram. Johnny, their son would be six by now. Bet would never lose the image of that small coffin. She woke up to it every morning. She could never love anyone in the way she loved Johnny. She felt guilty leaving the memory of him behind. The house was his home, and they'd had happy times before he was ill, but she needed to start afresh and besides, the house in Mitcham had a garden.

'I can't imagine what it feels like to give a child up voluntarily,' Bet said, swilling the pot.

'Well if there's no father around . . .' Sam said.

Bet was pouring the tea, she looked up at the clock. 'Shouldn't you be at the shop?'

'Jack's filling in. I told you. I'm seeing the bank manager about the loan for the car dealership.' He picked up a scone, cut it in half, buttering one half and handing it to her.'

'I'm really not hungry,' Bet said. When she'd looked in the mirror that morning she'd hardly recognised herself. She'd been slim as a girl. She blamed the grief. Grief makes you hungry.

'I ought to get going, I suppose.'

The telephone rang.

'I'll get that,' Bet said. She was expecting the brash tone of Jack's voice, one of Samuel's work colleagues.

'Mrs Abbott, it's Peter Clark from the Crusade of Rescue and Homes for Destitute Catholic Children.'

Bet ran her finger around the edge of the telephone table, noticing how the polish had dulled off. 'I can offer you an appointment next Monday,' he said.

'I think you have the wrong number,' Bet said.

'Who was that?' Sam asked, his mouth full.

'Wrong number. Why don't you take some of these scones into the shop?' she said. 'I've got plenty.' She didn't want to adopt and that was that. She put the wireless on, hoping to listen to the news while washing up.

She missed her boy. How could anyone replace him?

THREE

Kitty stalled at the traffic lights, pulled the choke all the way out and tried to start the car again. The Morris spluttered, coughed, then stopped. She'd wrenched the cable too far. Hardly surprising under the circumstances. The windscreen wipers struggled against a fresh onslaught of rain. The seats smelt of mould from the car having been parked in the wet for weeks. Alexandra was whimpering. What the hell had she done? If it hadn't been for Alexandra she'd have opened the window, let the smell of rain fill her with hope. Her mother was right: keeping her daughter was irresponsible. *She'll be known as the Campbell bastard.* She wondered if the mother and baby home would call the police.

She thought back to the night of Tom's wedding. A marquee had been erected in the garden. Tables were draped in white and laced with ivy. Large vases of lilies were stationed about the house filling the place with their perfume. Clarissa was in her element organising everyone, but Kitty felt distanced from all of it. Months in London had given her hope for another life. She hated Beecham.

After the wedding breakfast, she'd changed into a green silk ball gown and descended the stairs for the final round of socialising.

'Kitty, darling, you look absolutely splendid.' Georgie, her closest friend from art college, took hold of her arm.

Georgie was wearing a short lacy black dress. 'I can't believe your darling brother is married to such a plain Jane.'

'It was supposed to be black tie,' Kitty said, tugging at her friend's dress.

'This is as black tie as I go, I'm afraid.'

'And don't be rude about Anne.'

Georgie rolled her eyes. 'Where can one get a drink around here?'

Kitty pointed to the rows of champagne glasses.

'Have you lost *all* your marbles? I was being ironic.' Georgie held open her handbag and showed Kitty a packet of Players and a miniature bottle of gin.

'That's like bringing coals to Newcastle,' Kitty said.

Henry looked at them both from across the room and for a minute Kitty thought he was going to raise his eyebrows or laugh, but he didn't. She had the feeling that everyone could sense their attraction, as if it were a tangible thing. She strode across the dance floor, caught her mother watching her but ignored it.

'You don't appear to be having fun?' She took his glass and sipped from it before handing it back. 'My mouth aches for all the smiling.'

'I think it hurts more when you don't mean it.'

'I need to powder my nose.' She gestured for him to follow.

She slipped into the library. A solitary desk lamp lit the desk. She took a moment to absorb the rows upon rows of hardback books, the smell of damp paper. The Campbells were not literary, but years of wealth meant that the library was well stocked. She picked one out: *The Decline and Fall of the Roman Empire* by Edward Gibbons. She opened it and pressed her nose up to the paper. She had always liked the smell of books. This one smelt of mould. As she closed it, she saw that she had left the imprint of her mouth on the pages and imagined someone finding it years later. She put it back just as the door opened.

'This is an odd place to powder your nose,' Henry said. He walked over to a small table by the chesterfield and poured himself a whisky from a decanter.

'It's hard work, isn't it?' she said.

'Nonsense, you're marvellous with people.'

Kitty perched herself on the edge of her father's desk, sipped her champagne. The sudden tension in the room made her feel woozy. Henry sat beside her, his body so close that his leg was making her skirt rustle.

Kitty blushed. 'Sorry. I'm not very good at intimate situations.' She laughed. Enticing him to follow her had seemed a little forward. And yet, everything over the years seemed to point to this moment.

'Should we go back?' she said. She turned to face him then, smiling brightly.

Henry was looking straight at her, his eyes demanding something they weren't supposed to. He said, 'I've been away for two years and a day hasn't gone past when I haven't thought of you.'

'Well I would never have guessed it.'

'Why do we always do this?'

Kitty felt the sweetness of his breath, the tartness of the whisky. 'I don't know,' she said.

Their faces were so close that Kitty thought he might swallow her up. She couldn't breathe, her heart was racing so fast. He cupped her chin with his hand and gently pulled her towards him. She closed her eyes, felt his lips on hers. They kissed hungrily after that. There seemed no end to it until Saunders walked in.

'Your mother asked me to fetch the cigars,' he said.

Henry whispered into her ear. 'Boat house. Ten minutes.'

She felt his breath on her neck, held his hand until the last second as she walked away. Saunders discreetly turned his back to them. Kitty blew Henry a kiss.

'Henry, oh Henry. Why does it have to be like this?' Kitty banged her fists on the steering wheel, then flicked a glance in the direction of the neighbouring car to check the driver hadn't noticed. How could he be so cruel? She wondered what this other woman looked like. Did she have blonde hair? Was she pretty and unbelievably intelligent? Oh God, of course she was.

Kitty had been driving for ten minutes and still had no idea where she was going. She wondered if Tom's baby had been born, and if he'd got back from Kenya. She'd not heard. Why was it Tom got to keep his child and she didn't? Just because of a silly gold band. She pressed her foot down, legs still weak with fear and the effort of running. Her eyes settled on the rear-view mirror half expecting to see Nurse Wilmot in pursuit, still clutching the aspirin. Perhaps if she just kept driving she could outrun the nurse, the Sister, her mother and, for that matter, Tom.

Alexandra croaked little noises of complaint on the back seat as the car juddered into life. Kitty had no choice but to go home to Beecham. The closer Kitty got to her family home, the more impossible the task of keeping Alexandra seemed. Maybe she should call Georgie, her closest friend. She'd met Georgie at the Slade in her first year and had wholeheartedly taken to her wild social scene, a contrast to Kitty's own upbringing. During a rather hedonistic year they'd grown close. But, as close as they were, Georgie knew nothing about Alexandra. She, like everyone else, thought Kitty was in Paris. It wasn't because Kitty thought Georgie would judge her, she'd just been too ashamed to admit she was foolish enough to get pregnant.

Kitty saw a phone box and pulled over. Leaving Alexandra in the car sleeping, she made a dash to the telephone box. The rain was getting heavier so that it splashed onto the pavement. She realised then that she'd left her raincoat behind in the ward. The telephone box smelt of urine and stale cigarettes. She took a penny out of her purse, picked up the receiver and dialled Georgie's number. She shivered while she waited, the endless ring tone echoing in her ear. Nobody answered.

'Damn!' Kitty slammed the receiver back in the cradle. 'Why doesn't Georgie ever answer her phone?'

She couldn't just turn up at Georgie's tiny place. No, she had to face it: she was on her own.

FOUR

Kitty stopped at yet another set of traffic lights. Some genius piece of civil engineering meant that the journey was all stop and start. She hadn't expected Georgie to answer but all the same it left her feeling terribly alone. She'd driven too far to turn back and knock on Georgie's door. And she couldn't very well just turn up, baby in arms. She watched as a hawk circled above them, probably with an eye on some poor unsuspecting rodent. Kitty was heading in the direction of Beecham. Where else could she go? She hoped to God her mother hadn't come back from Kenya for Anne's birth, although who was she kidding? Of course Clarissa would be there waiting for her first legitimate grandchild while pretending the illegitimate grandchild didn't exist.

She'd been four and a half months pregnant when she'd moved into a house for unmarried expectant mothers in Kensal Rise, telling everyone she was off to Paris. After that she went to St Helen's when the girdle she'd worn got too tight and she began to show. On her mother's instruction, she told no one, not her father, nor Tom or Henry. Not even Georgie. She sent letters to a pen friend of her mother's in Paris who forwarded the correspondence with a French stamp – a plan her mother had concocted. They all believed she'd gone to Paris on a whim. Georgie had written to say how jealous she was and could she come to visit. No one asked about the Morris.

She imagined Henry had written letters to the Paris address but of course she'd never received them and she supposed her mother's friend had been instructed to destroy hers to him. Perhaps he hadn't even bothered. Finally, she took the initiative to write to him in Boston from London but never received a reply. She wondered if that letter had been found and destroyed by the Sisters in the mother and baby home. She'd believed the Sisters' warmth had been a sign of compassion, but her mother put a stop to that fantasy when she explained in one of many letters that she'd made a large donation to ensure Kitty was comfortable. How could she be comfortable knowing she'd have to give up her child whose father was with another woman?

The lights turned green. Kitty stalled again. Alexandra let out a tremulous cry.

'Shhh. Shhh.'

Alexandra's cries reduced to a whimper.

'It's okay, I'm here,' Kitty said.

Someone tooted while she tried to start the car. Kitty reached into her handbag for a cigarette, wound down the window a touch, lit it, watched as the smoke escaped in a flurry through the crack. She wrenched off her ring, remembering her mother had bought it in Woolworths, wound the window down further and was about to throw it when she realised she was being impulsive. Her mother's voice: *such a volatile girl*.

Somebody pressed on their horn again.

'All right, all right,' she said, slipping the ring back on and putting the car into gear. She'd have to go to Tom and Anne's house. Kitty wondered what it was like to be Anne: be pregnant and not have to hide it; give birth and have visitors bring flowers to your bedside. To be a Campbell without the bother of actually *being* a Campbell.

She started off as the lights turned to red, head cocked to one side. She thought back to the day when she'd first told Clarissa about the pregnancy.

She'd decided not to tell her about the pregnancy until Henry returned from the States. Kitty knew her mother would be bound to insist on marriage. She was terrified that she'd respond with her usual aggression, tell Kitty that she'd destroyed everyone's life. She needed to tell Henry first but then her mother made a surprise visit to her flat in London. Kitty had opened the front door aware that she looked awful. Clarissa was dressed in a fitted green cotton dress, elegant as always.

'I was in London so I thought I'd drop by,' she said, walking straight through to the kitchen. It wasn't until they were both standing next to the cooker that she looked Kitty in the eye.

'You look dreadful, what's happened?'

'It's the weather. It's terribly hot. Would you like some lemonade?' Kitty said. 'I've made pots of the stuff.'

Kitty felt herself floating, that 'swimmy' feeling she'd had since she was a child. It took her a while before she remembered where the tumblers were stored as she pottered around, absently going to the cupboard to hunt for biscuits. She stuffed one into her mouth to stave off a bout of sickness, turned to see her mother's horrified expression.

'I wanted to talk to you about Henry,' Clarissa said. She was standing in the doorway lighting a cigarette.

'Henry? Is he back, do you have any news?'

Her mother took a long drag of her cigarette before answering. A circle of smoke wafted between them. 'Kitty, I thought you should know.' She picked at an invisible thread. 'I've heard Henry is seeing someone. A fellow student at his university.'

'Who told you that?'

'Henry wrote to Tom boasting about it. I had half a mind not to mention it, but I just had this odd feeling he'd tried to seduce you. So. I thought I'd better tell you.'

Kitty couldn't stop the tears pricking at her eyes. 'I'm sorry, I'm not feeling myself.'

'Oh dear. Don't tell me I've left it too late.' Clarissa took the jug of lemonade and poured them both a glass. 'Why don't we sit down?'

'What do you mean too late?'

Clarissa perched on the armrest of the chair. 'Am I right in thinking you're pregnant?'

Kitty let the tears roll down her face in a moment of surrender. She hadn't wanted to cry; she'd been happy at first but she could see the utter failure of her situation.

'I dreaded it coming to this. Don't think I didn't notice you both disappear on the night of Tom's wedding.'

'We're happy to get married,' Kitty said. This wasn't strictly true. Henry didn't even know she was pregnant.

'Well apart from the fact that he's made his intentions clear with this other girl, I'm afraid that your father won't accept it. Henry is not like us, and besides, people will talk.'

Kitty felt physically sick. Her mother's body had grown taut and the atmosphere in the room was crackling. 'What do you mean, people will talk?'

'Good grief,' Clarissa said, her head shaking back and forth, 'you know exactly what I mean. And I had hoped to talk to you before anything as devastating as pregnancy happened.' She looked up, her eyes impenetrable. 'Kitty, we are not these kind of people. God knows what kind of family his mother came from. If you remember I met her aunt at the funeral. Dreadful woman.'

'Well that doesn't mean . . .'

'Kitty, there are things about Henry you don't know.'

'Like what?'

'I had hoped I would never have to tell you this, but one of the girls in the village fell pregnant a few years back. Rumour has it that it was Henry's. Lillian is actually frightened of him. She won't be in the same room with him alone.'

'Oh, Mother! Lillian is half-witted!'

Clarissa held up her hand to silence her. 'Whether it is rumour or not. Rumours aren't generated from nothing.'

'What was her name?'

'Pamela Watson. You remember her, don't you?'

Kitty sat down hard onto the armchair. She felt as if she'd swallowed something heavy. She did remember Pamela. She was a girl known for putting it around. Typical that Henry should be accused. 'People are just jealous,' she said.

Her mother sighed, stubbed out her cigarette in a nearby saucer. 'Henry isn't who you think he is. Young girls have a propensity to invent the opposite sex.'

Kitty buried her head in her hands.

'You're such an innocent, Kitty.'

'But . . .'

'This' – Clarissa waved her hand in the general direction of Kitty's stomach – 'is the last thing we wanted for you. It's perfectly expected of someone like Pamela, but it is not what is expected of you! Apart from the damage this will do to your reputation *and* ours, I just don't want you to be hurt,' Clarissa said, her mouth tight and her eyes sharp with intent. 'He's clearly irresponsible.'

'Stop it!'

Her mother reached out and touched Kitty's shoulder. 'Kitty, I'm trying to protect you, *and* the child. Henry is damaged goods and he's trouble. And he's clearly not the type to settle!'

39

'I said stop it!' Kitty was shaking. Tears stained her face but her mother didn't flinch.

'He's not like that,' Kitty said.

'Oh don't be so bloody naïve, Kitty. They're all like that.'

'If he was that awful why did you take him in?'

'After his mother died, he had no one. He was Tom's best friend, what else could we do? Besides, all of these . . .' Her mother stumbled on the words, took a drag of her cigarette, '"traits"' – she made quote marks with both forefingers – 'came out later, after his mother's death.'

'But there's no proof.'

'I saw him with Pamela, Kitty. One summer when he was back from Edinburgh, they were laughing and he had his arm around her. Next thing we know, she's pregnant.'

Kitty began to cry again. She had always loved Henry and couldn't imagine him with another woman. Yet if she thought about it, Henry had known what he was doing on that fateful night. It clearly wasn't his first time.

'I'm presuming Henry doesn't know about this?' Clarissa pointed to Kitty's stomach, again. 'Let's face it, it doesn't look as if marriage is on the cards with this other girl in Boston hanging around. Quite popular, our Henry.'

Kitty looked up to see her mother's closed expression. 'I was waiting for him to come back from the States. It's not something you write in a letter is it?'

'Then I think it's best if we don't tell anyone. Let's face it, Henry is more interested in his life in America. It won't be long before he forgets you. It seems as if he already has. He's a very ambitious man.'

Kitty sobbed openly.

Her mother passed her a handkerchief. 'Kitty, I'm not angry but you need to know what kind of man Henry is. Apart from anything, if you tell him, you could ruin his chances in that newspaper and at least that would make an honest man of him and we wouldn't have totally failed. To be honest it's rather undignified to force his hand, especially as he's dating someone else.'

'So what shall I do?'

'Adoption is really the only option you have. It will be best for the child, and best for everyone concerned.'

'But . . .'

Clarissa held up her hand. 'Being a mother means putting yourself and your own needs second.'

Remembering her mother's expression that day made Kitty push her foot down on the accelerator. She still didn't want to believe the things her mother had said about Henry and Pamela, and yet she'd done everything her mother had told her to, except for doing what was best for Alexandra. The Morris whined and the speedometer hit sixty-five. 'But it isn't best for everyone, is it?' Kitty said, turning to see if Alexandra was asleep. Henry had probably assumed Kitty had run away, but if there was another woman, then presumably he didn't care. She didn't want to believe that Henry had deceived her. She still loved him, whatever her mother said, and found it so hard to accept that he didn't love her back. Perhaps her mother was right, she was naïve.

She drove on, her future getting darker with every second.

FIVE

Henry Roberts wrapped the gold sovereign Howard Campbell had given him on the day he turned sixteen inside a white cotton handkerchief, and buried it deep in the top drawer. The gesture had been kind, a way of making Henry feel like he belonged, but Henry wondered what Howard thought of him now that Kitty had run off to Paris. Did he think it was because of him? He knew that neither Clarissa nor Howard wanted him for a son-in-law. They'd adopted him out of pity. When he turned twenty-one, they'd given him one of the worker's cottages and this was how he'd repaid them, making love to their daughter. But what could he do? He loved Kitty, though he was beginning to feel an idiot for doing so. He walked to the window, the rain pelting against the glass. Across the meadow he took in the flat plain cut deep by the river Adur, the grassy verge of the banks, the church steeple shrouded in mist. His gaze moved to Beecham Manor and a shadow passed inside him. Beecham Manor wasn't just a house; it *was* the Campbells. Despite the few years he'd lived there, Henry had never felt that he belonged, either to the village or the Campbells, except, of course, to Kitty.

The memory of his mother hovered, as it usually did when he was alone. That smile she used to disarm people, the way she would pinch his chin and wink just as she did on that first day his new friend Tom Campbell invited him to Beecham. His mother had gathered her skirt, swishing it back and forth as she danced around in the kitchen: *the Campbells, they think they're a cut above with all their airs and graces but they have their secrets just like the rest of us, I can tell you. Believe me, they'll love you, you watch.*

And they had.

They'd given him elocution lessons to help him blend in, knocked the American accent out of him, paid for his schooling at Worth where he had boarded. He wasn't proud of what he'd done. Seducing their daughter would no doubt be seen as betrayal.

He thought back to the first time he became conscious of his own deep attraction to Kitty, different to the sly glances they'd exchanged, the unspoken flirtations inside the arc of the willow tree, the fumbling efforts of their teenage years.

He'd been in his final year at Edinburgh and she was completing a foundation at the Slade. Everyone had been ordered home one Easter weekend for Tom's engagement party, no excuses of final exams were allowed.

He'd walked into the sitting room to find her laughing at something Georgie had said, her hair pinned up, her mouth painted. She was dressed in an elegant close-fitting skirt. The blouse was exaggeratingly the opposite, the sleeves puffed out and the collar framing her long slim neck. She was every bit Clarissa's daughter and yet when she turned and smiled, she was a stranger to him. As their eyes locked he understood that she felt the same as he did.

'Hello, Henry.'

Henry forgot to smile. 'You look like . . .' He couldn't find the word. 'Yourself.'

Kitty smiled, a gesture so genuine it seemed to reach into him. Tom was standing by the fireplace with Anne at his side.

43

'And this coming from the future best man. I thought you'd be good at speeches,' Tom said.

'Tom, you haven't even asked Henry if he's happy to be your best man yet,' Anne said.

'Who else is as qualified?' Tom said.

Henry gestured his acceptance with a tip of his glass. That was when Howard and Clarissa joined them, sweeping into the room with parental authority. He watched the worried glance Clarissa threw at her daughter, the nervous twitch of her eyebrows.

'Let's raise a toast to the newly engaged couple. To Anne and Tom,' Henry said.

They all raised their glasses.

Kitty sidled up to him. 'Thank you,' she said.

Her hair was glossy and swept skilfully to one side.

'For what, exactly?'

'For noticing.'

When he held her gaze her eyes showed him that she had indeed found agency. Art school suited her.

He wondered if Kitty would return from Paris before Anne gave birth. Tom didn't seem to know and he didn't dare ask Clarissa, who had grown aloof. He had the feeling it was her meddling that had sent Kitty off to Paris. It had been months since he'd last seen Kitty and he'd received no news. He'd expected Kitty to wait for him when he went off to America to receive his Masters degree but instead, she went to Paris without warning. He'd gone over the reasons why she might have shot off like that, even confronted Kitty, as much as one could by airmail, but paper is an unsatisfying place on which to squabble and she hadn't replied to any of his letters. What had gone wrong?

He slipped on his knitted waistcoat, heard the grunt of a tractor as it trundled up the hill, could see the headlights spill over the road even though it wasn't dark. The wind whistled its high-pitched tune. A bulbous black cloud threatened another onslaught, the skies cluttered and chaotic. Despite the violence of the weather the future held promise. She'd be home soon to meet her niece or nephew.

He threw his jacket onto the stool, rolled up the sleeves of his shirt, turned on the wireless. The newsman talked about Martin Luther King and then locally warned about the possibility of severe flooding. Henry hesitated over the day's mail, there was one from America. He found the letter opener, the newsreader's voice drifting away, his mind obsessed, unable to shift from the possibility of Kitty's return. It was an offer of a job from the *Boston Herald*. The telephone rang.

'Henry, is that you?'

'Tom.'

'I can't seem to get hold of Anne. The phone lines are down. She hasn't gone into labour has she?'

'Nobody's called. Isn't your daily supposed to be with her?'

'I suppose so,' Tom said.

Henry could hear Tom's hurried breathing. The phone clicked as he put in another coin. 'How was Kenya?' Henry asked, more to fill the void than anything.

'Fine. Listen, I'll be on the next train down. Do you think you could check in on Anne, see if she's all right? I just can't understand why the phone's not working.'

Henry looked out of the kitchen window. The Downs on the other side of the valley were barely visible, the church steeple had disappeared. The rain was so heavy that large puddles had formed on the garden path.

'It's probably the weather,' he said.

After he put the phone down, he picked up his jacket, wondering where he'd left the keys to the car. He tried not to let his anger get the better of him. He'd wanted to write the letter to the *Boston Herald* accepting the position they'd offered. He had to do something other than wait around for Kitty, for Christ's sake. He found the keys in his corduroy jacket and raced out just as another onslaught of rain slammed against the front door. On the doorstep, next door's cat had left a dead bird, the feathers scattered across the garden path. He jumped across the puddles, the rain and the wind stinging his face.

Damn animal, he thought. And damn the Campbells. He wished he didn't love Kitty like he did, but nothing was going to change that.

SIX

Kitty pulled up outside a tea shop in Purley. It was eleven o'clock. Alexandra was hungry. Her crying was at the melodic stage, but Kitty knew that if she didn't feed her soon she would grow hysterical. By the smell of things, she was in need of a change as well. Kitty's hair was a mess, her floss of curls flattened by the damp. She teased it back into shape with one hand and smoothed her skirt down as best she could before she entered the tea room.

A bell rang as she walked in holding Alexandra all bundled up in her pink hospital blanket, Kitty's handbag swinging underneath her, stuffed with a nappy and Sudocrem. The café's tables were decorated with tired lace tablecloths. The woman behind the glass counter looked up from her sandwich-making, welcoming Kitty with a small gesture of the chin. Photographs of shire horses and Shetland ponies stared into the room.

'Do you mind awfully if I change my baby's nappy?' Kitty asked.

'Do what you like, dear,' the woman said. 'Bathroom's over there.' She gave Kitty a warm smile, her hand buttering the bread, mechanically moving from side to side.

'I'd like a pot of tea if it's not too much trouble,' Kitty said.

Kitty went into the bathroom, laid Alexandra down in the basin. A mustard stain leaked out of her rubber pants. Alexandra's head shifted from one side to the other,

47

her mouth searching for milk. She was kicking her legs, punching the air. Kitty wasn't sure what to do with the soiled napkin and tried to tackle it while holding Alexandra in one arm, finally laying her on the floor. Alexandra's face grew pink with rage. She hadn't been fed for four and a half hours. Kitty rinsed her nappy under the tap and rolled it up as neatly as she could, washing her hands again, scrubbing her nails to get rid of the smell. Alexandra was on full throttle, her cries echoing inside the tiled bathroom. Kitty pulled off her jumper, unhooked her bra and unwrapped the bandages the nurse had put on that morning. Her breasts had grown hard. The milk started to leak straight off. She was just lifting Alexandra up when she heard a knock.

'Are you all right, dear?'

'Just got myself into a bit of a pickle,' Kitty said. 'Nothing to worry about.'

'Well, if you need anything.'

'Thank you.' She sat down on the loo, stockings crumpled at her ankles where she'd undone her suspender belt so that she could breathe. She hated the moment when Alexandra latched on. It was like being bitten and burnt at the same time. Her mother had stipulated that she wasn't to breastfeed, but Kitty had circumvented that one with a bribe of her own. She hadn't meant to love Alexandra, wasn't allowed to, but she couldn't help herself the second she was born. Wisps of hair veined across Alexandra's head. Kitty stroked her, felt the softness of her downy skin and wondered again if Anne had given birth. Nothing like this would ever happen to someone like Anne. Dear nicely behaved, Anne. Secure in the knowledge that her baby was welcome. A ring on her finger. Not from Woolworths.

When Kitty came out of the bathroom the woman behind the counter looked up at her and frowned. 'Not the most hygienic of places to feed the little 'un,' she said.

'Yes, I realise that.'

'Could have tucked you into a corner, no need to put yourself through that.'

Kitty blushed. An elderly couple was seated in the window eating scones, their mouths full. A group of young girls was huddled around a pile of toasted teacakes and a large red teapot, legs outstretched, their sweaters loose, cigarettes wedged between fingers. Looking around her at all the Toby jugs and china teapots, Kitty let a fantasy unfurl. Living here in this suburb she could be someone else. It was as if the place and all the knick-knacks offered her protection against the grey weighty tide of her past. She'd felt so free and ready for anything once, but now all she wanted was comfort. Perhaps she could get a job as a part-time waitress, find someone to help with Alexandra. Start again. But the horror stories of single mothers were horrendous, the girls at the mother and baby home had filled her head with all kinds of nightmares: mothers forced into prostitution. The story of that baby found abandoned on the Downs. *At least if she's adopted no one will know.*

She leaned across the counter. 'You wouldn't have anything to put in that would you?'

The woman raised her eyebrows, wiped her hands on her apron.

'It's illegal to sell liquor without a licence.'

Kitty felt the heat rising up her neck. 'Yes, of course. I'm sorry.'

The woman opened a cupboard and pulled out a small bottle of brandy, looked across at the couple. 'I use it for

49

cooking,' she whispered, then winked before dropping a dash into the pot.

'Thank you.'

'I thought you seemed a bit peaky,' the woman said. 'I'm Bet, by the way.'

'Kitty. I'm visiting a friend in Sussex, well, Bramber.'

Bet raised an eyebrow. 'That's down by Upper Beeding, isn't it?'

'Yes, that's right.'

'Not sure you're going to make it. Whole county is flooded. Upper Beeding has been in the news. My in-laws live down that way.'

'What do you mean – flooded?'

'Been on the wireless all morning. They reckon people have actually drowned.'

'Oh,' Kitty said.

'Come straight from the hospital have you?' Bet said, looking at Alexandra's shabby pink blanket.

Kitty blushed, she found herself fiddling with the wedding ring in order to make it visible. 'My husband's abroad.'

'Quiet now she's been fed,' Bet said, nodding at Alexandra. 'What's her name then?'

'Alexandra,' Kitty said, as a moment of pride hit her. It was such a beautiful name – a strong name, she thought.

'Why don't you find yourself a quiet corner, I'll bring this over for you.'

Kitty nodded, looked around for somewhere to sit. Bet followed her with a tray.

'Would you mind holding her while I pour myself some tea?' She held Alexandra out, feeling instantly foolish while Bet looked on.

'I'm a bit busy,' she said. 'I'll pour.'

Kitty didn't know what to do when she saw the tears spring up in Bet's eyes. She wasn't exactly sure what she'd done wrong but her own eyes welled up as well. Of course, why would Bet want to hold her daughter? She sniffed, trying to keep control, but the tears seemed to fall of their own volition. All that had happened to her, not just the events of that morning but the things that had happened since that first day she'd thrown up down the loo; months of it seemed to explode like a busted water pump, so her body was heaving and snorting and making sounds she didn't recognise as her own. Alexandra started to cry, her face all creased with panic. Suddenly Bet was putting her finger over her lips and taking Alexandra from her, cradling her into her ample bosom and leading Kitty into a room at the back that connected to the neighbouring house.

'I'm sorry if I was out of sorts. It's just we lost our child a few years back,' Bet whispered. 'Influenza. I'll go and see if someone can cover for me.'

Kitty looked straight at Bet expecting to apologise, bluster her way back out of the door. But confronted with the loss in the woman's eyes, she felt herself unravel into the armchair as Bet took the now quiet Alexandra back into the tea shop.

When Bet returned, Alexandra was asleep in her arms. She popped her down on the armchair and disappeared off again, only to return minutes later with a tray of scones, a pot of tea and a small bottle of brandy. The warmth of Bet seemed to absorb the fear that had begun to settle in Kitty's middle region. Her breasts felt sore and without thinking she rubbed them.

'You need cabbage leaves for that,' Bet said.

'I'm sorry?' Kitty said.

'Cabbage leaves help with engorged breasts.'

Kitty felt herself redden. 'I haven't really got a husband,' she found herself saying.

Alexandra let out a little squeal, probably wind, Kitty thought. Bet picked her up, expertly rubbing her back until she let out an enormous burp.

'Very ladylike!' she said and tucked Alexandra into the crook of her arm. 'Now, why don't you start from the beginning.' Bet leaned forward, put her hand on Kitty's knee. 'I'm not one to judge.'

Kitty had drunk so much tea her stomach was full of liquid and a feeling like cold porridge stirred inside her at the thought of leaving the safety of Bet's parlour. She wanted to stay put in this tiny room, with the fire crackling and the sound of the kettle steaming in the kitchen.

She felt safe.

Bet reminded Kitty of the girls at the mother and baby home, all uptight like a knot, unravelling in a blink of an eye as soon as they got near an infant. She had listened to Bet's story, how she'd lost her boy at three years old. How she woke up thinking about him every morning. Kitty had liked her instantly and had told her everything, even how she'd escaped from the mother and baby home. The words poured out of her and in doing so, Kitty realised how she'd acted without thinking of the consequences. *Such a volatile girl, Kitty.*

Bet slopped a little more brandy into both of their cups. 'Maybe you should go and see your sister-in-law, first,' she said. 'She's bound to sympathise if she's just had a baby herself. Perhaps your mother, seeing them both together, will change her mind.' Bet added a little sugar to their cups. Kitty didn't like to say that she'd been brought up to think of sugar in tea as sacrilege because her father imported it and knew more about tea than anything else.

'I'm not so sure. Although maybe Tom could talk some sense into her,' she said, thinking out loud.

'Tom's your brother?'

'Yes, he and Henry are good friends.'

'And you say your parents adopted this young man after his mother died,' Bet said, wrinkling her forehead. 'Perhaps your mother knows something you don't.' Bet settled her gaze on Kitty, her eyes steady as a freight train.

It hadn't occurred to Kitty that her mother hadn't told her everything. She'd told her so much.

'Let's face it, no mother wants their daughter to be pregnant out of wedlock and if he's done it before, that doesn't put him in a good light, does it? Your mother is just trying to protect you, that's all it is,' Bet said, patting Kitty's knee while focusing on Alexandra.

'I just don't believe Henry's like that, I suppose,' Kitty said.

Bet ran a finger under Alexandra's chin so that Alexandra smiled in her sleep.

She laughed. 'Well you won't be the first woman to think the best of a man. Have you thought to ask him?'

'I can't,' she said. 'It's too late now, really.'

When Kitty finally left she went to shake hands but Bet surprised her and pulled her into an embrace.

'I think it's fate meeting you, Kitty. My Samuel has been pushing me to adopt and I've been reluctant up until now. After meeting Alexandra, I've changed my mind.'

Kitty's arms were barely able to reach around Bet and yet Kitty felt so secure in those arms. Bet looked down at Alexandra. 'She really is the sweetest little girl.'

Kitty found herself coming out of the front door of the neighbouring house. She walked past the tea shop, a warm feeling radiating through her as she got into the car.

SEVEN

Henry was driving towards Anne and Tom's house after Tom's panicked phone call. He had tried to call Anne himself, but the line was dead just as Tom had said it was. Someone should have stayed with Anne at a time like this, not just the daily. But paid help was all the Campbells knew. Perhaps that was why Kitty had gone to Paris, to get away from the pressures of being a Campbell. No, he was convinced that this was all part of the same dance they'd been playing since the start. She was always just out of reach.

He wasn't looking forward to seeing Tom: that smile that never quite connected with his eyes. He drove towards the bridge, noticed how the river had bucketed onto the road bringing with it a tangle of broken branches, rubbish, the white dust that spewed out of the cement factory. Someone had stopped in the middle of the road. There was a commotion down by the water but Henry couldn't quite see what was going on, so he parked and waited.

The sight of the water took him back to one specific afternoon Kitty and he had spent on the lake. After his finals, he'd returned to Beecham to find Kitty in the boat house slumped up against a pile of picnic rugs, reading. He hadn't seen her in six months.

'Congratulations,' he said.

'For what?' Kitty asked indignantly, turning the page of her novel.

'For getting into the Slade.'

'That was ages ago,' she said, cupping her hand over her brow, straining to see him before looking back down at her book. 'What is it?' she asked.

'Shall we take the boat out?'

Reluctantly she agreed. He lifted the oars off the hooks and slipped them into the rowlocks, stepping into the boat so that it swayed and dipped into the water. He held out his arm to help her board.

'I'm perfectly capable,' she said.

He threw his hands up and stepped aside. The boat rocked as she sat down so that he almost fell. She laughed.

'Serves you right,' she said.

'For what?'

'You know full well what,' she said.

Henry cast off, throwing the moss-covered rope back onto the jetty so that it landed with a thud. He started to row, pulling at the oars so that the boat glided across the surface. The carp darted out from underneath as they cut through the inky water. Ripples fanned out. The water was covered in a dusty film, the lilies, a shocking pink, were crowded around the island, but the boat pushed them hither and thither.

'You should have written,' she said.

'I know.'

'Why didn't you?'

'I don't know.'

He looked at her then, but he found her so intense his eyes went back to the cool of the lake. 'Kitty Campbell you are hard work sometimes.' He pushed the oars deep into the water.

Kitty blushed. 'You will never admit it, will you?' she said.

He turned away, looking out onto the fields. A red admiral danced around their heads but she didn't appear to notice. He rowed towards the island. All that could be heard was the rhythmic plop of the oars, the sound of indolent insects drunk with heat. Henry lifted the oars above the water so that the blades hung in the air and the boat continued silently towards the island. Dragonflies danced around them. He heard the rumble of a tractor in the distance. Sometimes Beecham was heaven.

'I've been offered a place at Harvard to do a postgraduate degree,' he said. 'I'm going to America late August.'

Kitty laughed. 'Is that why you've brought me out here?' she asked. He could hear the mocking tone to her voice. 'To break the news.'

'Yes, probably. I suppose I thought you'd be sad.'

'Why?'

'No reason at all,' he said.

'So, congratulations all round. Is my father paying for this?'

Her words hit him like a punch.

'I'm sorry,' she said. 'That was uncalled for.'

'Actually, I received a scholarship.'

'Well done you.' Kitty flicked her hands in the water, splashing him lightly so that water spots fell on his trousers. Henry looked at her, scooping out a handful and splashing it so that it fell on her face and hair. She laughed, but it had taken everything he had to push past her defence.

Later that afternoon she'd sketched him sitting by the lake, leaning on his elbow, his knee bent. He had watched how her hand moved across the paper. There was nothing but the indolent sound of late summer insects and the fervent scratching of her pencil. She barely looked at her drawing, so intent she was on studying the shape of his body, her eyes flicking back and forth. His heart cracked open at the sight of her concentration. There was something so incredibly ethereal in the way that her hand danced across that page. He remembered how he had had to shift himself to hide his erection and she had chastised him.

'Don't move a muscle,' she said and he'd laughed.

'Show me,' he said when she had finished.

She flipped the sketchbook over. The black marks of the pencil made one continuous line and as if by magic he saw a version of himself. His thick hair black on the page. She had caught something in his expression: a sadness, or was it desire?

EIGHT

Kitty drove the Morris towards Tom and Anne's house, her mind churning over what had just happened in the tea shop. She stretched across for a cigarette, remembering again that fateful day of Tom's wedding: how the water lapped against the jetty as she approached the boat house, the planks creaking. Slipping off her shoes, she'd opened the door to the smell of oiled wood. She could hear Henry breathing.

'You were ages,' he said.

'I was careful.'

Henry struck a match and she saw the contours of his face lit by the warm light. He licked his thumb and extinguished the flame. She ran towards him, crashed into his embrace. They kissed silently, first slowly then hungrily. Their breathing pooled, echoing in the hollow space.

'Why have we waited so long?' she said.

He took her face in his hand. 'They won't accept it, Kitty.'

'I know.' She laid her head on his chest, felt the warmth of him.

'I didn't know what "in love" meant until now.'

'Only now?' She felt his smile in the darkness.

'I want you to come to America.'

She closed her eyes, thought of the Slade – she was in her final year – of her life in London and then of the art movement in New York. 'I will,' she said. They kissed again.

'We can just disappear,' he said. He ran his hand through her hair, cupped it in his hand.

'You mean elope?'

'If that's what you want.'

She ran her fingers to the arch of his back. Henry let out a groan.

'Kitty.'

'Don't worry,' she said.

'This isn't the way.'

She lifted the layers of her ball gown and for a second all she could hear was the rustle of silk taffeta and her own rapid breathing. Henry swept her up onto an upturned boat, pressed his body onto hers, their desire egging them towards unknown territory. She felt herself bring him closer and bit him gently, the rush of their longing, the tears, breath and sweat, the sheer hunger of their touch pushing them towards abandon. She cared for nothing other than the moment. Neither of them did.

'Oh, Kit.'

Only Henry called her Kit.

The roads were narrow, the hedgerow dense so that at times she lost the horizon. 'There's something very special about this child,' Bet had said. Kitty felt hot tears prick, which blurred her vision. She flicked the cigarette out of the window and wiped them away with the heel of her hand. She was five minutes away from The Old Priory, which wasn't far from Beecham, probably because Tom had wanted his mother close to hand. Of course Anne was obliging and a little in awe of the Cambpells, Kitty thought. Some people are impressed by money.

Down in the valley the fields were like black glass. So far she'd driven through puddles of water six inches deep but the Morris had behaved itself. When she got to the village though, water was spilling into the street, spreading its reach. The river had always divided the village in two, the small terraced cottages being on the far side, along with the grocer's and the post office.

Tom and Anne's house was on the near side where the road gently sloped towards the castle. The flint-stoned house was covered in wisteria; white roses grew around the front door. At the back, a garden went all the way to a brook.

Kitty parked up the hill away from the village. If anyone saw her with Alexandra, the gossip would spread faster than knotweed. She got out, buttoning her cardigan against the cool air, cursing herself for leaving her raincoat behind. She took off her scarf, wrapping it around her head because she imagined her hair looked frightful. Down in the village two small children were hanging out of their bedroom window. Kitty could just make out one of Tom's neighbours pushing the water back with a garden broom. She could see a crowd of people at the far end of The Street huddled by the bridge and was seized by the fear that Clarissa was there, serving soup and doling out food parcels.

She bundled Alexandra up in her blanket and walked briskly towards The Old Priory. All the while Alexandra made staccato gurgling noises. Kitty consoled herself with the possibility that people would think it was Tom's child.

Surrounded by chaos and destruction and all she could think of was the usual, imagining her mother looking out of every window. She'd experienced the feeling of being watched by her mother often: her first kiss, the day she'd cheated in her French exam, and that time she'd stolen a sherbet. She'd had to swallow the thing straight off for fear Clarissa would appear from nowhere and snatch it out of her hand.

As she drew closer to the river she could just make out Anne and Tom's handyman, Glynn, in the huddle of people. A filigree of water branched out of Tom and Anne's driveway, running into the gullies of the road. It started to slurp under her ill-fitting shoes. She headed towards the front door which was at the side of the house. The ground was raised so it was dry and she felt oddly grateful. She rapped the brass knocker. A faint flutter of fear flushed through her at the thought of her mother opening the door. Maybe Anne was giving birth right this minute. Through the chink of a closed curtain she saw the ground rippling, a glint of shifting light. Her eyes settled on legs.

'Anne!'

She tried the door, pushed it once, twice with her shoulder. Alexandra began to cry. She picked up a rock and smashed it against the handle. The lock splintered and the door fell open. Water flowed out of the house onto the driveway, trickling over the step. Kitty took off her shoes, stepping inside on tiptoes. Cold, muddy water slopped around her ankles. By the Aga Anne's head was half submerged, her mouth gaping open. A dark mass of curls shrouded her face.

'Christ!' Kitty padded across, fell hard down on her knees, aware of the filthy water swilling about her. Alexandra let out a squeal. She tried to cup her hand under Anne's head to lift it onto her knees, but it was impossible while holding Alexandra. Finally, she grabbed a tuft of Anne's hair to at least twist her head so that Anne's mouth was away from the water. She bent down to hear if Anne was breathing, but what with Alexandra's grumbling and the slosh of the water, she couldn't hear a thing.

'Oh please, God,' she said. There was nowhere safe to place Alexandra so she ran upstairs, her heart hammering.

61

Above Alexandra's rhythmic cries she heard another noise coming from Anne's bedroom.

'Who's there?'

She swung the door open. The first thing she saw was a basin full of blood. The room was littered with blood-stained towels – the place looked like a slaughterhouse. The horror of it rooted her to the ground, forgetting for a minute that Anne was downstairs. In the middle of all the paraphernalia of a home birth a baby lay cocooned in the most beautiful shawl. She, at least she thought it was a she, was crying gently. The two babies began to stutter as if suddenly aware of each other. Kitty lay Alexandra down beside Anne's child so that their two bodies were touching. Alexandra reached out her hand as if to calm her cousin. They both grew quiet.

The branch of the medlar scratched against the bedroom window making Kitty jump. She ran downstairs, untying her scarf as she went, dropping it on the stairs, tripping on the last step because she couldn't see the ground. She crawled over to Anne, picked up her head again and brushed the black web of hair away from her mouth. There was a cut on Anne's temple that curled across her cheek. Her skin was grey and lifeless. Kitty tried to find a pulse.

She had no idea what to do next.

NINE

Henry was still parked by the river. He heard someone shouting, 'Get back will you!' A crowd had formed by the river path. Some fool on a bicycle had fallen over by the telephone box. People gathered around. Henry craned his neck to get a better view, saw a flash of red, the lining of a cape spread out. He pressed on his horn.

'For goodness sake will someone let me through?'

The thin chiselled face of a labourer yelled back at him, 'What's got into you? Can't you see what's happened?'

Henry jumped out to lend a hand, a renewed sense of urgency about him. The woman had a deep gash across her forehead. She was wearing a nurse's cloak. Poor girl, Henry thought. But he needed to get to Anne.

By the time he was free to leave, the river was gushing onto the road and he couldn't cross the bridge. The engine choked under the water, he could feel its hesitation. He pressed down the accelerator, pushing the Humber through the torrent like a frightened mare. An arc of water sprayed around him. Angry villagers turned away from their own waterlogged drama to see what the racket was. He changed down a gear, throwing the car round the bend, a growing sense of urgency pushing him to drive faster.

He parked behind Kitty's Morris, a tremor of rage running through him at the thought she might have been here for days without telling him, then felt the liquid presence of fear at the thought of seeing her. When he arrived at The Old Priory, the door was open. He stepped in and saw Kitty bent over Anne. He was so shocked to see her it took him a few seconds to register what she was doing. She was trying to open Anne's mouth.

'Wait!' Henry said.

'Oh, thank God,' Kitty said.

'Is she breathing?'

'I don't know. I've just got here.'

He knelt beside Kitty and raised Anne's body up onto his thighs, sliding his fingers in between her lips, wrenching open her jaw, holding her nose and breathing into her until his lungs were emptied out. He concentrated hard, trying not to be distracted by Kitty. He couldn't get a proper angle. He brushed aside the cups and plates that cluttered the kitchen table, so that they fell and smashed onto the pooled kitchen floor, and put his hands under Anne's arms, her head lolling as he hoisted her up and laid her down. Her body was heavy and lifeless. He pressed on her chest, careful not to crush her swollen stomach. First a slow deliberate rhythm and then something frantic and urgent that left him drenched in sweat. Gently he shifted her face towards his own, his hands under her chin. Her lips were blue and he felt the need to force life into them. He inhaled, gave her his breath again and again until, quite violently, foam and spit spewed out of her, frothing and curdled. She opened her eyes briefly.

He saw a pool of red around Anne's crotch.

'Oh God,' Kitty said. 'Is she all right? She's given birth.'

'She seems to be losing a lot of blood,' Henry said. His hands were shaking.

'Do you think the baby is upstairs? Perhaps I should look.'

'No, you need to call an ambulance,' he said.

Kitty stood up, her breath was short as she went to the phone and picked up the receiver. 'There's no connection,' she said.

'Then try the village telephone for Christ's sake.'

Kitty jumped. 'But . . .'

'Quickly!' he shouted.

She grabbed her shoes and put them on in the hallway under the water. Her wet skirt clung to her legs. The telephone box was right on the other side of the bridge, if she didn't get a move on, it would be too late, he thought.

'Hurry, Kitty. I can feel her slipping away.' Kitty ran out of the door. Where was Tom for heaven's sake?

*

Kitty ran to the river where the telephone box was stationed by the bridge. Of all the reunions she'd imagined, this was inconceivable. Her mind was racing. What if Henry found Alexandra? How could she ask him about this other woman now? Someone had abandoned a bicycle, its handlebars misshapen, and leaned it up against the telephone box. It took Kitty two attempts to open the door and as she did, the bicycle fell. There were three inches of water inside and the weight of the door seemed to have doubled. The smell of urine had been replaced with something even more sinister. She dialled the operator amazed the phone still worked. 'Ambulance, please.' Cradling the receiver.

A woman answered, her voice irritatingly calm.

'I have just found my . . .' Kitty hesitated. Her throat thick and stiff. 'My sister-in-law has drowned. I found her submerged under water in her home. We've managed to give her the kiss of life.' Kitty was panting. 'She needs help.'

'Address please, madam.'

Kitty gave the address through a veil of impatience. She wanted to get back to Alexandra before Henry found her. God knows she wasn't ready for the explosion of truths that would have to be told, and now this. 'Please hurry,' she said.

'The ambulance will be with you as quickly as possible,' the operator told her.

She returned to find Henry crouched beside Anne on the chaise longue, rubbing her arm as if he could warm her up. Already Anne had acquired an ethereal beauty.

'Thank God,' Henry said. 'I thought I heard a child crying.'

Kitty felt a wave of anxiety. 'The ambulance is coming. I'd better go and see.' She turned to go but on seeing Anne felt suddenly filled with fear. 'Is she breathing?' she asked.

'Yes, but she hasn't opened her eyes again. Perhaps you could get a blanket while you're up there.'

'Yes of course. Where's Tom for heaven's sake?' Kitty asked. 'I thought he would be back by now.'

Henry wiped his brow, his face was streaked with sweat and dirt. 'He arrived at the airport early this morning, called from London to ask me to check on Anne. God knows why he had to go to Nairobi with Anne in this condition. Why all of them had to go. What about you? How come you're back from Paris? Why didn't you write?' His voice was clipped.

'I did write. I thought you'd gone back to Boston. Mother said . . .'

'How could I when you just disappeared? Why Paris, for Christ's sake?'

When their eyes met it was as if for the first time, like strangers. Those brown eyes, wounded, made her want to cry.

'You were in America. I thought you were just getting on with your life. I don't know, you felt so far away.' She knew if she mentioned this other woman, told him the things her mother had told her, he'd react badly. Now wasn't the time.

'But I told you I was coming back.'

A trickle of sweat ran under her arm. She could only think of the babies upstairs. 'I just thought you'd had a change of heart. That it was for the best.'

'I see.' He looked coldly at her, and Kitty sensed there was another side to Henry she hadn't wanted to see. Her mother was right – she saw him with rose-tinted glasses. All the while she was thinking of the babies upstairs. If one cried, the other would as well. They'd been alone for ten or fifteen minutes. Why weren't they making a sound?

'I'd better get that blanket.'

'What is it?' he asked. 'There's something you're not telling me.'

Kitty shook her head. 'I'm upset that's all, it's just that . . . you have no idea of the day I've had.'

He laid the back of his hand on Anne's forehead. 'I'm sorry I was abrupt,' he said. 'It's just that I think I deserved some kind of explanation. I came back from Boston and your mother told me you'd gone. Why couldn't you just write? You could have saved me the price of a bloody plane ticket.' He shook his head. 'I'm sorry,' he said again. 'This isn't the time.'

Kitty dropped her gaze to the floor, she could feel her face was red and tear-stained. God knows what she looked like. 'How long have you been in England?' she asked.

'Four months. I didn't know when you were coming back. Nobody seemed able to tell me. I've been offered a job.'

Kitty wondered if the girl he was seeing was waiting for him, but why had he come back if this girl was important? 'Honestly, I had no choice.' She sniffed, all sense of decorum had evaporated. 'Mother insisted.'

'*She* sent you away?'

'Yes.'

'Kitty, when are you going to be your own woman?'

He turned back to Anne. Kitty saw the greyness of Anne's skin. Then she heard the small cries of an infant from upstairs. She knew within seconds both babies would start up. It happened all the time at the nursery. Kitty could hear the siren from far off.

'I'd better go,' she said.

She sat down on Anne's blood-stained bed, exhausted. She'd wanted to accuse him of seeing someone else, talk to him about Pamela who got pregnant. She wanted also to tell him they'd had a child, but the doubt was festering inside her, her mother's words churning over and over. *You don't want to force him into marriage.* But why had he been so bloody indignant at her not writing when he'd written to Tom boasting about another woman?

What she really wanted was for her mother to be wrong.

It was Anne's baby who had started to cry. Alexandra was quiet, swaddled in her pink blanket, her eyes looking around as if Anne and Tom's bedroom was the most interesting place. Meanwhile, Anne's child was working itself into a rage, breaking free of the beautiful shawl, no doubt a present from Clarissa. Cradling them both she felt so utterly overwhelmed. She'd been a fool to come to Beecham. She knew her mother could deal with death, betrayal even, but she couldn't possibly manage shame. Thinking about her mother's reaction made her want to vomit. The constant presence of butterflies in her tummy was beginning to wear her down.

She got up, found a handkerchief, pulled herself together, then changed the baby's nappy. She was indeed a girl. Odd to think they were cousins. In normal circumstance they would have grown up together, she thought. She found a pile of fresh thick new terry towels stacked in Anne's wardrobe. Alexandra had never known such luxury. Giving Tom's child some of her milk felt strange, but what was she to do? She watched as the girl's mouth worked in much the same way Alexandra fed, her toes curled. She willed her to drop off, but she kept suckling. Alexandra, who sometimes slept so deeply Kitty had found herself checking to see if she was alive, was wide-eyed.

Kitty wondered about Anne. She couldn't imagine the news was going to be good. Not after losing all that blood. She watched the rain dripping off the branches of the tree outside, remembering something Bet had said: 'Of course keeping the child will give your mother more purchase, and she seems quite controlling as it is. She'll probably do everything she can to stop you. It's harder when there's no father. People talk. They're unkind.'

A crow flew past the window, its wings fanned out.

The girl stopped feeding. Kitty felt the emptiness of her left breast and thought she'd give Alexandra some from the right. She was still sore from having her stitches out and couldn't get comfortable. She put Anne's little girl down, noticing the slackness of her mouth. She was dark like Alexandra, with black birth-stained hair, but she had the Campbell forehead, and there were similarities in the shape of their lips and hands. It was obvious, to Kitty at least, that they were related. She picked up Alexandra and watched as she latched on. It would have been so lovely if they'd grown up together but that couldn't happen. She saw that now. There was too much tragedy for her family to face and she wanted peace for her little girl. She had to do the right thing. It was then the thought came to her.

TEN

Henry saw the blue light of the ambulance reflected on the windowpane of the house opposite. He hadn't been able to leave Anne. He was worried about the amount of blood she was losing. It felt to him as if she was close to death. What was Kitty doing? he wondered. He got up and went to the bottom of the stairs to call her.

'Kitty, the ambulance has arrived.'

The front door pushed open. There were two men in uniform and a nurse. They waded through the water without comment.

'Good afternoon, sir. Is this the patient?' said the older man. He took off his cap, tucked it under his arm.

'Yes.' Henry splashed past them to be by Anne's side.

The nurse, who had been unpacking her bag, took hold of Anne's wrist, picked up the watch that hung from her uniform. 'Get the stretcher will you, Bill.' She stood timing Anne's pulse, hardly seeming to notice the brown fluid swilling about her feet.

'I think she's given birth,' Henry said, wiping his face with the back of his hand. 'The baby's upstairs.'

The nurse looked down at Anne.

'Anne Campbell. Her name is Anne Campbell.'

The nurse nodded, not taking her eyes off the watch. 'And you are?'

'Just a friend, a family friend.'

The nurse placed Anne's wrist carefully across her chest. 'Her pulse is very erratic. We need to get her away quickly.' She was rifling through her bag of instruments.

'Was Mrs Campbell conscious when you found her, sir?'

'I didn't find her. Kitty did, her sister-in-law. When I got here she didn't appear to be breathing, so I resuscitated her. She seems to be losing a lot of blood. Have I mentioned that?' He was finding it hard to concentrate, he couldn't stop himself thinking about Clarissa's meddling. Of course it had been Clarissa that had interfered. He wondered if Howard knew about any of it. Probably not.

The nurse looked up, her gaze steady, patient. 'Lucky you were here,' she said.

Henry watched as the two men carefully manoeuvred Anne onto a stretcher. She was pale, her hands mottled with purple splotches, her lips colourless. They placed a blanket on her, carefully lifting her arms so that her hands sat neatly across her chest until the nurse picked one arm and started running her thumb across Anne's pale flesh in search of a vein. A sense of panic swept over him.

'Is she going to be all right?'

The nurse frowned, her concentration focused on the tangle of veins running under the flesh. He watched as she pushed the needle deep into the crook of Anne's elbow.

'It's hard to know. Did you say the infant was upstairs?' The nurse looked around the room, as if a child might be tucked into some unseen corner.

Henry gestured towards the bedroom. 'Kitty is with the baby now.'

The nurse gently turned Anne's head and cleaned the wound.

'Could you ask Kitty to bring the baby down?'

★

Kitty heard the voices of the ambulance crew downstairs. She felt as if everything was breaking up into tiny fragments.

'Kitty, are you there?' Henry was calling from the bottom of the stairs. 'You need to bring the baby down.'

'I'm coming,' she said. She bent down and kissed Alexandra, then picked her up and pressed her tightly into her chest. Her daughter began to make soft moaning noises. 'Shhh, you need to be quiet now.' Kitty wanted to weep, but the emotion sat inside her, weighing her down. What had she been thinking coming back to The Old Priory with Beecham Manor just up the road?

Anne's child began to whimper. She bent down and whispered in her ear. 'Believe it or not, you're the lucky one.' She laid Alexandra down stroking her cheek, watching as she drifted back off to sleep. Then she picked up Anne's child and carefully made her way down the stairs, wary after her fall. The nurse flicked a glance towards her, while injecting something into Anne's arm.

'Ahh, you have the baby,' the nurse said.

'It's a girl,' Kitty said. She was finding it difficult to breathe. 'I've been busy changing her, poor thing hasn't been washed very well.' Kitty heard the tremor of her voice, looked at Henry who was bent over in the armchair, his elbows digging into his bony knees. He stood up and she supposed he wanted to see the baby but he went to the window instead, shoving his hands deep into his trouser pockets.

'Another child to belong to the Campbell clan.'

'You say that as if it's a bad thing.'

His eyes were full of pain. It occurred to her that Bet was right: her mother had lied to her or not told the truth. The way he was now, wasn't the behaviour of a guilty man.

'What if her mother dies?' he asked.

Kitty turned away, unsure what to say. She said to the nurse: 'The bedroom looks as if there's been a massacre. Is it possible she gave birth alone?'

Henry's face creased up.

'Sorry, that sounded dreadful,' Kitty said, realising by the closed expression the nurse wore that she'd said something inappropriate.

'I'm really not sure,' she said. 'Okay, ready, Bill? We can't waste another minute.' She placed Anne's arm across her chest before the men went to move her. Kitty watched as Anne's body rocked about. Her neck looked long and slender, a large bruise was blossoming down one side of her face. Just then some of the village boys ran past the window. There was such an air of expectancy about the place that Kitty felt as if in a trance. It was as if every minute of her past was compressed into that room. A couple of Tom's novels were floating about the nurse's feet. What did it matter with life and death present and the room on the edge of darkness? Everything felt out of kilter, from another world.

'Is Anne going to be all right?' A small part of her wondering if Anne died, would she be allowed to keep *her* child and bring them up together with her mother. What was she thinking? Of course Clarissa wouldn't allow it.

'She's lost a lot of blood,' the nurse said. 'It also depends how long she was unconscious for. Was she conscious when you found her?' The nurse frowned. 'It's important.'

Kitty envied the woman's composure, the stiffly held smile, the warren of lines on her forehead fashioned by years of professional concern. She shook her head. 'No, she was unconscious. Her face was partly under water. It was an awful sight.' She wasn't really sure if she was crying because of Anne, because of what she was about to do, or because of the things Henry had said, or simply because of the impossibility of it all. *When are you going to be your own woman? You must do what's best for the child.* Voices entered her head and every part of her just wanted to run.

The nurse looked at Kitty.

'She'll need to go with Mrs Campbell,' the nurse said, nodding at the bundle in Kitty's arms. 'I'd like to check the baby over but we haven't the time.'

Henry followed the ambulance men out, picking up his discarded jacket.

'I'd better come with you,' he said. He turned to Kitty, frowning. 'Do you have everything?' he asked.

'I think I should wait for Tom, don't you?' She felt a rush of heat travel to her neck. The idea of Alexandra all alone upstairs making her breathless. She pushed Tom's baby into Henry's arms. He accepted the child like a gift, all fingers and thumbs. He looked down at Tom's child and she saw his face soften. She thought she heard Alexandra and looked up the stairs.

'I'd better get some of the baby's things,' she said. 'Don't go yet.'

*

Henry walked to the ambulance carrying the baby, careful not to drop her as he stepped inside, his mind batting away any thoughts of Kitty's odd behaviour. Right now, he had to concentrate on Anne. He thought she looked more comfortable in the sanctuary of the ambulance. The nurse took her pulse again, her frown deepening. 'Is the young lady bringing the child's clothes or what? We need to get some blood into this woman.'

What was Kitty doing? He was just about to jump out and fetch her when he remembered he was holding the baby. Then Kitty came flying out of the front door, a basket hanging from her elbow. Tears were streaming down her cheeks, her lips moist and bloated.

'Here,' she said. 'There's some extra napkins and nightdresses.'

'Aren't you coming?' he asked.

'Someone needs to be here for Tom.' She put the basket into the ambulance, then looked up at him: so much hidden behind her blue eyes that he was forced to look away.

'Are you okay holding the baby?' the nurse asked. She was busy checking Anne's blood pressure.

'Do I have a choice?' he said. He'd never held a baby before. The sweet little girl put her hand up to her ear and scrunched up her lobe. When the ambulance took off up the hill, he held her tight.

'Step on it, Bill! Sirens, blue light, the works. She's fading,' the nurse said, counterbalancing as they chugged up the hill.

Anne's skin was ashen. Henry looked down at the baby and felt the wrench of his past. This child might lose her mother, just as he did.

The memory of his mother laid flat, dressed in a corn-flower-blue tea dress came to him, as always, unwelcome. He remembered how he had made his way from school that day, a weight bearing down on him as he got near his home. 'Just feeling a bit poorly, that's all,' she'd said that morning, but he'd seen her like that before when she'd brought home bottles of liquor. He'd arrived home and looked up to see his mother's bedroom curtains were drawn. The sight of them made him feel heavy. On days like these, she'd always turn towards the door when he brought her

75

tea, fumbling about in her purse, handing him a few coins to buy a pasty, the smell of sleep sticky in the air.

He walked into the kitchen to find the usual sight of unwashed plates. His heart sank.

He called out, 'I'm back.'

His mother didn't answer. He washed the dishes, put the kettle on, careful to scrub the wooden drainer clean so that no mould grew. He warmed the teapot, put some tea inside, pouring on the water, then got his satchel and laid out his homework. He stomped up the stairs, angry for having a mother who wasn't there to greet him. He walked into the bedroom, held his hand up to stop the stench of alcohol and stale breath, saw his mother in her best blue frock. Her skin was pale, flawless. He'd never realised how beautiful she was before. He touched her face with the back of his hand, then felt her forehead with his palm, knowing that she wouldn't wake.

'Mum,' he said. 'Can you hear me?'

He rushed to the wardrobe to get the extra blanket she kept on the top shelf, careful to tuck it around her. Then he ran downstairs and went straight to Burtanshaw's corner shop.

'My mother's not well,' he said as he charged through the door.

Mrs Burtanshaw was slicing ham. The machine purred and crackled as paper-thin portions fell onto the grease-proof paper.

'So you said this morning. And it wouldn't be the first time, would it?' Mrs Burtanshaw said. 'Now look what you've made me do. I've lost count.'

'But she's really ill this time. I can't wake her up.'

Mrs Burtanshaw raised her eyes. 'Well try harder.'

'I did, but she didn't move.'

The woman she was serving swivelled round, her bulky body pressing at the cloth of her coat. He recognised her then as Mrs Carpenter who had four children whose father had died in the war.

Mrs Burtanshaw wiped her hands on her apron. 'Bill,' she called out. 'You'd better come.'

'What is it now?' Mr Burtanshaw growled.

'Now!'

Mrs Carpenter held out her hand. 'You come with me, luv,' she said.

Henry took the woman's hand, feeling the squashy surface of her plump fingers. He thought of his mother's bone-thin wrists and the feathery texture of her skin.

Mrs Burtanshaw buttoned up her coat so quickly the buttons were all wrong and the collar askew. She hastily wrapped up the ham. 'Here take this,' she said to Mrs Carpenter.

Mr Burtanshaw arrived, puffing and wheezing with the effort of ascending the stairs.

'You'd better call Doctor Harris,' Mrs Burtanshaw said. 'I have a funny feeling.'

Mrs Carpenter nodded at Mrs Burtanshaw. 'I'll take the lad up to Beecham,' she said.

When they arrived, Saunders, the Campbells' butler, opened the front door and led them into the kitchen. Henry had always liked this room. It was warm and filled with the smell of burnt sugar and onion. On the Aga a pile of folded sheets was being warmed and a pot of stew was bubbling.

'Look who's joining you for tea,' Mrs Carpenter said to Kitty who was sitting alone at the kitchen table. Agnes was by the stove rolling out some pastry. Kitty looked up, her face open as a prayer book.

'Hello,' she said. 'Agnes helped me to make this splendid cake.' She pushed a fluffy Victoria sponge across the table.

77

Henry saw how she read his pain by the way she flashed a questioning look as Mrs Carpenter disappeared down the hallway with Saunders. He sat at the kitchen table opposite Kitty with his hands in his lap, wanting to be invisible. Kitty's pencil shook as it hovered above the page.

'I hate mathematics,' she said.

'Do you want me to help you?'

Kitty shook her head.

'I wouldn't refuse an offer like that, Miss Kitty,' Agnes said, putting a plate of ham sandwiches in front of them.

Henry couldn't face a sandwich even though he was famished. Kitty pushed the exercise book across the table, a smile inching up her cheeks.

'You don't have to eat anything if you don't want to. I'd be happy if you helped me with my homework.'

Henry looked at it. The work she was doing he'd done years back. Long division had been easy for him. He was now working on algorithms that even Tom couldn't do despite going to that posh school.

'Have you a spare piece of paper?' he asked. 'I'll show you how to make it simple.'

'You don't mind?'

Henry shook his head. 'I'll need some paper.'

Kitty handed him a clean sheet. Henry settled down to explain the process. For a while he forgot about his mother, the smell of her bedroom, the polished smoothness of her skin. Kitty seemed to relax as he took her through each stage of the equation. Then he heard the cry of a siren down in the village. He didn't look up but kept working, even though tears were running down his cheeks. Kitty quietly handed him her handkerchief and touched his arm. Both of them watched the pencil as if it was working out the sum all on its own.

Later, Kitty and he waited for her mother on the stairs, the smell of lavender furniture polish about them. Clarissa brought a small suitcase that belonged to his mother and parked it in the vestibule. She stood whispering words to Saunders before walking into the hallway busily removing her gloves as she went.

'Hello, dear,' she said. She crouched down beside him. 'I've just popped to your house to pick up a few things. You're going to be staying with us for a few days.'

'Where's my mother?' he asked.

'They've taken her to the hospital.'

Henry turned round and buried his head into Kitty's shoulders. He sobbed, feeling his body cave in to the fear. Kitty stroked his head. 'She will be all right, won't she?' he asked.

Clarissa crouched down.

'Oh dear, Henry. I'm afraid it isn't good news. No, it isn't good news at all,' she said. She placed one hand on his knee and the other on Kitty.

The ambulance stopped. The doors were thrown open, bringing him back to the present. He watched as Anne disappeared into the cavern of the hospital building, the nurse beside her, leaving him alone, the child buried into his chest. He wasn't really sure if he was holding the baby correctly, his coat still looped over his arm. He could smell the metallic salt air. The baby's face wrinkled as if she could taste the salt of the sea. His heart ached at the girl's innocence, at the thought of Anne giving her life and possibly losing her own. The seagulls hollered above, the pavements were black with the afternoon's rain. He had never liked Brighton, not since reading *Brighton Rock*. He thought of Kitty. Something was different about her, he knew distress when he saw it and he suspected it had nothing to do with Anne. There was something she wasn't telling him; he was sure of it.

The driver jumped out, swung the doors of the ambulance closed. 'Make your way up to the maternity ward. They're expecting you. Here, take this,' he said, handing Henry the basket. Henry clutched the baby close, grabbing the basket and looping it over his arm.

Inside, the chambers of the building were ringing with a deep hushed silence. Henry had been here before: the same hospital, the same smell of illness pressing down on him. Clarissa had brought him, but by that time his mother was already dead. He pushed the memory aside, but his mother's ghost followed him down the airless corridors as he punched at the swing doors leading from one department to another.

He stopped an orderly who was pushing an empty wheelchair.

'Could you direct me to the maternity ward?' Henry said. The baby had started to cry.

'Fourth floor,' the orderly said.

A midwife and a doctor were waiting. He could hear a woman grunting behind a closed door in the clutches of birth. The midwife, a woman in her forties with a neatly coiled bun, took the girl, gripping around her tiny frame.

'Certainly has a pair of lungs on her.'

Henry winced at the cliché.

'Perhaps you can tell me where they might have taken Mrs Campbell?'

'Intensive Care, most probably,' the midwife said.

Once again the image of his mother returned to him unbidden. He looked back at the little bundle he'd handed over to the midwife, knowing that the future had more to offer him. He'd enjoyed holding the baby – the idea of new life – he just prayed Anne was going to be okay.

ELEVEN

Bet was in the kitchen preparing supper. She hadn't been able to stop thinking about the girl and her baby all day. She'd wanted to scoop the two of them into her arms, but that wouldn't have been appropriate. She picked up her pinafore and wrapped it around herself before starting work in the kitchen, running her knife down the stomach of the trout, slitting it open so that the innards spilled out onto the draining board. She gave them a quick tug, then scraped down the blood line. The heads she cast aside into the open newspaper along with the potato peel. Their watery eyes stared blindly up at her, their mouths gaping. She cut the flesh away from the bone, trimmed the fat. A spot of blood went onto her pinny and she dabbed away at it. She couldn't get the girl off her mind, the way she'd gabbled, the words gushing out of her, telling Bet the whole story, her body shaking as she'd led her into the parlour of the house next door, away from the interested gaze of her regulars.

The potatoes were bubbling away; she gave them a prod to test them but the centres were still hard. It was the child that concerned Bet most. Poor mite growing up in the wake of the scandal and from that type of family as well. She threw the fish onto the skillet, smiled as the flesh made a satisfying hiss, opened the window to get rid of the smell. She looked up at the clock: six o'clock. Sam should be back soon. Fish needed to be served up fresh.

Five minutes later, Samuel walked through the door just as she was loading up the plates. She heard him wipe his feet, hang up his coat, brush it free of the day's filth. She quickly wrapped up the peelings and heads and whipped them into the bin outside.

'Hello, luv. What we got 'ere then?' Samuel took off his suit jacket, hung it on the back of the chair. 'It's not Friday.'

Bet poured them both a glass of Guinness. 'How was the bank manager?'

'I got my loan. Mr Carter has been very generous. He said I'd proved myself a good businessman. That's quite a compliment coming from a man with an established background such as the bank. Of course he was a bit concerned what with the mortgage on the new house, but I told him I could handle it and the figures stack up.'

'Well that *is* good news,' Bet said. She picked at her fish. She'd lost her appetite.

Sam looked at the pile of boxes she'd stacked in the kitchen. 'You've been busy,' he said.

'Someone's got to do it. We've got four more days in this house and six years of stuff collected. I've thrown out so many things.' Bet forced herself to eat the fish. She was anxious and she couldn't stop herself thinking of the girl and her baby.

'Well don't throw out too much,' Sam said. 'We've a big house to fill.'

'Well we don't want to fill the new place with broken china that we should have thrown away years ago.'

Sam had already drunk half of his Guinness. She could see he had a lot on his mind by the way his fingers were drumming the glass in between bites of his food.

'I went to see about that showroom I was telling you about in Croydon.'

'Croydon's a long way off.'

'Just on the outskirts, but it needs to be where people can stop off and have a look.'

'It's closer to Mitcham though. You'll have to drop me off at the tea shop first.'

'We'll worry about that later.'

Sam wolfed down his fish while Bet continued to pick at hers. His table manners had never been up to much. She kept thinking about Kitty and how she'd seemed broken despite her cheery aspect. Sam was still wittering on about second-hand cars but she found herself unable to listen.

'You look different,' he said. 'What's up? It feels like we're celebrating, what with the Guinness.'

'Well, we are. There's the loan for one thing and a new start.' Earlier she'd put on a bit of lipstick and looked in the mirror wanting to feel like a woman again, teasing her hair a little to get height. She thought to tell him about the girl who'd come into the tea shop. She knew her change of heart would mean a lot to him.

'A funny thing happened today. A woman came into the tea room. She was holding this dear little baby and I could tell she wasn't married from the second I clapped eyes on her.'

Just then she heard the cries of an infant and turned towards the front door, her heart pounding hard as if she'd run up a flight of stairs.

'Did you hear that?'

'What's that, luv?'

Bet assumed it was a passing pram, took a deep breath and started again. 'But she wasn't, you know, a woman of a certain kind. She had a cut-glass accent for one thing, and I thought to myself, how can a girl like this end up in trouble?' Bet hesitated, the tears pricking her eyes as she looked at Samuel, his face open. 'Anyway, poor thing. Her parents had told her she'd have to get rid of the baby because they didn't approve of the father. Poor girl did as she was told, put the baby up for adoption . . .'

'And don't tell me, you took him off her hands.'

Bet rolled her eyes and put her rubber gloves on ready to wash up. 'Actually, it wasn't a him, it was a girl. It just made me think, that's all, about what you said this morning.' The water was steaming hot, just how she liked it because it made everything clean without much effort. What with the clatter of the pans in the sink and the tap running, she didn't hear anything until the water stopped running.

'Was that someone knocking?' Sam asked.

There was a definite baby's cry this time followed by another knock on the door.

'She must have come back,' Bet said, walking towards the door.

'Who?'

'Kitty. The girl I was telling you about.'

And she opened the door still wearing her rubber gloves.

TWELVE

Kitty swung onto Beecham's gravel drive with blurry eyes. She'd cried the whole way. It didn't matter if Henry was seeing someone else, and it didn't matter if he had a girl in Boston, she told herself. They would never be able to be together now. It was too late. How could she have faced her mother? Too many mistakes had been made, they'd let desire take the lead and paid the price. She didn't want the same for Alexandra. Didn't want her anywhere near her mother, all that bitterness she'd have to swallow. Despite Henry's apparent confusion she no longer trusted him, even that was her mother's doing. She turned off the engine. She wasn't sure how long she sat there staring at the house, at her bedroom that looked out onto the forecourt and the spinney across the road. Tom's handyman, Glynn, had handed her his handkerchief after she'd explained what had happened to Anne. Now it was sodden. The windows were steamed up and there was an oval of condensation just behind the steering wheel. In that moment everything seemed clear. Not the future that was muddy and difficult, but the past. She hadn't really considered how she was going to feel.

She felt numb.

She wondered if she could slip into the kitchen and find Cook's supply of brandy. The emptiness she felt inside had grown so large that it pressed on her lungs. She opened the car door. It all depended on who was there to greet her. Usually it was Saunders. Tom would be at the hospital by now unless something had happened.

Something *had* happened.

When nobody answered the doorbell she leaned on it heavily, then crossed the driveway, stepping over the fence into the kitchen garden. She wrenched off the Woolworths wedding ring, remembering the day her mother gave it to her. *Just in case you begin to show.* She strode down towards the lake, passing the boat house, ignoring the feeling that climbed up inside her chest. She looked into the well of the water, the mucky surface, the clutter of plants falling around it, and threw the ring, relishing the small 'plop' as it entered the water.

Then she went over to the vegetable patch to check for cabbages. Finding some she broke off a few outer leaves. It was probably an old wives' tale but Bet had seemed convinced and Kitty knew that in a few hours she'd be in a lot of pain.

The back door that led into the scullery was open. Kitty crossed the threshold and a jelly-like feeling came over her. Someone had locked both the dogs in the boot room and they were scratching to get out.

'Is anybody home?'

Nobody answered. She went straight to Cook's cupboard and pulled out the brandy, didn't bother with a glass. When she went to put the bottle back another flutter of fear made her uncork it again. The dogs were agitated. She could hear them thumping against the door, barking. She half expected her mother to be watching, but when she turned the place was empty.

The kitchen had always been Kitty's favourite room because it was chaotic, full of jars and tins with all kinds of goodies. Above the range, copper pots hung on hooks and there was always the smell of pastries, bread, or soup hanging in the air. It was the warmest room in the house. She remembered a time before Henry's mother died when they'd not long known Henry. He'd just arrived from America and still had a bit of an accent. They were all sitting around the table eating teacakes. She remembered it because she'd just started her period. It was shortly before Henry's birthday party.

'When's Daddy coming home?' Kitty asked. She was careful not to lick her fingers even though the butter ran down them.

'He'll be back soon,' her mother said.

'But it's today, isn't it?'

Clarissa nodded. She was distracted by a pile of toasted buns.

'Where's he been?' Henry asked. He always ate hungrily with his elbows on the table back then, but years with the Campbells knocked that out of him.

'He's been in the West Indies,' Clarissa said.

'Buying sugar and tea' Tom added. Tom was proud of their father and it embarrassed Kitty because she knew that Henry didn't have a father.

'Is that what he does, buys sugar?' Henry asked.

'Not like in the shops, silly,' Tom said.

'He knows that, stupid.'

Tom stuck his tongue out, so she did as well.

'Kitty Campbell I will not tolerate bad manners at the table,' Clarissa said.

'What about *your* father?' Tom asked Henry. 'What does he do?'

Henry blushed then and looked down at his plate. 'He works in a car factory,' he said.

'The Carpenter boys said you don't have a father,' Tom said, 'but I told them that he's American.' Tom stretched out the word *American*.

'They're just jealous because you don't play with them any more,' Kitty said.

'Some children lost their father in the war, Tom,' Clarissa said. 'Like the Carpenters.'

'I know,' Tom said, indignant.

Kitty recognised the way Clarissa looked at Henry. She'd witnessed her mother's pity before. 'Don't you miss your father?' she asked. Tom kicked her. She elbowed him back.

'Yeah, sure do, but my mother and he didn't get along and she said it would be better if I forget him.'

'How can you forget your father?' Kitty said. 'I couldn't forget mine.'

Tom kicked her again. Clarissa was buttering a teacake for Tom, careful to wipe her fingers on the napkin before she slapped her hand on the table to bring a stop to their quarrel.

'Mom said that he was sending me something big for my birthday,' Henry continued.

'We say Mum,' Kitty said, knowing Tom would start to copy him in no time at all.

'When's your birthday?' Tom asked.

'Next week.'

'Are you having a party?' Kitty asked.

Henry shook his head, wiped the butter that had collected on his lips with the back of his hand. Clarissa handed him a napkin.

'Mum said we haven't the space.' He winked at Kitty after he'd pronounced the word 'mum' correctly.

'We could have it here?' Kitty said. 'I'll make the cake.' She turned to their mother. 'He can, can't he?'

Her mother thought for a minute. 'I don't see why not. I'll speak to Cook, and of course you'll have to ask your mother.'

Just then Howard walked in.

'Daddy. You're back!' Kitty rushed into her father's arms. He embraced her. She felt instantly relieved by his presence despite the bitter smell of London on his suit. He turned to shake Tom's hand who stood waiting patiently beside her.

'Henry's going to have his birthday party right here in this house. Mummy said so,' Kitty said.

Howard raised his eyebrows, bent down to kiss Clarissa's cheek.

'How was your trip?'

'Long.'

'I'll make a fresh pot of tea,' Clarissa said.

Howard winked at Henry who hadn't said a word. 'What's all this about a birthday?' he asked.

'I'm going to be fourteen next Friday, Mr Campbell.'

'That *is* a fine age.'

'Is thirteen a fine age as well?' Tom asked.

'Very fine,' their father said. 'So you moved into the village not long ago, is that right?'

'Yes, sir. We came back from the States in the autumn.'

'The States, wow!' Their father looked pensive. 'You must miss it?'

'Yes, I do.'

'Come on,' said Tom. 'Let's go down to the village.' Tom pulled at Henry's jumper. Kitty jumped up to join them.

'Where do you think you're going, Kitty Campbell?' Clarissa said.

'Down to the village with Tom.'

'You're not to play with boys, Kitty. Not now you're a young lady.'

★

The memory played before her eyes. The feeling of being confined by her mother making her feel angry, and here she was, still controlled by her. *Kitty, when are you going to be your own woman?*

She blushed at the thought of Henry looking at her with a puzzled expression. She'd admired him even then, but *he* had probably thought her silly. As for Henry's accent, the Campbells knocked that out of him with elocution lessons when he came to live with them after Dorothy died. Kitty had been proud of their generosity once but Georgie had scoffed when she'd told her the story of how Henry had come to live with them. She had listened while chipping away at some piece of wood in a sculpture class. 'They probably like to be seen as generous. It allows them their wealth,' she'd said. She'd given Kitty a coy look under her fringe, cigarette slipped in between nicotine-stained fingers. 'Either that or they're hiding something.'

Kitty thought about Bet's comments: 'Maybe your mother knows something about Henry that she hasn't told you.' She thought about Henry and the girl in the village.

Walking into Beecham's hallway Kitty felt overwhelmed by the vastness of it, as if seeing it for the first time. 'Hello, is anybody there?' she said again. She popped her head round the library door. Everything felt hollow, as if the place was bare of furniture as well as people. The grandfather clock ticked its bass tone. 'Is anyone home?' Her voice was swallowed up by the emptiness of the place.

'Beecham is never empty,' she muttered to herself as she climbed the stairs. The phone started to ring and she moved to answer it but stopped at the thought of her mother, or worse, the mother and baby home. What did she care? Alexandra had nothing to do with them now.

It was over. Alexandra was safe.

THIRTEEN

Bet was cradling the sleeping baby while Samuel paced up and down, stopping to stoke the fire, more out of nervousness than a need to keep the room warm. Her rubber gloves were still on the floor. She kept looking at the tiny girl. Before, she'd been wrapped in a scruffy old hospital blanket and a badly knitted cardigan, whereas now she was swaddled in a beautiful lacy shawl with scalloped edges, the likes of which Bet had never seen before. The suitcase gaped open, taking up a large portion of the room. Kitty had provided a change of clothes, formula milk, a bottle, still in its box, and several napkins.

'That's an expensive suitcase, that,' Sam was saying, throwing his hands in the air. 'I mean what kind of woman dumps their baby in a suitcase at a stranger's doorway?'

'A desperate woman.'

'But the letter and everything.'

'It's a gift.'

'How did she know it's a gift we wanted?'

'It's fate Sam. Look at her, she's the sweetest thing you ever saw. It was you who wanted to adopt.'

Sam threw a glance, but she could see he was too troubled to take the child in. 'Not like this, Bet. Not like this.' He unbuttoned his waistcoat. 'Don't go getting ideas into your head.' He kept pacing back and forth, refusing to catch her eye.

'And that letter. I mean, it's a little bit presumptuous. We're going to have to call the police. You can't just bring up someone else's child, there's paperwork to sort out. Adoption is a long process. It needs to be formalised.'

'So, we'll formalise it. Will you sit down, Sam, or better still hold the baby while I make up some milk. I mean at least she had the good sense to leave her equipped. You got to take your hat off to her. I can see what she's done: all her options were being taken away, and she thought, damn the lot of you. I'm going to choose my daughter's mother, and, Sam, she chose me!'

Sam turned round on his heel and looked at her open-mouthed. 'She's run away from her responsibilities, that's what she's done!'

'What choice did she have? By all accounts her parents had threatened to disown her. That class of woman can't be seen to sleep around. Poor girl was beside herself. Said her mother thought the father was a bit of cad, but she didn't want to believe them. Of course she didn't. Now take the baby while I boil the kettle.'

Sam shook his head. 'I'll put the kettle on. I might drop her.'

'Don't be daft. You've done it before.'

'The police will take her into care. There are procedures to follow.'

The headlights of a passing car passed through the room. Bet shuddered and stood up, surprised by a sudden agility. 'Samuel, don't you go start being negative. We need to stay strong.' She grabbed his elbow to stop him in his tracks. 'Stop this patrolling about will you.'

'Bet, this is law breaking.'

'We haven't done anything wrong, Sam.'

'Not yet, we haven't.'

'You've got contacts in the police and you've already been in touch with the adoption services.'

Samuel was rubbing the back of his neck, something he always did when he was stressed.

'How do you know that?'

'They called, that's how.'

Then Sam broke free and strode out into the hall.

'Where you off to now?'

'Calling the police.'

Bet followed him, propping the baby against her shoulder. 'Sam, no, not yet. Let's have one night with her. You never know, Kitty might change her mind and come back.'

'Bet, we're moving house in a few days, we haven't got time for this! And if she comes back and we've moved house, then what?'

'Tomorrow morning we'll take the baby down to the police station. We can take the letter, the papers, all of it. And you can call the Crusade of Rescue and Homes for Destitute Catholic Children. They'll probably have some idea what to do. But leave it till the morning. Let's just have one night with her before the trouble begins.'

Sam was standing in the hallway, his hands hanging limply by his sides. He let out a long sigh, shaking his head. 'I'll do it, Elisabeth, but against my better judgement.'

'Good. Now go put that kettle on.'

Samuel went into the kitchen. From there he shouted. 'Again, what type of woman leaves her baby on a doorstep?'

'She had run out of choices for heaven's sake!'

'Even so.'

'She was beside herself this morning and yet it seemed to me she wasn't quite connected, like she didn't have her feet firmly planted.'

'And now we're sitting here with *her* baby.' Sam was standing frowning in the doorway. 'Funny old life!' He raised his eyes and went back into the kitchen. 'We can't get involved, Bet. We're moving.'

She could feel the girl stirring and she cupped her hands under her arms and rocked her again. 'Put on a pan of water, will you. We'll need to sterilise the bottle and the teat. There's such a lot to do.' She rubbed the baby's cheek and watched as she chewed in her sleep. Kitty had asked for her to be named Alexandra. Alexandra Abbott, she liked the sound of that and the fact that the girl was dark meant she could easily be Samuel's daughter. The baby's small hand reached up to her chin, one finger protruding. She opened her mouth and yawned. Bet ached with the desire to feed her.

She loved her already.

FOURTEEN

Henry was in need of a drink. He'd only been allowed to see Anne for a short while after waiting to speak to the doctor. Anne was in a room of her own, comatose, all manner of things wired into her. Afterwards, he'd driven back to The Old Priory in a daze, hoping to find Kitty, but she'd already left and there was no sign of Tom. He'd gone up to Anne and Tom's bedroom, which had been torn apart in Kitty's hurry to get the baby's things. Whatever must she have thought when she found Anne's baby? All that blood like a scene out of *Sweeney Todd* – nothing could have prepared him for the carnage. He'd cleared everything up. It wasn't fair for anyone to have to face that, except for perhaps Tom who had probably stopped off to see Kitty's friend Georgie rather than face his pregnant wife. But it was Kitty, her frayed nerves, her hysteria, that had shaken him most.

As he finally drove down the curved driveway to Beecham Manor, the wheels biting at the newly laid gravel, he noticed Kitty's car parked sloppily at an angle. He continued on to the back of the house glad to see someone had left the garage door open. He parked inside, sat in silence listening to the rain battering against the roof of the garage, unable to face Kitty just yet. He thought about all that water and the destruction it had caused, and the woman who had fallen off her bicycle and the brown contents of the overflowed river sloshing about in Tom's living room. He thought about Kitty standing there while he nursed Anne, her jaw clenched and her body rigid. All that effort she made to appear brave and free, yet she was far more vulnerable than people realised. He had been so determined to find out why she ran away and had failed. He leaned onto the steering wheel and let his head drop. He needed to think before facing her again.

He crossed the kitchen garden making his way wearily towards the back door, exhausted yet alert. The peaty scent of damp earth, fresh and hopeful, clashed against the memory of Anne lifeless in the hospital. Henry imagined Tom beside her, probably still smelling of that woman in London. He let himself in through the back door. The place was in darkness. The dogs were barking non-stop in the boot room. He let them out, crouching so that they licked his neck before pushing the kitchen door ajar gently. Henry had looked after the dogs since first coming to Beecham. When he was younger, he used to get up early and walk them before school. As Howard was in Kenya they'd been his responsibility once again and he'd been grateful. He loved the Campbell dogs. Someone was in the kitchen.

'Kitty!'

But it wasn't Kitty. Lillian, the Campbells' housekeeper, was standing by the stove in the dark dressed in her coat. She jumped, covered her mouth, which Henry realised was full.

Irritated, he said, 'Why were the dogs locked up?'

'I'm not sure,' she said. 'I was just about to leave.'

'Is Kitty about?' The dogs were bouncing around him. He held out his arm to stop them. 'Where's Saunders?'

Swallowing, Lillian said, 'He's probably gone to the village.'

'And Kitty?'

Lillian's blank eyes were fixed on the dogs. 'I don't like the dogs in here.'

He hustled them both back into the boot room. 'Is Miss Kitty here?' he said again.

'I'm not sure,' Lillian said, her voice shaky. 'Someone called asking for her just a minute ago. A man who left his name, he said something about a mother and baby home. He asked to speak to Clarissa as well. I left a note on Howard's desk.'

'Probably some charity event most likely, if they asked for Clarissa,' Henry said, thinking aloud.

'Everyone is down in the village. There's been a flood,' Lillian said.

'I'm aware of that,' Henry said.

He walked to the drawing room to check Kitty wasn't there. The room crackled with lack of use. Someone had thrown sheets over the furniture and the Chinese rugs had been rolled up, tied with string and stacked in the corner on their end. They must be in the process of spring cleaning, he thought. As he went back down the hall, he popped his head into the library but she wasn't there. He climbed the stairs and was about to walk past the old nursery when he noticed Kitty slumped in the armchair sitting in darkness. He saw then that her blouse was undone and her breast exposed. He stopped outside on the landing. He couldn't see clearly but he thought she was holding a tea towel, as if she'd collapsed with it in her hand. She was still wearing her mud-stained shoes and her stockings were caked as well. He stood inert, incapable of movement, unsure what he was seeing, the memory of her earlier that day as she handed him the child and the sight of her now like a collision. Kitty looked up.

Pulling her blouse together she said, 'Isn't it awful?'

'So you came back here?' he said. 'What about Tom?' Kitty's eyes pinned him down. A deep silence surrounded her that seemed to move towards him, an invisible lake of feeling. All he could hear was the thrumming of his own hurried breath.

'I thought someone ought to contact our parents.'

'I've already sent a telegram to Howard,' Henry said.

'Right, good.' She was looking down at her lap as if something were there. He wanted to run up to her, ask what the heck was going on, but there was something intangible stopping him.

'I went back to The Old Priory.' He realised he wasn't making sense.

'I didn't know what to do. In the end I thought it best to come back to Beecham. I've made so many mistakes, Henry. I couldn't make another one. But you can't undo the past can you?'

He wasn't sure if she was talking about Paris or before. He was trying to piece everything together in his head when he saw the reflection of a blue light on the nursery wall.

Kitty looked up. The space between them felt even denser.

'It occurred to me Anne was probably dead. Is she?'

'No.'

He stepped forward. There was a rap on the door, three short firm taps that felt intrusive. The dogs started to bark again, he could hear them running about in the kitchen. Outside, Henry heard a man cough. Kitty didn't appear to notice any of it.

'Lillian,' Henry called. 'Can you get the door.' He turned and walked towards the banister. 'Lillian!'

Kitty dropped her head back on the chair, her face scarred with emotion, her cheeks wet with tears.

'She's a darling little girl, don't you think? A real darling.'

The blue light reflected all around her. There was something about her tone, that hysterical edge. How had they gone from the boat house to this?

Kitty remained slumped in the armchair. She didn't seem to notice the kerfuffle going on downstairs. Time seemed to have stopped, but he looked at his watch to see that it was nine o'clock. It had been such a long day. He went down the stairs far enough to see Tom in the vestibule flanked by two policemen. Lillian scuttled past them. He heard her leave through the back door.

'Thank you so much, you've been awfully kind,' Tom said. He shook both of their hands.

'Anytime, Mr Campbell,' he heard one of them say. They both stood astride, their caps tucked under their arms as they left.

Tom took off his hat revealing hair that was freshly cut. What kind of man would get his hair cut when Anne was waiting, heavily pregnant? Henry turned back to Kitty. Even in the darkness he could sense the weight of what she was feeling reach into him. She tilted her head upwards and was about to say something, her mouth open.

'It's Tom,' he said.

'I'll be right down,' she said.

Henry took the stairs two at a time. 'Did they give you a lift home?'

'Yes they did,' Tom said. 'Terribly nice chaps. They came to see how Anne was; whether she was well enough to answer any questions. Apparently the midwife's mother reported the woman missing. Then while we were driving back we heard news that the nurse had had an accident down by the river. Godawful this flood. People have actually drowned.'

'And how is Anne?' Kitty asked. She was standing behind Henry.

Tom shook his head, his shoulders rolled forward. 'She's still unconscious.' His face was flushed. 'Apparently you saved Anne's life,' he said to Henry.

'Is that what they told you?'

'Yes, lucky you were there.'

Henry had swum for the county, been a lifeguard during the school holidays. If it had been Tom, Anne would be dead.

Tom turned to Kitty. 'And it was you who found her.'

Henry could sense his unease. Kitty slipped past him and stood with her arms crossed, holding onto the cuff of her shirt.

'Anne was in a terrible state, we thought she was dead. And where were you? What on earth were you thinking buggering off to Kenya when Anne is that heavily pregnant? I can't believe Mother didn't stay with her either. What is wrong with this family?'

Tom bowed his head. 'Didn't anyone tell you about the fire in the plantation? How come you're back from Paris, anyway?'

'Well someone had to be here for Anne. It's about time you woke up, you're a father now and you can't just go off gallivanting about.'

They all stood still. Of course she was right, but it was a shock to feel the intensity of her anger.

'I need a drink.' Kitty walked towards the library. Henry noticed that she'd taken off her stockings. Tom followed. 'I got to see the baby briefly before we left. A pretty little girl, isn't she?'

'Yes. And you need to damn well look after her.'

'The paediatrician said we could probably bring her home next week. Anyway, this business with the midwife explains why Anne was alone.' Tom wrung his hands. 'Apparently she'd lost a lot of blood because of the birth. They think that's why she fainted. You're right, I shouldn't have gone, I told Mother it was awful timing.'

Kitty slumped down into an armchair, staring blindly into the fire.

'Let me take your coat.' Tom hesitated before shifting himself out of the sleeves. Kitty turned to Henry. Their eyes locked and he saw then that whatever he'd felt upstairs in the bedroom was now buried.

'I'll make us a sandwich,' Henry said.

'Can't Agnes make something?' Tom said.

'I imagine she's gone to bed. It's been a long day for everyone.'

'Well get her up then,' Tom said.

'For God's sake, Tom,' Henry said.

Tom frowned, his eyes bruised. 'You're right. I'm sorry.'

'I could do with a drink,' Kitty said again.

Henry turned on another table lamp, poured them all a whisky. He noticed Kitty's hands were shaking when she took it. Tom was finally silent.

He strode down the hall in darkness. The smell of tobacco and wood polish added to an overwhelming sense of nostalgia. The three of them hadn't been together for years. He sensed something had changed in Kitty, not since Paris, but since she'd handed him the baby in the ambulance. Her hair was in a tangle, piled high on her head. Salt dried on her cheeks. Her eyes were narrowed and hard. When he reached the pantry he saw the sandwiches were already laid out on a plate, a fan of tinned salmon and cucumber. He remembered the feeling of wonder when he had first visited Beecham Manor. But luxury wears thin against a tide of loss.

He pushed open the door of the library with his foot and laid the tray on Howard's desk, shoving the letters aside.

'They think she's going to live, but there's a chance of brain damage,' Tom was saying. He pulled out a packet of cigarettes from his trouser pocket, tapping one out before offering the pack to Henry. 'They can't seem to tell me anything conclusive. Apparently the next twenty-four hours are crucial. Looking at the baby I thought there's a chance she will never know her mother.' He turned away to face the fire, dipped his head, exposing red marks left by the barber. The veins on the back of his hands protruded like the roots of an old tree. 'Oh God,' he said and drew heavily on his cigarette, his mouth revealing a masked vulnerability. A waft of smoke spilled out of his mouth. He began to cry, real tears that somehow brought relief to all of them.

FIFTEEN

Bet was humming the tune of 'Heartaches by the Number'. She'd no idea how that track had found its way into her head. Alexandra hadn't accepted the bottle and she was getting hungry, wriggling about, her head going from one side to the other. Samuel was strutting in front of the fire, his waistcoat undone, his tie thrown across the arm of the chair. He'd poured himself a second beer and was drinking it with a thirst she'd never seen before.

'What are the neighbours going to think?' he said. 'The whole street is probably awake by now. Can't you quieten her down?'

'Why don't you do something useful?'

'Like call the police?'

She threw him a look. He rolled his eyes.

'Like go and get the cot out of the loft,' she said.

'For heaven's sake, Bet. We don't know if we can keep her yet.'

'Samuel! We have to get it out of the loft on Friday anyway, or were you expecting me to do that as well?'

Samuel held up his hand. 'All right, all right. What's wrong with her anyway?'

'I imagine she's missing her mother for one thing and more likely her milk. Formula isn't quite the same. She'll take it when she understands there's nothing else, poor mite.'

Sam stomped up the stairs, intent on waking the neighbours if they weren't already awake. She could hear him swearing up in the loft, throwing things from one side to another.

The baby was dozing, but she knew it wouldn't be long before she started off again. She went into the kitchen and put the pan of boiling water back on, holding the baby in the crook of her arm. She needed to warm the milk. It was ten o'clock. It was going to be a long night.

'There's a box of all Johnny's linen. You might as well bring that down.' She could hear Samuel in Johnny's old bedroom erecting the cot. 'Sam, did you hear me?'

'I heard you.'

Five minutes later, he walked into the kitchen, his hair all up on end and his shirt smudged with dirt.

'I think you're getting ahead of yourself,' he said.

The baby started to stir.

'What is wrong with you, Sammy? Have a heart.'

'It's hardly surprising, is it? This morning I was on my way to being an entrepreneur and now look.' His words trailed off and he let out a sigh.

'Just get a grip and wash your hands. You're going to give Alexandra her first bottle of milk.'

'Oh, Bet, no. You know I can't do that.'

'You don't know until you've tried. You used to be brilliant with Johnny. At least hold her while I warm the milk. You need to wash first though.'

Sam went to the kitchen sink, scrubbed his hands with carbolic soap, his body hunched as he rubbed all the way up to his elbows. Alexandra had opened her eyes and was looking around her. She seemed to prefer the kitchen to the parlour.

'There, there. It's going to be all right,' Bet said. 'Sit yourself down.'

Sam went and put himself in one of the kitchen chairs and Bet handed him the baby. 'It's not like you haven't done this before, is it?'

Alexandra wriggled her head, her eyes searching around. 'But she seems so delicate.' Sam frowned, but Bet could see his body sink into itself, his features soften.

'She's a pretty lass, I'll give you that.'

Bet checked the temperature of the milk on an upturned wrist. It was just warm enough. Perhaps it had been too hot before, she thought. 'Here,' she said. 'Try her on this.'

Sam put the bottle to the girl's lips. They both held their breath as she guzzled it down.

'Don't let her rush it,' Bet said.

Sam pulled the teat back a little. 'Bless her,' he said. 'She was hungry, that's all.' He looked up at Bet, his face taut with fear, his eyes liquid. 'Oh God, Bet. Why us?'

★

Kitty was obsessing about Alexandra, hoping to God she was safe in Bet's arms. She wanted to tear into Tom, slap him hard for having everything she could not. Henry had gone off to make them all a hot drink and she'd been left to face Tom, when all she wanted to do was wrap herself in a blanket and sob. All she could think about was her baby, the sound of her crying outside Bet's door a constant internal echo. The memory of Bet's door knocker, the hearty sound of it. That momentary feeling of relief as Bet opened the door and then the horror as she watched Bet stoop down to pick Alexandra up. Kitty's limbs had felt like liquid, as if the bone, the flesh and the muscle had melted.

The fire sputtered and crackled. She watched mesmerised

for a second. The flames dancing, smoke contorting at the pull of the chimney.

'Is everything all right?' Tom asked. 'Henry seems tense.'

Kitty blinked the tears away. 'We thought Anne was dead.' She took the pins out of her hair and gathered them in the lap of her jumper. 'Why did Mummy have to go to Kenya for God's sake?' she said, threading some of the hairpins through her jumper.

'She went to support Dad.'

'Weren't you support enough?'

'I told you, there was a fire.'

'Was it bad?'

'What?'

'The fire, was anyone hurt?' She knew the answer to this, remembered her mother talking about Adamu.

'It's not good.' He ran his foot along the hearthrug. 'There was a lot of damage. One of the workers was badly burnt. We'll have to pay compensation. Dad wanted Mum to help the family. Adamu has been with us for a long time and his wife and children are devastated. He thinks it was arson. We sent in an accountant to check out why the company was making a loss and the next thing you know the office goes up in smoke.'

'It wasn't a good idea to leave Anne alone.'

'I was gone a week, Kitty.'

'It was the wrong week.'

'I know, but Anne was fine with it.'

'Of course Anne would say she was fine.'

'How was Paris?' Tom was hunched over, nodding. He wasn't his own man, any more than she was her own woman. Henry was right about that.

'Oh fine. It was fine. Everything's fine.'

'I was just asking.'

'Then fine.' She looked down at the pins in her hand.

Tom reached for another cigarette. 'I'm sorry, I'm not very good company.'

'None of us are.'

They sat there, the smell of their parents about them. Snatches of their past prying into the moment: the way their father would tap his pipe against the grate, his legs permanently crossed as he sat in the armchair.

'Tom, what did Henry tell you about this girl he's met in Boston?'

'What girl?'

Kitty knew it wasn't the right time to bring up her mother's accusation but there was something about Henry's tone – a sense of injustice. She was clutching at straws. 'Nothing, I must have misheard,' she said.

'Henry's probably got hundreds of girlfriends, good-looking chap like him.'

Kitty couldn't help it. She was crying. 'Do you mind if I slip off? I'm absolutely whacked.'

'No, no of course not.'

Henry was standing by the door watching her with his dark eyes. 'I've made you a cup of Ovaltine.' Kitty shook her head.

'I can't,' she said, and tears slipped down her cheeks.

SIXTEEN

Bet was beside herself. It was the middle of the night and she hadn't been able to sleep, her mind was racing away into the future. This baby couldn't have arrived at a worse time. How was she going to get everything packed up and move house? She'd have to close the tea shop for a while. She turned to see Samuel sleeping on his back, a soft hum escaping his lips. She envied him. All that fuss and the man was able to close his eyes and switch off like a clockwork soldier. His hair was ruffled and she felt a wave of appreciation at the memory of him feeding the baby. He'd not stopped looking at her, comforting the child with gibberish so she'd drifted off. Alexandra was asleep beside her in the suitcase – she'd managed to make up a bed inside it, worried that the cot was too big. She'd dropped off after she'd given her a second bottle just past midnight. Now Bet was wide awake. She pushed back the bedsheets, threw on her dressing gown. She looked at the baby swaddled in that beautiful shawl and wondered how Kitty was feeling, imagining her in a terrible state. There'd been a stack of envelopes. One containing a letter confirming that Katherine Victoria Campbell had officially requested that Elisabeth Abbott and her husband formally adopt her child, Alexandra Dorothy Campbell. How had she known Bet's surname? Kitty must have gone to the bother of looking them up in the telephone directory.

Then there were papers from the mother and baby home in North London. In amongst the baby's things she'd found a pair of booties with chiffon laced through. Who the hell on earth uses chiffon? But it was the fine lacy cuffs that had clearly been knitted by someone who knew what they were doing that puzzled Bet most. Surely they hadn't been knitted by Kitty. She wasn't the knitting type.

She went to the window and pulled the curtains back. She thought Kitty might be there waiting but the street was empty, except for a cat sidling down the middle of the road. Imagine if the baby was still outside and they hadn't heard her, the cat could have climbed into the box and suffocated the poor child! Bet clasped her hand to her chest at the thought and went downstairs to make herself a cup of hot chocolate. She struck a match, turned on the gas and while she waited for the milk to warm, took out the letter addressed to her, which Sam had scoffed at on first reading. The girl's hand-writing was immaculate. She was clearly educated, but that had been obvious the minute she'd spoken in the tea shop. What a decision to make after one brief meeting, to choose to give your child away just like that. She heard a noise and felt her pulse quicken. She went out into the hallway to find Samuel standing there bleary-eyed.

'What's up, pet?'

She heard the milk spit onto the range and rushed in to find the gas had gone out and the milk had boiled over. 'Blast,' she said. She turned to Sam.

'What if Kitty changes her mind? Oh I couldn't live without her now. I can see her running around in our new garden.'

He opened his arms and she folded herself into his embrace. 'Try not to worry. It'll turn out for the best.'

But Bet wasn't so sure. They'd had bad luck before.

SEVENTEEN

Henry had wanted to comfort Kitty; seeing her in that state left him feeling very distressed but he felt as if she didn't want his comfort. He returned to Beecham early the next day to take Howard's dogs out at dawn. It was Tuesday and yet it seemed as if a whole week had passed in one day. Throughout the night he'd listened to the trees rustle, to the crack of branches, the spiteful howl of a vixen on heat, the creak of his cottage responding to the wind. Unable to sleep for thinking of Kitty. And when he'd finally drifted off into a light sleep, his thoughts battled just under the surface, his body wired with confusion and longing. He was hoping to catch Kitty after he'd walked the dogs. At breakfast.

He walked the Campbells' dogs across the South Downs towards Chanctonbury Ring. On the brow of the hill, the trees, hewn out of their continuing battle with the wind, appeared to be kneeling in prayer. He'd grown up with this terrain, yet never belonged to it, but still he had come here to wrestle with his feelings in the same way the trees wrestled against the elements. A cluster of houses and farms huddled together below. Fields carved out of the landscape, bringing order, so quintessentially English. He wondered if Kitty would come away with him. It was hard to imagine now. She seemed to have closed down so intensely she was someone else entirely.

The dogs were barking, running down into the woods, chasing the scent of an animal. Henry crossed the stile, dipped down under the canopy of branches, followed the track until he found the torn body of a young partridge, twitching. He reached for a fallen branch, laid it across the bird's neck and stamped the last breath out of it until it lay lifeless, the feathers coated in dust. He saw blood on the bitch's lips. Howard's young Saluki. You can't scold a dog for its instinct, he thought. He imagined the hen searching for its chick. He had better get back.

Henry walked into the kitchen just as the phone rang in the hall. He picked up the receiver. After he had spoken to the doctor he realised Kitty was standing in the vestibule buttoning up her mother's coat.

'Is it good news?' she asked. She seemed to deliberately make herself busy with the fastening and buckling of shoes.

'It seems so,' he said. 'Anne is awake.'

Kitty didn't look at him. She was putting on lipstick using the hall mirror. 'That *is* good news,' she said, rolling her lips in and out. She turned to him then, offered him the briefest of smiles. 'I was just on my way out. I have the most awful headache.' She tucked a stray bit of hair behind her ear. 'Had it since yesterday. I thought if I just got some air.' She waved a dismissive hand as he gave her an umbrella. For the first time he began to wonder if she'd met someone, that her indifference was about something else entirely, and nothing to do with Clarissa and Howard's class issues.

'I'll just go and tell Tom the news and then maybe I can join you with the dogs,' he said.

'But you've already been out. I was going to take the car down to the seafront. Do you mind?' she said. 'I really can't wait.' She opened the front door before he had a chance to reply.

'Kitty, wait.'

'Later,' she said, without looking back.

'What about Anne? Will you come to the hospital?' She waved.

He watched as she strode across to the Morris. She seemed to have replaced her girlish coquettish gestures with slow womanly assuredness.

After she'd gone he felt the sense of failure like a wave that left him physically exhausted. He went to find Tom, knocked, didn't wait for him to answer. Tom, still in his underwear, was putting on his socks. He looked up, startled at the intrusion.

'I don't have any clothes,' he said. 'Can you take me home later? My car is in the garage at The Old Priory. In a terrible state I imagine.'

'The hospital has just telephoned. Anne's no longer comatose.'

Tom's eyes widened. He dipped his head, turning away from Henry. 'Thank God. Did they say anything about the baby? Has Anne seen her do you know?'

'They didn't mention it. I'm assuming as they're at the same hospital, they would bring the baby to her.'

'I can't believe I have a daughter.'

Henry walked across and laid a hand on his shoulder. Tom nodded, acknowledging the gesture. 'You need to call Dr Mosse. I've written the number on the notepad by the telephone.'

'I'll be right down.' Tom's voice was thick. But all Henry could think about was Kitty. He felt sure something had happened but he couldn't figure out what.

EIGHTEEN

Kitty stood across from the tea shop, shaking. A cream blind with Bet's Tea Shop inscribed across it in green had been pulled down to cover the front window. Of course it was too early. The grocer next door was open though and Kitty was tempted to go in and ask about the tea shop. The night before, she'd waited until Bet had opened the door, watched her dip down and scoop Alexandra up before turning the engine of the Morris. Mr Abbott must have taken the suitcase, she thought. She stepped off the kerb and heard the frantic ringing of a bicycle bell too late as the cyclist swerved to avoid her.

'Oi! Watch out will you!'

'Sorry.' Kitty gave an apologetic wave of the hand. She had no idea what she was doing. She thought perhaps she could talk to Bet, explain why she'd left Alexandra on her doorstep.

The grocer, dressed in a dark blue apron, was laying out all the fruit and veg. Mounds of carrots, potatoes, cauliflowers, broad beans and cabbages that looked invitingly fresh. He heaved a stack of crates onto his shoulder, plonking them down onto the pavement just as she went to walk into the shop. She dug into her pocket and realised she'd left her purse in the car. She turned on her heel and walked back, checking the road properly this time. As she crossed, she looked up at the house, noticing a flutter of movement as someone drew the curtains. She put her head down, skipping to avoid a bus, her heart hammering.

The greengrocer nodded. 'Morning. Can I help you, miss?'

'Half a pound of Cox's, please. Oh and a green cabbage,' Kitty said.

'Right you are.'

While he made a show of picking out some apples, she wandered into the shop. There were rows of tinned products neatly arranged in pyramids and a cheese counter as well as a range of hams. For a brief moment she let the fantasy unfurl of being married to Henry. Alexandra waiting for her in a pram outside while she bought them all something delicious for supper. Then she heard the cries of an infant coming from the back room. It was Alexandra. A mixture of relief and sorrow clashed inside her. She looked up and behind the counter there was an open door and a hallway. Bet was staring right at her. They stood holding each other's gaze, neither of them able to speak, Kitty's tongue coarse as sandpaper until the greengrocer swept in, bringing with him a cheerful aspect.

'Samuel,' Bet cried.

'It's all right, Mrs Abbott,' the grocer said. 'I got this.' He twisted the brown bag over and handed it to her along with a cabbage. 'That'll be one and thruppence ha'penny, my luv.'

Kitty dug around in her purse hunting for the exact change, her hands shaking so much she was unable to count the coins. It was clear Bet didn't want to talk to her by her stony expression. She heard Alexandra cry and caught her breath. When she looked up, Bet had gone.

'Thank you, lovely.' The grocer winked and stooped down to pick up a stray carrot from the floor. Kitty didn't know what to do. Already it felt as if Alexandra belonged to Bet. A simple act of desperation meant Kitty had forgone any right to ask anything of anyone.

'Can you tell me when the tea shop next door opens?'

The grocer shrugged. 'Around eleven o'clock, normally, but I'm not sure about today, though.' He stepped a bit closer. 'I think there's a spot of bother.'

Kitty, suddenly horrified that Bet might call the police, turned and fled.

She drove towards Beecham, the memory of Bet's face as she clutched hold of Alexandra on repeat. She parked in the woods, under the arc of a horse chestnut. She needed to think about what to do next. The light pushed its way through the thinly covered branches. No sign of last night's rain just the odd shiver of water dropping. The sky was stained blue, fragile as thinning cotton. She watched the branches sway, the young leaves supple and green, trembling in the blustery weather, staining the countryside with optimism. The verges were dotted with primroses. She pushed the seat back as far as it would go and stretched her legs. She wanted to cry but couldn't. The sway of the branches reminded her of a time when she and Henry had played hide and seek with Tom. She had been hiding inside the canopy of the willow tree and the branches had shifted in the wind. Henry had crept in and stood looking at her, his eyes reaching into her soul. Her heart had pounded because she knew that he was looking at her in a different way, there was a longing to him and when she went to shout to Tom that she'd been caught, Henry had stepped closer and put his finger on his lips to silence her.

'Shh,' he said. 'Let's just wait.' And then he had put his hand up to her face and kissed her, very lightly on her lips and she had felt a tingling in her breasts and a wash of shame. The willow had been their place.

That was before he went to Edinburgh, and presumably before Pamela Watson got pregnant – which she still didn't quite believe had anything to do with Henry – in much the same way she had. The shame was back, it trailed behind her like a hungry dog.

It started to rain, big drops thrummed on the roof of the car. She thought of Anne. A hard knot forming inside her. Of course Anne had survived and would get to keep her daughter. Then inevitably she thought of her mother. It seemed to Kitty that wherever her train of thought started, it ended with Clarissa: always the shadow, omnipresent like pollution; that impenetrable sadness that Kitty had slipped around for most of her life. This ancient wound that her mother carried about had now successfully passed on to her. How on earth had her mother envisaged Kitty living alongside her sister-in-law watching Anne mother her child while Kitty's child was brought up by strangers, never to be seen again? And Tom's reaction to her question about Henry had been vague, as if he hadn't known whether to say yes, or no. She needed to leave. Walk away from all of them. This thought made her yank the seat back into place, snagging her stockings and cursing. The Morris started first time and she spun off, mud spitting off the wheels into the newly sprouted fern.

She got back to Beecham to see Henry's car had gone from the garage. Her father's dogs did their usual thing of slamming against the boot-room door as soon as she entered. It was always left up to Henry to walk them when her parents were away and she remembered how he'd turned to those dogs for comfort when his mother had died. Their helpless pleas for freedom didn't reach her. She left them whining to find Lillian sifting flour in the kitchen.

'Cooking, Lillian? Where's Agnes?'

Lillian blushed. 'Down in the village, helping.'

The flood had receded in Kitty's mind and it took her a while to register what Lillian was referring to. 'Of course,' she said. 'Saunders as well?'

'He's gone to the airport to pick up your parents, miss, but a telegram arrived to say there's been a delay.'

Kitty felt her stomach constrict, the sharpness of anger clashing with a sticky amorphous grief waiting for her attention. 'Any news on Anne?'

'Your brother and Henry have gone to see Mrs Campbell in hospital.'

'Oh good.'

She watched as Lillian went about her duties, rolling out pastry, sprinkling the marble surface with flour.

'Do you know Pamela Watson?' she asked.

Lillian looked up, a shock of red flushing her cheeks. 'Yes, miss.'

'And presumably you're aware of the rumours?'

Lillian turned back to her work. 'It's not good to gossip, miss. Anyway, Pamela has long been married to one of the farm hands at Carpenter's farm.' She turned to Kitty. 'Will you be staying for lunch, Miss Kitty?'

'That's very kind of you to ask, Lillian, but no. I won't be here for lunch.'

Kitty went upstairs, found her old school trunk and stuffed as much into it as she could. She cleaned out her wardrobe, not because she needed clothes but because she wanted her absence felt. Then she took one of the cherished Globe-Trotter suitcases, her mother's this time, and filled that. She had no idea what she was going to do. A solitary tear wheeled down her cheek. She squeezed her eyes shut and resumed packing: hand-knitted jumpers, woollen stockings, a black dress, most of it she hadn't worn in years. She packed anything she could find. Then she went into her mother's dressing room and fished through the contents of *her* wardrobe. If she were a scorned lover, she would take a pair of scissors to the lot. But Kitty knew a more rational stance would do more damage. She picked out her mother's black Jaeger suit which she'd worn to Henry's mother's funeral, and her pink shot silk suit from Dior, and the bouclé pink suit as well. She'd need some winter options, she thought, and chose a couple of her mother's favourites.

She laid them on the back seat of the Morris then went into the library. On her father's desk was a pile of mail, including the letter she'd written to her mother telling her about the birth and the date she was due to leave St Helen's Mother and Baby Home. Another of her letters lay unopened with a French stamp on it. She picked up her father's fountain pen, snapped off the lid, sliding open the drawer of the desk to retrieve a piece of headed paper.

Howard and Clarissa Campbell,
Beecham Manor,
Steyning

Dear Mother and Pa,
I gave birth to a beautiful baby girl who is now being cared for by someone else. The birth was quick but painful and I had several stitches. You have no idea what I've been through, the sense of loss I feel. She was my daughter, your granddaughter.

I cannot forgive you for making me give her up so I must leave.

I never want to see either of you again.

Kitty

She carefully folded the paper and slipped it into the cream envelope. Then she picked up another sheet of paper and addressed a missive to Henry.

Next she went to the conservatory where all her art materials had been left boxed up. She tore open the boxes and dug out her paints and charcoals. Beside her easel there was a portfolio of her drawings she'd done as a young girl before she'd gone to the Slade. She untied the bows and leafed through the drawings of dogs, of the garden and flower arrangements, stopping at a pencil drawing she'd made of Henry. She remembered the day she'd dragged him down to the lake and begged him to sit still, but he had been hopeless and wriggled, picking up pebbles and tossing them into the lake while she tried to sketch him using a soft pencil.

'Look at me,' she'd said.

'You're taking too long,' he'd said.

'We've been here all of ten minutes.'

He smiled at her then and she noticed the gap in his front teeth. He was sixteen and had not long lost his mother. She could see the pain of loss in his eyes, but she did not know how to translate the sadness of them to paper. In the end he looked away and she caught him with his thick black hair hanging over one eye, and his chin resting on a knobbly knee, his calf bulging with muscle.

Her whole body stiffened at the memory. She felt as she had done then, the sadness emanating from Henry off the page. She could see how well she'd caught his mood, or perhaps it was that she'd always understood his sadness in the same way she had come to accept the shadow of it around her mother.

Kitty scooped up the rest of her drawings and decided to take them with her. God knows when she'd get back to her art, but this was all she had.

As she struggled across the driveway hauling the trunk over the gravel, she caught sight of Lillian staring at her from the kitchen window. The quizzical way the girl watched infuriated Kitty. She rolled up the sleeves of her mother's coat and beckoned her over, waiting as she shuffled out of the back door with her pigeon-toed gait, slowly making her way through the herb garden, wiping her hands on a tea towel.

'Will you give me a hand, Lillian?'

'Yes, miss.'

They lifted the trunk, Lillian struggling as the weight shifted towards her, dropping the tea towel in the effort not to lose her grip. Kitty took the weight with her knee, pressing it underneath and shoving the trunk into the boot of the Morris. Next she went to pick up her art materials. The car sunk under the weight of it all.

She arrived at the A23, indicating towards Brighton, not really knowing where she was heading. The indicator sprung out, the light blinked. The sound: *ticker tick, ticker tick*, indicating that she was about to turn right. She stopped at the give way sign.

A car sounded its horn.

'Oh shut up,' she screamed.

Kitty flicked the indicator the other way, towards London. She would start her life again. Call on Georgie, that's what she should have done in the first place. She would disappear if she had to. The Morris hammered along as fast as the wind and she felt for a brief second like she might outrun the feeling that had settled like a dull ache in her sternum. She'd only been one night without her daughter but that one night had changed everything. She missed Alexandra, she missed her with every cell in her body. But at least she knew her daughter was safe.

NINETEEN

Bet was still in a state of shock. She hadn't known what to do when she saw Kitty. The girl was clearly strung out and yet she was talking to Jack in a light and breezy manner. Bet had told Samuel immediately and he'd run out into the street to find her. Kitty had already gone. Bet was relieved that she'd disappeared but she didn't let on. She'd been surprised by the way her legs buckled at the thought of losing Alexandra. Kitty had stood looking at Bet as if their lives hadn't collided and she was just popping in to buy apples. Apples, for Pete's sake! And a cabbage.

Samuel persuaded Bet to go with him to the police station, she hadn't wanted to but Sam said they should be willing to give the baby up if the law insisted. They left by the back gate that led out to the alleyway. Bet thought it best just in case anyone should see them, but mostly she was worried that Kitty would be waiting. The lane that ran down the back gardens was damp. Green mould and mud made walking tricky. Bet was forced to stretch across a puddle, pressing Alexandra close, but the high fencing afforded them privacy. She'd not been able to put the baby down all morning, not even for a minute, since seeing Kitty.

As they drove off Bet found herself crying. Everything seemed impossible.

'What's up, luv?'

'They'll take her away, Sam. I know it.'

'They might do, which is why we're going to see Bill in Clapham. But you need to be realistic, Bet. We can't just take her in. It's not that simple.'

'But won't they think it's odd not going to our local station in Purley?'

'I've already called Bill,' Sam said. 'He said the fact that we go a long way back will help but we'll have to line a few pockets to get things put through as quick as possible. We're not doing anything illegal. It's all here.' He patted his suit jacket pocket which is where he'd put Kitty's letter.

'What's with the change of heart?'

Sam looked in the rear-view mirror and gave her a wink.

While he drove, she looked out of the window at the rows of grocers, shoe shops and hardware stores already bustling while her tea shop remained closed. *What was Kitty doing? Had she come to get her baby back?* Despite everything, she felt calmer now she was locked in the car. Sam had never let her down, she reminded herself. Streatham Common seemed cluttered with school children on their way to school. She used to do everything she could to avoid seeing children after Johnny died but now she felt she could bear to watch as they skipped and ran around.

'I don't understand what she was doing in our shop.'

'I told you, she'd probably been parked nearby all night and wanted to make sure the girl was all right.'

Kitty had seemed highly strung. It was hardly a surprise given the circumstances, but it was clear to Bet that she loved her daughter, and it was possible she'd want her back. Maybe she'd persuade her mother to change her mind. Normally, girls in Kitty's situation shut up and put up, but Kitty wasn't normal. She'd realised that much.

'If you want my opinion, she's done the sensible thing. I mean this way she chooses who adopts her,' Sam said.

'Sam, that's exactly what I said last night. I'm not so sure now.'

Samuel indicated to turn right. Even though the indicators worked he still put his arm out of the window, his chubby forefinger pointing in the direction he was turning.

She'd have to learn to drive, she thought. Perhaps Sam would buy her a second-hand motor at the car auctions he went to. She imagined the pram she'd buy. They'd sold Johnny's, which she was glad of because it had been a constant reminder of their loss. They'd be able to buy a more modern one. She'd seen them about, more box-shaped with smaller wheels than the one Johnny had. They drove down Streatham high street, past the bus station and the Odeon where she and Sam had gone on their first date. She hadn't loved Sam straight away, he wasn't all that good-looking when he was younger and it wasn't as if his family were that much either, but his generosity and charm had won her over. He'd always made her feel special. They'd been through so much. And now this.

'We're here,' Sam said. He turned round. 'Let *me* do the talking.'

TWENTY

Henry was growing increasingly nervous. A permanent lump of anxiety had formed in his chest. He was driving Tom back after seeing Anne, aware suddenly that the car smelt of Tom's Brylcreem. He wound down the window, let the breeze catch his face, changing down a gear on a tight corner and pressing his foot on the accelerator. The engine strained, letting out a high-pitched mechanical roar.

'I must say, Paris has had an odd effect on Kitty,' Tom said, continuing on from the conversation they'd started earlier. 'I wonder if she hasn't got in with the wrong sort of crowd. Of course you do realise Kitty's in love with you, don't you? She was asking if you were seeing someone else last night. Completely inappropriate. She'll grow out of it soon enough.'

Henry offered him a sideways glance.

'Do you worry about Anne finding out?' he asked. He'd known about Tom's affair with Georgie for some time and was so keen to see Tom's reaction that he just missed a bicycle coming over the hill. The woman stopped, took off her hat and waved it at them.

'What are you doing?' Tom said, turning to see if she was all right. They were driving so fast she disappeared as they turned a corner. 'You've gone and missed the turning for Bramber.'

'Well, do you?'

'I don't know what you're talking about.'

'Georgie,' Henry said.

He saw Tom clench the door handle. 'Look I . . . it's just a flirtation that's gone too far, that's all. Now's not the right time.' He pointed to a lane up ahead. 'We can turn round up there.'

But Henry drove on towards Beecham. 'It wasn't the time for a haircut either was it? You don't care a toss about Kitty. You just wanted to avoid talking about Anne's state and your own bloody guilt.' Henry felt the spittle leave his mouth. 'Meanwhile, we have no idea where Kitty buggered off to this morning and why she's behaving erratically.'

He skidded round another corner.

'Slow down!'

Henry hit the brakes so abruptly that they both jolted forward. Tom held out his hands to break his fall against the dashboard.

'Christ, Henry, what's wrong?'

Henry leaned his head on the steering wheel. 'I've got an awful feeling about Kitty,' Henry said. 'And I think it's my fault.'

'What on earth has been going on?'

'I love her, Tom, and I thought she felt the same way.'

Tom looked at Henry, a frown rippling across his face. 'Is that why she went to Paris?'

'I think your mother had something to do with it. She probably didn't approve.'

'Probably not.' Tom let out a long sigh. 'I know my mother and what she wants for her daughter. For sure she had someone stable and well heeled with a title or inheritance of some kind in mind. They are shockingly conservative, my parents, not to mention ambitious.'

The car creaked as the engine cooled down. A cuckoo was making itself heard. Henry felt a rush of shame. He had nothing to offer Kitty.

'I'm well aware of my standing, Tom,' he said. He realised in that moment why he had gone to the States. He would never match up to the Campbell expectations. He had an urge to leave, get away.

'Christ, what a pickle,' Tom said.

They arrived back to find no Morris. A pie was cooling in the kitchen. Lillian must have made it and gone home. Saunders had left a note to say he was picking up Howard and Clarissa. Then they found a telegram announcing their delay.

'Kitty!' Henry called up the stairs. The house felt empty and a feeling of dread came over him.

'Probably on her way to the hospital,' Tom said, picking at the pie crust. Then Henry noticed Kitty's hat in the vestibule by the mirror but no coat. His heart ached at the impossibility of it all. He went upstairs to find her bedroom door closed. He knocked, entered to find the wardrobe gaping open, her room turned upside down. Everything gone, even the hangers.

'Good God.' Tom was standing behind him.

The telephone rang and Henry rushed downstairs to pick it up, hoping it was Kitty. 'Hello, Steyning 5436.'

'This is Sergeant Coleman from Brighton police station. Is that Mr Campbell?'

'No. Mr Campbell isn't here. I'll pass you to his son.'

Tom took the telephone. 'Hello. This is Tom Campbell speaking.' He was coiling the wire around his finger as he listened to the man on the other end. 'Oh dear,' he said.

Henry could hear the crisp tone of the other person on the line. Tom was frowning.

'I see,' he said. 'No, she was here last night but it seems she has taken everything and buggered off.'

Henry felt a bolt of anxiety. Perhaps there'd been an accident. He realised then that already he was preparing for the next incident, as if the flood, like some biblical prophecy, had precipitated a long run of inevitable disasters.

'Yes, of course. Can I take your number?' Tom scrawled a number on the leather-bound notepad. 'Remind me of your name, again.' He scrawled down PC Coleman.

Henry's pulse quickened.

Tom put the phone down and turned to him, his face drained and grey-looking. He ran his fingers over his newly shorn hair.

'What is it?' Henry asked.

'Someone has reported Kitty as missing. Someone in South London. I thought she'd been in Paris for heaven's sake! I'm beginning to wonder if something else is going on. Honestly, if anything happens to me Kitty always tries her hardest to remain the centre of attention.'

'Somehow I think this isn't an attention-seeking matter,' Henry said. He believed Kitty was withholding information, something important enough to leave like this, taking everything. Could it be another man? He remembered her art materials in the conservatory and went to see if she'd taken them as well. He saw that the door had been left open. The only art-related object she'd left behind was her easel. Henry knew that this wasn't just some desperate cry for help. She was leaving for good.

He went to find Tom, who was in the library, standing over Howard's desk.

'She's left my parents a letter and, look, there's one for you. Nothing for me of course. I'm just her bloody brother whose life has fallen apart!' He handed Henry Kitty's letter.

Henry tore it open, ignoring Tom's self-pitying rant.

Dear Henry,

I have decided to do exactly as you suggested and 'be my own woman'. I heard about the woman you were dating in Boston. Of course I forgive you but I'm afraid I don't want to play second fiddle. I know about your misdemeanours in the past, but in the end I don't care about that. But, you have a new life now, away from here and the past. You need to start afresh and so do I. We both knew that my parents would disapprove and much as I am angry with them, I feel it will be some time before I can trust anyone again.

Too much has happened.

Love always,
  Kit x

He looked up to find Tom staring at him.

'Well?' Tom said.

'She's seems to think I've got another woman in tow. God knows how she came to that conclusion.'

'Yes, I told you, she asked me about it last night. Honestly, that can't be what this is all about, can it?'

'Can you take me to the train station?'

'Why, where are you going?'

'I need to find Kitty.'

'Where to start!' Tom said, throwing up his arms. He started shuffling through the pile of mail again. 'Do you have to leave now? We've only just arrived.'

'Tom, this is important.'

Tom stared at him, his eyes wide, his mouth tight. 'Look, I know this isn't what you want to hear right now, but there could be some other reason my parents are against you and Kitty getting together.'

'What do you mean?'

'Well, I've often wondered . . .' Tom shook his head. 'I know it sounds absurd and maybe this isn't the time, but I've often wondered why my parents adopted you. I had this fantasy as a child that that you were really my brother. Silly, I know. But I heard them arguing one night about your future, and it sounded as if . . . as if . . .'

'Go on,' Henry said. His mouth felt dry.

'It was as if my father knew your mother before we met.'

'That's absurd,' Henry said. 'They're hardly likely to have met socially.'

'Look, I'm just telling you what I think. I've always suspected that we weren't told the truth. My parents fought a lot around that time.' Tom stood, leaning on the desk, as if all the air had gone out of him. 'I just thought you ought to know, that's all,' Tom said.

'I need to find her, Tom.'

Tom sighed. 'That much is clear.'

'I'll start with your girlfriend.'

'She's not my girlfriend, Henry,' Tom said, his voice gaining authority. 'Accusations like that destroy marriages.'

'Yes, you're right, sorry. Right now, Georgie is our best chance of finding Kitty.'

'Is that what Kitty said in her letter?' Tom asked. 'That she's going to Georgie's.'

'No, I'm just guessing.'

Tom stuffed some of the envelopes into his coat pocket, held out his palm. 'Keys.'

Henry threw the keys and Tom caught them. Henry looked at his watch. He paced down the hallway, aware of Tom close behind him. 'Steady on, old boy.'

Opening the front door and jumping down the steps of Beecham, Henry said, 'There's a train in twenty minutes.'

TWENTY-ONE

Kitty arrived in Maida Vale later that afternoon, exhausted and emotional. She'd driven up the London Road, past Purley and the tea shop. Past the old London airport, then Croydon. When she arrived at Hyde Park Corner she drove round several times in a blur before driving up Park Lane towards Marble Arch and Maida Vale, hoping to God that Georgie hadn't moved again. She would never forget driving with Alexandra in the back, the little mewing noises she made as they drove down to Beecham. All that was left was her daughter's ghost, the Polaroids in her pocket and the sketches she'd drawn.

She parked outside a greengrocer's and remembered the bag of apples and the cabbage she'd bought from Bet's grocer's. She couldn't shift the image of Bet's startled face as she stood waiting. She'd write to her, explain that she hadn't known quite what to do. There was a public house on the corner, The Elgin. Kitty was tempted to have a drink but it was likely she'd attract the wrong sort of attention and anyway she must look a frightful mess. She stepped out of the car and went round the passenger side to retrieve the suitcase.

A gang of children were kicking a ball about in the forecourt of the block of flats. She watched as two small boys scuttled after it, pushing and shoving, their eyes fixed on the makeshift goal. A woman was bouncing a pram outside a house opposite, draped against a pillar, looking exhausted. Kitty turned away, felt the crush of pain spread inside her chest.

When Georgie opened the door she was wearing a bra and knickers and nothing else. Typical, Kitty thought. The sight of her standing akimbo before her, so familiar, brought tears to Kitty's eyes.

'Do you always answer the door dressed like that?' Kitty said, struggling with one of the suitcases as she squeezed past her.

'Staying long?'

'Forever, if you're not careful.'

Georgie closed the door, scratching her head as she leaned against the door. 'Are those for me?'

Kitty stood still, unable to move. Finally, she handed the brown paper bag full of apples and the cabbage to Georgie who put them on the hall table.

'Have you brought these all the way from Paris?'

Kitty turned, the sound of Georgie's voice and the fact that she knew nothing of what Kitty had put herself through was the final straw. She broke down.

'Kitty, whatever has happened?'

Kitty fell into Georgie's thin arms. Hiding her face in her friend's bony chest, she breathed in the smell of lavender and gin. The comfort of Georgie's embrace, combined with the odd mix of perfume, made Kitty cry harder. Georgie pulled Kitty into the room, undoing the buttons of Kitty's coat as if she were a child.

★

Bet couldn't get Alexandra to settle. It had been a long day, what with the visit to the police station and then they'd gone shopping to buy some more powdered milk and all the paraphernalia of baby care. She'd happily bought Alexandra a new nightdress and some mittens to stop her scratching her face, but then Sam insisted they bought a pram as well, even though there was nothing to say they were keeping her, and an even stronger possibility they'd have to take her to the mother and baby home and wait to see what the court decided. Sam's friend had suggested that they reported Kitty as missing. He said it was best to say that she'd left the child with her and not returned. Bet didn't like to lie, but she didn't want to risk losing Alexandra either. She was angry with Sam for buying the pram.

'It's tempting fate.'

'If they take her, they can take the pram as well,' he'd said. 'I want her to know we cared for her.'

'As if she'd know,' she said. But she knew buying things made him cheerful. It was his way of putting the world to rights. When they got back to the house, Sam had popped into the grocer's and returned twenty minutes later to help with packing. Most of the house was done except for the parlour and the basics in the kitchen.

Now she paced back and forth with Alexandra in her arms while Sam was in the pub talking to a man Bill had suggested could help. A solicitor who might be able to tie things up quickly. The police had registered Kitty as missing and had called the mother and baby home to confirm she had indeed absconded.

'We'll have to put a search out for the mother,' Bill had said. Bill was an old school friend of Sam's. They used to meet once or twice a month before Bill got transferred to South London.

Bet didn't want them to find Kitty. She had half a mind to up and run, take Alexandra to her aunt in Cornwall.

Fear got the better of her when she was tired and right now she was exhausted.

She put Alexandra over her shoulder, gave her a little pat. Finally, she let out a throaty burp and Bet had to laugh. 'Very ladylike,' she said. 'Like father like daughter.' Then she chastised herself. She liked the name Alexandra Abbott, thought it lucky even. It would get shortened for sure, and if that was the case she'd steer everyone to call her Ally. She felt Alexandra's body relax and her head go heavy and knew then that she'd dropped off. She was just drifting off herself when she heard Sam's key in the door.

She jumped up, wrapped her dressing gown around her waist and buttoned up the collar against the cold. Sam was in the kitchen making himself a warm drink.

'You can make one of those for me as well,' Bet said.

Sam jumped. 'Good grief, woman. You gave me a fright!'

'Well, what did he say?'

Sam was putting some more milk in the pan and got out the hot chocolate, shovelling into the tin with a spoon and sprinkling it into the pan. 'He said it's not going to be as straightforward as we'd hoped, but he thinks we have a good chance. There's a lot of things going for us.'

'What does that mean, for Pete's sake?'

'Well, Bill was right when he said we should say Kitty left you with the baby promising to return and when she didn't, we found a letter. That demonstrates we knew Alexandra before Kitty disappeared. Then there's the girl's letter. She very clearly states that she would like *us* to be the adoptive parents. But they need to go through the usual channels and procedures. The procedure of adoption I mean. We're going to have to take our case to the juvenile court, but the fact that we're experienced parents and have lost a child will act in our favour. He said if the mother and baby home don't kick up a fuss then it's likely to run smoothly, but we might have to take the child back there while it goes through court. A lot depends on whether Kitty has signed papers at the mother and baby home. Apparently they'd already allocated suitable parents – that's the word they used, "suitable parents".' He rolled his eyes.

'Has he been in touch with the home already?'

'Yes, as soon as Bill rang him. That's what we pay him for. Anyway, he only spoke to a secretary who couldn't seem to find the paperwork, which could mean that Kitty left without completing the process.'

'And that's good for us or not?'

'If she didn't sign the form at the home, then we have a good chance. But they'll need to conduct a formal interview and they may insist we hand her back while they decide.' Sam turned back to the milk, dipped his knuckle into it to test its warmth.

'Oh God. I hate the idea of her going back to the mother and baby home.'

'It won't be for long, Bet.'

'What if they find Kitty and she changes her mind?'

'Then we have to hand her back.'

Bet slumped into the kitchen chair.

'But she's not going to do that, Bet. She wants this child to be ours, she's said as much.' He was making himself busy wiping a perfectly clean surface.

'But surely as a mother who has abandoned her child, she has no rights. And what if they don't find her?'

'He said what was more important was that we were also "suitable parents". They probably will find her. Apparently they're in touch with the girl's mother.'

'And if she changes her mind?'

He stopped then and turned to look at her. 'Yes, there is that possibility.'

She could see the worry in his eyes. 'I knew we shouldn't have bought that pram.'

'Now, Bet, don't start fretting. We both knew this wasn't going to be easy but she's still here, isn't she?'

'Is this man going to help us, or not?'

Samuel poured the hot chocolate into their cups, handed her one.

'Yes, he's going to help us, but, like I said, it's not straightforward.' Samuel put his arm around her shoulders. 'Don't worry. I'll think of something.'

'She feels like my own,' Bet said.

TWENTY-TWO

Kitty sat curled into a ball, her knees drawn up to her chin, watching Georgie mix up another drink. She felt like a rag doll that had lost its stuffing. Georgie had thrown on some slacks and a polo neck. Even when she didn't try she looked chic. Her hair was backcombed into a bob, the remnants of her eyeliner smudged, yet still she looked glamorous.

'This would never have happened to you,' Kitty said.

'It could happen to anybody.' Georgie poured a slug of gin into Kitty's glass. 'I still don't understand why you didn't tell me?'

Kitty shrugged. 'Mother thought it best to tell no one.'

'Oh, Kitty!'

'I felt I'd let her down,' Kitty said. 'She told me Henry was seeing someone else, which made me feel such a fool. She told me that there was a girl, Pamela Watson, who lived in the village that had got pregnant. Apparently, everyone believed that Henry was the father. Basically, she implied he was a scoundrel and I was the idiot daughter!'

'Oh, Kitty! You should have at least told him about the pregnancy.'

'Mother told me not to.'

Georgie rolled her eyes. 'The problem with your family is that everything seems to revolve around money, church and clothes! That's why this whole story of why they adopted Henry . . .' She shook her head. 'I'm sure it's not what it seems.'

'What do you mean?' Kitty asked. Her head hurt after crying so much. It was easy for Georgie to show bravado; she'd been brought up to be outspoken and unconventional. Her father was a psychoanalyst, her mother a painter, she was one of five children and none of them were the least bit materialistic.

'I've always suspected the gesture was to cover up some sordid bit of their past. I mean who adopts a child out of the blue? It just seems odd, that's all. Why is your mother so against him?' Georgie continued, stirring the drinks with a cocktail stick.

It wasn't the first time Kitty had heard Georgie ask this. She'd always been cynical when it came to Henry's adoption. Kitty wondered if Georgie was right, was there some dark secret her mother was hiding?

She felt utterly confused.

Georgie handed her the gin, a slice of lemon floating on top so that Kitty could only sip it. She poked the lemon further into the glass. She'd half a mind to gulp the whole lot down. She lit her third cigarette. It was going to be a long evening. They were already on their second drink and it hadn't even got dark yet.

'In their defence, Henry was Tom's closest friend.'

'Yes, but they could have offered to be guardians and yet they went for full-on adoption. Why? And now your mother is accusing Henry of all kinds of dreadful things. The truth of it is, she doesn't think you should be with Henry but what isn't clear is, why.'

'They're snobs.'

Georgie plonked herself down on the floor, sat cross-legged, all arms and legs. 'If it were me, my mother would have insisted on keeping the child, then probably brought her up herself while she hummed her way through yet another atrocious painting, while the child was left to run around naked in the garden just like we did. Honestly, feral cats had more parental interaction. The fact that my father was a psychoanalyst made it all the more absurd.'

'My mother kept going on about how getting pregnant wasn't the way to catch a man, and how Henry was completely unsuitable and clearly not interested.'

'And you believed her?'

Kitty remembered how indignant Henry had been. She looked down at the handkerchief Georgie had given her, all scrunched up. 'I don't know.'

'I can well believe that your mother thought she was doing the right thing, but then again so did Mussolini.'

'What's Mussolini got to do with anything?'

'All dictators believe they're right,' Georgie said. She was on a roll. Kitty realised how impossible it would have been if she'd turned up with Alexandra. She thought about Clarissa. Why did her mother have such a hold over her? 'I only know I miss my baby,' she said, burying her head into her hands.

Georgie reached out and squeezed her ankle. 'I understand,' she said, but Kitty knew that Georgie couldn't possibly know what it was like to lose a child.

'Parents pass on their wounds like kings do their crowns,' Georgie said.

'What's that supposed to mean?'

Georgie stood up and glided back towards the collection of glasses and bottles on the sideboard to add another slice of lemon and a cube of ice to her glass. 'I'm just saying that maybe the reason she disapproves of Henry is because of something to do with her past, or your father's, and nothing to do with you and Henry.'

'Oh, Georgie, please don't go all weird on me.'

139

'She's right about one thing,' Georgie said, pointing her finger at Kitty. 'A baby would change everything. Men are not so keen to take a woman who has a child, you know.'

Kitty spat out a laugh. 'Oh please! You're as bad as she is. The truth of it is my mother would rather cause misery than have the Campbells seen as anything but a cut above.'

'Oh, Kitty, your life, your daughter's life, it would have been a disaster, let's face it. Even if there is no real reason to stop you being together and your mother is making it all up, you'd have always worried that Henry married you because you were pregnant.' As Georgie spoke, she waved her hands around, smoke curling off her lit cigarette. Kitty thought she was tipsy, which was odd because she didn't feel the slightest bit drunk herself.

They heard a door slam, and then a neighbour turned on a wireless at full blast. They both heard the thrumming of drums and a double bass.

'Whoever it is, has good taste at least,' Kitty said.

Georgie went and banged on the wall with a curled fist. 'Be quiet, will you!' She turned to Kitty. 'He's such a cad.'

The volume was turned back down.

'Well, at least he listened.' Kitty stood up and went to find the small case she'd brought back from the mother and baby home, digging out the sketchbook filled with drawings she'd made of Alexandra and handing them to Georgie, along with the Polaroid.

Georgie held out the sketchbook, turning it this way and that, before she looked at the photograph. 'Goodness! I can't believe you've had a little girl,' she said. 'What did you call her?'

Kitty felt her eyes brimming with a fresh bout of tears. 'Alexandra. She was the dearest little thing.' She started to choke, the sobs reaching up her throat. Georgie pulled her into a hug.

'Oh, you poor thing.'

'I keep thinking that somehow she'll come back to me.'

Georgie stroked her head. 'I know.' She squeezed Kitty's shoulder. 'You did what was best for her, darling. You couldn't have brought her up alone, you know that.'

'Why not? People do.' Kitty looked up at her, feeling childlike.

'Well, what life would she have had? And you can forget being an artist. Pram in the hall and all that.' Georgie waved the sketchbook around so that it arced above her backcombed hair.

'I don't care about being a bloody artist. I could have worked,' she said.

'And who would look after the baby?'

Kitty walked towards the window. She could see a couple down below. They were having a row. He was pointing his finger at her while the woman was smoking nonchalantly beside him. 'We're forgetting Henry,' Kitty said.

'Henry, who doesn't even know you've had a child. Who possibly has another woman in America and who your mother is adamant you don't marry!'

Kitty walked back to the ice bucket and picked up another cube, sighed as she dropped it into the glass. 'I take your point.' She noticed a silver cigarette case that was very similar to Tom's, tucked behind the decanter. Picking it up, she flipped it over and saw his initials. *T.C.* She swivelled to face Georgie who was wistfully poking at the slices of lemon in her glass and swirling the drink around, watching as the bubbles in the tonic sprang to life. They were both slowly getting drunk.

'Has Tom been here?' Kitty asked.

Georgie blushed. Pulling herself upright, she said, 'He popped in yesterday, on his way home.'

'You mean he came by to see you while Anne was giving birth?'

Georgie continued swilling her drink, refusing to look at Kitty. 'We've grown rather close, it seems.'

'How close?'

Finally, Georgie tilted her head and faced Kitty, her cheeks still pink. 'Not *that* close. I know it's foolish, but there's a chemistry between us that's hard to ignore.'

Georgie was rarely vulnerable but Kitty could see a chink in her armour.

'Oh, Georgie. My brother will never leave Anne, especially now they've had a child.'

Georgie's shoulders stiffened. 'Who said I needed him to leave Anne?'

'Infidelity is a bit of a raw subject right now.'

'Don't worry. It hasn't come to anything.'

Kitty slumped down and rocked her head back and forth. She honestly didn't know if she could bear the prickling reality of human behaviour. She pined for the innocence of Alexandra, her little hands grappling for something to cling on to while she fed, her toes curling with pleasure. Just thinking about it made her breasts leak.

'Do you have any tissues?'

Georgie walked to the other side of the room and proffered a box of tissues. Kitty took a few and stuffed them into her bra, which was already sodden.

'Mother said Henry had boasted about another woman to Tom, but when I asked Tom he didn't seem to know what I was talking about.'

Georgie curled her feet up underneath her. 'Well, there is the strong possibility your mother is lying, but you need to ask yourself why.'

'Alexandra is her granddaughter for Christ's sake!'

'Kitty, I'm the first person to criticise your mother, but I honestly believe she thought she was protecting you. Besides, if she is this bloody prejudiced, maybe Alexandra is better off away from the family.'

'Oh, Georgie, that's exactly it. I don't want her having to grow up with the same awful constraints I did.'

'Well yes, but you hardly know Bet either, let's face it.'

'I trust Bet. I couldn't tell you why but I do. She has a heart of gold, that much was obvious. I just thought, as she'd lost her son . . .' Just the thought of Alexandra in Bet's arms made her sob.

'You thought there was space in Bet's heart,' Georgie said.

Kitty nodded, unable to speak, her mouth filled with saliva. She snatched another tissue. Her chest heavy again.

'Well then, you've done the right thing. You won't be the first woman who has had to give up her child.' Georgie stroked Kitty's hair, wiped the tears away with the back of her hand. 'And don't you worry about Tom and me. I think he's scared of commitment, that's all.'

Kitty sat up, took a slug of her drink, stubbed out her half-smoked cigarette. She looked around at the bareness of the room, the stark lines of the chair, the neatness of the sideboard with its collection of artefacts on one end and bottles of spirits on the other.

She would have to stay for a while. If Georgie let her, that is.

TWENTY-THREE

Henry slammed the train door shut with a thud and inhaled the metallic smell of the empty carriage. He saw Tom standing by his car having a smoke and waved, fishing out his own pack of tobacco. They passed a level crossing. In the queue of cars, a hearse led by four horses waited patiently for the train to pass. He remembered the day of his mother's funeral. A few villagers, the Burtanshaws and the Carpenters, joined them at the church. Howard was in Kenya and it seemed that his mother didn't have many friends and only one relative, a sister who lived in Yorkshire who he'd never met. She sat in the front pew, patting her eyes constantly with a handkerchief. She wore a brown coat that looked too big for her and a rather drab knitted hat. After the ceremony the aunt introduced herself to Clarissa.

'You've done my sister proud, thank you,' she said. 'I'm afraid we're unable to contribute, in case you were wondering.' His aunt clutched her handbag to her stomach.

Henry watched as a feeling of disgust rippled across Clarissa's face. He felt a flush of shame. This was his mother's only relative.

'That won't be necessary.'

'Can I ask the cause of death? Your husband wasn't very clear when he called.'

Clarissa pulled Henry towards her, while scowling at his aunt. 'Influenza, I believe.'

'Shame.' His aunt looked at Henry, her eyes twitching, her mouth rolling in and out as if she'd just put on lipstick. 'This must be Dorothy's boy,' she said.

Clarissa gently pushed Henry towards his aunt who was holding out her hand. Henry shook it, noticed the clamminess of her hand.

'You were that high when I last saw you,' she said, indicating a low point. 'I don't suppose you remember me, your auntie Joan?' Henry shook his head. He felt hot. Clarissa had bought him long trousers and a new navy wool jacket.

Clarissa signalled to Tom. 'Tom, darling, why don't you and Henry go outside for a bit.' Tom beckoned Henry to follow with a quick flick of his head. Henry sauntered down the aisle, his hands wedged deep into his pockets. Mrs Carpenter and Mrs Burtanshaw stopped talking, watching him pass. Even without looking he knew their eyes were full of pity.

'Selfish, that's what it is. Poor chap.'

He stopped by the church door, turning as he heard Clarissa whisper something to his aunt.

'I'm afraid not,' his aunt said. 'I barely know the boy and my Bert hasn't a way with kids, and he wasn't a fan of my sister if I'm honest. Met her a few times, that's all. She was a funny one, Dorothy. Too good for the likes of us, especially when she went off to America.' His aunt sniffed, dabbed at her eyes. 'You see, we used to be close, share lots of secrets, but then she got married and upped and left. I never really saw much of her after that. I'm not sure she even loved what's-his-name, the American, but she was so keen to get away, make a better life for herself.'

Clarissa tilted her head in that scrutinising way she had. 'Don't you care what happens to him?' she said.

'Oh, it's not like that. I just wouldn't know what to do. My Bert would kill me if I brought him home. We haven't the money for one thing. And there's the dogs.'

Clarissa folded her arms, her handbag swinging from the crook of her elbow. 'Dogs?' she asked.

'You see my sister got about.' She bent closer to Clarissa. 'She knew how to have her way with men. Have you been in touch with . . .' She hesitated.

'Charlie Roberts?' Clarissa offered.

'Yes, that's him.'

Clarissa opened her handbag, pulled out a ten-shilling note. 'I'm well aware of the circumstances,' she said. 'It's for *that* reason I'm asking. We wrote to Charlie Roberts and, as yet, haven't received a reply. The poor child is an orphan.'

His aunt dabbed at her eyes again, eyeing up the note as Clarissa dropped it into the charity box on her way out. 'I'm sorry,' she said and scuttled off, nodding as she passed Henry.

In the car on the way home, Henry looked out of the window and longed for the solace of the woods and the Campbells' dogs. He could tell by the way Kitty clutched the hem of her coat that she was crying. Every now and again she'd sniff. Eventually, he handed her his handkerchief and she took it. He wanted to cry but couldn't. It was as if Kitty was doing the crying for him. He watched her hand fingering the handkerchief, her skin pale and transparent, a thread of veins laced across her wrist. He'd seen her do this before, her hands working away at a piece of cloth. As Saunders drove, the trees and fields became a blur and he thought of his mother in the coffin. He wondered if she was still wearing the tea dress. Clarissa had squeezed Henry's shoulder when they'd lowered her into the ground.

'Time will heal,' she'd said.

Henry knew that wasn't true. It was the usual thing with adults: they lied because they wanted you to feel better. He kept thinking that if he'd gone home sooner, his mother would still be alive.

'Kitty, do try to control yourself, dear,' Clarissa said. She smiled at Henry, but her eyes didn't match her mouth.

'Home,' Clarissa said as they pulled into the driveway.

But it wasn't his home, was it? He jumped out and ran inside.

'Henry,' Kitty called.

'Leave him!' Clarissa said. 'He needs to be on his own.'

Henry raced upstairs to the room he was staying in. He flung his coat across the bed, the sound of his aunt's voice ringing in his head. He had worked so hard to forget his father, which is what his mother had wanted, but that day all he wanted was to remember him, feel the weight of his large hands on his shoulders, press against the roughness of his donkey jacket.

He woke up just as the train was crossing the Thames. He had a sinking feeling that he would never find Kitty in this vast metropolis. What if she hadn't gone to Georgie's? He thought about the Campbells. He didn't imagine Clarissa was happy about his and Kitty's relationship. He knew he was poor stock, and knowing Clarissa, she had someone rather more well heeled in mind: a banker or barrister or some profession other than a journalist. Someone with a private education and a large inheritance. He felt ashamed that somehow he'd replaced Clarissa's generosity with a betrayal of some kind. He needed to find Kitty if only to get her to return to Beecham. He imagined that somehow her disappearance would be attributed to him. It was him she was running from; he was sure of it.

He was astonished to see that Victoria was still buzzing with commuters even though it was after six. He started to walk towards the bus stop but there was a queue of people who had clearly been waiting for some time, so he flagged a taxi just by Hyde Park Corner. London was an assault on the senses with its stream of traffic and people pounding the pavement, different to Boston, more claustrophobic. The street lamps were flickering orange even though it was not yet dark. It was a city that never slept, a world away from the quiet leafy lane he lived in.

He arrived in Maida Vale to see Kitty's Morris parked outside Georgie's bedsit and felt a calm descend upon him. He paid the driver. When he looked up at the window he saw it was in darkness. He rang the bell, but nobody answered. A feeling of despair overwhelmed him. He felt as if he were chasing his own tail.

TWENTY-FOUR

Kitty woke up in Georgie's bedsit to find her friend gone. She must have dozed off, thanks to the gin. It was dark outside but she could hear footsteps and voices. She checked her watch. It was eight o'clock. She had an awful headache, but what hurt her most was the feeling of hollowness that seemed to echo the sparseness of Georgie's room. She wondered whether Alexandra was still sleeping in Tom's suitcase. Kitty felt a deep sadness and realised that this feeling was never going to go. How could it? She switched on the standard lamp and a low orange glow filled the room. She wondered if she could quickly pop to the bathroom and went to the door dressed in her knickers and bra. She tentatively turned the doorknob, fumbled around for the light switch on the landing, thought she heard Georgie laughing. Her bladder was about to burst, she felt sure she was going to vomit and her breasts were hard and on the point of exploding. She was going to have to tighten the bandages and use fresh cabbage leaves.

She crept up the stairs and found two doors firmly closed. There was a door on the next half-landing. Kitty turned the handle just as the light on the stairwell switched itself off. By the smell of things, an odd mix of bleach and urine, she'd found the right place. Her hand reached up into the darkness until she felt a cord on the tips of her fingers.

Back in the hallway, she found the light switch and made her way to Georgie's room. The door was closed. After trying to open it, she realised she was locked out.

'Bugger,' she said. She could hear Georgie in the room next door, her high-pitched tone cracking the silence. Voices wavered between whispers and outbreaks of laughter. Something about the cadence suggested Georgie was flirting. Their shared merriment seemed to make her feel lonelier. Kitty, in her knickers and bra, didn't feel like interrupting them. She slumped down on the stairs. The light snapped off and she was left surrounded by an inky blackness. The need to hold Alexandra close, smell the top of her head, filtered out into the darkness – the ghost of her motherhood. She let her body slide to the bottom step. Her mouth filled with salty saliva. Only Henry could console her, and where had she left him? In equal darkness and no understanding of the cause, and her mother's slander of his character had worked away at any feeling of trust. She had never felt so utterly broken.

She remembered another time when she'd waited on the stairs like this. It was the day Henry had found his mother dead. She woke up to the roar of her father's voice coming from downstairs.

'How was I to know she'd do such a stupid thing?' he said.

'Shhh. You'll wake the boy up,' her mother said.

Someone, probably her mother, clicked the library door shut. Their voices were muffled but forceful. Kitty pulled on her dressing gown and searched for her slippers with her toe, fishing them out from under the bed. She went and sat on the stairs.

'You can't abandon him now. He's your responsibility. You owe it to him.'

'That stupid woman got greedy, that's all it was.'

'She didn't even know who you were at first. You said so yourself.'

'Of course she knew who I was,' her father said. 'But it was you who invited her into this house.'

Kitty heard the sound of skin being slapped.

'Clarissa, I . . .'

'You know this is the end of us, don't you, Howard?' her mother said, spitting the words out like bullets. 'Don't think I didn't see you both at Henry's birthday party. I did, and you seemed pretty familiar to me.'

Then there was silence. Kitty got up and crept towards the hallway. Moonlight shone onto the carpet. Shadows of trees moved across the lawn outside. She could feel her mother's stifled rage leaking out of the library.

'And put him in Harrow with Tom?' her father said. His voice thin and shaky.

'Good God, no. That really would be too much. People will talk.'

Her father didn't answer. Kitty lifted her hand to the door handle, her heart pressing against her chest. When she opened the door, she saw that her father's shirt was dishevelled and his hair bristled up like a toothbrush.

'Kitty, what are you doing up? Go back to bed,' he said.

Her mother strode over, her face strained.

'I didn't hear anything, Mummy, I promise. I just wanted to know what happened to Henry's mother that's all.'

'You're too interested in that boy,' she said. 'It's embarrassing for all of us.' Her mother bent to slap her on the leg, then took her by the shoulder and grabbed her hair, winding it around her hand so that Kitty yelped. Her mother made her look at her. 'What have I told you about eavesdropping?'

'I didn't, Mummy. I promise.'

Clarissa shoved her back through the door. 'Back to bed!'

Kitty closed her eyes, weary. How many times had she replayed that scene while in the mother and baby home? She knew there was something her mother wasn't telling her about Henry. And then there was the time she'd seen Dot and her father in the kitchen garden squabbling on the day of Henry's birthday, when they had apparently only just met. A couple of years after that, Dot, who appeared carefree and beautiful, died. Georgie was right, her parents were hiding something.

One of the doors upstairs opened and Kitty instinctively hid in the shadows. As Georgie let herself back into her bedsit, Kitty jumped up and just caught her, her finger clutching hold of Georgie's sweater, before Georgie slammed the door shut.

'What on earth are you doing?' Georgie said, turning on the light in the communal hallway and yanking her into her bedsit. 'You're not dressed.'

'I could ask the same of you.'

Georgie gave her a cock-eyed smile. 'Talking to the neighbour,' she said, tucking her hair behind her ears and smiling broadly. 'He's rather a dish.'

'I thought you said he was a cad!'

'Well he does play the wireless rather loudly. It was because of that I went to see him, he turned it up again and I didn't want him to wake you up – he was making a hell of a racket. Anyway, it turns out he's a journalist and a poet. Very political, knew all about Martin Luther King. Very left wing.'

Kitty went into the kitchenette and turned on the tap, splashing water onto her face. 'Oh that *is* good news. At least your parents will approve.' Kitty hadn't meant to sound sarcastic, but Georgie seemed to have forgotten the state she was in.

'You look awful, why don't you have a bath,' Georgie said, ignoring her tone.

They both heard the front doorbell. Peeking through the gap in the door, they watched as Alan, the noisy neighbour, went to open it.

'You're right, he is rather handsome,' Kitty said. Something about Georgie flirting with the neighbour made her feel very sad. Her life had become tragic and she felt so utterly alone. It seemed nobody understood how awful she felt.

TWENTY-FIVE

Henry had walked to stay calm. Pounding the pavements allowed him to gather his thoughts, so he chose to go down to the canal, his collar turned up against the cold night air. He'd slowed when he got to Regent's Park and took in the zoo. From the other side of the canal you could just see the giraffes, their small heads swaying rhythmically in the dark. He was overwhelmed by the combination of their grace and innocence and found himself absorbed by their movements.

When he got back to Maida Vale for the second time that evening he bought a newspaper in the stationer's opposite and saw the light of Georgie's bedsit was on. He'd rung the bell and finally a rather dapper-looking chap answered it. Georgie joined him soon after.

'Kitty said she'll be down in a jiffy. Why don't you wait in the pub?'

Henry felt a wash of relief. 'Thank you,' he said. 'I'll wait for her in the saloon.'

The pub was empty except for a couple of men in the public bar. He ordered a whisky and sat down, spreading out his newspaper, watching as people strode past. There wasn't much in the news, just the continuing angst about railway closures. Some baby had been found on a doorstep, and there'd been a robbery in a bank on the high street in Islington.

A woman was pushing a pram, a scarf tied around her backcombed hair, a toddler tottering alongside her on reins. It was late for a youngster to be up, he thought. He looked at his watch. It was almost eight o'clock. A young boy was dragging an empty barrow down the road, a grey apron wrapped around his coat, a blue cap balanced on his head. Henry thought London rather grotty. There were still areas that hadn't been dealt with after the war, the empty shells of houses, their walls blown clean off to expose the houses' innards: faded wallpaper, a broken sink, the frayed wood flooring, held together by scaffolding bolted in. He didn't understand what Kitty liked about London. He reflected on how he felt when he was in Boston. Those big skies you got in America, the feeling of victory and hope, that air of optimism you could almost touch. He was just contemplating ringing the bell of Georgie's bedsit for the second time when he saw Kitty walk down to her car. Even from this far he could see she was unhappy by the way her body was hunched. He downed his whisky, scraped back his chair and dashed across the road. A bus stopped and a crowd of people got off. He weaved his way through the throng.

*

Kitty didn't so much see Henry as sense him. He was striding across the road, his coat flapping, black hair flopping down over his eyes. He looked handsome and sad. If only they were strangers to each other. She wasn't surprised he'd found her. She hadn't made it difficult for any of them; although she'd been convinced Tom would be the first, but of course Tom was busy with Anne and his daughter, and then there was Georgie. What fools they all were.

The street was busy with people on the way home from work, men in suits, lovers hand in hand, a group of young men kicking a ball against the railings of the house opposite. She caught Henry's eye, felt the pull of him like the tug of the sea. A stray dog ran out into the street just as Henry leaped up onto the kerb. A passing car hooted but it trotted on oblivious.

'Kit.'

Henry pulled her into his chest and she was comforted by his earthy damp smell. Just for a second she allowed herself to forget everything.

'What the hell is going on?' he whispered into her ear so that she could feel the heat of his breath.

She pulled away, turned her eyes to the road, not quite trusting herself to speak. All she could think about were her mother's words: *boasting about some girl he'd met in Boston. Don't be so naïve, Kitty.*

'Let's get a drink,' she said.

Henry held out his hand and she tentatively took it, threading her fingers through his, the action feeling so natural until she heard her mother's words again and reclaimed her hand, slipping it into her pocket. 'You may not like what you hear,' she said.

They ordered their drinks and sat down at a table by the window. She wiped a ring of water away from the oak surface with her hand. The saloon was starting to fill up. Men stood in raincoats, their trilbies poised on the bar. Smoke hung in the air, slices of lamplight breaking through. Kitty unbuttoned her coat, watched as Henry put his mackintosh on the coat stand.

'Not much of a spring, is it? Is The Old Priory still flooded?'

'Don't,' he said.

'Sorry.'

'Tell me.'

'Give me a minute.' She took a sip of her whisky, hoping it would settle her nerves. She'd already drunk two gins. 'How is Anne and the baby?'

Henry was running his finger up and down his glass. 'Anne's okay – in shock, but she's been reunited with the baby. They called her Emma.'

Kitty's stomach contracted. She allowed herself the thought that Emma could have had a friend in Alexandra, imagining them playing on the lawn in Beecham.

'They think Anne will be home in a week or so,' Henry was saying.

He proffered an open pack of cigarettes, shaking one free. She took it. He lit her cigarette and said, 'What happened, Kit? I thought you were coming to the States with me, but you disappeared. Why?'

Kitty heard the tremor in his voice. She leaned forward, steeling herself. 'What about this girl in Boston?'

He frowned, brushing his thumb around the rim of his glass. There were the remnants of a frothy moustache on his top lip left over from his Guinness. She wanted to brush it off but stopped herself.

'Yes, I read your letter.' He looked straight into her eyes. 'I don't know what girl you're talking about.'

Kitty felt herself blush. 'You wrote to Tom, boasting about some girl you'd met.'

Henry frowned. 'Did Tom tell you that?'

'No, my mother did.'

Henry rolled his eyes. 'Well, it's not true. They don't want us to be together, Kit. That much is clear.'

Kitty didn't know what to believe. She'd spent so long obsessing about this girl, trying to imagine what she was like. She felt real.

'What about Pamela Watson?'

'Kit!'

Kitty held up her hand. 'I just hate the idea that you left her in that state.'

'What state?'

'Please answer the question.'

Henry sat forward, both hands on the table, the anger in his eyes flickering like a freshly lit fire. She felt herself tense up, her stomach knotted ready for the slap of his confession.

'Yes, I heard that I was accused of fathering her child, but it's not true. I would never leave a woman in *that state*.' He lifted his fingers as if to quote her, his eyes burning with anger. He shook his head and when he looked back at her again all she could see were the wounds that life had inflicted on him. 'Pamela was just a young woman seeking attention. I was her friend, that's all. She clearly didn't want anyone to know who the father was.'

His fists curled, his knuckles smooth as young conkers. 'I've been the scapegoat in that village for years. The only person who was kind to me was Mrs Carpenter.' His eyes blackened, hair the colour of dark chocolate hiding one of them. 'Do you really believe I would leave a woman pregnant and not take responsibility for her?'

Kitty felt the weight of his words, an internal collision. She turned away.

'No.' She couldn't bring herself to tell him about Alexandra. Where would she start? And what was the point? It would only cause more heartache. Georgie was right, it was clear her parents didn't want them to be together and she wasn't sure what she felt any more. She wanted to believe him, but there was a foolishness to her desperation she couldn't ignore.

'Is all this gossip your mother's doing as well?'

Kitty felt the hot flush of shame. 'Yes, but why would she lie?'

'Because she wants you to be with someone like Tom,' he said. 'With a private education, maybe even a title and a proper job in banking or law, a barrister perhaps.'

'*You* were educated privately, in the end.'

'You know what I mean.'

Kitty had never seen him this angry, she could sense the rage simmering, his clenched fist on the table, the determined set of his jaw, all an indication to the peril of their relationship, or at least the volatile nature of it.

'Why Paris? Is there someone else?' Henry said.

'I didn't go to Paris,' she said. 'I've never been, in fact.'

Henry leaned back, ran his arm over the back of the chair next to him, gripping the wood. She had always loved the span of his hands, remembered them suddenly clasped around her face when they had made love that one time.

'What about the letters you sent home? They had a French postmark.'

'Paris was something my mother cooked up. I sent the letters to a friend of hers and she forwarded them with a French stamp.' Kitty looked out of the window, saw the same woman as earlier sitting on her front doorstep, rocking the pram. Swallowed down the feeling of remorse that was climbing up her chest. 'So, instead of going Paris, I was in London. I thought it was better if we, you know, stopped seeing each other.'

'Why, Kit? Why lie?' he said, his face bruised with emotion. She wondered then if she'd got it all wrong. 'Why let your mother control every aspect of your life? Jesus!' Henry leaned forward again. She wanted to reach out and touch him but instead her balled hands felt heavy on her lap.

'She guessed something was going on between us,' Kitty said. 'Of course I knew there would be an element of disapproval but nothing prepared me for what she said, nor how she said it.' Kitty took a deep breath, feeling the words sticking in her throat. She could so easily tell him about Alexandra now but something was stopping her, an invisible hand pressing against the throat. Things can never be unsaid. 'She told me you were seeing someone else, that you had fathered Pamela's child and denied it, that you were a scoundrel, basically.'

A look of confusion rippled across his face.

'Jesus! None of this is true, Kit, you have to believe me.' Henry's eyes were watering. He ran his palms over his face. 'Jesus,' he said again.

'When my mother told me, she made me feel so . . .' Kitty wrestled with the words '. . . dirty,' she said finally. 'She knew about the boat house, Henry. She made me feel an idiot for thinking that you cared for me, and the truth is I still feel an idiot.'

'Kit, look at me.'

Kitty felt her stomach clench, bracing herself, she turned and looked into his eyes. She saw the pain and yet still she couldn't trust him, she wasn't even sure why any more but the sense that something had irrevocably changed flooded through her. How could she love anyone now? She had failed her own daughter. She clasped her hands together, pressing the heels of her palms together, pushing them against her thighs.

'I still don't understand why you didn't write and tell me at least. I had a right to know you'd had a change of heart. I was waiting for you. Why didn't either of them tell me? I asked them again and again what had caused you to go off to Paris, just like that' – he snapped two fingers – 'and they would just shrug it away. Once you mother said how fickle you could be sometimes. If she knew about us, why didn't she just say?'

'I don't know,' Kitty said. She felt a stab of anger, seeing his pain when she was unable to express her own.

'God, if I thought someone was misleading my daughter I'd confront them.' He drew his hands up to his forehead, clutching at his hair then raking his fingers through it.

He had no idea what she'd been through, but then that was her fault. 'Oh, Henry, can't you see. They will never approve and I know that you want me to believe you but a part of me just can't. I keep seeing this image of you with another girl. I don't trust you any more. I don't trust my family either. I don't even trust myself.'

There was a terrible racket outside, cars hooting, someone ran in shouting. 'Anyone know who this blasted animal belongs to?' Everyone turned to see what the noise was all about, some of them shuffling towards the door, necks craning, laughing at the poor disorientated animal. Their mirth clashed against Kitty's wretchedness. Henry didn't appear to have noticed. He was looking at her – a wounded creature – with dark eyes.

'What's clear is they don't want us to be together,' he said, his voice suddenly rational and steady. 'Tom believed there was some other reason. He thought perhaps we were brothers.'

'Oh, Henry, that's an awful thought.' Her mouth filled with bile. She wondered if Henry was using this shocking news as a distraction. Surely her mother wasn't capable of keeping such a dreadful secret, but then she remembered her parents arguing around that time and felt physically sick at the thought. Was this what she'd suspected but hadn't been able to face? Surely her parents would have told them by now.

'Georgie believes there's something else going on,' she said, 'but I think the idea that we're related is a little extreme, don't you?' Her mind was suddenly unravelling. 'Good God. You don't think Dot and my father, you know . . .'

He was staring at her, his face blank. 'No wonder Clarissa is behaving like this. There has to be a reason.'

Kitty was suddenly filled with the horror that this could mean that Alexandra was a product of incest. She broke down, leaning on her elbows, feeling the pull of the sleeves on her coat. The lie was beginning to wear her down. She heard the scrape of Henry's chair as he stood up, imagined him walking away but then he was beside her, his arms pulling her towards the cave of his chest.

'It's not true, it can't be,' she cried. 'Maybe we're cousins, maybe that's it.'

'Let me deal with this. I'm going to speak to them.'

Kitty wrenched her body free of his embrace. The publican walked out from behind the bar.

'You all right, love? He treating you well?'

Kitty looked up, imagined her face bloated and frightful.

'Yes, she's fine,' Henry said, his tone curt.

'Just some bad news, that's all,' Kitty said, trying to smile.

'Sorry to hear that.' He bent down to get closer, his eyes sharp. 'But keep it down.' The publican wiped the surface of the table, collected an empty tumbler.

Henry sat up, braced himself, as if ready to confront an oncoming gale. He ran his fingers through his hair, took a long swig of his Guinness. She watched as his mind volleyed each potential avenue with renewed agility.

'I need to confront them,' he said.

Kitty took long deep breaths to steady herself. 'Basically we're assuming your mother *and* my parents lied. That's a lot of deceit if you think about it. I think there's some other reason, something my mother isn't telling me. Maybe she knows something about you, or your father. Does it matter? We need to let each other go, Henry, whatever way you look at it.' *It's for the best.*

Henry was staring out of the window. 'To think I thought they took me in out of kindness. There is nothing kind about Clarissa's defamation of my character.'

He was leaning on his elbows, his fisted hand pressed against his forehead. She ached with the desire to comfort him.

*

Henry felt the weight of their shared past descend: the memory of Kitty in the library, her release on the night of Tom's wedding, the years they'd shared, the forbidden nature of their love, came into focus. He couldn't believe Clarissa had lied so prolifically. Tom was right, there was something else and he was damn well going to find out.

'We were always part of a reaction to them, you and I,' Kitty was saying. She leaned forward, opened his pack of cigarettes, twisting one free. 'Maybe we found each other because of that.'

He believed as Kitty spoke she was excavating something deep in their collective soul. He would never stop loving her, he knew that much. He watched as she looked out of the window, although he could see that she was focused on some interior detail, not the activity outside: the open-topped car parked up with a couple of young girls in the back in plastic raincoats, or the man in the kiosk opposite selling newspapers. He knew that Clarissa was hiding something, he knew it in his bones.

'I'm not saying that I didn't love you,' Kitty was saying, 'but I have the feeling the attraction was because you weren't a Campbell.'

'And yet now you think I might be,' he said.

'What?'

'A Campbell.'

'You will never be a Campbell,' she said. 'Apart from anything, you look nothing like us.' She smiled and he saw her soften, a little of the old Kitty shining through, but then her body tensed. 'But the possibility of shared blood, what an awful thought.'

'Kit, we don't know that yet.'

She dipped her head. He watched helpless as she closed up like a clam. 'It doesn't change anything, Henry.'

'If I can prove they're lying.'

'About what? About you and this woman in Boston, or the fact that you maybe my long-lost cousin, or worse, brother. None of it looks good.'

'Let's get out of here,' he said.

They walked down to the canal, their bodies touching. Something about the way their footsteps synchronised made him want to weep. He thought about his father, the memory of him in a workshop making him a sledge, showing Henry how to hold the nail straight, use a hammer, then gently touching his head with his big hands. He missed him now more than any other time. Why had his father forgotten him?

They stopped to watch a narrowboat chug past loaded with coal, the driver nodded, tipped his hat, barely visible in the dark. Henry gave a short wave. The thud of its engine echoed down inside the tunnel. He pulled Kitty into an embrace, and she laid her head on his chest. He would never stop loving her.

Then she pulled away.

'This isn't right,' she said. He thought she might be crying but suddenly her hands came up to her face and he saw in her eyes a determination he couldn't argue with.

Silently they found themselves walking back towards Georgie's bedsit. It had grown dark and chilly and the sound of London rumbled like a threat – the grumble of traffic, the sharp whistle of a train, the patter of footsteps, the passage of progress.

He reached out to Kitty when they got to Georgie's front door but she shook her head. She took off her shoes, held them with two fingers. He noticed a spot of blood on her tights, a red island on her heel. They stood like that, both of them focused on her feet, until he pulled her towards him again and ran his fingers across her cheek.

'I've missed you,' he said.

She turned her head away. 'I know.'

'There was never another woman, Kitty.'

'It doesn't matter now, does it? The trust has gone.'

'I have to confront them, Kit.'

'I'm not sure I want to know,' she said.

'You should call Tom.'

'I can't,' she said. 'I need to make a new life.'

'I'll come back,' he said.

'I know,' she said, pulling away. 'But I'll be a different person by then.' She turned quickly, running up the steps, opened the front door, jamming the key in the lock. When the door swung open she looked back, her hand poised on the brass handle. Her slim wrist, the almond shape of her eyes.

'Henry. Don't tell them you found me.'

TWENTY-SIX

Bet couldn't believe it was Wednesday. She'd completely lost track of time. She was in the kitchen pacing back and forth, waiting for the milk to cool. Alexandra's body was erect and stiff with hunger. It had been three days since she'd turned up on her doorstep, two since they'd been to see Bill, and nobody had rung, yet the fear of someone turning up ready to take her remained. And then there was Kitty who had just turned up and then ran. She'd been expecting a visit from the police, even though Bill had said it wasn't necessary. She would be glad when they moved, although she felt bad for thinking it.

Alexandra had only been up once in the night, her little cries for help more like a kitten mewing than a human baby. Bet hadn't been able to sleep for the worry. She was awake when the milkman came, his float clinking and clanking down the road, the sound a comfort, as was the steady patter of rain.

'Dear little thing,' she said, kissing Alexandra's silky head. She could hear Samuel downstairs rattling about in the kitchen and was surprised to see that he'd already sterilised the bottles and teats.

'I thought I'd give the nipper her breakfast,' he said. He put out his arms. 'Here, let me hold her while you sort her milk.'

Samuel was cooing and making strange faces while Alexandra frowned and pouted. Bet busied herself with the bottle, testing the milk on an upturned wrist, finding a fresh napkin to use as a bib.

'There's more rain due. Country is sopping as it is. We need sun to dry it all up.'

'When *you* talk about the weather I know we're in trouble,' she said, wiping down the draining board, focused on the peeled varnish that was flaking in the grooves.

'I've been thinking, this mother and baby home depends quite heavily on donations. Maybe the best thing for me to do is to pop up to North London and see them.'

'Oh, Sam, isn't that bribing?'

'You know me, luv. I know how to phrase things.'

'Well, I prefer to go through the usual channels. We have to trust that this letter from Kitty Campbell holds in a court of law. Anyway, they need to find her, and if she's signed . . .'

'Money usually solves things more efficiently, Bet.'

'But can we afford it?' She handed the bottle to Sam, who sat himself down and offered Alexandra the teat.

'We're going to have to live lean for the next few months and I'll have to work my fingers to the bone, but this little girl's worth it.'

'But we need to do everything by the book, Sam. Bill said we needed to be as straight as a pair of policemen's trousers.'

'And risk losing her? What if Kitty comes back? She might change her mind, which is why I'm going to call the mother and baby home, today.' He withdrew the teat, and wiped the milk from Alexandra's chin. 'It's not over yet, Bet. She's perfectly within her rights to take her back.'

He looked up at her and she could see he'd made up his mind and nothing she said was going to change it. But she couldn't help thinking about Kitty. She must be beside herself, poor girl.

'I think we should call her Ally. Alexandra is a bit of a mouthful,' she said.

'Ally Abbott. I like that, but we should christen her Alexandra, don't you think?'

'Aren't we jumping ahead of ourselves here?' she said.

Sam looked back down at the child with tenderness. 'I'm going to do the best for you, don't you worry,' he said. 'The thing is that if she hasn't signed those documents, and if we use her letter, with a little help we could expedite the whole process.'

Bet felt a mixture of anxiety and pride. Sam's hair was still sticking up after his morning's ablutions. He'd missed a bit of shaving cream on his neck and so she wiped it off with her finger, smoothing down the rogue strand of hair. A bout of anxiety made Bet feel shaky again. She looked at the girl, her face already as familiar to her as Sam's. Her dark lick of hair, her sweet mouth and perfect nose and the way she clutched both hands at her chest as if in prayer. It was impossible to imagine a life without her.

TWENTY-SEVEN

Henry stood at the top of the stairwell at Beecham the morning after he'd seen Kitty, a knot forming in the pit of his stomach. He looked out onto the garden thinking about how she'd been the night before, remembering the look on her face, both adrift and defiant. He touched the glass pane, tracing raindrops of water that scuttled across the leaded window.

He had lost her.

Despite it being past nine, nobody appeared to be up. He'd returned to Beecham late last night hoping to catch Clarissa and Howard, but they'd already gone to bed. Tom had stayed up to greet him and asked after Kitty, but Henry had lied and said he hadn't seen her. After a nightcap, they had both ended up staying at the manor and of course he hadn't slept well, the sense that Kitty no longer trusted him, that there was something she hadn't told him dancing across his thoughts throughout the night.

A fine drizzle left the grass moist. He allowed himself a moment to enjoy the view: the willow hanging over the lake, the stepping stones arcing across to the island. The flowering shrubs: rhododendron, hydrangeas, the beech tree that stood at the far end of the fence and the box hedging that hid the kitchen garden. The tennis court with its frayed net and swimming pool that had turned an algal green from lack of use; all of it ingrained in his psyche as wealth just out of his reach, much like Kitty. Memories of his time as a young adult floated before him. He and Kitty held together by an invisible thread of longing.

He noticed one of the dogs had wandered underneath the willow tree, his tail sticking out as if the animal had got trapped in the tangled branches. He remembered how Kitty and he had often met inside the cave of that tree. The first time it happened she had slipped him a note at breakfast. *Inside the willow at 10. x*

He hadn't been living with the Campbells long, under a year he supposed. It was the summer before the Campbells sent him away to school and he'd been filled with a loneliness and anguish that sat heavy inside. He remembered how shortly after breakfast that day he had parted the fronds filled with anticipation – a kaleidoscope of butterflies in his stomach – at the idea of them meeting secretly. At ten, he found her leaning against the trunk, knee bent, her foot planted against the bark in an effort to look nonchalant. She smiled, eyes full of mischief, and he had felt the grief that had weighed heavily inside him floating away.

'You came,' she said.

'You knew I would,' he said. They had held hands, both of them trembling and then she pulled him towards her so that his face was buried into the flossy texture of her hair. He had never wanted anything so much in his life. Even then he couldn't contemplate losing her.

After that day, they often disappeared into the belly of that willow, hiding their desire, unsure of what to do with it. Touching each other guiltily, fumbling and nervous.

He felt a wave of sadness at the memory of those days and the clandestine nature of their feelings, and the comfort she'd given him, always playful. He had seen none of that side of Kit last night, just the melancholy presence of betrayal and fear.

The tree shivered and the dog bolted across the lawn, startled by a magpie that had landed nearby.

'What a ghastly day,' Clarissa said.

Henry started from his reverie and turned to see Clarissa standing behind him watching the same spectacle. She smiled, as if they were watching children playing gently in the sun rather than a dog bolting across the lawn on a miserably wet spring morning.

'Good morning,' she said.

'How was your journey home?' he asked.

'Exhausting. Tom told us that you went to London to look for Kitty. Any luck?'

'I'm afraid not.'

Her cold blue eyes locked into his. They both knew he was lying.

'How was your trip?'

'Difficult,' she said, pinning a stray piece of hair into place.

Tom appeared at the bottom of the stairs, a petulant look on his face. 'Everyone seems to have forgotten that my wife is in hospital. Once again, Kitty's at the forefront of your concern. We need to get going soon.'

'Oh, darling, I'm so sorry. Let's all have a quick coffee in the library,' Clarissa said, kissing his cheek. 'Then we can make our way to Brighton.'

Tom led them down the hallway, footsteps echoing on hard wood. The question on Henry's mind was how to broach the question of his parentage, or whatever it was. If Tom and Georgie had been right about there being a reason for them not to be together, it would change everything. The door to the library creaked as Tom opened it. Howard was already there reading the *Financial Times* in his armchair.

'Have you had breakfast?' Tom asked Henry.

'Bit late for that now,' Clarissa said. 'We can have coffee in here. Agnes has made some buns.' Clarissa went to Howard's desk and started running her hands over the mail. Henry watched as she fingered the envelopes. He saw a letter from Kitty with a French stamp on it – what a farce that was – and then the handwritten envelope that Tom had spotted yesterday afternoon. He'd recognise that curled neat handwriting anywhere. Clarissa picked up the penknife, tore the envelope open.

'Can't you open that later?' Tom said.

'It's from Kitty,' Clarissa said. 'I didn't think to look at the post last night.'

Henry knew that this would irritate Tom, who'd been describing the state of The Old Priory to Howard, presumably he'd talked about nothing else since his parents had returned. Howard looked bored. Everyone waited as Clarissa silently read the contents. It must have been a short note, much like the missive Kitty had penned to him, because she put it back in the envelope seconds after she'd opened it. Looking at Henry, she said:

'Did you know anything about this?'

'No,' he said. Her skin had browned while in Kenya, mottled with freckles. Her hair was curled into a pleat but he could see that she had taken less care than usual. Her lipstick had bled into the lines on her top lip. She looked tired.

'She's probably gone back to Paris?' Tom said. 'I thought she'd at least want to see Anne.' He was restless, pacing back and forth.

Clarissa's eyes went back to Kitty's letter. He had to act quickly, think how he could broach the question of her accusations without revealing that he'd seen Kitty.

'Kitty's not out of sorts, she's behaving like she always does when there's a crisis,' Howard said, folding his newspaper and tucking it down the side of the armchair.

'Do shut up,' Clarissa said.

Howard recoiled.

Tom gave an indiscernible shake of the head. The steady rhythm of the grandfather clock was the only sound in the room. Saunders came in with fresh coffee.

The moment passed.

Clarissa took a sip of her coffee before sitting on the arm of Howard's chair. Henry thought there was something about their body language that suggested they were about to confront him about Kitty, that everything would spill out into the room. That is what he wanted: life to be messy and real instead of mannered, but this was the Campbells.

'I suppose we'll have to wait for visiting hours to see our first grandchild,' Clarissa said.

Tom smiled, glad that his daughter had been acknowledged. Henry watched as Clarissa picked at some invisible spot on her sleeve. He looked at the envelope sitting on the desk, keen to read the contents, believing the note contained the missing piece to the puzzle. The clock rumbled into life marking the half-hour.

'Bun, anyone?' Clarissa said.

Henry felt a need to sort out his flight to the States, write to the newspaper in Boston and get the hell out. He remembered his aunt saying how his mother had wanted to go to the States, and here he was feeling the same thing. There was something that he wasn't being told about his past, and he was determined to get to the bottom of it. He and Kitty would never be free if he didn't.

'Would you have my father's address?' he asked. He watched as Howard flicked a glance at Clarissa. It was enough to tell him that Tom and Georgie could be right. Howard and Clarissa had been hiding something.

'Is there something you're not telling me?' He noticed the muscles rippling in his forearm and unclenched his fist. Wherever he put his hands, they felt cumbersome.

'Well, I suppose now is as good a time as any.'

'Howard . . .'

'No, Clarrie, he has a right to know.'

Tom, who had been standing by the mantelpiece with his hands in his pockets, flashed a look at Henry. 'Can't this wait?' he asked.

'No,' Henry said.

Howard said, 'I'm going to get straight to the point.' He hauled himself out of the chair. 'It's been on my mind for some time. You see, there's a possibility that *I'm* your father.'

'Good grief,' Tom said, turning on his heel and gaping at Howard. 'I knew it.'

Henry waited, the feeling of weightlessness forcing him to steady himself on the chesterfield.

'Judging by your reaction, you already had an inkling,' Howard said.

Henry pushed his hands in his pockets in attempt to look more relaxed. 'Well, I thought there had to be a reason for the adoption, yes, and it would make perfect sense of your disapproval regarding Kitty and me . . .' Howard went to speak, but Henry held up his hand. 'But I think you're wrong. I know my father.'

'Well, your mother seemed to think . . .' Howard said, but Henry interrupted again.

'My mother was desperate.' It was clear Howard believed he was his father but Henry *knew* he wasn't his son. It occurred to him then that his mother was clever enough to use the Campbells for money. He remembered how poor they were. To think that this was what was keeping him and Kit apart.

Howard retreated back into his armchair, his rheumy eyes looking downwards.

'Well, that doesn't change the fact that your mother believed there to be a possibility.'

'Are you aware of the circumstances surrounding your mother's death?' Clarissa asked.

Henry sensed that Clarissa was about to hit him hard. There was no warmth to her face, she was tight-lipped. He looked down, unable to meet her eye, the image of his mother dancing around the kitchen conflicting with the image of her laid out on her bed, a beauty radiating from her even in death.

'Your mother committed suicide,' Clarissa said. 'Why do you think she did such a thing? She was blackmailing us. Did you know that?'

He'd always known of the possibility of his mother having committed suicide but he'd pushed the thought away. Clarissa's words had meant to wound him and she'd succeeded.

'And, as you know, when we wrote to your father, he failed to reply,' Clarissa said. 'Which, I'm afraid to say, suggests that he wasn't interested.' Clarissa took a sip of her coffee.

Henry blinked back the tears. This whole story was beginning to frighten him, the idea that one incident should follow him into the future scarring the chance of love and freedom. Clearly there were things about his mother he didn't know and the thought that whatever it was might have caused her to take her own life made him feel instantly weak.

Tom, after gawping at his mother, put his head in his hands. 'Christ,' he said to Henry. 'I'm so sorry.'

Henry had no idea if Tom was apologising for Clarissa's bluntness, or his mother's act of suicide. He pulled himself up, reached for a cigarette. 'I'm not sure why this wasn't done at the start but there's one way to settle this and that's to have a blood test. Withholding this information has already caused enough damage. Kitty is obviously completely broken and I think once we've cleared this mess up, she and I would like to get engaged.' As Henry said this, he knew in his gut that Kitty wasn't going to come back to him easily. He turned his gaze to Clarissa.

'Thank you,' he said.

Howard looked up weakly, unable to speak.

'I'll be in touch regarding the blood test,' Henry said. He went and patted Tom's arm before heading to the door. 'I'd better go and walk the dogs. Give my love to Anne.'

He was careful not to slam the library door. He wasn't going to give Clarissa the satisfaction of witnessing the rage coursing through his veins. But it was his mother that haunted him, and the idea of her ending her own life, and for what?

TWENTY-EIGHT

Kitty woke up with a familiar feeling of emptiness the morning after she'd seen Henry. She was heartened by the hiss and crackle of eggs frying, although she had no appetite, but felt a wave of love for Georgie who was trying her hardest to offer comfort.

After Kitty had said goodbye to Henry she had oscillated between feelings of self-pity and outbursts of rage. Georgie had been the epitome of patience, feeding her tissues, cigarettes and gin. She was already dressed in slacks and a polo-neck jumper, standing over the stove in the kitchenette. Kitty had slept heavily and for a second, before the brutal attack of consciousness, she forgot why she was there. Then the image of Alexandra came to her and the pain registered in her chest.

'Oh good, you're awake. I thought a cooked breakfast might do you good,' Georgie said, scooping the eggs out of the pan. 'Why don't you pop into the bathroom. This will be ready in a couple of minutes.'

'That's kind, although I don't feel all that hungry.'

'Nonsense. You need sustenance.' Georgie was laying the table. 'Chop, chop.'

Kitty obediently got up. She went to her suitcase and fished out her own pair of slacks, wondering if she would fit into them as she hadn't worn them since before the pregnancy.

'I have to go to the studio as I'm behind on a commission,' Georgie said. 'What are you going to do?'

'I thought I might go and see Alexandra,' Kitty said.

Georgie didn't answer, but Kitty saw how her shoulders squared up as if someone had touched her back.

Breakfast was a challenge. The tea was too milky and for some unfathomable reason Georgie had put sugar in it.

'Eat up. The egg will settle your tummy.'

'How do you know my stomach is out of sorts?'

'You look pale and emotional. I'm trying my best to be maternal and you know how that doesn't come naturally to me.'

Kitty smiled at the idea of Georgie being maternal. It *was* incongruous. 'I lied to Henry, Georgie. It feels so wrong. My parents lied, now I'm doing the same.'

'Nonsense. At least now Henry can get on with the rest of his life, and so can you,' Georgie said. Kitty found herself thinking about Bet in the shop yesterday. The way she'd held on to Alexandra protectively.

'I thought I would go and see Alexandra today,' she said again.

Georgie leaned forward and touched Kitty's wrist. 'Oh, Kitty, do you think that's a good idea?'

Kitty pulled her wrist out from under Georgie's hand and picked up a piece of toast, biting into it with a loud crunch, the butter wetting her lips. 'I just want to see her, that's all.'

Georgie rolled her eyes, lit up a cigarette, her shoulders hunched. Kitty thought how expressive Georgie's shoulders were, how endearing her best friend could be.

'What we want and what's best don't necessary correlate. You need to put the baby's welfare first, Kitty. This isn't the right time to have a child, you're ill prepared. Children

178

need stability.' All the while she was talking her hands were arcing above her, this way and that, fingers positioned like a ballerina's. She made gesticulation an art form.

'What do you know about stability?' Kitty said.

'I know what it's like to live without it.'

Then the phone rang.

'Someone else can get that,' Georgie said.

'It might be Henry or Tom. If it's Tom, tell him you have no idea where I am.'

Georgie stood up, her cigarette dangling from her long fingers. 'There's something I have to tell you about Tom.'

'Oh, Georgie, I don't care, it's your life and I won't judge, but whatever you do don't tell him you've seen me.'

By that point, the phone had stopped ringing.

Later that morning, Kitty took the bus to Purley because the Morris was low on petrol. She sat on the top deck so that she could smoke. She watched London from a distance, the people threading their way through Marble Arch, down Oxford Street, a purpose to them she no longer possessed. She changed at Victoria realising then that the car would have been a better option. The iron smell of the bus made her feel a little queasy. She reached for a cigarette and realised she'd left her matches back in the Morris. A young chap was sitting next to her, his mackintosh buttoned to the neck.

'Could I trouble you for a light?' she asked.

The man dug out some matches from his pocket. 'You can keep 'em,' he said.

Kitty went straight to the tea shop. When she got there it was closed. Apologising for the inconvenience, the sign said: *Closed until further notice*. The grocer's was open, though, and the young chap who'd served her the day before was busy charming a queue of customers. Kitty walked past, casually eyeing up the activity inside the shop, looking to see if she could catch sight of Bet. She could just make out another girl behind the counter, a slim brunette, nothing like Bet, serving up slices of ham. Now that she'd arrived she realised that she had no plan, no conversation worked through in her head. She'd expected to walk into the tea shop to find Bet behind the counter buttering bread.

She crossed the street and stood waiting, hidden behind an old beige Standard. She crouched down and contemplated going to the greengrocer's again to buy more fruit. But then Bet's front door opened. Bet was manoeuvring a pram through it, which seemed to involve lots of pushing back and forth. The pram was a navy blue, a shining beacon of motherhood. How had they managed to buy that so quickly? What had she been thinking? Georgie was right. *Children need stability.* What could she offer her daughter? A life of struggle and shame. The thought of Alexandra made her breasts feel more solid and painful. She ached to see her. She smelt of cabbage.

Kitty watched as Bet finally managed to get the pram down the front step, bending down to peek inside the hood before walking up the road. Kitty followed, her heart thumping, leaving her short of breath. It started to spit with rain so she pulled out Georgie's umbrella from her bag and made sure to hold it low over her head. Bet nodded at a couple of neighbours as she strode along the pavement, the carriage of the pram bouncing gracefully in front of her. Someone stopped and bent down to look inside. There was lots of cooing and laughter. The woman kept touching Bet on the arm, swinging her basket back and forth. Kitty felt a stab of anger, followed by a wash of sadness. This was *her* daughter. Bet swung round suddenly, her focus right in Kitty's sightline. Kitty ducked out of sight, turning sharply into an alleyway. The comfort she felt being close to her daughter suddenly gone. She waited a couple of minutes. When she turned to go out again, she saw Bet had travelled up the road, a distant spot on the landscape. She was so busy watching Bet that she didn't notice that the woman who'd been talking to Bet was standing right beside her.

'You lost, luv?'

'I was just waiting for a friend.'

'Oh yes, who's that then?'

Kitty felt herself flush. 'Katherine Walters,' she said.

'There's no Katherine Walters down here, luv.'

'Oh no, she's not local.'

The woman nodded, wrinkling her nose. 'Mind if I get past? Not enough room for two umbrellas to pass down 'ere.'

Kitty let down her umbrella and stepped aside. By the time she'd waited for the woman to pass, Bet had disappeared. Kitty felt oddly relieved. She knew she couldn't do it. She couldn't put her child through the turmoil of her life after imagining her so safe and secure in Bet's pram, Bet's home, Bet's stable marriage and the neat little terraced house that looked utterly appealing compared to the shambolic homelessness Kitty had to offer. She hadn't told Henry about Alexandra because of the shame she felt. Alexandra needed love that was free of the Campbells, she thought. She would visit again. She picked up her step, some possible vision of her future bringing her to life, and walked past the safe walls of Bet's house towards the bus station. She would buy a new easel and start to paint, find some work as a waitress somewhere, so that she could send money to Bet. She would come to visit Alexandra again so that her daughter knew she wasn't far.

Maybe, if she got her life together, she could get her back.

TWENTY-NINE

Henry got back to the cottage after walking the Campbells' dogs to find it damp and unwelcoming. The image of his mother laid out in her bedroom in her best frock accosted him like never before. How could Clarissa be so cruel to tell him about his mother's suicide? She'd delivered the devastating news as if she were discussing the weather.

It was just after two o'clock and he hadn't eaten. He was too anxious for hunger. He sat at his desk and pulled the lid off his pen before placing it down on the blotting pad, his palms flat against the smooth wood. His mind kept batting away the thought that Kitty had withheld something, that perhaps she already knew that there was a chance that they were related, but then again she'd seemed so shocked. But there was something so dramatic, so final, in the way that she had packed everything she owned. None of it made sense. He wanted so desperately to be free of his past and to take Kitty as far away from Beecham as possible.

Of course Kitty had done as she was told and run away from him. All children think their parents know better, but Henry had learned young that parents are fallible. The only way he was going to get to the bottom of this whole mess was to find his father and to sort out this blood test with Howard. The doctor had sounded sceptical when Henry had spoken to him on the phone. In the end he'd made an appointment to see him the following day.

From the window he could see the valley, drenched and glistening. The clouds, various shades of grey, were bulbous, threatening another onslaught. He heard a dog barking, probably the spaniel that belonged to the Carpenters, and then a car make its way towards the farm, the pull of the outside world a distraction. The need to escape the confines of the cottage was growing harder to ignore. God, he was ready to leave this place, find his father, try and unravel his mother's dodgy past, but what to write to Kitty. He couldn't face calling her, and anyway, he thought it wise to respect her need for distance. He knew Kitty well enough not to push.

He jolted as the door knocker rapped, jumping up to answer it, expecting it to be one of the farm hands that worked for the Carpenters looking for the unruly mutt. The last person he expected was Howard, who took off his hat and stepped inside before Henry had a chance to welcome him.

'You'd better go into the sitting room.' He realised his voice was shaky and took a deep breath. Howard remained in the hall, making a song and dance of wiping his feet.

'No point in all of us going to the hospital. I thought this would be a good moment to talk,' Howard said.

Henry felt himself shrink against the weight of Howard's presence. He was surprised to see that Howard was nervous, his hands balled into a clumsy fist.

'I think I know why you're here,' he said.

'Right,' Howard said. They stood for a minute, heads bent, until Henry gestured again for them both to move into the sitting room. 'I thought it would be good to talk things through alone.'

'Does Clarissa know you're here?' Henry watched as Howard contemplated his answer.

'No.'

'You see . . .' but Henry didn't know where to start. The thought of his mother's past pressed against his chest, made him feel weak.

'Go on,' Howard said.

'I don't believe you're my father for one minute,' he said. 'I don't know about the relationship you had with my mother, but I know Charlie Roberts *is* my father.'

Howard's eyes locked on to his. Henry saw the fear, and something else he couldn't quite recognise. 'Well I can understand this is hard. But I didn't just come to discuss this. I came to talk to you about you and Kitty.' Howard was folding his coat, placing it over the back of a chair. 'But if that's what you would like to talk about, I think a drink would be in order.'

Henry crossed the living room with a couple of strides, picked up the decanter and poured them both a drink. 'How can you be so sure you're my father?'

Howard ran his hand over his thinning hair. Henry noticed the mottled texture of his skin. He had the weathered look of a man who had spent years in Africa, age spots spattered across his forehead. He handed Howard his drink.

'I'm not sure,' Howard finally said. 'But your mother told me that was the case.' They stood facing each other, the sound of the fire crackling. The Carpenter dog continued to bark from some far-off field. Henry's heart was beating fast, suddenly realising that his mother's death was rooted in this web of lies.

'Are you going to tell me?' He hesitated, unsure how to phrase his thoughts. 'About my mother, I mean.'

Howard sighed, wrapped his arms around himself as if he was defending his body from something cold and unpleasant, one hand cupping his drink. 'Your mother and

I spent some time together just at the end of the war. We met at a tea dance, that's all. It wasn't anything sordid, if that's what you think. I was genuinely intrigued by her. Every man in that room wanted to dance with Dorothy. She was so full of life.' He shook his head. 'That smile of hers. She could have ended the war with it.' Howard walked towards the window. Whatever he was recalling was better remembered looking out at the landscape. 'She was captivating,' he said. 'Your mother was quite a woman.' He turned to Henry, offering a faint smile. 'My father brought it to an end, of course. I was engaged to Clarissa you see, and Dorothy to Charlie Roberts. It would have caused quite a scandal, and Clarissa's father was a friend of my father's. He was right, it would never have worked, but some part of me regretted leaving Dorothy. It was the closest to love I ever got.'

He held Henry's gaze, a weary look to him. 'After she committed suicide, I never forgave myself.'

Henry flinched. 'I didn't know about that until earlier this morning. I must say it came as quite a shock.' He was unable to contain the emotion any longer. Tears rolled down his cheeks and he quickly wiped them away with the sleeve of his shirt. Howard stood rooted to the floor, unable to break free of his reserve.

'I'm sorry, I thought you knew,' Howard finally said, his voice cracked. 'You were young, Henry.'

'I suppose I did know, deep down, but to hear it like that.'

'Yes, well you know how Clarissa can be.' He coughed. 'I came here hoping that I could persuade you to help us find Kitty.' He looked at Henry with troubled eyes. 'I know what you must think, that we disapprove of you and Kitty because of your background, but it's just not right, can't you see?'

'She doesn't want to be found,' Henry said. 'I saw her yesterday and I made a promise.'

Howard nodded, his mouth sloped into a frown. 'Then you must honour it,' he said.

'It would have helped if you'd been honest,' Henry countered.

'Yes but . . .' Howard rubbed his forehead. 'You're right. We should have told you sooner. You'd have to be pretty stupid not to see something was going on between you two. But I think the best thing you could do now is leave her be. Kitty needs to heal her wounds.'

Henry had never seen Howard so rigid. What wounds? he wanted to ask. It was he who had been rejected. 'I remember my father. I remember how he was with me,' he said.

'He probably thought you were his back then.'

'You can't be sure my mother was telling you the truth. I mean, it's not as if we look alike, nor do I bear a resemblance to Tom, or Kitty for that matter.'

'Well, yes. I would agree with that.'

'Has it ever occurred to you that my mother might have lied? Did you give her money? God, we needed it and my father wasn't a great earner and probably wasn't able to send that much. I'm presuming she blackmailed you.' Henry watched Howard's expression shift. It was obvious to Henry his mother had used Howard and surely Howard would want to know the truth. He needed that blood test as much as Henry did.

'You needn't worry. I've looked after you . . .'

'I don't want your money. I want you to have this blood test so we can put this bloody awful business to bed.'

Howard finally flopped down into one of the armchairs. He looked spent. Henry could see that all of this had taken its toll: the fire in Kenya, the flood and Anne's accident, and now Kitty's disappearance. Howard was a man who kept everything together with a regimented daily routine, but once that routine was broken he fell apart.

'I don't know anything about this blood test, what is it?' Howard asked.

It occurred to Henry that a small part of Howard wanted him to be his son, but he didn't care to know why. 'I read once that this test was used to prove that Charlie Chaplain was the father of Joan Berry's child. Apparently, blood grouping follows some immutable rules.'

'I'm afraid I have no idea who Joan Berry is.'

'She's an actress. It was a huge scandal in Hollywood.'

'How on earth did you learn about that?'

'If you want to be a journalist, you need to have a broad knowledge of pretty much everything. Besides, it was a famous paternity suit in California in the forties. I read about it in one of your newspapers, I seem to recall. It works something like this: if a baby has type AB blood and his mother has type A blood, then the father must have B or AB blood.'

'You've lost me already,' Howard said, shaking his head.

'I think it was the first time judges could use actual science to determine if a man could realistically be a child's father.'

'Impressive.'

Henry let the silence work its magic. The farmer was working a field in the distance, the dog still barking. 'I know I'm not your son. I'm going to find my father and hopefully a blood test will prove I'm right.'

'So you're going back to America?' Howard asked.

'I've been offered a job at the *Boston Herald*.'

'Well that *is* good news,' Howard said. Henry imagined this news would bring relief to Clarissa. *Out of sight out of mind* was one of his mother's favourite idioms, and he supposed it was Clarissa's as well.

'We did try to contact Roberts, but as you know he didn't reply. It's possible that your mother had already told him of course. About me, I mean.'

'Maybe, but something could have happened to the letter.'

'I suppose so. How are you so sure that this can be done in England?'

'I'm not, but I'm determined to find out. If we have to get this done in the States, then so be it.'

'I'd prefer it if we used my doctor in London,' Howard said.

'I've already booked to see my doctor in Steyning, tomorrow,' Henry said.

Howard nodded, reached for his coat. 'Tell me what you need me to do.'

THIRTY

Bet waited for Samuel in the parlour while Alexandra slept soundly in her pram. It was Thursday and even though she'd had the baby for just four days, she felt this is how their life had always been. The fire glowed, reminding her of her childhood. She'd bought wool, a soft butter yellow that she loved, and a pattern for a baby's cardigan with a little decoration around the neckline. Nothing too difficult as it had been some time since she'd picked up a pair of knitting needles. She knew once they got to the new house she'd never get around to going to the wool shop, and anyway, she'd wanted to take Alexandra out in her new pram. The woman in the wool shop had been helpful and made a fuss of Alexandra. As she cast on several stitches, Bet thought about Kitty. She knew it was Kitty who'd followed her yesterday, there was something about the way she walked that was unmistakable – a finishing school type of grace – but Samuel hadn't believed her when she'd told him.

'Don't be daft,' Samuel had said. 'What would the girl gain from following you?'

When they woke up this morning he'd refused to discuss it further. 'Don't start with your fretting, Bet, it'll invite trouble.' He'd gone off shortly after that to the mother and baby home having made an appointment, whistling 'Love Me Do'.

She counted the stitches. Eighteen. She needed four more.

Several neighbours had peeked into the pram and congratulated her on such a pretty daughter. She'd found herself able to say quite easily that the girl was adopted. Even Joan Watson had said how happy she was to see Bet with another child. Now she began to fret about what she'd say to them all if they took Alexandra away. What did it matter? she thought. But it did matter. On the way back from the wool shop she'd half expected Kitty to appear out of nowhere and snatch Alexandra right out of the pram. At home, she anticipated a knock on the door. Sam was right, her fears were getting out of hand. She'd be glad to leave Tivertone Street.

She lost count of the stitches and started again, pushing the looped wool between finger and thumb. Twenty-two. She switched needles and knitted into the back of the first row to give it a neat finish. She knew it was Kitty, she'd even pointed the girl out to Joan, although she hadn't explained the full story, just that she'd noticed the girl loitering. She looked at the needle decorated with a row of stitches. The more Bet thought about Kitty, the less easy she felt. She jumped at the sound of the key in the lock, putting the wool carefully down the side of the armchair and plumping up the cushion as she went to greet Samuel.

'How was it?'

Samuel took off his hat and brushed the rain off his raincoat. 'What, not even a hello?'

'Sorry. I'm all over the place.' She took the coat and wrapped it around a hanger.

'Where's Ally?'

'She's in her pram, asleep.'

She followed Samuel. 'Did you remember the sausages?'

He handed her the wrapped meat. 'We weren't thinking straight when we bought the pram, were we?'

'What do you mean? Are they going to take her back?'

'No, I didn't mean that, luv. I meant the pram's too big for the hallway. Still, it'll be fine in Mitcham.' He gave her one of his cheeky smiles, then bent down and gave Alexandra a kiss.

'Will you tell me what happened at the mother and baby home, Samuel Abbott? Or I swear your dinner will end up in the dog's belly.'

'We haven't got a dog.'

'Samuel!'

'All right, don't get your knickers in a twist. Fetch me a beer and I'll tell you all about it.'

Bet went out into the back yard to the outside pantry. When she got back, she found Samuel in the kitchen with the baby in his arms. She put the beer down on the table.

'Oh, Samuel, how could you? It took me ages to get her down.'

Samuel looked up at her. 'I've made a sizeable donation, but the long and the short of it is, she's ours.'

'Oh, thank God.' Bet leaned onto the back of a kitchen chair. 'How much did you give them?'

'Enough to oil the wheels.'

'How are we to afford it, what with the move and everything?'

'I don't know, Bet, but we'll manage somehow, we always do. They want to meet you. Apparently they have to vet us both for the authorities, but it's as good as done. The fact that Kitty disappeared works in our favour and then there's the letter, which states that she wants us specifically to adopt Alexandra. Anyway, we're to go in and see them after we've moved. Nice chap, as it happens. He said that it was all highly unusual, but from what he'd heard about Kitty Campbell she wasn't one to follow procedure. It's got to go through the courts, but that's a done deal.'

'What about the other couple?'

'That's not our business, Bet.' Sam was still cooing over Alexandra.

'I swear it was her yesterday.'

'Who?'

'Kitty. The girl's mother.'

'We've been through this, Bet. Did she say hello? No.'

'Why follow? Why not just say hello? She did exactly the same when she came into the shop. I'll be happy to leave this place, I can tell you. She'll get a shock when she comes after tomorrow. We'll be long gone.'

'You don't want to start down that road, luv.'

Bet felt a shiver run down her back. Sam was right, she needed to calm down. 'But I'm concerned, Sam. She's given up so much and she must feel devastated. I just find myself worrying that one day she's going to snatch Alexandra out of the pram.'

Sam beckoned her to stand next to him and took her hand in his, pulling her down towards him so that he could give her a peck on the cheek. 'It'll be all over soon. You're the girl's mother now.'

Bet looked down at his strong arms cradling Alexandra and felt herself relax. She nodded, blinking to suppress the tears, and went to unwrap the sausages, then lit the gas to boil the potatoes. All the while she felt Sam's eyes on her back.

'I've been thinking, what with the new car showroom and, well, the tea shop and me having too much on my plate – goodness knows when we'll find someone to take my place and the profits weren't much in the first place. Why don't we sell the tea shop?'

'We won't get much for it and besides, I was thinking of extending the grocer's. Mind you, what with the money I've just put the mother and baby home's way, we'll be eating Spam and baked beans for Christmas lunch!'

Samuel started to pace back and forth. Bet was worried he'd make the baby all anxious. 'I was thinking of putting in a proper cheese counter and having a deli counter.' He stopped, looked directly at Bet, his eyes full of concern. 'What's this really about?'

Bet looked down at the girl swaddled in the shawl Kitty had delivered her in. Her small hands were curled into a fist and her nose was buried into Samuel's chest. She had this need to protect them all. The truth was she wanted to be somewhere Kitty couldn't come back to and the tea shop was like an open door. She didn't want to be looking over her shoulder all the time but she knew Samuel wouldn't like it if she admitted that. 'There's always my bolt money,' she said, speaking her thoughts out loud.

'Your what?'

'I've been putting some money aside for quite some time now. And there's the money my grandad left me.'

'Why haven't you told me before?'

'I was waiting for the right time.'

'And that's now?'

Bet nodded. She was pricking the sausages and popping them into the pan.

'How much exactly?'

Bet thought for a minute, remembering her mother's words of advice: *Always keep your bolt money, Bet. You never know.*

'Bet.'

'It's not much, a few hundred.'

'How many hundred exactly?'

Bet turned round, put down the fork and wiped her palms on her apron. 'About three hundred. It was money grandad left me.'

Sam sat down with a thump. 'Crikey, and to think of all that grovelling I did at the bank! It's that money I paid off the home with.'

'Oh, Sam, we're up to our neck as it is.'

'Well, we had to fight our corner. All we need to do is pay the juvenile court and she's ours. But the new house is going to put us under financial strain, so we could do with the money.'

Bet went and sat down. She was feeling weak and vulnerable. 'I can't wait to leave here, Sam. I want to keep Alexandra safe.'

'From whom?'

'From Kitty,' Bet said. 'There's something not quite right about her. I don't want her to find her way back to me because someone at the tea shop told her my address.'

'Forget the tea shop. The grocer's makes more money anyway. Bet, can't you see this is madness? She's not going to find us.'

Bet looked up at him. She knew he was right, but something told her this wasn't over. 'She won't let go, Sam. I know it. A part of me will always feel that Alexandra deserves to be with her mother.'

'But she left the baby on your doorstep, luv.'

THIRTY-ONE

Henry sat in the doctor's waiting room, Howard beside him, his brown spotted hands locked tightly in his lap, his body twitching every time someone entered. Neither of them bothered with the magazines on offer, nor did they exchange pleasantries – they were past that. When Henry's name was called, Howard insisted on going in with him. Henry imagined some lie would be told to establish the reason for this test, but he didn't care. All he needed were the results.

When they entered the doctor's surgery, the doctor was washing his hands in a small basin, his shirtsleeves rolled up, soap still visible on his arms.

Howard went and sat down, still clinging to his neatly folded coat but Henry waited to be asked.

'Ahh, Mr Roberts. Do sit down.' The doctor gestured to the chair next to Howard and continued to rinse his hands. Henry sat. The doctor made no comment on Howard's presence. He set about drying his hands, patting his arms with a paper towel and rolling down his shirtsleeves.

'Last patient had influenza. I like to take precautions.'

Henry thought it strange to have Howard sitting beside him and for the first time he sensed a parental bond forming, which he didn't want, but at the same time it stirred in him a belief that he wasn't entirely alone. The doctor sat down, slipped on his spectacles and read the notes he had on file.

'I'm already aware of your predicament,' he said. 'I believe you had words with my secretary earlier. It seems there are some issues regarding paternity.'

'That's right,' Henry said, feeling uneasy that his relationship with Kitty was behind his need to press forward. Something about the doctor's demeanour, the casual laissez-faire way in which he brought the subject of paternity up, made Henry wonder if Howard had also spoken to him before they arrived. He supposed the question of Henry's paternity had been at the centre of Howard's life for many years.

'Have you been able to telephone my doctor?' Howard asked, which revealed that he had indeed spoken to the doctor.

'Yes, I have.' He turned to Henry, a warm cheerful smile inching across his face that felt incongruous considering the gravity of the situation.

'I've just spoken to Doctor Winterson, Mr Campbell's own doctor, and he is calling me back with details of Mr Campbell's blood group. But we will still need to take blood for the test.'

'Are you aware of this test?' Henry asked.

'Of course. Group testing. It's been done before, though not in this practice. I believe there was a case recently reported in the papers. But for the test to be accurate, we will also need to know your mother's blood type as well as your own and Mr Campbell's. There's no point in doing it, otherwise.'

Henry felt a total fool. He had no idea of his mother's blood group and thought it unlikely she had any idea herself. 'I'm afraid I don't know what my mother's blood type was,' he said.

'Well, why would you?' the doctor said. He was scribbling down something on a piece of paper. 'We'll need to send samples up to a lab in London – obviously that's impossible as far as your mother is concerned.'

Someone knocked on the door. The receptionist entered and handed a note to the doctor, before slipping quietly back out. All the while, Howard sat with a stony expression, his body a tense knot of self-consciousness.

'Well, according to this and my records, you both have the same blood types. Blood type A.' He looked up and smiled with a closed mouth.

'What does that mean?' Henry asked, leaning forward, his pulse running faster.

The doctor sat forward, his hands forming a steeple. 'Well I'm not entirely sure of the complexities of blood grouping but basically . . .'

'It means there is a possibility that I'm your father,' Howard interrupted, 'isn't that right, Doctor?'

'Yes, that's about the long and the short of it, although obviously it's not conclusive. As I said, if we knew your mother's blood type, then that would help to provide a more accurate result. It's complicated to explain but . . .

'Yes, we're both aware of how it works,' Howard said.

The doctor raised his eyebrows. 'Good. So if we can try to track down your mother's records, she must have had something on file, somewhere, and perhaps you can write to any relatives she had. They might be able to shed some light.'

Henry's heart was pounding so hard he felt fit to burst. His mouth felt dry. He had been so convinced that he'd be able to disprove Howard's claim in the space of an afternoon but if anything, the likelihood of Howard being his father seemed more possible. What a fool he'd been.

The doctor handed a piece of paper to Henry. 'This is the address of the doctor in London who deals with this kind of thing, especially if it's linked to the courts.'

'Well this isn't a legal matter,' Howard said, standing up and taking the piece of paper.

The doctor stood up, held out his hand. 'Don't worry, I'm sure this will be sorted at some point.'

Howard reluctantly took his hand out from under the protection of his folded coat and shook hands.

Henry stood beside him, unable to speak. He nodded. 'Thank you,' he said. He shook the doctor's hand, still confused as to what would happen next.

Howard squeezed Henry's arm as they made their way to the car park. 'Don't worry,' he said. 'We'll sort this out in no time. You're right, we should have done this a long while back.'

'You appear to have done a bit of research since this morning,' Henry said.

Howard smiled reassuringly. 'A good friend is a surgeon, he had a friend who is a pathologist. I learned a lot after two phone calls. Try not to worry. I know this is important and I will try my hardest to help.' He unlocked the Bristol and they set off for home.

As they drove through the country lanes, Henry noticed the primroses spotting the grass verges. Everything he had dreamed of was hanging by a thread. He wished to God he could walk away, but he couldn't, not from Kitty. Something in the core of his being knew he would never be free of this unless he tracked down his mother's blood group. It was then he had a sudden flash of knowledge. Perhaps his father – his real father – Charlie Roberts, might know it. But what if he'd disappeared? Or worse: he believed Henry was Howard's child.

Howard indicated to turn right. The lane leading up to the farm was long, but Henry wanted to clear his head. 'No need to take me all the way, I could do with the fresh air,' he said.

'Well, if you're sure.' Howard delved into his inside pocket and handed Henry a folded piece of paper.

'Let's hope Charlie Roberts responds this time,' he said.

Henry got back to his cottage to find the cat had left a small vole by the doorstep, so he went and found the shovel by the shed, scooping up the stiff little corpse, his mind skimming the list of tasks he had to do.

Once indoors, he sat down at his desk, not bothering to remove his coat or make a fire. He needed to write to Kitty, explain how he had confronted her parents and how he was determined to find out what was at the root of Clarissa's lies. His pen worked across the page until he sat up, stiff from the cold, aware suddenly that Kitty would look at this differently to him. She would assume that her parents were trying to protect her, that they were telling the truth. He held his head in his hands, noting the coolness of his fingertips, the way the house had chilled. He stood up, went into the kitchen and lit the gas hob to warm the place up, then went back into the sitting room to make a fire. His hands made quick work of the newspaper and kindling. The coal scuttle was full from this morning. As he watched the fire spit and crackle into life he churned over all the possible avenues. He thought then of his aunt who had been at his mother's funeral. He would write to her to see if she knew anything that might help. He unfolded the piece of paper Howard had given him, his father's address was penned in an untidy scrawl. Boston; the same place he'd been offered a job. What were the chances of that? Somehow this coincidence sparked hope. He remembered the contents of his father's last letter written months before his mother died. He had invited Henry over to America for a visit. After his mother's death, Henry hadn't been able to stop thinking of him until Clarissa called him into the library and explained in that soft palatable manner of hers that their attempt to contact him had failed. He remembered the feeling of rejection and how he worked hard to forget him.

The flames were dancing now, their violet fingers licking the chimney breast. Henry went and poured himself a whisky, took off his coat and picked up his pen once more. His flight was booked for Saturday. He had two days left to put everything in place.

The only way for them both to have a future, was to unravel the past.

THIRTY-TWO

Kitty was alone. There was no sign of Georgie, so she assumed that her evening with Alan, the neighbour, had extended into the next day. She scrambled out of bed feeling rotten, the familiar wave of nausea pushing for attention. It had been five days since she'd left Alexandra on Bet's doorstep, three since she'd said goodbye to Henry. All of it felt a lifetime ago but there seemed no end to the feeling of loss.

While Georgie had spent the evening with their neighbour, Alan, Kitty had stretched and primed a new canvas from scraps she'd found in Georgie's wardrobe, drinking gin as she stapled the cloth to the wood, staving off an alcoholic wave of self-pity. She found the idea of painting offered relief.

Outside, the dawn was just breaking. The street lamps emitted an eerie orange light against the urban greyness of London. There was a hue to the grey of Maida Vale, a muddy tone that was a mixture of smoke, fumes and rubble. She'd grown used to it over the past few days, but in the mother and baby home, London had appeared greener. She rolled up the sleeves of her pyjamas and pressed her forehead against the window. She could see the milk float trundling down the street, the creamy bottles shining under the lamp-light, the empties rattling in their cages. The milkman was whistling a tune she recognised but couldn't place. Listening to the lightness of the melody, she felt a fleeting moment of hope that was quickly dashed. Hope was dangerous in a landscape as barren as the one she'd created.

She parked the canvas on a makeshift easel, which she'd stationed by the window and ducked down under the bed to pull out her collection of paints which she kept in an old biscuit tin belonging to Beecham. The bedsit was already crowded with clothes and make-up and Georgie's knick-knacks, so Kitty was careful to keep her art equipment, which she'd smuggled up from the boot of the Morris the night before while Georgie was with Alan, out of sight. Kitty wasn't ready to expose herself to her friend's critical eye just yet. She knew Georgie would probably appear around lunchtime, exuberant and full of advice, so she set to work straight away, keen to make her mark, unsure what was driving her other than a need for the obliteration and articulation that art offered.

She added a spot of cadmium green deep along with cobalt blue on a chipped plate she'd picked up at a junk shop and slid the palette knife between the two colours, crushing and pressing them together, so that little islands of green on blue spread onto the china plate. She turned the mixture over as if she were folding butter into flour, adding just a touch of yellow and white, until she'd got the colour she wanted: a blue that was green in a different light. She closed her eyes, imagining the final piece – a spread of soothing colour and a string of violent red – and pressed the knife onto the canvas.

Yesterday she'd telephoned her old tutor asking if he could offer her a teaching post. She knew she'd sounded distressed but she'd been one of his favourites. He didn't ask any questions, didn't ask if she was painting either. His nonchalance was such that she wondered if he was expecting her call after hearing rumours. He offered her a trial day and because of that she'd set about reminding herself what art meant to her. It was a language and she had to remember how it was spoken. She hadn't told Georgie about the job or the art. Georgie would be excited and Kitty didn't want to be excited about anything.

Later that afternoon, she went to Victoria station and took a train to Purley. The train was busy with tourists. Day trippers visiting the big city. Mothers holding the hands of their small children on family outings. As the train pulled out of the station she felt a surge of anxiety grow in her chest. She'd bought Alexandra a new cardigan and hoped Bet wouldn't mind if she posted it through the door. She knew it was unlikely she'd see her daughter, but she just needed to be close, a glimpse was enough. By the time she got to Tiverton Street she could see the grocer's had a queue of people waiting to buy fruit and veg despite the fact it was five thirty. A trickle of water ran down the gutter. She took a sharp intake of spring air and shivered. Braced against the chill she made her way towards the familiar gold lettering of the tea shop wedged between Bet's house and the grocer's. She crossed the road, her eyes focused on the pavement. It wasn't until she was on the other side of the street safely tucked behind a car that she saw the 'Sold' board clamped to the front of the house. She hadn't even realised it was for sale. She looked right and left to check she hadn't made a mistake, a feeling of dampness around her neck making her alert. The house was empty and the tea shop had been boarded up as well. A familiar dull ache blossomed inside her as she walked towards the front door and climbed the same steps she'd left her daughter on. She knocked, then hammered the door knocker. The emptiness of the place echoed in response as if the house itself had died. She was breathless, edging towards panic, so that her heart kicked inside her chest.

They'd taken her daughter.

She didn't bother with the grocer's. The young man was busy serving people and didn't look like he wanted to be interrupted, so she went to the pub on the corner, the Fox and Hounds. Wiping her face with the cuff of her coat as she walked in, to see a room full of men; a rowdy bunch, all of whom fell silent as she entered. Each and every man eyed her up as she made her way to the bar. Her skin felt prickly with perspiration. The barman was attending to someone and took his time before giving her his attention.

'You lost, luv?'

'Not exactly. I'd like a whisky if I may. A single malt if you have one.'

There was a pause. 'Afraid we're fresh out.'

A small chuckle came from a couple of men stationed by the bar, their donkey jackets grubby with grease, their faces shadowed with growth.

'That one will be fine,' she said, pointing to a bottle she recognised from her father's drinks cabinet.

'Want water with it?'

'Just ice.'

A man whistled, followed by a ripple of voices and low, base laughter. The barman passed the glass across. 'One and six, luv.'

Kitty opened her purse and took out a half-crown. She looked at the drink, took a sip. She didn't want to make more of a spectacle of herself than she'd already done.

The barman gave her some change. As she took it she smiled, aware that she was flirting rather ineptly. She couldn't seem to take her eyes off the muscly arm exposed under his rolled-up shirtsleeve, the edge of a tattoo just showing. But it was the way the cotton was rolled tight against his forearm that brought back a memory of Henry rowing.

'You all right, miss?'

'Yes, I'm fine. I see Bet and her husband have moved house and they've closed the tea shop. Where did they go?'

The barman frowned. 'Can't say I know them all that well.' He turned towards a chap who was on his own in a well-cut suit. He was leaning against the bar in the far corner. 'Any idea where the bloke who owns the tea shop has moved to?'

'Who wants to know?'

'This young lady, boss.'

The man eyed Kitty up, his hazel eyes taking in her mother's camel coat, which Kitty knew gave a sense of propriety and was out of place in a public house such as this one.

'They moved up towards South London. They're extending the grocer's, so tea shop's closed for good, so I've 'eard. Samuel's put a manager in now that he's running the car showroom.'

'A car showroom?'

'Yeah, he's a funny one, Sammy.'

'Any idea where they've moved to?'

'Christ knows. South London somewhere. Car showroom's probably on the London Road. There's quite a few of 'em down that way.'

'Thank you,' she said, a small bubble of hope forming, which she instantly crushed. She picked up her glass and downed the whisky in one and walked straight out to the chorus of whistles and jeering . . . 'You're in there, mate.'

'Bit posh for you, lad.'

She pulled her coat tight around her neck and made her way towards the station. So they hadn't moved far. That was a small comfort. She'd take the Morris down and have a look for that showroom. It couldn't be that hard to find, surely. She'd bought the cardigan on the large side so she had time. But she couldn't ignore the relentless wash of despair that churned inside her. The possibility that she would never see her daughter again was unthinkable.

PART TWO

—

Six months later

THIRTY-THREE

Kitty had spent the day working with her students, teaching them the language of colour. She'd set them the task of understanding the tones in flesh: the purple, the greens, the blues. Skin, black or white, is not one colour, she said as she paced around the studio. As she watched them mixing oils, she felt the emptiness swill about – an ache that came and went like an internal tide – she had learned over the past few months to stay busy.

She hadn't seen Alexandra in six months.

After the class had finished, she strolled in the direction of Bloomsbury, grateful for the cold snap of autumnal air that spoke of the winter to come. Its sharp sting bruised her cheeks. She still had no idea where the Abbotts had moved to, despite spending many weekends driving around Croydon looking for a car salesroom with the name of Abbott. She even asked at the grocer's. The nice young man who was usually always friendly had been hostile the last time she'd paid a visit on a weekend.

'I can't tell you where they are, miss. It's more than my job's worth,' he'd said, which suggested that Bet hadn't wanted to be found. That hurt Kitty most of all. After all they'd been through. 'But they still have the baby?' she'd asked, while he threw dusty potatoes into a brown paper bag.

'Yes, they do. That's when the trouble began,' he said,

handing her the produce and popping the coins she'd given him into the till.

After the lesson, Kitty made her way to visit an art studio that belonged to an art co-operative Georgie had put her in touch with. She still kept her work hidden and Georgie didn't pry, because she was too busy with Alan. Kitty had been walking for at least five minutes churning over her next move to find her daughter when she became aware of a presence behind her. She turned to see Tom staring, wide-eyed. It reminded her of that game they'd played as children: *What's the time, Mr Wolf?*

'Why not just stop me and say hello?'

'Sorry, I . . .'

'She sent you, didn't she?'

'If you mean our mother, then no. I know about the baby, Kitty.' He hesitated, distracted by the passing traffic, mostly black cabs and buses. 'Georgie told me. I'm so dreadfully sorry,' he said.

'Poor Tom, you'll always feel guilty that you were mother's favourite.'

'Can't we just talk?'

Kitty thought for a minute. Tom did look stressed. 'There's a public house not far from here, although it will probably be full of students,' she said.

'We could go to Dad's club.'

Kitty sighed. 'No, Tom. Apart from anything, Mayfair is quite far.'

'We could take a cab.'

She rolled her eyes. 'Let's find somewhere nearby.'

She started to walk away but he gripped her arm.

'I've missed you so much, Kitty. We all have. Mother's not well. That's partly why I'm here.' He stood there, shifting from one foot to the other. At last, they started walking towards Soho. He didn't mention Emma and she certainly wasn't going to ask, but it made conversation terribly awkward. She could feel a fiery knot settle in her stomach, wondering why Georgie hadn't mentioned Tom.

'So you saw Georgie?'

'We met for a drink. Don't worry, nothing's going on . . .'

'Well you'd be a fool if it is.'

'Things have been tense at home. Mum hired a private detective. I knew you wouldn't just disappear for no reason and so I confronted her. She broke down. She's terribly worried about you, Kitty.'

'Tom, please don't. She feels guilty, that's all.'

Passing through Seven Dials they decided on The French House, more bar than pub. Of course it was packed. Filled with artists and actors. Kitty felt herself relax. This, she had to admit, was not neutral territory and she was pleased to see that Tom wasn't altogether comfortable.

'What can I get you?'

She was tempted to ask for a Pernod but that was showing off. 'I'll have a glass of house red.'

He pushed his way forward. He seemed to have shrunk since she last saw him. When he returned, there were no tables so they squeezed themselves into a corner of the bar that ran alongside the window. Kitty perched on a stool and Tom stood leaning against the window. He was wearing his city coat with a velvet collar and looked out of place. Kitty was shaken up, her legs felt wobbly and she resented it.

'So, what else do you have to tell me?' she said.

'Mother's been unwell.'

'So you said.'

'It could be psychosomatic, although I have this terrible feeling she's going to die.' Tom looked away, more comfortable with the view of Dean Street.

'We're all going to die, Tom.'

'She seems filled with regret, that's all. I've never seen her so sad.'

'She's been sad all of her life. You just haven't noticed.'

Tom turned back to face her, his eyes unfocused. 'It's not her fault, Kit. She was trying to protect you. If Henry *is* our half-brother, then your daughter is a product of incest. It would have been a disaster.'

'It *is* a disaster!' Kitty shook her head. 'So you know everything. Henry doesn't know about the child, so I'd appreciate it if you didn't tell him. At least *he* can be free of this mess and live his life.'

'Gosh, you must really care for him.'

She turned away, not wanting him to witness the tears. 'He's trying to find his father. He seems to think he may know something, but it doesn't really matter because nothing can be proved now that Dot is dead. They should have done a paternity test when she was alive. Then none of this would have happened.'

'I know.' He reached for her hand. 'Come back, Kitty. Beecham is so dull without you. Anne needs you. I haven't been the best of husbands.'

'Then try harder.'

'I don't think I know how. Did you know about Georgie and me?'

'Of course, I just had other things to worry about. Presumably that's over. Anyway, she's seeing this new chap, Alan.'

Tom smarted. They sat in silence until Tom said, 'Anne confronted me about Georgie. She said she was on the

212

point of leaving me and asked what I wanted to do. I told her I was devastated at the idea and that I was sorry.' He looked down at his half-empty glass. 'Nothing actually happened between us.'

'The problem with Anne is that she was the kind of woman our mother expected you to marry,' Kitty said.

'I do love her. I don't know what's the matter with me.'

'You're afraid of commitment.'

'That's what Georgie said.'

Kitty found herself feeling sorry for him and chastised herself. Tom was a pest and yet her mother had never judged him in the way she did Kitty. 'What are you going to do?' she asked.

'Stay of course. I couldn't bear the idea of leaving Emma for one thing.' Tom blushed, put his hand up to his face. 'Oh God, I'm so sorry.'

Kitty felt her mouth go dry. It was careless of Tom, typical even, and yet she saw how hard her situation was for him.

'Are you in touch with Henry?' he asked.

Kitty's hair was coming loose. She pinned it up, catching the eye of a man sitting alone by the bar. 'We write, yes. I wanted to ask you. Is it true that Henry boasted about a girl he was seeing in Boston?'

'You asked that on the day of the flood. I don't remember him mentioning anything of the sort, why?'

'Mother said you told her he was boasting about some girl he'd met.'

He rolled his eyes. 'God she can be meddling sometimes. She was probably just trying to put you off. Pretty obvious if you think about it.'

'The truth would have been kinder.'

'Not for the Campbells it wouldn't!' He smiled, as if this was some shared joke. It was obvious to Kitty that he had no idea of the pain their mother had caused. She'd believed her mother, but of course she'd lied.

'We're thinking of moving to London. Start afresh.'

'Gosh, that's a brave move. How will you cope without Mother?'

'Sarcasm doesn't suit you, Kitty.'

She knew she should ask Tom about his daughter, Emma, go through the pleasantries. That's what they'd been brought up to do, be dutiful and polite, but after Tom's faux pas it was hard. He'd always been tactless, but this was perhaps the first time she'd seen him ashamed. She pulled out a cigarette, offered one to Tom. She lit it, passing him the lighter, the cigarette still between her lips, catching the eye of the man by the bar for a second time. She smiled, feeling rather attractive. He winked at her.

She let the rest of the wine slip down. 'We were never a happy family, were we?'

'I don't think that's true.' He paused. 'Kitty, I need to tell you something.'

'Go on.'

'Anne's given me a chance because she's expecting another baby. She's desperate to see you but . . .'

Kitty felt a sudden jolt of anger. 'Don't tell me, she's too embarrassed.' Kitty couldn't bear the idea of Tom having two children, when she wasn't even allowed to keep the one child she loved so deeply.

'Well, actually, she's probably more embarrassed about this thing with Georgie. And of course she knows you must be devastated finding out that Henry could be our brother.' Tom leaned across, his hand squeezing hers. 'I'm sorry, Kitty. Really I am. Anne didn't want me to tell you, she feels so bad about what's happened.'

'Does she now? Poor Anne.' She took in his furrowed

brow, the familiar confused expression that had become Tom. 'I lost my child, Tom. All I have now is my art, and the hope that my daughter might know me one day. It's all the other mothers and I talked about in the mother and baby home, the chance that we might get to meet the children we were forced to give up. You cling to the most absurd things. Most of all we spent the time trying to forget. We'd watch the television all huddled together in the sitting room, a programme called *Z Cars*. All types drawn together by the absurdity of our situation. It was the first time I'd felt like I belonged, probably because nobody judged.' She took a deep breath, trying to stay calm. 'I know that I'm expected to put this behind me, forgive my mother, make everyone feel comfortable, but you see I can't. I love Alexandra, even if she was a product of incest as you so tactfully put it. Losing her has changed me. I'm afraid I don't want to see your happy family, or not so happy, let's face it. And I don't want to see our mother either, and let her phantom illness override the loss I've suffered. There isn't a day that goes by when I don't think of Alexandra, her sweet little face looking for mine.' Saying the words made her fill up with a rage so terrifying she thought it best to leave. She gathered up her bag, put on her mackintosh. It had started to rain and the people who'd been drinking outside pushed their way into the small room. It felt as if they were closing in on her. 'Can't you see I've lost too much?'

Tom said, 'I know, it may seem hard now but it will change, the pain will fade.'

'The girls at the Crusade said the same. We were all armed with platitudes but we had to be, didn't we?' She sighed. 'I have to go. I'm supposed to be seeing a studio.' She pushed past the thickening crowd, stepping out into the onslaught of rain. She was desperate to see Alexandra and had no idea where she was. *Her* baby was gone. The fiery knot that had formed in her stomach was beginning to burn. *You need to put that emotion into work*, Georgie had said.

As she laced her way through the crowds in Soho, Kitty tried to imagine the colours she would use: red. Scarlet, Rossa Corsa, Dutch Orange, a scandalous shocking pink. She needed to get to Kensington.

She needed to paint.

THIRTY-FOUR

Bet looked out of the front window at the fading light of South London, red-tinted fingers of cloud threaded a greying sky. Autumn was showing signs of arrival, leaves blocking up the gutter; the back yard with its pocket-handkerchief lawn needed a good clear-out already. She loved their new home. It still felt new even after six months. Since the adoption papers had been signed and everything had gone through the juvenile court, Bet had grown calmer. But a part of her still expected to see Kitty loitering across the road like she had in Tiverton Street for those few days. Sam said there was no way Kitty was going to find her in the back streets of South London. It was true that Bet found the anonymity of the rows of identical houses comforting. She hadn't expected to like Mitcham, but Samuel had a nose for property and she realised he'd been right – it was a move up.

She put on the radio. 'Slow Twistin'' was playing and she found herself dancing around the kitchen and down the hall until she caught sight of herself in the mirror. She'd lost weight and had bought herself some slacks. She looked younger and felt the stirring of desire move her swinging hips towards the kitchen.

She'd ordered thirty invitations for the christening. They arrived wrapped in brown paper early that morning, a stack of thick cream cards her mother would be proud of, stiff enough to stand on any mantelpiece, with a little gold cross in the centre of the page. Samuel hadn't been keen but he knew better than to argue with Bet when it came to religious ceremony. She'd managed to get Alexandra to bed early so she took out the packet of envelopes she'd ordered. The first card would go to her in-laws, after that she'd write to her mother and auntie Carol. October seemed late for the christening of a baby born in April, but at least the weather had held. Alexandra wasn't a big baby, so the christening gown Samuel's mother had contributed still fitted, and of course the shawl she'd arrived in was perfect.

An hour later Samuel arrived, his body stooped with fatigue.

'It's still so muggy,' he said.

'What's up?' she said from the kitchen.

'I almost sold my first car today, but in the end he had a change of heart.' Sam walked into the kitchen, smelling of traffic.

'That showroom is costing me a fortune. I need to sell two cars a month to break even. It's been open a month and I haven't sold one.'

'What about the grocer's?'

'If it wasn't for the shop, we'd be eating the remains of the dishcloth.'

'I could start working again, save on staff.'

'What about Ally? We can't have her neglected for a few pennies.'

'Mum could step in.'

He nodded. 'Let's not get hasty about work. Your mother's not as spritely as she was.'

'My mother is perfectly capable thank you very much.' She unwrapped the chops she'd bought and put on her apron. Samuel was pacing back and forth in the kitchen making her nervous. She tried to keep the mood she'd had before, swinging her hips while cooking, but Sam turned the radio off.

She handed him the cutlery. 'Do something useful while I mash the potatoes,' she said. 'I got these chops for a good price, the butcher was just about to close so they were cheap.'

'Saving money on food isn't going to help pay for this christening. What with the food, the invitations, the vicar; it's costing a pretty penny.'

'Don't make me feel guilty, Sam.'

'We're running close to the bone, that's all.'

'Then best you sell another car before Sunday week, or better still, sell two.'

Samuel rolled his eyes. 'When you say it like that, you make it sound easy.'

Bet turned round, hands on her hips. She wasn't feeling in the least bit sexy now. 'People don't just go and buy cars willy-nilly, it's not as if you're selling apples. You can't just stick them in the window and wait for people to walk in. Cars need to be sold, in fact, the idea of cars needs to be sold. Why don't you advertise like they do in the papers?'

Samuel stood staring at her, his face blank. 'You're right. I'm going to advertise in the local paper. And we can put up an announcement for the christening while we're at it.'

Bet wondered if this was a good idea, she didn't want to attract attention, but Sam seemed so set on it and the conversation had lifted his spirits.

THIRTY-FIVE

Henry hadn't been at the *Boston Herald* long before he was offered a post at the *New York Times*. He'd snapped it up because the pay was good but more importantly it was a portal to a different life. So far, he loved it. The office was alive with a sense of urgency. The girls in the typing pool could be heard hammering away, the constant rush of delivery was about him, the post boys whizzing in and out. They were due to go to press within the hour, but he'd already given in his piece on 'What the English think of the American dream', and was now marking up an article one of the juniors had given him. His secretary swanned into his office and put down a mug of coffee on his desk, breaking his reverie.

'What's this?' he asked.

'You look tired,' she said.

'Thank you.'

She handed him a couple of letters. 'These landed on someone else's desk.'

One had a postmark from Leicester, the other was from Boston. He hoped the letter from England was from his aunt, he certainly didn't recognise the handwriting. It was neat and rather childlike. He opened it, steadying his shaking hand on the desk.

Dear Henry,

   I'm sorry to hear that you still have no news of your father. I would love to be able to help, tell you that I knew him well, but your mum didn't have much time for me once she was married and on her way to America. Yes, I was aware that there was a man she met in Brighton, a rather well-to-do man I seem to recall, who fell for her quite deeply. He might well be Mr Campbell but as I never met him, I couldn't tell you for sure. I remember the relationship began just before my sister was due to get married, so the timing wasn't good and I think Dorothy was torn. Your mother was an attractive woman; men fell for her all the time, but I knew this man was different. I think she really liked him but of course she liked the idea of going to America as well. She waited for a proposal, but nothing came. Charlie was due to go home to Boston and I'm guessing by that time she was already pregnant with you because you were born about eight months after that. I barely had time to take a train down for the wedding as it was all so last minute. I was the only guest, apart from a friend of Charlie's. After the ceremony we went down to the pier and took some snaps and then went to the local to celebrate. Your mum seemed happy and there was no mention of the British soldier after that. So, in answer to your question, there is a possibility that the British soldier (possibly your Mr Campbell) is your father. However, I don't want to cast aspersions or anything on the dead, after all Dot was my sister and we used to be close. But she could be cunning in her own way and if she thought making a well-to-do man think he was your father to give you a better life, I wouldn't put it past her. As for your mother's blood type I'm afraid I can't help. Looking at these photos (enclosed) I see a striking likeness between you and Charlie Roberts.

I hope this helps
Yours,
Aunt Joan

He'd written months back but it turned out she'd moved and so it had taken him this long to track her down. The same had happened with his father. The address Howard had given him had led to nothing. It seemed there was no end to the search for clues to his parentage.

The photographs were black-and-white snaps of his mother and Charlie Roberts on Brighton promenade. They were framed with a cream lacy edge. Henry was pleased to see that his mother looked genuinely happy. She was elegant and slim in a pale suit, smiling into the camera, holding a small bouquet of lilies up to her chest; a white ribbon floated in the breeze. Her hair was pinned up with a sprig of gypsophila. She was beautiful. His father was leaning against the balustrade, his arm wrapped around her waist, pulling her towards him. There was another photograph of the two sisters. Joan, a poor copy of her little sister, a few inches smaller in a floral dress. Even from the photograph you could tell Joan was less lively. But what struck him most was his father, it was like looking at a photograph of himself. His hair was dark, flopping over his eye just like his own. His hands were big and his fingers long. Henry was the spitting image. He felt the cruel blow of hope twist in his stomach.

Henry had been in New York for just a month and already he felt at home. He found the symmetry of the streets – laid out in logical order – reassuring. The skyscrapers seemed to represent the nation's ambition, the way they reached upwards. The cry of men selling hotdogs, or chestnuts, the general banter that seemed to happen between strangers echoed a collective sanguinity. He loved it all. But even though he'd reinvented himself, the past lingered – his father still remained a mystery to him and the blood test taken six months ago remained inconclusive. Now this letter.

From the sixteenth floor the chequered taxis looked like yellow-backed beetles slipping in and out of the lanes, pulling over on the command of a whistle, the throb of New York a comfort. Something about the constant movement, the frantic pulse of people and the pure optimism of America made him feel anything was possible. Looking down onto the street, at the people threading their way through the sidewalks, he thought back to Kitty's comment about the Campbell obsession with being above everyone and realised that, like her, he desired the opposite: to belong. He wanted to share this moment of realisation with her, give her the same sense of freedom he was feeling up here on the sixteenth floor, show her the photographs his aunt had sent and watch her face change as the recognition sunk in. But he knew that although everything that was contained in his aunt's letter gave him hope, it didn't offer proof.

The boy whose article he was supposed to be correcting caught his eye from the other side of the room. Henry beckoned him to his office and picked up his blue pencil. He ringed a sentence to be moved up a couple of lines. The whistle went and there was the usual flurry of activity. Henry handed the paper back to the young man.

'It's good,' he said. 'Just move this sentence up to get the point across earlier. See it gets down to the boys on the floor below.'

'Thanks, Mr Roberts.'

He picked up his coffee and took a gulp before attending to the second letter that was propped up against the pot he kept his pencils in.

He tore it open.

Dear Mr Roberts,
I'm sorry to tell you that a Mr Charlie Roberts no longer

abides at this address. We do, however, have a forwarding
address: 203 Bunker Hill Street, Boston, MA 02129.
   Sincerely,
   Mr Craig Potter

Henry felt the usual weight of disappointment but at least he had a new address. He should have known it wasn't going to be easy. He looked up to see the room was emptying, the floor littered with scraps of screwed-up paper, the aftermath of last-minute changes. Everyone headed to the bar on the corner of Seventh and Eighth without so much as a nod of the head. Words had become unnecessary, although it was the currency of the newspaper world.

'You coming, Henry?' Danny, one of the subs, shouted, hovering by the swing doors.

'I'll be right down.'

He felt sure Charlie Roberts was his father but what did it matter if there was no proof. Kitty had written to tell him about her new job teaching and rather than feel happiness, he felt as if her ability to carry on had divided their worlds further apart, but he couldn't let go.

He buttoned up his jacket and got his hat. Danny was still waiting for him. 'You go and call the elevator. I'll be with you in a jiffy.'

He threw the last bits into his briefcase along with his aunt's letter. What if all this searching was a waste of time and Kitty didn't want him? He had a horrible feeling that even with the proof, she wouldn't relent. There was something in the tone of her letters that made him suspect that whatever he did wouldn't be enough. He'd send her these photos. Surely she would see the resemblance.

Too much was resting on a blood test that felt impossible to complete and a father who seemed impossible to find.

THIRTY-SIX

Bet couldn't sleep. The noises were different in this house, the place creaked and there was a scuttle of activity from the roof she supposed was from a bird's nest in the eaves, although the constant purr of Samuel's breathing was as familiar as ever. She found herself thinking about Kitty, the way she had caught a glimpse of her every now and again for those few days. Bet never felt there'd been closure.

She was worried about money mostly. Maybe they'd taken on too much. She went downstairs and made herself a hot toddy. The kitchen still felt too big – never seemed to warm up and suddenly she longed for the comfort of their tiny kitchen on Tiverton Street.

She walked into the lounge, that was what the estate agent had called it, 'the lounge', and sat in one of the old armchairs that used to be in their old parlour. It appeared ridiculously small in this large room. They'd have to replace them with a three-piece suite at some point. The curtains from the old house were two inches too short and didn't quite wrap around the bay window. She snapped off a loose thread from a cushion. It was going to take a lot of work to get this house up to scratch, and years, probably.

She went to check on Alexandra. Ally lay on her back with her head turned to one side, both fists curled. She really was a gift from God. She was sleeping right through the night these days but what good was it if Bet didn't sleep herself! On her way back to their bedroom Bet saw a pile of letters on top of Samuel's briefcase. She picked up the one from the bank. A statement. Bet went straight to the figure at the bottom. £500. That wasn't too bad, she thought. Then she noticed the minus sign beside it.

'Good grief,' she said. She held her hand on her chest.

'You all right, luv. Can't you sleep?'

She jumped at the sound of Samuel's voice, and then waved the bank statement up in the air. 'How have you let things get this bad?' she said, leaning onto the bed. 'For Christ's sake.'

Samuel made a show of pulling back the sheets and sat beside her. He took the paper and curled her fingers around his, but she snapped her hand away.

'We knew it was going to be tight, luv, but you're going to have to trust me. The advertising is working. I sold two cars last week. It's just going to take time that's all.'

She stood up. She wasn't going to sleep now so she might as well go through the books herself. 'Let me have a look at these figures. I'm going to see what we can do.' She got to the door and looked back at the crumpled version of Sam.

'It's not just our life you're gambling, it's our daughter's as well.'

THIRTY-SEVEN

Kitty put the key into the lock of the mews house in Kensington. It had been two weeks since she'd seen Tom and yet she still found herself checking to see if he was walking behind her. The wood of the front door had split and bowed so that she had to force it back with her knee until it sprung open. The place was dusty and unkempt, the varnish on the floor dull, splashed with dots of paint and glue, but the rich smell of oil paint was like a calling. She stepped inside and immediately felt a wash of calm. The room was north-facing. Even on a grey day, the light was perfect. There were several easels dotted about. A pin-board covered in postcards, photographs, bits of fabric, colour swatches, notes written about whose turn it was to buy tea or coffee. Someone had pinned a stuffed bird in flight on the ceiling so that it hung, mid-flight. She felt as if she'd come home.

Kitty took out a sketch she had of Alexandra, and pinned it up on the board along with the Polaroid. She threw on an old shirt she'd stolen from Henry years back. The smell of him no longer lingered but she felt safe inside his clothes. She missed him, but the dream of them being together felt as if it had slipped down a crack. The fact that she'd lied put more distance between them than the Atlantic Ocean ever could, and now that she knew her mother had lied about the woman in Boston, she felt a deep shame.

She tied up her hair, slipping in a thin paintbrush to keep it in place. Then she unrolled her brushes, found a palette in a cupboard, squeezed a tube of aquamarine onto it, adding white together with the smallest squirt of cadmium green to create the colour teal. Just watching the brush gave her a feeling of release. She placed the loaded brush onto the canvas she'd prepared a couple of days back, remembering suddenly that feeling of anticipation she always got before laying down that first layer of paint. She'd learned to speak to her daughter with colour, she thought. She pushed the flat of the brush into the surface, closed her eyes, feeling the veil fall between the world outside and the one that lived inside.

She'd been alone for over an hour, when the door creaked open. She assumed it was one of the other painters, but when Kitty smelt her mother's Chanel perfume, she twisted on her heel. Clarissa was standing in the doorway, her handbag swinging from her elbow as she loosened her scarf with one hand. A gesture so familiar to Kitty that for a second she could have been in the hall at Beecham. Clarissa was thinner than before and her skin was sallow.

'I know you don't want to see me,' she said, pushing the scarf into her handbag, fastening it so that it snapped shut.

Kitty gripped her brush tightly. 'How did you find me?'

'I'm still your mother,' Clarissa said. She looked around for somewhere to sit. There wasn't anywhere that wasn't spattered in paint.

'You hired a private detective.'

'I was worried.'

'What are you worried about? What people would say? That your unmarried daughter was a hussy? That she slept with her possible brother for fun! Why didn't you tell us? Why did you let me believe Henry didn't care?' She was surprised by the violence of her questioning, the raised voice that felt as if it belonged to someone else.

Clarissa winced. 'I thought it best if you didn't know about your father and Dot. You had enough on your plate. I was trying to protect you.'

'The only thing I needed protection from was you.'

'Oh, Kitty.'

'No.' Kitty had an urge to flick her loaded brush onto her mother's neat pastel coat and splatter it with paint. She swept the brush across the canvas, a feeling like hot lava roared in her throat. Red would be good, she thought. Blood red.

As she painted, she spoke. 'While you were in Kenya, I gave birth to my daughter. Actually, I should tell you that I tore rather badly. Had to have quite a few stitches. They didn't bother with anaesthetic.' Kitty wiped the brush clean, put it down. 'How could I have come back to Beecham with Anne and her baby round the corner? A second one about to arrive so I understand.' She grabbed a stool, brushing aside a pile of paper balanced on it. 'I chose who I gave my baby to and it wasn't about money, respectability or social standing. I wanted her to know warmth and love.'

Clarissa's eyes grew large and fearful. She stepped forward, reaching out a gloved hand to touch her. 'I found her good parents.'

Kitty looked down and noticed a stain on her mother's glove. 'Yes, I think I saw them. A stiff and formal couple. Probably the daughter of a friend, knowing you.'

'Kitty, I . . . I was trying to protect you and the girl.'

'No, Mother, you were trying to protect yourself. It's clear that at some point Dorothy had an affair with my father, and you're ashamed of that, aren't you? You probably see it as failure.'

Clarissa shook her head. 'No, Kitty. It's not like that.'

Kitty went to the sink, turned the tap which hammered away at the plumbing, and dipped to get her face under it. When she finished, she wiped her mouth with the back of her hand, then picked up the hem of Henry's shirt to brush away the tears. 'I can't offer you a drink, there's not even a cup. You're supposed to bring your own.'

'It's a nice place.' Clarissa reached into her handbag and dug out a cigarette. 'Kitty, I promise you . . .'

'You can give me one of those as well,' Kitty said.

Clarissa handed her the packet. 'I didn't know you smoked.'

Kitty tapped one out. She could feel her mother sliding towards her, her grip getting tighter. 'Well, you wouldn't, would you?' She raised her eyes, found herself crossing her arms and leaning back against the window. She watched as her mother clocked the photo of Alexandra and walked towards it.

'Is this her? Oh, and a drawing as well.'

'Leave those alone,' Kitty said.

'She does look a dear. Although I'm not sure it's a good idea to keep photographs. You need to try to forget.'

'Stop it!'

Clarissa swivelled back to face her, a mad look in her eye. 'I suppose you're in touch with Henry. I hear he's still trying to find his so-called father, Charlie Robets. Of course the blood tests your father took are inconclusive, but you knew that I suppose.'

Kitty gripped her fingers into a fist, swallowing the pain as half-moons dug into her palms. 'Yes, I know that. Even if he can prove Daddy isn't his father, how can we be together now? You lied about there being another woman and I believed you. I rejected him because of the things you said. I believed you, I trusted you. Now, he doesn't even know our daughter exists.'

Clarissa's face was blank. 'It wouldn't have worked anyway,' she said. 'How could it?'

'You don't know that.'

'His mother was a bus conductor for heaven's sake.'

'Oh, Mother.'

'But what if he *is* your brother, Kitty? I know it's hard but . . .' Her eyes welled up. 'She got pregnant. How could I battle against that?'

'You managed it somehow.'

Clarissa shook her head, took a puff of her cigarette, elbow cradled in the palm of her hand, holding herself tightly in a stiff embrace. Then she flicked her ash into a cupped hand. Kitty used to admire that habit. 'I don't think your father ever really stopped loving her,' Clarissa said.

'Accidents happen mother, but Dot got to keep her child.'

'Oh, Kitty, and look what happened.'

'What happened?'

'She committed suicide, that's what.'

Only her mother could make her feel such conflicting emotions of rage and sorrow. Kitty remembered Henry on the day of his mother's funeral, lost and broken by grief, and the whispers of people in the church. '*Selfish, that's what it is!*' But just like everything else, the truth was kept from them.

'That's awful,' she said finally. She felt wobbly and had to lean on a stool.

All the while her mother stood smoking.

'Does Henry know?'

'Yes, we told him before he left.'

Kitty imagined the blow he must have felt, the guilt he probably carried. She felt herself crack open. The idea that he hadn't spoken a word of this, that he'd quietly got on with the business of finding his father made her want to weep. She threw her cigarette to the floor, stubbed it out, looked up to see her mother staring at her.

'Incest is pretty awful, Kitty. At least your daughter won't be the subject of gossip.' Her mother tilted her head. Kitty noticed the half-moon circles that bracketed her mother's thinning lips. She'd grown old.

'You talk about it as if we were supposed to know, but it's your fault. You kept the truth from all of us.'

Clarissa sighed. 'Do you remember Henry's birthday party?'

Kitty nodded, walked back to her painting and squeezed vermilion onto her palette.

'That's when Dot asked for more money. Your father had already given her a sizeable chunk. I wrote a cheque, and said that was the last of it. I'd never met her up until then.'

Kitty lifted her hand to her forehead, remembering her mother's rage the night Dot died, remembered also her father in the kitchen garden arguing with Dot.

'I often wondered if she would have taken her own life if I'd shown more compassion, but she got greedy.'

Kitty felt her pulse quicken. This was Henry's mother, Alexandra's grandmother, she was talking about. 'I'd like you to leave,' she said. It was as if the voice belonged to someone else. She had this vision of pushing her mother's face into a pile of fresh earth and shuddered. A violent rage she'd managed to still was resurrecting itself, an internal bloodied battleground.

'The fact that you feel free to say that means that I have had some measure of success as a parent,' her mother said.

'My freedom of speech means nothing. The currency of love is respect, and you lost my respect the day you told me that I would have to get rid of my child and lied to me. Now, all that is left is the aftertaste of pity.' Kitty went and spat into the sink.

'Pity?' Her mother's brow furrowed. 'Kitty, the pregnancy was unacceptable, even if it turns out Henry isn't your brother. You have your whole life ahead of you.'

'I want you to leave.'

Clarissa was fumbling about in her handbag. 'You could be someone, Kitty. I didn't want you to end up like her. Once you've had children it's over.'

'I *have* had a child. And it *is* over.'

Her mother had tears running down her cheeks. 'Anyway, you've done someone a tremendous favour,' she said. 'Giving a childless couple the chance to be parents. And she's better off, isn't she? The little girl. Better off with a mother who can provide her with stability? A father.'

Kitty thought about Henry. He would have been a wonderful father for Alexandra, only the possibility that he might be her brother – half-brother, half-uncle, half-father was horrific. But none of this was their fault. Her mother stood motionless as Kitty held the door open. Kitty's hand gripped the handle. 'Please,' she said.

When she was outside, her mother turned to speak. 'I'm sorry about your allowance. I'm perfectly happy to reinstate it.'

'I don't want your money.' Kitty closed the door and went back to her painting. She added turpentine so that the colour ran down the canvas, creating rivulets on the surface like veins. Red was the symbol of blood and good health. It was the first colour to be named in all primitive languages. Cadmium red, fire-engine red, blood red, madder red. It was the colour of war. It was the colour of death. It was the colour of love.

THIRTY-EIGHT

Kitty tried not to show her nervousness as she stood in front of a circle of art students, their faces blank and disinterested – an art in itself. Over the past month she'd gained more students, some of them in their final year who had heard about her methods and asked to join her class. She wanted to win the growing group over but the visit from her mother had left her wobbly, her confidence battered. There were a couple of brightly dressed girls stationed in the centre who wore zany mismatched outfits.

'So, you need to think of colour not just as a tool. Colour is language,' Kitty was saying. 'Jung interpreted Picasso's blue period as representing *Nekyia*.' She stood up, walked to the board and wrote the word in large letters. '*Nekyia* A mythic journey into hell'. She walked around the room, behind her students' stools and stopped next to one of the girls who was busy chewing gum. 'What does colour mean to you, Trixie?'

Trixie, her bleached hair stretched into high bunches, shrugged her shoulders.

'Oh come on, you love colour. You wear it like it's armour.'

Everyone laughed. Kitty had surprised herself with her articulacy.

'I guess I use it to look different.'

234

Kitty was just about to respond when another student interrupted. He was wearing a leather jacket. His thick black hair fell over his collar and she was reminded of Henry.

'For me every colour has an emotion. For example, indigo blue is melancholic, poignant, but cobalt blue is bold and indignant.'

Kitty felt the shuffle of footsteps as the room began to grow interested. 'Absolutely!' Kitty said.

'And what does cobalt blue signify to you, Trixie?'

Trixie blushed. She looked down at her feet. 'Pain,' she said.

Kitty ran her fingers over the wood of the table, feeling the grain of it under her fingers. How could she tell this girl that she knew all about pain.

'I want you all to think how blue makes you feel. The important thing is to find the right depth of colour, the right tone. Play with the feeling. Play with the colour.'

There was a flurry of activity, the scraping back of chairs, the rustle of paper. Her heart swelled with pride. She had inspired them and was proud of it.

On the way home the bus rattled along, the alchemy of movement filling Kitty with an unexpected vitality, a sudden joy at seeing London's lit shops, Piccadilly alive with people. The effect of her mother's visit was waning. She picked up an old copy of the *Standard* someone had left behind on the seat next to her, partly as a way to still herself. On the front page there was news of Harold Macmillan's resignation due to bad health. She found herself unable to concentrate so she flicked through the pages looking at the headlines. They were still harking on about the Keeler case. Someone had been run over by a trolley bus. The fashion pages had a spread on Mary Quant. Kitty realised how little she knew of the world, how locked up in her own worries she'd been. For once she felt as if she belonged, that she was part of the city. Then she came to the announcements. Her eyes went straight to it: Abbott, Alexandra Dorothy, to be christened at St Barnabas Church, Mitcham. Her heart galloped so fast she felt woozy. She folded the newspaper in half and tucked it into her holdall. She took a deep breath, leaned against the glass window to cool herself.

Her daughter had come back to her.

THIRTY-NINE

Bet dressed Alexandra in Samuel's christening gown and put on lace booties and a yellow cardigan to match the bedding. She laid her into the pram, careful to show the silk edge of the blanket. Alexandra's eyes fluttered open and she smiled, her gummy mouth spread wide, one tooth showing, her hands batting up and down with excitement, kicking everything into disarray. Bet was overwhelmed by a wave of love as Samuel came up beside her.

'You ready, luv?' He gave her a peck on the cheek. 'She looks beautiful, like her mother.'

Samuel opened the front door and gestured for Bet to follow with an extravagant wave of his arm. Despite the blustery weather it wasn't too cold, so her spring coat, yellow to match Alexandra's cardigan, was perfect. She pushed the pram down the garden path, aware that the church bells were ringing the call to service. A sudden vision of their life in years to come flashed before her.

She parked the pram by the vestry. The beech tree was covered in golden russet-coloured leaves. By the gate there was a maple, a glorious red. They were blessed with a beautiful sunny autumnal day, the branches offering pools of shadow. Yesterday she'd been to the cemetery in Purley to leave some yellow roses on Johnny's grave. She'd said a little prayer of thanks, kissed the stone as she always did.

On impulse she'd shown the gravestone to Alexandra so that she knew she had a brother.

Samuel straightened his tie.

'How do I look?'

'Handsome as ever.'

Bet knew he wasn't comfortable in his suit unless it resulted in some fiscal reward and he wasn't religious either, but he respected Bet's need to keep God on her side. He winked as they went through the doors.

The church was packed with their friends and family along with the usual congregation she'd got to know over the past couple of months. It seemed everyone had come: there was Mary who used to lunch at the tea shop every Tuesday, and Jan who she'd met at the park when Johnny was alive, and Joan, Tim and Kerry, Bob from the pub up the road on Tiverton Street. People she'd waved to, shared a life with but hadn't realised how much they cared. Samuel was shaking the hands of a couple who'd bought a car from him, patting the backs of friends she didn't even know. Bet was finally beginning to feel as if their small family had found a place in the world.

The vicar had suggested the christening took place on a Sunday after the service so that the whole Christian community could welcome their daughter, but she wondered if even he'd counted on the community they'd left behind coming as well. Of course Samuel would be doing the sums – all those people meant more food.

She looked up to see her mother sitting in the front pew talking to her aunt, both of them dressed in lilac, clearly happy that Bet's cousin had been chosen as a godparent, along with Samuel's brother. She wondered what her mother made of it all considering Samuel wasn't a match she'd approved of. Samuel guided her and Alexandra down the aisle. They sat beside her mother and to her surprise her mother squeezed her hand.

The vicar arrived. Everyone stood for the first hymn. Alexandra's eyes snapped open as the chords on the organ were struck. Bet held her on her shoulder so that she could see the congregation. She didn't know when she'd been this happy.

*

Kitty watched Alexandra from the back of the church, a hankie screwed up in a balled fist. Her body heaved with renewed grief. At least Alexandra was still covered in the Campbell shawl. But she'd grown so much. She had chubby little arms and legs and in some way was unrecognisable. It was good of Bet to respect her wishes. Alexandra Dorothy was a strong name. She'd chosen Dorothy for Henry even though he had no knowledge of her existence.

Bet appeared to glow, a much slimmer version of the woman she'd met at the tea shop, as if motherhood had reshaped her. How could she not have told her that she was moving? Of course, Bet had no way of knowing where she lived.

Kitty couldn't believe how full the church was. This is what she'd sensed that first day in the tea shop, even though she couldn't put a name to it. Bet's popularity was real, as tangible as the flesh on her bones.

At the end of the service, the vicar announced the christening of Alexandra Dorothy Abbott. Bet went to the font, swaying slightly in her yellow wool coat with Alexandra in her arms, her husband at her side, his hand in the small of her back.

She remembered Henry's palm pressed against *her* back when they returned to the ballroom at Beecham after their time in the boat house. It had been just one time and now everyone was gathered here in this church to celebrate a whole new life conceived by strangers.

The church was silent, motes of dust danced in a shaft of autumn sun as it reached down the aisle, the light tinted green and blue from the stained glass. This should have been her beside Henry, it should have been his face open with pride.

Kitty felt invisible in this world of wholesome people, until she caught sight of Bet and their eyes locked for one brief second. Bet looked sharply away as a man and a woman joined the happy couple. The godparents, Kitty presumed. If this had been a Campbell christening, there would have been at least four godparents, she thought, all of whom would bestow gifts and promises, none of which would be fulfilled. These were good people she'd found for Alexandra. Normal people. The emptiness was fierce inside her, a burning thread. She wanted Alexandra back. She wanted Henry by her side. She wanted to know for certain that he was not her half-brother. She wanted things she couldn't have.

★

Bet realised her hands were shaking as she saw Kitty slide out of the pew, slippery as silk as she dropped a few coins by the door and left. The sound of the door closing made her heart thud. How on earth had Kitty found them? Nobody noticed. While the congregation sang the last hymn, people congratulated the Abbotts as they made their way back to the front pew. Bet handed Alexandra to Samuel.

'I'll be back,' she said. She ran down the aisle, anxiety breaking open inside her like a parasol. She ignored the curious glances of family and friends.

'Sorry, sorry,' she said from one side of the aisle to the other.

The door handle was stuck. She cursed and got it open. She arrived just as Kitty was walking out of the gate into the road.

'Kitty!' she screamed. 'Kitty!'

Kitty stopped and turned to face Bet. Even from where she was standing, Bet could see the girl had been crying. Her face was creased and her make-up had run. Desperation had trumped any need for decorum.

'What do you want?' Bet was surprised by her own tears. 'Why did you come?'

Kitty looked down at her feet. Bet stepped closer. 'I saw you opposite the old house. Do you have any idea how creepy it is having someone follow you around?'

When Kitty faced her, her chin was high. Clearly she'd rescued some sense of dignity from the well of her upbringing.

'I just wanted to know she was okay, that's all.' She scrabbled about in her bag. 'I brought her some things. A pink rabbit and a cardigan from Harrods. Well they're both from Harrods, actually. *And* a silver napkin ring.' She grimaced as she stepped forward to hand the package to Bet.

Bet snapped it out of her hands. 'You can't just turn up like this, unannounced. Do you understand?'

'I meant no harm.' Kitty cocked her head. 'I just needed to see her that's all, on Sundays. She was born on a Sunday.' Then she turned and walked away.

Bet was overwhelmed by a terrible feeling of emptiness. She wondered if it would ever go away: this belief that she'd taken Alexandra from her real mother.

FORTY

Kitty was still shaking when she got back home after the christening to find Georgie and Alan sprawled over the bed, both reading the Sunday newspapers, a fug of cigarette smoke hovering above them like a dust cloud. Coffee cups littered the side table. She'd grown fond of Alan but she was tired of playing gooseberry. She was going to have to find a place of her own but money was short – the teaching didn't quite offer enough.

Georgie jumped up, still in her knickers and kimono. 'Thank goodness you're back. Your father's been here to see you. It was awful. You should have seen his face when he saw your mother's clothes sprawled across the floor.'

'Hell. Why don't they just leave me alone? I'm definitely going to have to move now.' She went straight to the kitchen and poured herself a coffee. 'First she stops my allowance; then she sends Tom. After that she turns up at the studio uninvited and now Pa has been ordered to hunt me down. It's relentless!' She took a sip of her coffee. Georgie was gawping at her. 'Did you welcome him dressed like that?' Kitty asked.

'Of course not.'

'Pity.' Kitty slumped down at the kitchen table. 'Afternoon, Alan.'

'Is it already afternoon?' He looked at his watch. 'So it is.'

'Isn't that your mother's suit?' Georgie said. 'Don't tell me you've been to church. Kitty, what is all this about?'

'You look interesting,' Alan said. He was tucking his shirt into his trousers.

'Never mind that, what did my father have to say?'

'Poor chap was very uncomfortable. Georgie offered him a whisky. We thought you'd just popped out, so we told him to wait,' Alan said. 'He seems very concerned about your mother and talked about there being some hurt on your side. He said you needed to consider everyone else now and I'm afraid I lost my temper.'

'Alan sent your father packing,' Georgie said, putting more coffee into the percolator. 'Want some hot milk with that?'

Kitty shook her head. 'What did you say to him?' she asked Alan, who freed the percolator from Georgie's hands and hurried her out of the way.

'Hey, this is *my* kitchen.'

'Your friend needs you,' he said. He set about filling the percolator. Over his shoulder he spoke to Kitty. 'I told him that his moral code was out of sync with modern values. That this was his granddaughter we were talking about and that you'd been very distressed.'

Kitty smiled in appreciation. 'Thank you,' she said.

'It wasn't easy because apparently your mother's ill, but Alan told him that if it was his daughter he'd have been honest in the first place,' Georgie said.

'Oh she's not ill. She's just trying to get my attention.'

'So where were you?' Georgie asked.

'I went to Alexandra's christening,' Kitty said.

Georgie's eyes widened. Kitty hated it when she appeared fearful – it didn't suit her.

'So you found Alexandra?'

'Yes.'

Georgie sat down, ignoring the kimono as it slipped off her shoulders. She gently turned Kitty's chin forcing Kitty to look into her eyes. 'Were you invited?'

Kitty took a swig of her coffee and stood up. 'Not exactly. But I did chat to Bet. I wanted to give Alexandra her christening present.'

Georgie jumped up and stood, hands on hips. 'Kitty, what were you thinking?' She threw her arms up and started pacing back and forth, her bare feet sticking to the linoleum. This is what Kitty had dreaded most, the way Georgie had of putting the innocent need to see her daughter up for inspection.

'Oh God, I just had to find out if she was okay, that's all. There was an announcement in the *Standard*, it was practically open to the public. There were so many people.' She turned away, unable to face Georgie's earnest expression.

Georgie reached out, pulling at Kitty's shoulder 'Kitty, I thought we agreed it was best not to visit when you found her.'

'What's to stop me going to church on a Sunday, just to check she's okay?' Kitty watched as Georgie and Alan exchanged a look.

'I've not seen her in six months!'

Georgie picked up a mug of coffee and started tapping the edge of it, the sound resonating, as unpleasant as a tin can rolling down the street.

'You chose Bet because she could give your daughter the best chance in life. You need to stop this obsessing. You know she's safe and now you need to move on.'

'I miss her, that's all.'

Georgie stood up, running her hands over Kitty's head. 'I know you do. But you're an artist, Kitty. One day you're going to make your daughter proud. Right now, you have to let Bet do the job of being her . . .' She was going to say mother; Kitty was sure of it.

'I need to get another job. The teaching is just two days, and it's not enough. I saw an advert in the newsagent's for a cleaner the other day. Two mornings a week and it fits around college.'

'Cleaning! Do you even know how?'

'I need the money. The teaching pays just enough but if I want to get a place on my own, I need a bit more to live on,' Kitty said.

'You have here,' Georgie said.

'It's a little crowded.' Kitty tried to smile.

'Not for long, I'm moving in with Alan.'

Alan, who'd been busying himself in the kitchen, turned round, a tea towel in one hand, a coffee cup in the other, eyebrow raised.

Georgie reached out her hand and he walked towards her. They both hauled Kitty into their arms but she slipped out of the embrace.

'Keep me out of this,' she said. All she wanted was Alexandra, and perhaps Henry, and they were both gone.

She'd go to church every Sunday, she thought, and in some deep throbbing part of her, she was comforted.

FORTY-ONE

Bet washed up the last of the plates while Samuel gave Alexandra her milk. It had been a long day and she'd managed to make the house look festive with flowers and a framed photograph of Alexandra. People congratulated them on their new home, but she could see a few raised eyebrows at the mismatched furniture. It was a step up from Tiverton Street, but it would have been obvious that they were penny-pinching, although there'd been sherry to wet the baby's head and Sam had handed the beers around as if he'd won the pools. But what was making her squirm the most was her mad dash out of the church.

'I was trying to catch an old friend who isn't well,' she'd said every time someone had asked.

Anxiety had got its claws in again. What if Kitty found out where they lived? Bet remembered Kitty's tear-stained face. Did it really matter? Perhaps *she* was the one being hysterical.

She put her best china cups away. The place had looked okay filled with people, but now it looked shabby. Truth was, she had a hankering for one of those Danish style three-piece suites and a teak gramophone to match, but there was no money for such luxuries.

Back in the kitchen Samuel picked up a tea towel and started to help dry the stack of china.

'Don't worry, luv. I can get on with this,' Bet said.

Samuel stood his ground, tea towel wrapped around a plate. 'I want to know what went on today.'

'Oh, Samuel, didn't you see her?'

'See who, Bet?'

'The girl's mother.'

'We've been through this. How many times do I have to tell you, you're legally Alexandra's mother?'

'It was the announcement; she must have been looking out for it.' She was wiping down the Formica surface.

'So, it's my fault.' Samuel was drying up the plates in that methodical way that he had, wrapping the tea towel around the plate and turning it anticlockwise.

'Did I say that?'

'It was my idea to make an announcement.'

'And because of that the church was packed.'

He'd made a pile of small plates on the kitchen table and had aligned the patterns. 'Did you catch her?' he said.

'She was all dolled up, but her face was puffy and desperate. She looked like a bloody mad woman the way she dresses up in clothes that are too big, and too old.'

'What do you think she wants?'

Bet took off her rubber gloves, let the water out of the sink, watching as it curled down the plughole. 'I don't know.' She turned to Sam. 'But I get the feeling it's complicated.'

'Seems pretty simple to me: she can't quite let go and wants to check up on her.'

'That's what *she* said.'

'We should call Bill. It's not right her turning up like that.'

Bet turned away. She felt nauseous at the idea of threatening the woman who'd given them a child. 'No, Samuel. Not yet.'

'Bet, it's harassment.'

Bet took off her pinafore and put the kettle on. 'We had a cat when I was a girl. Had six kittens. My dad gave them all away and the cat went around the house looking for them for days afterwards. Maybe Kitty just wants to be part of her life in some small way.'

'And you're okay with that? Because I'm not.'

'No. I'm not either, but calling the police feels wrong. I mean what harm can she do?'

FORTY-TWO

Kitty stood outside the newsagent window on Clifton Road two weeks after the christening looking at the ads for part-time work. The cleaning job was still on offer. The only way she was going to afford to pay the rent for Georgie's bedsit on her own, and have money for food as well, was to earn more money. There were several cards, all written with a neat hand, advertising secretarial posts and shop work. The florist was looking for an assistant, the bakery needed help at the counter.

The cleaning job was every Monday morning and Friday afternoon. It was a hectic household. A young family with three sons. On her third morning she let herself in, picking up the cereal packets and putting them away before taking off her coat. She'd just finished polishing the lids of the jars on the top shelf that were grimy with dust, when Felicity, the woman who had employed her, arrived home, a young baby boy in her arms.

'Gosh, you've done a good job,' Felicity said, plonking her child down in the highchair and handing him a rusk. Kitty looked at the boy, his chubby little fingers wrapped around the rusk. Her heart began to drum hard; she couldn't stop looking at the boy until the woman interrupted her.

'Would you like a cup of coffee? I'm making one for myself.' Felicity wore avant-garde clothes with swirly fabrics in bright colours. She looked like one of Kitty's students. There was nothing maternal about her at all.

'No, I'm fine, thank you,' Kitty said.

'I must say you clean very well. My husband thought you were a bit posh, but I think you've done a fabulous job.' Felicity pulled out a jar of instant coffee.

'Thank you,' Kitty said. She bent down to retrieve the polish from under the sink, her heart still hammering at the thought of this child who was around the same age as Alexandra.

'How old is he?' she asked. She noticed then that Felicity was pregnant.

'Will? Oh he's just nine months old. He's big for his age.'

Kitty watched as the boy munched on his rusk, his face plastered and sticky. She walked over to the sink, looking for something to clean his face with. 'Do you have his face flannel handy?'

'Oh, gosh, you don't need to worry. His face is always grubby with bits of food. I think there's one in the downstairs bathroom if you're that bothered.'

Kitty believed that Bet wouldn't have left Alexandra's face like that, but what if she did? What if Bet was as careless? She went and fetched the flannel and ran it under the hot tap, rubbing the bar of soap across it and then more hot water until she was satisfied it was clean enough to wipe the boy's face.

She walked over to William, at least she assumed he was a William and not a Willis or Wiley. She wiped his face and hands. The boy cried out when she took the rusk out of his hand.

'Don't worry, little one. You can have it back. We just need to clean you up a little bit.' She dabbed his nose and winked and the boy chuckled. She could feel the tears well up and tried to swallow them back. When she'd finished, she gave him his rusk and turned round to find Felicity staring at her.

'You're very good with him,' she said.

'I have a younger brother,' Kitty said, unable to look her in the eye.

'Would you be interested in babysitting at any point?'

Kitty felt herself stiffen. 'Well, I am quite busy,' she said. She could feel Felicity sizing her up.

'It's just so hard to find good babysitters.'

Kitty wanted to say something about mothering being a privilege but she knew by now that she'd do well to keep quiet. 'Well, I had better go and clean the bathroom,' she said and rushed upstairs. Once in the bathroom she pushed the door shut. She got on with cleaning and polishing the taps, wiping the sink. She tried hard to let her mind go blank but the boy's goofy smile seemed etched into her mind, somehow layered with Alexandra's sweet face. She kept cleaning until her hands were red. It wasn't until she'd finished stripping the beds, changing the sheets and vacuuming the bedrooms that she realised the hours had gone by and she'd been there for five hours when she was only supposed to be there for three.

She went downstairs to find the house empty again. Her money was in an envelope. She took the money out, found a pen and scribbled a quick note.

> Dear Felicity,
> Thank you so much for the money. The sheets are in the top loader and you will need to buy yourself some more bleach. I'm afraid I won't be able to come again. I've been offered more teaching work.
> Kitty x

She ran to the studio, desperate to put the feeling of anguish into something. She threw the door open expecting to see one of the other painters, but the studio was empty. She went to find her canvas and lifted it up onto an easel. The red blob she'd painted was still sticky where she had layered it on thick. There were ridges where the paint had given way to gravity. The smell of turps and linseed oil brought calm, as did the steady process of mixing the colours as she worked them onto the palette with a knife. She felt her pulse slow, the feeling of Alexandra's absence drifting back to a place that was manageable. She threw on Henry's shirt, remembering his body in it as a young boy, the sleeves rolled up to his elbow, the hair on his arms bleached by the sun. She ached with the need to see him and at the same time she wanted him to have never existed. She picked up a brush and dipped it into marine blue. She wanted this painting to be layered, to have depth, to seduce the audience without words. She remembered her student who said cobalt represented pain. Was blue melancholic? The blues, the beat and rhythm of acceptance, that is what Henry had once said. She brushed the colour on the canvas and was immediately stilled.

She wasn't sure how long she'd been working, but it was dark outside when she finally stepped back from the easel. She hadn't noticed the gloom of the studio, the cold icy air. She went to clean her brushes, enjoying the methodical nature of the process, her mind blank as threads of colour ran clockwise into the butler sink. She watched the stained water spiralling down the plughole, heard the door scrape open and turned to see Georgie standing in the entrance, a baker's boy cap pulled over her bobbed hair.

'Had you forgotten you were supposed to be cooking supper?' Georgie said, switching on the light, illuminating the hollow space with cold harsh neon.

Kitty dropped the brushes and ran up to her, throwing her arms around her neck.

'Oh, Georgie it was awful. She has three children and was pregnant with another. She brought the baby back to the house and he was just so gorgeous.' She could smell Georgie's lacquer and the lavender talcum powder she used on her skin. Georgie unpeeled her arms.

'Who, Kitty? Who has three children and is pregnant?' she asked, tucking Kitty's hair neatly behind her ear and holding her face still.

'The woman I clean for.'

'Hasn't this woman heard of the pill?'

'What do you mean, the pill?'

'Contraception, silly!'

'Well obviously not if she has three children and is pregnant with a fourth, no. But, Georgie, I saw the baby today and I couldn't bear it.' Georgie guided her towards a stool. 'Sit down,' she said, taking off her own coat. 'You're clearly exhausted. Tell me all about it while I tidy this up.' Georgie had that concerned lopsided expression that usually meant trouble. But instead of walking to the sink and finishing washing the brushes, she walked towards Kitty's painting.

'The woman I clean for has this big house just down the road from your flat. It was fine when I didn't see her, but then she came back today with the little boy and, Georgie, it broke my heart.' Kitty's mind jumped back to Georgie's mention of contraception. 'Do you mean to say that this pill stops you from getting pregnant?'

Georgie nodded. 'It's a bit late for you to be thinking

about that.' She circled the painting. 'Why haven't you shown me any of these before?'

Kitty felt a wash of shame, not just because she'd deliberately avoided showing Georgie her work, but because she knew nothing about this pill. 'I don't know, probably because it didn't occur to me.'

Georgie was cupping her chin in the palm of her hand, reaching out to touch the surface. 'You need to do something with this. It's brilliant,' she said.

'You're not listening,' Kitty said.

'You're the one who isn't listening,' Georgie said, twisting to face her. Kitty hated it when Georgie offered that doleful look of concern. But this was something else she was reading in Georgie's face. She couldn't quite put a finger on it.

'I'm going to speak to John who owns a small gallery on Cork Street. I think it's time you showed the world who you are. He's going to love this.' She turned her gaze back to the painting. 'God, Kitty. You're going to be a star.'

FORTY-THREE

Bet arrived at the church gate with a slippery feeling in her tummy. She was expecting to see Kitty again, although she'd not seen her since the christening two weeks ago. Samuel had stayed behind to go through the books but she wished he'd come. She could see a scattering of parishioners chatting outside the church doors. Alexandra was sitting up in the new seat attachment Samuel had bought, her reins clipped in place so she didn't fall. She looked around her, dazzled by the light falling through the freshly sparse trees, the leaves dancing about as they fell, and she reached out to them.

'Good morning,' Bet said to the vicar.

The vicar shook the hands of a young couple and turned towards her. 'Good morning, Elisabeth. How's Alexandra this morning?'

'In good spirits,' she said, unclipping her reins and pulling Alexandra free of the blankets. Alexandra's brown eyes darted around until falling on the vicar with a small frown of concentration.

'Will you be joining us for coffee afterwards?' he asked Bet.

Bet didn't want to leave Samuel poring over the figures alone. 'We'll see how the little one behaves,' she said.

'Good, good,' the vicar said. As if one 'good' wasn't enough.

She followed him into church, her eyes taking in the parishioners. A hush fell over them as the vicar entered.

The turning of heads except for one. Bet knew immediately who it was. Her heart battered away as she walked past Kitty's pew. Kitty looked up but Bet refused to acknowledge her. If this was how it was going to be, then so be it. But I'm not going to make it easy for her, she thought.

Alexandra, as if sensing her anxiety, let out a garbled cry. Bashing her arms up and down she started to make cute little noises.

'Da, da, da, da, da, da.'

Bet watched this latest development with pride and saw Kitty's face crumple. *Well, if she insists on following us about.* Jill from the corner shop stood up to let her through, holding Alexandra's hand for a second. Bet turned to Kitty, saw her distress and felt a smug satisfaction, then felt guilty immediately afterwards.

After the service Bet charged up the aisle to catch Kitty to give her a piece of her mind. But the vicar stepped into her path.

'I must congratulate you, such a well-behaved baby,' he said. 'The coffee pot is waiting.' The vicar made his way to the door as the congregation shuffled towards the exit. Bet watched as Kitty slipped past him, head down. She followed, dipped past the vicar.

'She needs a change,' she said, pointing to Ally's rear end.

'Kitty!' She pounded up the path, ignoring the commotion as she brushed past a family. 'Kitty.'

Kitty finally turned to show her tear-stained face. 'I don't mean any harm,' she said. 'I just want to see her every now and again. I've brought her a new dress. It's yellow. I know you like her in yellow.' She handed her a cardboard box with a ribbon.

Bet felt as if every cell in her body was being tugged and scrambled, the anger dissipated, a swell of pity caught her unawares. Ally gurgled, batting her arms up and down. Kitty offered a tearful smile. Bet wished Samuel had been with her as she took the box, unsure whether to open it there and then.

'Thank you,' Kitty said, her voice cracked. As she turned away, Bet could see how unsteady she was. She held on to Alexandra, nuzzling into her neck.

*

Kitty sat in the Tube station at Colliers Wood watching a grey mouse scuttle around in circles on the track. A sweet wrapper was caught up in an eddy of wind. The Northern Line always felt gloomy on a Sunday, and yet it seemed everyone around her was cheerful, their chatter unnaturally loud. The rumble of the train grew louder until it whined into the station. Kitty watched as everyone boarded and the train left the station. She stayed sitting on the bench, enjoying a solitary moment before a group of Sunday school children arrived with a nun. She watched the little girls all dressed in their Sunday best, chattering away to each other and felt the tug of loss pulling. Kitty understood why Bet was angry, but she wasn't asking much, just to see her daughter on Sundays. What harm could it do? And yet it wasn't enough. She wanted to feel the flesh and blood of her own child close to her chest.

The next train thundered into the station. Kitty felt compelled to run into its path and her whole body started to shake with the desire to do so. The feeling was over-whelming. *Would it hurt?* What would happen to her body? She saw the unsuspecting face of the driver and clutched the seat. She closed her eyes and was surprised that Henry came to her mind. His kind face smiling at her from across a room full of people on the night of Tom's wedding. She had hoped that his face would fade.

'Excuse me, miss. Are you all right?'

Kitty's eyes snapped open. A young man was crouched down beside her, wide-eyed, his red curly hair floppy around his ears.

'You look awfully pale,' he said.

'I'm not feeling well.'

'Why don't I find someone to help, or I could take you home if you like.'

Kitty smiled at his generosity. 'Oh, that's very kind,' she said. 'But I think if I get on the next train I'll be fine.'

'Well, I'll wait with you,' he said. Kitty nodded. She was thinking about the vermilion red on her most recent painting, how the stain she'd created by thinning the paint had changed the meaning behind it.

PART THREE

—

1965
Two years later

FORTY-FOUR

May

Kitty walked into the gallery on Cork Street, stepping away from the buzz of London's rush hour into the sanctuary of the hushed austere space with its expectation of money. She was hoping Georgie would be waiting for her. Instead, Georgie's close friend John, the gallerist, was arranging the biggest vase of lilies she'd ever seen. It seemed to fill the whole room.

He turned to give her a kiss on each cheek, his eye on some detail that needed his attention. 'Presentation, darling, is everything,' he said, excusing himself. He'd insisted that all her paintings were framed in thick ornate, gold frames. Kitty felt embarrassed by their ostentation – they no longer felt as if they belonged to her – but John brushed her comments aside. He always wore velvet, smoked with a cigarette holder and never looked anyone in the eye. Typical of Georgie to have a friend like him, Kitty thought. His boyfriend, Jules, who was John's opposite, a shy unassuming man, probably blunted by John's exuberance, was admiring Kitty's paintings.

'Your work is good,' he said in a flat unassuming voice that served to emphasise John's eccentricity. 'Filled with rage.'

'Thank you.' Kitty pined for Georgie's presence. She needed her shining personality so that she could stand calmly in her shadow. 'Have you heard from Georgie?' she asked.

'No, and she's not answering my calls, but it's her job to be difficult,' John said as he instructed the waitress where to line up the glasses. 'All you artists are alike.'

John was tall and looked more so in his velvet green suit and red silk cravat. His hair was cut close to the scalp to hide the fact that he was bald. Jules was short and rather cuddly with a mop of black curls.

'She'll be here soon,' he said. 'She never misses these events.'

The opening was to be at six. Georgie arrived with two minutes to spare, Alan looking dashing at her side in his checked jacket and polo neck. Georgie was dressed in a little black dress and kitten heels, her hair backcombed into a high bun, her eyes painted with kohl. Kitty wanted to burrow into the protection of her wool coat and thin arms. She felt dowdy in comparison, in slacks and a polo neck. She'd been good at performing once, but that was before Alexandra.

'Darling!' Nobody was quite sure who Georgie was referring to, but Kitty obliged her with a kiss.

'You look nervous,' Georgie said.

'I *am*,' Kitty said.

'Here, take one of these, they'll help,' John said as he breezed past. He held out his palm and offered her a blue pill.

'They're not going to make me hallucinate are they?' Kitty asked.

'They're Valium, honey, not LSD!'

Georgie squeezed Kitty's hand. 'Come on, it's just a couple of hours, that's all.'

Alan drew Kitty into a hug. 'It's going to be okay,' he said.

Twenty minutes later, the gallery was full of people with deep plummy voices and shrill laughs. A fug of smoke billowed above the chattering crowd, the waitresses flitted about dressed in tails and shorts. There were already a few red dots claiming Kitty's paintings, which made Kitty feel numb. In her head every one of those paintings belonged to Alexandra.

Still, Kitty was quite enjoying herself thanks to the wine and that little blue pill. People wanted to talk to her. When they asked what her paintings meant, she said she didn't know.

'They're an expression of something I haven't interpreted yet,' she said to one keen admirer who turned out to be an art critic.

'Oh, that *is* interesting,' he said.

Kitty laughed but her smile faded when she saw Anne and Tom saunter in. Tom in his city suit and Anne in a ghastly lilac mini-skirt and matching coat. How on earth did Tom hear about this exhibition? she thought. Surely Georgie wouldn't have invited him. He wasn't exactly the arty type. Tom, who nodded at Georgie with a tight-lipped smile, walked straight towards Kitty. Kitty could see he was nervous by the way he stooped. Anne was beside him, her hand clinging to his arm like a child does its mother at kindergarten. Kitty hadn't seen Anne since the day of the flood, nor had she seen Tom for two years. For a second everything seemed to recede and it was just the three of them standing in the room: the Campbells.

'The paintings are wonderful,' Anne said, avoiding Georgie with dramatic purpose. Georgie nodded with just the right amount of propriety, wearing the sweetest of smiles.

'You've been busy, little sis,' Tom said, hands slung deeply into his pockets until he was offered some wine.

'How did you know about this show?' Kitty asked.

'Mother has bought paintings from John for years,' Tom said. 'Didn't you know? She received an invite.'

'So, she sent you to spy on me.'

'She's too ill to come herself, Kitty,' Anne said. Kitty resented this news coming from Anne. What did Anne know?

'This doesn't mean I'm coming back,' she said to Tom.

'Oh, Kitty, we didn't mean to impose.' Anne reached out to touch her but her hand slid off Kitty's arm. 'Tom misses you, that's all. We both do.' Kitty felt tears prick at the sight of Anne's compassionate expression, softening her resolve. She imagined their two children probably being looked after by a nanny and her anger spiked again.

'Your poor mother would have loved to have seen this but she really isn't well,' Anne said.

'We do need to talk about Mother at some point,' Tom said. 'She's ill, Kitty.'

'She's been ill for years.'

'I'm thinking about you as much as her. You'll regret it if she dies and you haven't resolved the problems between you.'

'They're irresolvable,' Kitty said. She preferred Tom's frank tone to the sickly stickiness of Anne's rhetoric. Everything about Anne had the texture of a blancmange, and then it occurred to Kitty that motherhood had probably changed her.

'I don't think now's the right time, do you?' Georgie said.

'It was wrong of you to come,' Kitty said to Tom.

Anne looked contrite.

'We've already reserved one of your paintings,' Tom said.

Kitty rolled her eyes. 'You can't buy your way back into my life. Just remember that every single painting here was for Alexandra,' she said.

Anne smarted.

'I'm sorry if that makes you feel uncomfortable,' Kitty said. Kitty was feeling slightly dizzy. It was as if all the versions of herself were competing for attention at the same time.

'Tom, Anne. May I introduce you to my husband,' Georgie said.

Alan held out his hand, towering above Tom. Kitty glanced across to see John stick another red dot on one of her favourite paintings, but it didn't mean a thing. She'd give up all those red dots to be Alexandra's mother.

FORTY-FIVE

Henry was shuffling through his paperwork in an attempt to make order of the increasing pile. It was one of those days when the heat shimmered on the pavements and the ice cream stalls were more popular than the hot dog stands. It was May but there was a freak heatwave that brought out summer dresses and short sleeves. The office was emptying out, people were threatening to meet at the bar and he thought he should probably join them. He could do with a drink. In amongst the papers, he came across one of Kitty's letters. Folding it carefully, he slipped the envelope into his inside pocket. He carried on wading through the paperwork, filing various receipts into relevant piles so that he could hand them all to his assistant to deal with the next morning.

He was just about to pack up and leave the office when his telephone rang. Switchboard must still have an operator working, he thought as he picked up the receiver.

'Henry Roberts,' he said, his other hand still working through the papers.

'Hello, this is the operator speaking. We have a call from London, England for you. Can you take the call?'

Henry's mouth went instantly dry. He thought of Kitty and stilled himself.

'Yes,' he said.

He heard the machinations, the burr and buzz of the

line, which he imagined was all the way under the Atlantic. Then there was a click.

'You're through,' the operator said.

'Henry, it's Tom.'

At the mention of Tom's name, Henry plonked himself down in his chair.

'What's wrong?' he asked, not bothering with the pleasantries.

'Our mother is dying. Look, I don't want to worry you but I'm concerned about Kitty.'

'Couldn't you have written?'

'Not really, not for something as important as this. Clarissa's dying, Henry.' Henry recognised the thick choked quality of Tom's voice and realised Tom was crying. 'Kitty doesn't seem to be registering what's happening.'

Henry saw his briefcase had toppled over and he reached to grab it, his coat catching a nail that protruded from the chair. 'How do you know?' he asked.

'I saw her the other day. She had an exhibition in Cork Street.'

'Yes, she mentioned that in her last letter.'

'She was so hostile, Henry. Even to Anne, who has done nothing.'

'She feels betrayed, Tom. There's not much I can do about that.' He didn't bother to mention how he felt betrayed as well.

'Clarissa is dying for heaven's sake.'

Henry felt hollowed out, as if all the air had been punched free of his lungs. He knew he should fly back, pay his dues, but the thought of returning to Beecham before finding his father, drowned him in a sense of failure.

'Sorry, I didn't realise her health was that bad,' he said.

'Well, I don't want to worry you, but the thing is that she's desperate to see Kitty and you're the only person who can persuade her.'

'I'm not sure about that,' Henry said.

'Perhaps you could call.'

The idea of speaking to Kitty, of hearing her voice, filled him with dread. He had somehow managed to compartmentalise his feelings for Kitty, for England, even for his future. He patted his jacket in search of a cigarette.

'I shouldn't be the one to be telling you this, but someone has to,' Tom was saying. 'I should have told you years ago. But you need to promise that you didn't hear it from me,' he said. 'In fact, you didn't hear it from anyone.'

The line was silent. Henry realised there was a delay happening. His mind was flitting through the possibilities, expecting to hear about some unsuitable gentleman.

'Of course,' he said.

'The reason Kitty ran away is because she had a child, your child.'

Henry felt the tremor of his pulse racing. He wasn't sure how to respond. 'I'm sorry,' he said. 'What did . . .'

'You have a daughter,' Tom said, louder this time.

Nothing prepared him for the shock of a child. He felt himself start to shake, a collision of emotions flying through his veins. Kitty had lied, Clarissa had lied, so had Tom. They had a child. A daughter! All this time he'd read her letters with the faintest glimmer of hope, but now he couldn't quite grasp the words that had been spoken: a daughter.

'Where is she?' he asked. 'Where is our child?' A surge of anger made him tighten his hand into a fist. His thoughts seemed to tangle like fine cotton, his mind thick with possible outcomes. He just couldn't quite believe it.

'Henry, please,' Tom insisted. 'The child was adopted, but Kitty doesn't seem to have accepted this and well . . .'

Henry heard Tom's hesitation, fireworks of thoughts still sparking off in his head. 'Why wasn't I told any of this?'

Another delay and then: 'Because of this dreadful business with my father and your mother,' he said.

Henry tapped out a cigarette and lit it, took a long drag. 'Go on,' he said.

'According to Georgie, Kitty is practically stalking the family who adopted your daughter. She can't seem to let go, and if her behaviour on Saturday is anything to go by, then I would say she's close to madness,' Tom said. 'She doesn't speak to any of us, just Georgie. She lives most of the time alone in some squalid apartment in Kensington. Apparently, the only time she sees people is when she's teaching, or when she goes to church to visit your child.'

'Church?'

'Yes, apparently she goes to church in Mitcham just to get a glimpse of her daughter. Georgie is worried the girl's mother is going to call the police, or worse, Kitty is going to snatch the child back,' he said. 'Apparently Kitty hoards toys that she buys for the girl.'

'Are you still seeing Georgie?' he asked.

'Of course not. Georgie's married, hadn't you heard?'

'Yes, yes I had.'

'Anyway, I told you in my letter, things are good with Anne and me.' Tom coughed. Henry could hear the rattle of phlegm in his throat, and then the hammering of a typewriter in the background. He imagined Tom was in the Campbell office in London.

'When are you going to come back?'

Never was the first word that came to Henry's mind, but then he thought about his daughter, their daughter. 'I wasn't planning to come any time soon,' he said. 'I still haven't found my father.' He realised how futile that sounded.

'Well, I would think of coming back sooner,' Tom said.

269

Henry tried to marshal his thoughts into some cognitive response. What did Tom mean, sooner? He needed to find his father and now it seemed it was more important than ever.

'I'll come back late summer,' he said.

'That might be too late,' Tom said.

'Yes, you're right. I'm sorry. I'm not thinking straight. I'll come back as soon as possible,' he said.

Henry went straight to the bar on the corner of 7th and 8th. He ordered a Scotch and soda. He had taken to finishing his day in the local bar where he could always find one of the boys from the newspaper to unwind with, although right now he couldn't face anyone. The room was sticky with heat, the ceiling fans whirred above them, ticking a steady rhythm, without much effect. He'd only been at the *New York Times* for two years so it was hard to tell, but this heat felt unusual. Time had passed quickly and yet he was still no further in his search. Jesus, he had a child. No matter which way he looked at it, he couldn't seem to absorb the news.

Tonight everyone was crowded around the television where some baseball game was televised but Henry wasn't in the mood to lose himself. He popped a couple of ice cubes into his glass and downed half of the shot in one. The group of young men, mostly journalists, were cheering and slamming their hands on the bar down the other end. Henry was trying to piece together those last few days in England when he had seen Kitty in London. She'd sat in the pub in Maida Vale and lied to him. Bare-faced. Had she already given the child away by that point?

A girl from Features came up to him.

'You look pooped,' she said.

He offered a small nod, the air of certainty about her making him shudder slightly. 'Been a hell of a day,' he said, knowing that wasn't quite enough to generate a conversation.

'Why don't you come on over and join us?'

Henry looked across at the tight little bunch in the corner who seemed disinterested in the game. He tried to remember the girl's name. Her nails were painted red. She had short hair that was backcombed high at the crown, and wore a plaid skirt. On any other night, the crowd of journalists, their banter thrown back and forth in competitive exchanges, would have been a welcome distraction. Now he was a senior editor, there was little time for anything other than his work. Sure, he'd often have a quick drink, then there were the occasional visits to 42nd Street for the jazz, and of course, the continuous search for his father.

'You're from England, aren't you?' Gracie, that was her name. He'd spoken to her once a few weeks back. He looked up to see Gracie's keen blue eyes smiling at him. He knew it was going to be the usual pattern of exchanges, the questions about London and the Beatles, about the Queen and whether he missed home or not. He could bet his bottom dollar she'd ask if he went to Oxford. She was pretty and as tempting as a freshly made bed.

'I don't believe that guy Harvey Oswald shot the president, do you?' she said.

'Wow, are people still talking about that?' he said.

'Seems so. It was pretty major.' She parked up beside him, climbing up onto the bar stool. 'Personally I think we should be focusing on more personal stories. Everything we write is about the economy, or politics, or crime, but people want to read about ordinary life,' she said. 'By the way, I loved your story on "What do the British think of the Kennedys?"

'Perhaps you should work on women's magazines,' he said, not really concentrating.

'Hey! That's unfair!'

Henry leaned against the bar, his elbow supporting the drink he was cradling. 'I'm sorry,' he said, unable to open up. He hadn't meant to sound brusque.

'I'm just trying to start a conversation, that's all.' The girl smiled. He liked her frank way of talking, the subtle way she was flirting, but he didn't want to feel obliged, not now, not when he'd just learned he'd fathered a child, and there was something about this girl that made him feel obliged.

'Sorry,' he said. 'It's been a long day.' He leaned forward and squeezed her arm, realising the gesture probably appeared to be patronising. 'I've just received some news. Apparently I have a daughter.' He lifted his glass of Scotch and swallowed it down. 'But you've given me an idea,' he said. She sat with her hands in her lap, her eyes widened.

'Wow! That's one way to end a conversation.'

'Get the girl a drink will you, Jack,' he said, slamming down a couple of dollars on the bar. 'Don't take it personally,' he said.

He picked up his briefcase and walked out, aware that the group in the corner were looking at him. He was thinking about his father, wondering whether he read the *New York Times*. Gracie had given him an idea. He could write an article about looking for his father and what it felt like to find out you have a daughter you had little chance of meeting. He needed the results of that blood test more than ever. He thought then about his daughter. Maybe one day she would need to find him.

FORTY-SIX

June

Bet was late for church. She felt queasy and incapable of rushing. Perhaps it was the blancmange Sam had insisted on the night before. She could still taste the milky vanilla. But she'd missed last month's period and the one before that. A worm of hope was beginning to work its way into her head. They hadn't been careful – why would they when they'd tried so hard before? Samuel was downstairs cooking a fry-up, the last thing she felt like eating. She could hear Alexandra's sweet voice twittering away downstairs.

The dress Bet had put on felt tight, she had to hold her stomach in and even then the zip protested. 'Blast.' She went to the mirror and saw that she had, after losing all that weight, begun to put it on again. 'Oh Lord.'

'Breakfast is on the table!'

She arrived to find Alexandra already in her high chair, a dribble of egg down her front. It was the cardigan Kitty had bought for her. Bet hadn't told Samuel. 'Oh, Sammy, you forgot her bib. Look she's covered and I put her in her Sunday best.'

'Why do that before breakfast?' Samuel gestured for her to sit down. 'Anyway, she's too old for a bib.'

Bet felt dreadful. She had an awful feeling she was going to be sick – that and the thought of the extra pounds put

273

her off eating anything. She grabbed a cloth and rubbed away at the stain. 'I don't feel at all well today,' she said. 'But I'm worried about Kitty.'

'Who gives a fig what Kitty thinks? If you're ill, you're ill. Personally I could do with a day off. All those people. I spend my life chit-chatting. It'll be nice to just sit and read the Sunday papers instead of sitting in that stone-cold church.'

'Then stay here.'

'I could tidy up the garden.'

'I worry that if I don't go, she'll go and do something stupid.'

'Like what?'

Bet tasted a bit of bacon. The salt wiped out the taste of iron that filled her mouth. She didn't want to discuss Kitty. Samuel didn't know about the occasional presents she gave, nor the money the Campbells had sent after Clarissa had tracked her granddaughter down, though God knows how. The letters she received from Kitty's mother had been short and to the point. She asked for the occasional photograph. Bet had sent her a couple and asked politely if she could keep details of her address to herself. Clarissa explained how she no longer saw Kitty and was glad to have news of Alexandra. Hypocrite, Bet thought. She looked down and saw that Alexandra already had her new shoes on that Clarissa's money had paid for.

'Samuel Abbott, I'm going and that's that. It's just one hour.'

Sam swallowed and put his cutlery down, his hands clasped together. 'Bet, how long is this going to go on for? Until she's eighteen for heaven's sake. I mean if you want her in your life, then invite her around, but this Sunday nonsense . . .' He looked down at his half-finished egg, pushing it away. 'It's madness. How long before she asks questions?' he said, nodding in Ally's direction. 'Have you thought of that?'

'I hate it. You know I do. But I feel sorry for her. What if something happened? She has that wild look in her eye, sometimes.'

Alexandra was batting her spoon into a squashed egg, watching as the yoke spilled out. 'Let me cut that for you,' Bet said. 'How many times have I told you to cut everything into small bits, Sammy?'

Bet stood up, leaned over to help Alexandra. The sight of the egg made her stomach churn. 'Sammy, I think I'm pregnant. I must be to feel like this.' She didn't dare look to see his reaction.

'Are you sure?' His voice softened.

'As sure as any woman,' she said.

'Mummy not well,' Alexandra said.

'Get her ready for church,' she said as she rushed upstairs to the bathroom.

'I'm coming too,' he said. A small part of Bet wished he'd stay at home, especially if Kitty brought Alexandra a present.

★

Kitty's favourite day was Sunday. That was the day she allowed herself to be a mother. Alexandra was talking, she loved to see the changes in her. She'd decided on Clarissa's pink suit. She hadn't worn that in months. Sunlight streamed through leafy trees as she walked to the station. She felt a flutter of excitement at the thought of seeing her little girl. She'd bought her a doll in Hamleys, which she'd named Aggie. Of course she'd have to give it to Bet, but

Bet was always gracious. Kitty had turned down Georgie's offer of lunch and decided she'd come back and spend the afternoon painting. Her new basement flat in Kensington wasn't far from the studio. Since Georgie's marriage to Alan she'd begun to wonder if Henry would ever return. When her own life would start. She hadn't spoken to him in two years, but his letters still arrived like clockwork every month. She glanced down at her handbag where his latest letter sat unopened. She'd been too frightened to look at it in case he'd met someone else. She wasn't sure why this thought had occurred to her now. He'd been away long enough and probably had a load of girlfriends.

She arrived at the church to find Alexandra's pushchair alongside another pram. A warm wash of relief filled her as she walked inside. She took her usual place in the back pew next to the aisle. Bet was in the front talking to one of the other parishioners. She'd nodded at Kitty but neither of them ever exchanged a word. Kitty preferred it like that. She knew that Alexandra noticed her and that was all that mattered. Bet's husband was sitting beside her, one hand holding Alexandra who was keen to run around, her whole body leaning away from him in an attempt to free herself. Kitty willed Mr Abbott to let go, and when he did Alexandra ran straight towards her.

'Hello,' she said. She looked up at Kitty with Henry's large brown eyes and a smile that was broad enough to create two dimples. 'My name is Ally.'

Kitty's heart swelled. She dipped down to speak to her. 'Hello, young lady,' she said. 'I thought your name was Alexandra.' She put out her gloved hand and Alexandra looked down, a ripple of confusion showing before she seized it with both hands and shook, jumping up and down. Kitty wished she'd removed her glove so that she

276

could feel her daughter's soft skin, feel the flesh and blood of her. Memories of the day she escaped the home came flooding in. Alexandra pressed to her chest as she leaned out of the window.

She looked down at Alexandra's shoes. They were new and exactly like the shoes her mother used to make her wear as a child. Start-Rite, Mary Janes in brown. How she had hated the colour of those shoes when she was young. She reached into her handbag and pulled out the doll. Alexandra's eyes grew large as Kitty walked the doll across her lap and up to Alexandra's cheek to give her a kiss.

'For me?' Alexandra asked.

Kitty nodded. 'For my special little girl,' she said. 'She's called Aggie.'

Alexandra took the doll and hugged it, her dimples so pronounced Kitty wanted to kiss each one. She took off her gloves and held out her arms, inviting Alexandra for a cuddle, unaware that Mr Abbott had come to collect her. She saw his highly polished shoes first.

'Come on now, Ally. Leave the nice lady alone.' With his dark hair and brown eyes, he could have easily been Alexandra's father. He looked at Kitty, his eyes direct and steady, then nodded before taking the doll and handing it back to Kitty. Kitty thought the gesture a little curt.

Alexandra started to cry, her frown deepened and she pouted. 'I want my dolly.'

Kitty felt as if she'd swallowed a hot burning thread. She handed the doll back to Alexandra.

Mr Abbott bent down and whispered in her ear. 'This won't be happening again,' he said. He led Alexandra away, who turned and waved, clutching the doll to her chest as she went back to the front pew. Kitty had wanted to press her nose up against her daughter's silky hair. Bet stood up abruptly, pulled Alexandra close, shook her arm and flashed a look at Kitty which left Kitty feeling bruised.

'Will you behave,' Bet said, smacking Alexandra's leg and sitting her down hard. Alexandra began to cry and Kitty stood up. The idea that Bet smacked her daughter had never occurred to Kitty before. How could Bet chastise her just for saying hello? She went running to the front pew. Everyone stood up. The hymns began. Hot and breathless, Kitty felt the eyes of the congregation on her as she pushed her way towards Bet.

'Please don't do that,' she said.

Bet continued to sing with gusto while Alexandra clung to her leg. Kitty walked down the aisle, aware of the sideways glances.

FORTY-SEVEN

Henry arrived at his desk to find two half-drunk coffee cups stationed on a pile of paperwork he'd collected over the week. The cleaners had either missed them or this was some kind of silent protest. A stack of unopened letters had been left on his chair. Hundreds of them. His secretary was standing by the door with another handful.

'What's this?' he asked.

'I'm guessing it's a response to your article,' she said, pouring them onto his desk. 'People haven't stopped talking about it. The chief is raving about you. He's asked for you to go and see him.'

'Crikey!' he said. Henry was chuffed. He knew he was a favourite but he'd taken a risk with that article and had pulled it off.

He hung up his coat and took the cups to the kitchen. He was determined to get through the pile of envelopes by the end of play. Somewhere in that lot, his father might have contacted him. He put a fresh coffee down and opened the first. In normal circumstances he'd hand the lot to his assistant, but these weren't normal circumstances by any stretch.

Late afternoon, when the office was winding down, he opened one of the last letters, feeling elated that the public had responded so openly but at the same time despondent that the one letter he wanted hadn't arrived. The one in his hand was a handwritten envelope with a Charleston postmark. He sliced it open with a letter opener bought for him last Christmas by his team. The first word that spun off the page was '*son*'.

> *Son, I've been trying to track you down for many years now, your mom didn't make it easy for me. I read your article last week and knew I'd found you. Turns out there are hundreds of Henry Robertses, but not many who have lived in England and returned to the States. It's lucky that I picked up that paper when I was in New York. I'm not an avid fan of the news, seems to be mostly depressing, but I'm glad fate intervened.*
>
> *We'd love to see you. Number's at the top.*
>
> *Love Dad*

Henry looked at the address, his heart racing. His father had just happened to be in New York. What were the chances? He'd moved from Boston to Charleston, South Carolina. No wonder he hadn't been able to track him down. He'd been looking in Florida, Los Angeles, Houston and San Antonio. Charleston was in the same time zone and he hadn't thought of it. It was driving distance, a day away. A fluttery feeling in his stomach meant he had to force himself to pick up the phone and ask the operator to put him through to the number he'd been given. He hadn't spoken to his father in years and yet memories flooded in: his father's hands showing him how to thread a line through a fishing rod, put a hook onto it; peeling an apple so that the peel stayed in one piece; helping him to paint a toy soldier that sat on his windowsill for years. He could picture that toy soldier as clear as anything. How angry he'd been with his mother when it was left behind in the move to England. He put the phone down.

He would wait until the end of the day. Let the idea breathe a little.

By six o'clock the office was empty. The operator put the call through. The ringing tone was flat, consistent. Henry began to feel anxious. He was a step closer to a dream he'd lost touch with. Finding his father could set them free.

'Hello, Robert's residence.' The woman was breathless. 'Sorry. Just had to run to get the phone. Hank, will you put that ball down now, you're driving the dog crazy! I'm sorry. Can I help you?'

'I'm looking for Charlie Roberts.'

There was a silence on the other end, the breathing had slowed down, but Henry could still hear an intake of breath. 'Charlie, it's for you.'

Henry heard the crackle of the line, the receiver being put down and then picked up again. 'He's just coming.'

'Thank you,' he said.

There was a second when the silence seemed unnaturally loud, before the woman asked: 'Is that by any chance Henry?'

'Yes, it is.'

'You sure as hell have an English accent,' the woman said.

He would have to postpone his trip home.

FORTY-EIGHT

Kitty was desperate to buy Alexandra new sandals. The image of her wearing shoes her mother would have chosen had left her fretful, that and the red mark on her daughter's leg. At the shoe shop there were rows and rows of plain brown leather sandals but Kitty wanted red for her daughter. She found a pair with diamonds cut into the leather and asked the lady who was serving to bring her a pair for a three-year-old.

'Do you have an exact size, madam? It is customary for us to measure the foot.'

Kitty rolled her eyes. 'That would be all very well and dandy but she's not here, is she?'

The assistant, who had blonde hair clipped back with two black grips, searched for a colleague but they all appeared to be busy. Kitty was beginning to lose her patience.

'Perhaps, you could bring your daughter back? It's just that children's sizes vary. The width especially.'

'It won't be possible to bring her in so please bring me three or four pairs that are likely to fit. Then I can return the ones that don't, can't I?'

The woman's eyes darted around. Kitty didn't know what was wrong with the girl.

'Come on. I haven't got all day!'

The girl trotted off to the back room and returned with options. She put the boxes down and was about to unpack them when Kitty waved her on.

'Just wrap them up. It's fine.'

Kitty went to the cashiers and wrote out a cheque while the girl packaged the shoes.

Then she walked to the studio and spent the entire day painting. Ever since Bet had scolded Alexandra, she'd felt a contorted energy surging around her body. The canvas was the only place for it. She loaded the palette, using a knife to mix the paint colour. *Red shoes. Pillarbox red. Blood red.* Then she made up an orange and turned to the easel. That first mark was always the most nerve-racking. She felt a rush of excitement as she spread the paint across the blank canvas. Without thinking, she pressed her hand into it.

After that first brushstroke, she barely stopped, forgetting to eat or even make tea. She stepped back as the light shifted towards dusk, surprised by the vigour of the work and the blood-like quality of the paint. She got home to find a note from Georgie on the doormat. 'Come over, we have something to tell you.' Kitty wondered if Georgie was pregnant. She'd been thrilled when Alan and Georgie moved into a mews house a few streets along but sometimes it felt as if they were too close. She was too exhausted to go now. She went and put the bag of shoes for Alexandra in the bedroom and changed.

Later, she sat down on a stool, heavy with exhaustion, pulled out a letter from her bag she knew was from her father. It had arrived the day before and she hadn't felt able to open it. They'd been incommunicado for two years now. It could only be bad news after what Tom had said. She heard the tread of people passing, looked up to the pavement to see just legs. She had to stand right next to the window to see the crack of sky. She decided to open Henry's letter first. His missives were always fact filled: details of his daily life, the office, New York and evenings spent listening to jazz. Occasionally he would break off to respond to her news. *I'm happy to hear that your exhibition went well.* The communication felt false but that was her fault.

As soon as she opened the envelope, she could tell this letter was more introspective by the density of the prose. He reflected on their past, how much had happened to both of them, how he had learned to accept their separation, but then she came to the real news. He had found his father, or rather his father had found him. *This could set me free, Kit, if I can prove he's my father. We've been waiting for this. My life has been on hold as if a great operator in the sky has pressed a button and I am left waiting to start my real life, perhaps with you or maybe not. We both need to be free of this shadow, Kitty. I feel because of this we have not been wholly honest with each other. Do you remember that day on the lake? I've been thinking about it.*

Of course she remembered. What did all of this mean? '*Perhaps with you or maybe not.*' What did he mean by that?

She read on. *Why couldn't we admit our feelings then? Because we both knew they'd disapprove or because we thought it was wrong? Perhaps we were simply scared.* She could feel her pulse racing. She'd waited so long for this news, hoping it would change everything, but it didn't, not in the way she needed it to. How could it? He was right, she hadn't been totally honest. He had no idea he had a daughter. She looked at the letter from her father, wondering if it would make her feel better or worse. She sliced the envelope open with a palette knife.

Worse, most probably.

My Dearest Kitty,

I have tried to call many times but I just can't seem to get through. It is with great sadness that I write this

284

letter. Your mother has been diagnosed with pancreatic cancer and has very few months left on this planet. I know how much pain we have caused you, and I have always respected your decision not to see us. I know Clarissa can be difficult, but perhaps what you don't understand is the part I played in her growing frustration. I haven't been a good husband, not always. That aside, for both of your sakes (she doesn't know I'm writing this letter) I feel it is time to make amends. Anne and Tom have been down on several occasions. But it is you that your mother asks for day after day, tirelessly. Regret is something that visits us when faced with our own mortality. I do believe you will regret not seeing your mother before she dies. Please come, my darling girl.

Your loving Pa

Kitty went to the phone, picked it up and dialled Beecham's number. It rang and rang until finally Clarissa picked up. Kitty listened to the broken quality of her mother's voice. She'd expected her father, or Saunders, and found herself unable to speak. Quietly she replaced the receiver in its cradle. She felt a dull ache spread across her chest and went to the drawer where she kept a small vest that belonged to Alexandra. She held it up to her nose.

She must have slept for a couple of hours. When she woke up, Georgie was standing over the bed, her hands resting on her hip. Kitty slipped Alexandra's vest under the pillow.

'You were supposed to drop by,' Georgie said.

'I'm sorry. I don't know what happened.' And then she remembered the letter. 'My father wrote to me. He thinks my mother is going to die soon. They just won't leave me alone.'

Georgie sat down on the bed, stroked Kitty's hair away from her face. The gesture made Kitty think of her mother. 'Oh, Kitty, I really do think you should go.'

'I can't face it,' Kitty said. Tears tracked down her cheeks.

'Maybe it won't be as bad as you think,' Georgie said. 'What was your news?'

'John wants us to have a shared exhibition. He said the press want to do a piece on female artists. It's happening, Kitty. Our life is changing.'

Kitty was just glad to hear Georgie wasn't pregnant. She knew it was selfish and the guilt left a bad taste in her mouth, but she couldn't quite face being an aunt-like figure just yet.

FORTY-NINE

Bet felt even more nauseous the following week; she staggered through her days in a blur. She'd dropped off a urine test at the doctor's and was due to call them, although as far as she was concerned there was no doubt she was pregnant. She picked up the telephone and after several minutes waiting, the doctor took her call.

'Good morning, Mrs Abbott, how are you feeling?'

'Terrible,' she said, impatient to hear the results.

'We have some good news,' the doctor said.

Bet wondered how much longer this man was going to torture her for. 'And?'

'You are indeed expecting, Mrs Abbott. Congratulations. By my calculation you should be close to fifteen weeks.'

After she'd made an appointment to see the doctor, she sat down to read with Alexandra. Sun flooded the lounge making everything in the room seem faded. She could see dust on every surface. Alexandra was struggling through her words. Bet felt a wave of contentment. She was proud of this room. They'd bought a new teak three-piece suite and she'd made the curtains herself.

By the time Samuel got home she was exhausted. Toad-in-the-hole was waiting in the oven, Alexandra's favourite. Samuel kissed the top of Alexandra's head and gave Bet a quick peck before sitting down.

'Sold two, today,' he said. 'I'm going to need some more help soon.'

'Don't get ahead of yourself, Samuel. We need to be careful.'

Sammy was about to fill his mouth. He stopped and looked up, wrinkling his nose. 'Did you speak to the doctor?'

She sat down opposite him and let him wait. His fork was mid-air and he gently lowered it down. 'What is it?'

'We're going to be parents for a second time,' she said.

Sammy stood up, rushing round the table to give her a hug. 'I knew it,' he said. 'You've been all over the place this week! I could have told that doctor before he did the test.'

'Ally, you're going to have a little brother . . .'

Alexandra laughed.

'Or sister,' Bet interrupted.

'It doesn't matter which,' Samuel said. He went over and gave Alexandra a hug. Bet felt a sudden moment of panic. 'We must love them both equally,' she said.

Samuel frowned. 'There's no doubt in my mind,' he said.

'Eat up,' she said to Alexandra, signalling to Samuel to end the conversation.

After they'd eaten, Bet busied herself with cleaning up the kitchen. 'Why don't you pop upstairs and get into your pyjamas, poppet.' She gestured to Samuel to help. 'We need to talk,' she whispered.

When Samuel came down after reading Alexandra her story, he poured himself a beer. Bet switched off the television and patted the chair next to her. Samuel sat down with a sigh. Bet felt her heart quicken. She knew what she had to say wasn't going to be easy.

'I'll need to tell Kitty,' she said.

'What on earth for? It's none of her business.'

'That day Kitty came into my shop, you and I had had words because I said I wouldn't adopt. I told her all about it, I told her how unhappy I'd been since losing Johnny. How you wanted another child, and I wasn't sure I could love anybody else's, and as I held Alexandra I knew I was wrong. Kitty said as much. She said: "Well it looks like you could love another from where I'm sitting." We were together not more than an hour and in that time we changed each other's lives. How can I forget that? I owe that girl so much.'

'I think it's time Kitty moved on,' he said. 'She can't keep dipping into our life like this. If she suspects we're going to have another, in her mind it'll give her the right to visit more often, maybe even steal her back.'

Bet felt the crush of his words. She knew that somehow they'd all danced to Kitty's tune but she would never stop being torn between gratitude and fear.

'I want to tell Alexandra she's adopted,' Samuel said.

'I don't know, Sammy. We don't want her thinking she's different just yet,' Bet said. 'Sometimes, when I see Kitty in church, a part of me is scared that Ally will find out who she is and love her more than me. Kitty is glamorous and pretty. I'm just ordinary.'

Samuel put his arm around her, pulled her towards him. 'You are not just ordinary! But this is what I'm saying. Maybe she will want to meet Kitty when she's older, but all the more reason to get Kitty out of our lives now. If we tell Ally she's adopted and Kitty carries on appearing on Sundays, it won't take Ally long to put two and two together. She needs to know at some point,' Sam said.

Bet felt her limbs soften, the panic reaching into her body. 'I think we should wait until she's older, when she can understand. When she's an adult. I don't want her fretting when this one's born,' Bet said.

Sam gave her a little squeeze. 'I'm not sure if there's ever going to be a right time, luv.'

'Just not now,' she said. 'I want her to feel the same as this one.' She patted her stomach. Bet felt fear as a physical thing that climbed up her body. Sam was right, when she began to show, she'd stay away from church.

They had to get Kitty out of their life soon.

FIFTY

July

Kitty felt flustered and hot. She hadn't been able to find anything to wear and consequently arrived late to church. Her mother's clothes felt wrong and she'd ended up wearing a plain cotton dress of her own. She crept into the back pew just as the congregation sang one of her favourite hymns. It wasn't until she stopped singing and everyone sat down that she realised she couldn't find Bet. Kitty stood up, pacing around at the back of the church, hoping to find the Abbotts hidden behind a pillar. She could hear the melodic chant of the vicar as he gave his sermon, then realised the whole congregation had turned to watch her.

'Sorry,' she said, sitting down. Had the Abbotts moved *again*?

She went through the service, singing the hymns but hitting the wrong notes. Her hands shook as she turned the pages, her mind wading through the countless reasons for their absence. Supposing they'd taken Alexandra far away? Supposing she was ill? Perhaps they'd gone on holiday, but they hadn't gone away before now. She thought they had an understanding.

Afterwards, she waited to shake the vicar's hand. She put down the bag of shoes.

He leaned forward, offered her his hand. 'You've been coming for quite some time, but I've never had the chance to speak to you.' He smiled, gazing at her with unwavering conviction. It rather took her by surprise.

'I'm usually in such a hurry to get back home.'

'Where do you live?'

'Kensington,' she said.

'That *is* a long way.'

Kitty looked at this man's kind face, the softness of his skin, the way a fuzzy layer of down stuck up on his rose-coloured cheeks, the veins mapped across them.

'Do you know if the Abbotts still live near here?'

'Why don't you ask them?' The vicar looked about.

'Really?' she said, unable to resist the prick of hope his misguidance brought.

'No, wait a minute. I saw Elisabeth only yesterday in the high street and she was feeling unwell.' He clasped his hands together.

'Oh that *is* a shame,' Kitty said. 'Would you have her address? I'd like to send her a card.'

'Of course,' he said. 'We're a tight-knit community here, and I know she'd like it if we all sent her best wishes.'

'I can sign it from all of us, but I need the address.'

The vicar turned to wave at some of the parishioners as they made their way out of the gate, his arm lifting his cassock off the floor to reveal brown brogues and grey trousers. 'If you're prepared to wait while I close everything down, then I can help you.'

Kitty felt a surge of elation. She would make sure she visited the Saturday before church. She wanted to make sure Alexandra tried on her shoes.

★

Bet had spent the week agonising over their holiday after receiving Kitty's card. How had the girl managed to get their address? It was unsettling. What was odd was that it had arrived only yesterday, which meant that Kitty had obviously sent it to ensure Bet went to church on Sunday.

It was Saturday and they were off to Brighton for a week's holiday, so she would miss church for a second time. She was flitting around the bedroom picking up socks, making the place nice to come back to. She wiped Ally's fingerprints off their new teak wardrobe with the back of her sleeve. She knew, or hoped – she couldn't decide which – that Kitty would be panicked by their absence. She picked up the get-well card again and was unnerved by the neatness of Kitty's handwriting, the familiarity of her tone: *You were missed on Sunday at church. We all hope you get better soon.* If only she'd given a return address, then Bet would have given her a piece of her mind. She hadn't told Samuel, didn't want to upset him. What if Kitty resorted to hanging around outside their home like she did last time?

But Bet was prepared.

Samuel was polishing their shoes downstairs on the back step. She could hear the rhythmic sweep of the brush through an open window. Ally was watering the plants, chattering away, and Bet was packing the last of their things for the trip. It had been *her* decision to go away. Not going to church had been hard for Bet and being on holiday made it easier, but the shift in the way she felt, an unburdening, had been enough to keep her on track. Samuel had been delighted and booked a family suite at the Grand Hotel.

The knock on the door took her by surprise. Instinct made her call out. 'I'll get it.' She raced downstairs. When she opened the door to Kitty she was tempted to slam it shut again. Kitty was holding up a bag. 'I bought Alexandra some shoes,' she said. 'I've had them for over a week now. What size is she? I bought a few for her to try.'

'I beg your pardon?' Bet could hear Samuel and Alexandra chatting on the back doorstep. She hoped to God neither of them came to see who it was. She closed the door until it was only ajar, so that she was left talking through a narrow gap.

'I'm sure I can return the ones that don't fit.'

'No,' Bet said. 'You'll take them all back.' Her voice wasn't her own. She was shaking. 'Kitty, you can't just buy her things and turn up. I'll call the police if this happens again.' She watched Kitty register her words, her brow wrinkling up.

'I just wanted to buy her some shoes, that's all. I missed her at church, you see.'

'She has perfectly good shoes.'

'They look like something my mother would buy her. I can't bear it.'

Bet felt herself grow hot. Quickly, she snatched the bag out of Kitty's hand. 'Fine.' She went to slam the door but Kitty put her hand out.

'Is Alexandra in?'

Bet thought for a minute. 'She's with her father.'

'I see. Will I be seeing her tomorrow? Perhaps you could bring the shoes that don't fit to church.'

Bet felt another rush of heat making her damp under the arms. 'Okay.'

'Do you smack her often? Please tell me honestly, I can't bear to think of her crying like that.'

Bet was so shocked she was unable to respond. Finally, she slowly shook her head.

'Good. I'll see you tomorrow then.'

Bet slammed the door. If Kitty knocked again, she'd tell Samuel to answer it. Sod it.

'The case is ready for the car,' she shouted as she ran upstairs to hide the shoes. 'I just need the bathroom one last time.'

'Who was that at the door?' Samuel asked as he came into the hall.

'Jehovah's Witnesses.' Her heart was galloping. She felt sticky and couldn't remember what had been said. She took a peek out of the bedroom window and saw Kitty marching off in the direction of the Tube station. Looking at her you'd think she was walking down a catwalk not traipsing back to central London. Bet had a quick look at the shoes. There were three identical pairs in different sizes. One of them was Alexandra's size exactly. She slipped them out and decided to take them with her. They were Start-Rite, a beautiful red. Bet quite liked them.

The day was bright, a perfect summer's day if only the cloud of Kitty's appearance wasn't hanging over it. They drove past the old tea shop where she'd met Kitty. Samuel had extended the grocer's so the shop had one long façade. From the look of it, it was packed. How their life had changed, she thought.

Alexandra was jumping around the back singing: *We're going to the seaside, the seaside*. The roads were busy. Bet tried to imagine where all these people were going, perhaps they were on their way to Brighton as well. Inevitably her mind went back to Kitty.

'Penny for your thoughts,' Samuel said.

'I'm hoping Kitty doesn't flip out when she realises we're not there tomorrow.'

He flashed her a sideways glance. 'I thought that was exactly what you wanted.'

'I know, Sammy. But I worry. She seems to have got worse.'

'What are you talking about? She's been "barking" since day one. We've got *her* to worry about.' He stuck his thumb in the direction of Alexandra.

'I feel for her though. Remember how I was when I lost Johnny? Grief is a hard thing to bear.'

'It's hardly the same, Bet.'

'She's mad with grief, that's what it is.'

'Are you talking about that pretty lady again?' Alexandra asked.

FIFTY-ONE

Kitty was excited to see Alexandra in her new shoes. She'd thought Bet would be pleased with the purchase, but she hadn't seemed that happy at all. It was rude to slam the door like she did but at least she'd taken the bag. When Henry returned from America, Kitty planned to tell him about Alexandra and then she would take him with her to church. He could talk to Mr Abbott about everything.

She flicked through her mother's collection of clothes. Everything looked tired, out of date. She thought of her mother ill and put the thought away like she would her brushes. She tied her hair back from her face with a black Alice band. She'd had it cut in a bob at Sassoon's and loved the way, with a bit of back-combing, it curled and flicked up around her neck. She fished through her wardrobe and decided to be bold and wear a new orange dress she'd bought. She decided she'd take the Morris for a change, packed her casual clothes so that she could go straight to the studio after church. There was an unfinished painting waiting for her attention at the studio. She'd promised Georgie she'd pop round later and she needed to call Tom back after hanging up on him again. Georgie had insisted it was time for change and although Kitty knew she was right, she struggled when it came to Tom.

As she drove through Kensington, she noticed the streets were deserted. It always took longer for the city to wake up on a Sunday. The few people on the street were either eager tourists or night workers on their way home. The day was so warm that she was forced to take off her jacket. She wound down the window. The wind blew through her hair and she found herself smiling as she crossed the Thames. As she approached the suburbs, she saw families on a day out, men walking their dogs.

She was filled with hope.

The church was packed, and it wasn't until Kitty sat down that she realised there must be another christening. The sound of a baby crying up front, the rows of women in spring hats, the cluck of casual chatter. She stood, forgetting to pick up the hymn book, scouring the pews for Bet. There was no sign. She pressed her hand against her chest and couldn't believe the rapidity of her heartbeat. Everyone sat. Kitty remained standing. Alexandra was nowhere to be seen, neither was Bet. Bet had distinctly said she would see her tomorrow. Kitty went straight to the door and marched back to the car.

The Morris was keen to move, racing past the rows of Victorian houses with a volition of its own towards 54 Dalesbury Road. Perhaps Bet was still ill, or maybe she didn't like Alexandra's new shoes. Thoughts collided so fast that Kitty didn't see a woman with a pram walking on the zebra crossing until the very last minute. She braked, the tyres screeching on the tarmac. She sat, her heart racing, her fingers clutching the wheel. The woman with the pram looked startled.

When she arrived at Bet's house, she was drenched in perspiration. She thought perhaps Bet would be angry with her for turning up out of the blue. She'd explain that all she wanted to do was take back the shoes that didn't fit. It was only fair. Yesterday she'd been surprised by the neatness of the front garden, with its small apple tree planted in the centre. A chequered path led to a highly polished red front door. Today she felt slightly angered by its order.

Kitty knocked. Then knocked again and tried to peek through the letterbox. When nobody answered, she hammered at the door until the brass knocker grew warm in her hand.

'Can I help you,' an old man's voice asked. He was standing the other side of Bet's garden hedge. Kitty could just see the top of his bald head. 'They're away on holiday. Gone to Brighton.'

'Brighton!'

'That's right.'

'Do you know when they'll be back?'

'Next Saturday I think. Are you a friend?'

'Yes, yes I am,' Kitty said.

'Shall I tell them you called by?' He was standing on his tiptoes so that she could see half of his face. She knew he was smiling by the light in his eyes and the crinkled edges of his lids.

'Oh, I wouldn't worry. I'll pop by another time.' She hurried down the path. 'Thank you,' she said.

It was as if the Morris took her to Brighton all by itself. She parked the car in Kemptown, not far from the seafront. She needed to change and was beginning to feel hungry. Realising then that she hadn't had any breakfast, she walked into the first café she came to. Next door was a newsagent, so after ordering breakfast, she bought the papers. For a minute she felt just like everyone else.

After breakfast she went to a telephone box, wedged the door open so she didn't have to inhale the urine, and called all of the major hotels asking for a Mrs Abbott. She discovered that they were in the Grand Hotel but weren't in their room. She'd call again later.

It was sunnier down on the front, the sea a shimmering invitation. There was a gaiety about the place that was hard to ignore. People were ambling along the promenade. Screams of delight came from the water. Kitty wondered how on earth she was going to find Alexandra in all this chaos. Still, she knew where they were so it was just a case of waiting. She decided on the pier and felt a little woozy looking down through the cracks at the move-ment of the sea below. She stopped for a minute, closed her eyes and listened to the sound of the water crashing onto the pebbles. She walked up and down the pier for a good hour, bought an ice cream when she grew too hot. She was strolling past the penny arcade, thinking of booking herself into the same hotel as Bet, when she heard Alexandra's sweet voice.

'Daddy, are there fishes down there?'

Kitty didn't move. She was partly hidden by a couple of girls beside her larking about. She waited until the Abbotts moved in the direction of the funfair. Kitty followed. Alexandra was wearing a floral dress and the yellow sweater Kitty had bought her. Her hair was tied in bunches and she was wearing her new red shoes. Alexandra ran up to the edge and stepped up onto the balustrade. She'd grown so tall in the last couple of weeks.

'Ally, come down, you'll fall.' Bet held out her hand. Kitty remembered the reprimand Bet had given her at church. She watched as Alexandra ran up to Bet, hugging her leg. Kitty rummaged about in her handbag for a handkerchief to wipe her sticky fingers on. When she looked up, she saw them walking in the direction of the carousel. She arrived just in time to see Mr Abbott put Alexandra in a car.

'Mummy come too,' Kitty heard her say. Kitty slipped to the opposite side, out of sight behind a pillar. The machine started up. The man in charge wore a soft cap and baggy flannels. He rang a bell and the thing slowly shifted round. Alexandra was laughing, waving to Bet and Mr Abbott. A minute passed before she noticed Kitty. Her face broke into a smile of recognition and she waved, her bunches bouncing up and down. Kitty couldn't resist lifting her hand. Alexandra stood up, deciding to climb out of the car, ignoring the spinning carousel, busy with the business of making her way towards Kitty, climbing over obstacles. Bet was crouching down and Samuel bent over her. They weren't even watching.

Kitty went to help Alexandra and held out her arms.

'STOP!' Bet cried, her hand up to her mouth. She started to run alongside the carousel.

Alexandra looked up at Kitty a second before she tumbled off the merry-go-round. Kitty ran towards her. 'Oh, Alexandra,' she said. She stooped over to pick her up, hugging her close. She kissed her head, felt her soft hair on her face. The smell of her daughter filling her nose.

'Mummy,' she said. Kitty's heart thumped hard. But then she saw that Alexandra's arms were outstretched towards Bet.

'Have you gone mad? Can't you see what's happening here? This has to stop, and it has to stop NOW!' Bet was trembling. She pulled Alexandra away from Kitty. Kitty wanted to pull Alexandra back but then she saw the swelling in Bet's stomach.

'You're pregnant!' she said.

Bet was holding Alexandra tightly, shaking her. 'Silly girl,' she said.

'You weren't even watching her!' Kitty said.

'I wasn't feeling well,' Bet said.

'The shoes look lovely.'

'Pardon?'

Alexandra watched Kitty from Bet's shoulder, her thumb stuck in her mouth. Eventually Bet handed her to Mr Abbott who was shaking his head and muttering. Kitty watched as they exchanged a few words out of earshot. Mr Abbott took Alexandra away. Kitty didn't dare move, aware suddenly that the man who ran the merry-go-round was talking to her.

'You all right, luv? Not sure what happened there.'

Bet tramped back and took hold of Kitty's hand, pulling her in the way she did Alexandra sometimes. She addressed the carousel man.

'It's not your fault. Our daughter recognised this lady, that's all.' She pulled Kitty to the side. The sound of the organ music faded and in its place the seagulls shrieked. Bet twisted Kitty round to face her, her arm gripping her thin shoulders.

'Kitty, do you know what happened? She was trying to say hello to you. I don't know what's going on here, but you left your child on my doorstep because you weren't able to look after her. She's legally our child now and you should leave me to do the job you trusted me with. You need to get on with the rest of your life and let Alexandra do the same. At some point she's going to get very confused if you keep up this stalking, and then what?'

'I could take her back,' Kitty said. 'After all. You've got your own child coming now.'

Bet slapped her face then felt herself crumble. Kitty held her cheek.

'Is that what you do to Alexandra?'

302

'How dare you!' Bet said through her tears. 'I've done everything you asked. I named her as you wanted and I've allowed these stupid Sunday visits. But she *cannot* grow up confused. Do you understand that? I will not allow it. If you love her, you will not allow it either.'

Kitty closed her eyes. When she opened them they were glazed over.

Bet went on, 'If you love her, you'll let her go. Over these past couple of years, I've tried, really I have, but how long do you think we can keep this up? If she finds out you're her real mother now, she's going to wonder why she's living with me, don't you see?' She baulked at having to use the word, *real*. 'Worse still she's going to wonder why she's not with you. I'm going to have to tell her she's adopted at some point, when she's an adult, and that you left her on my doorstep, but she needs to know *I'm* her mother.' Bet pressed her index finger onto her chest. 'I don't want her thinking she's any different to this one.' She patted her swollen stomach.

Kitty was shaking. Her shoulders shuddered and she started choking into a sodden grubby-looking handkerchief. Her hair was all roughed up by the sea air, her eyes red-rimmed and swollen. Bet sighed, got out her hanky and handed it over. 'Here,' she said. Then she found a tissue for herself.

'Can I buy her an ice cream?' Kitty said. 'Then I'll leave you alone. I know you think I've behaved badly but can I be on my own with her one last time?'

Bet thought for a moment. Samuel would never agree.

'You know what it's like,' she said. 'You lost your Johnny.'

Bet felt a sting to hear Kitty remember her son's name. 'It's not the same,' she said. At some point, Kitty would be able to see her daughter again, whereas Bet and Samuel would never get that chance with Johnny. But that wasn't Kitty's fault. She knew what Kitty was feeling. 'Okay,' she said. 'But give me a minute. My Sammy isn't happy.'

Kitty nodded. 'Perhaps I should go and freshen up,' she said.

'All right. I'll meet you back here in twenty minutes. You can spend some time with Alexandra. After that, it's got to stop. No more Sundays. I need your word, Kitty.'

Kitty stared out to sea, and when she finally looked at Bet, her eyes belied the pain she was feeling. 'You have my word,' she said.

FIFTY-TWO

Bet found Samuel waiting in the penny arcade right at the end of the pier. Clutching a handful of coins, his posture was bent as he pulled the arm and watched the spinning fruit, waiting for the clunk as it came to a halt. Two cherries and one plum. Alexandra jumped up and down with excitement.

'Two cherries,' she said, holding up two fingers. Bet tapped Samuel on the shoulder just as he was about to pop another penny into the slot. Startled, Samuel twisted round, his hands pulling Alexandra close.

'You don't want to do that,' Bet said, indicating towards the penny in his hand. 'We don't want Ally thinking gambling is a good thing.'

'It's a one-armed bandit, not a poker table!' he said.

Bet took Alexandra by the hand and led her towards a game called Wonder Win.

'Give me one of those,' she said. 'At least this involves a bit of skill.'

Samuel handed her a penny. 'More like a flick of the thumb.' He popped the penny in and Bet tucked Alexandra under her arm. 'Watch this,' she said, and the silver ball spun up and around the coil of steel. They all watched, mesmerised as the ball whirled into the centre.

'Again,' Alexandra said.

'Has she gone? And what was that she said about a pair of shoes?' Samuel asked.

'Red shoes!' said Alexandra, pointing at her new shoes.

Bet turned and glared at Samuel and was surprised to see fear flash in his eyes.

'Where did these come from? She only just got a new pair.'

'I told you, I wanted a brighter pair for the summer.'

'You didn't tell me.'

'Oh, Samuel, you never remember these things. Let's have a look over here,' she said.

'Are you going to tell me what happened?' Sammy had stopped by Mystic Meg, a clockwork gypsy who apparently could see into the future. Bet was tempted to pop a penny in the slot.

'Come on,' he said. '*Something* must have happened.' He was standing very close to her.

'Kitty is going to take Alexandra for one last walk down the pier while you and I go and have a cup of tea. After that, no more Sundays.'

She watched him take in her words, reading his face, waiting.

'Are you mad?' he said. He snatched a penny, shoved it into a nearby slot machine in protest. She watched him roll his shoulders, an infinitesimal shake of the head.

Her hand inevitably reached under her bulge, wanting the comfort of her little miracle. Nobody could take that away from her. Alexandra started to whine. She was waiting for another go with the penny. Bet rolled her eyes.

'She's going to run off with her, you know that, don't you?' said Samuel.

Bet looked down at Alexandra who was distracted by running her wet fingers over the glass of the Mystic Meg machine. 'I don't think she will,' she whispered, the words thick on her tongue. She took Alexandra's hand and led her over to the penny drop machine, ignoring the weight of Sam's eyes boring into her back. 'Pop it in,' she said.

'It'll be me driving through the night looking for them.' He was running his hand through his hair.

'We'll call the police if it comes to that. But it won't.'

A few penny coins dropped into the trough of the machine. 'You've won,' she said to Alexandra. 'Look.' She scooped out her winnings. 'Sometimes it works to think the best of people,' Bet said. She watched a group of young girls laughing over a candy floss. She couldn't remember being that carefree. There wasn't time for thoughts like that, she told herself. Not now. Not ever.

'Here, give me that,' Sammy said to Alexandra.

Bet put her hand out and stopped him.

'What?' he said. 'I don't want her hands to get grubby.'

'Let's watch the horses,' she said, taking Sammy by the arm and holding Alexandra, pulling them all close into a bundle. They watched the green and red horses on sticks race to a jolting finish. She was convinced she'd felt the little one inside – a flutter more than an actual tumble – connecting them as four. This little human being inside her made her feel brave and powerful.

She agreed to meet Sammy in the Grand Hotel tea room. She thought it best he wasn't there to see Kitty, but as she watched him skulk off after giving Alexandra a hug, she felt swamped with doubt. She'd never forgive herself if Sam was right.

Waiting on the pier, Alexandra spun herself around to make herself dizzy. For once Bet didn't reprimand her. The roar of the sea washing against the pier echoed underneath them. The seagulls played havoc above. The late afternoon sun shimmered against the peeling paintwork of the Victorian scaffolding. Bet absorbed all of it, allowing herself a moment to think of nothing.

Kitty came up behind her. She bent down and gave

Alexandra a peck on the cheek. 'Hello, little one,' she said. 'Are you feeling better now?'

Bet heard the tremor in Kitty's voice. She'd almost forgotten about the tumble on the carousel. Her mind had been preoccupied with her own life and what was about to come. While she waited, she'd been working out how she was going to tell Kitty that she'd have to stay with them. Kitty stood up. Bet could see that she'd washed her face, put on some lipstick and a touch of rouge. She was a pretty girl, and although Bet saw traces of Alexandra in her, the heart-shaped face, the high forehead, her colouring meant she didn't look much like her daughter. Alexandra's eyes were hazel and her hair darker than Kitty's with streaks of blonde where the sun had touched it.

'I thought I might take her for an ice cream,' Kitty said. She bent down to address Alexandra. 'Would you like that?'

Alexandra looked at Bet, who tried her best to offer a smile of approval, but she knew it was forced and Alexandra would know it too. Bet felt a pinch of fear grip her stomach and then she thought of those carefree girls and the candy floss and something told her to go with it. To trust.

'And maybe a ride on the helter skelter.'

'I wouldn't recommend that *after* an ice cream,' Bet said, feeling the baby floating inside her. Why had he or she suddenly got so active?

'Yes, you may have a point there,' Kitty said. She held out her hand. 'Coming?'

'You're not going to let her go down on her own, are you?'

Kitty frowned. 'What do you take me for?'

Bet looked away. She wasn't sure how to answer but the anxiety had swollen and she was close to tears, wrestling with doubt like it was a physical thing, reminding herself what she believed: that Kitty would do the right thing.

'Mummy,' Ally said, holding out her hand.

'Would you like to come?' Kitty said. 'You don't have to go down, but you can watch.'

The feeling of relief was overwhelming. 'Okay, I will,' she said.

They walked to the end of the pier, both of them holding Alexandra's hands. Bet found herself filled with a feeling of goodwill, remembering that day when Kitty had walked into the shop. Looking at them all now, they could be sisters or two friends having a day out in sunny Brighton. She worried about Sammy. Soon she'd have to decide whether to leave Alexandra or not.

'Do you like your new shoes?' Kitty asked. 'I do love red sandals, don't you?'

Bet watched as Ally hesitated. 'Yes, red is lovely,' Bet said, 'but, Kitty, it was wrong of me to accept them. There's to be no more gifts.'

Kitty looked at her with that all-too-familiar perplexed furrowed brow. 'The other shoes were rather dull, that's all.'

Bet said, 'It's up to me to choose her things.' But her authority wavered. She thought it uncanny that Kitty had taken a disliking to the shoes that her mother had unwittingly paid for. She was going to have to put a stop to Mrs Campbell's interference as well.

'Of course,' Kitty said.

When they arrived at the helter skelter, Kitty paid the man for their mat and picked Alexandra up. It was such a natural gesture and yet Bet couldn't help feeling a stab of anxiety as she watched them walk up the steps. She's three for heaven's sake, she told herself, and she's loving it. If you want this to end, then let her be for a bit.

FIFTY-THREE

Kitty felt the sharp early summer sea breeze bite into her skin. She hadn't felt this alive in years. She climbed up the circular stairs. Halfway up the helter skelter she stopped, and through a crack, took in the sea that stretched out before them, the light dancing on its choppy surface. Now that she was out of Bet's sight, she squeezed Alexandra tight against her chest.

'Oh, Alexandra, I so want you to love life.'

Alexandra looked at her, concentrating on her face with a small frown. 'Are we going down now?' she asked. Kitty thought she might cry, but she reached out and touched her, pressing the palm of her hand on her cheek. Kitty gripped her fingers and kissed them, then brought her small hand to her heart. 'Let's do it.'

She could hear a group of children climbing up behind them, their voices echoing in the wooden cave. Bet was below, probably wondering what was keeping them.

'Come on,' she said. 'You're going to love this.'

Once at the top, she put the mat down, careful to hold Alexandra's hand, suddenly aware of how high they both were. Fighting the desire to look down, a part of her compelled to tumble over the edge. She sat and pulled Alexandra onto her lap, wrapping her arm snuggly around her.

'Ready?'

Alexandra nodded. And then she pushed them off and the wind blew through their hair so that she felt the strands tickle her chin. She bent down, breathed in the smell of her daughter's neck, the sea a blur, and then all too quickly they were coming to the end, floating onto a big doormat. She jumped up and there was Bet, holding out her smooth plump arms. Alexandra ran towards her.

'That was fun, wasn't it?' Kitty said.

Bet touched her shoulder then bent down to talk to Alexandra. 'Kitty's going to take you for an ice cream while I go and see Daddy.'

'Are you sure?' Kitty asked.

'I know you will do the right thing,' Bet said. She stooped down and kissed the top of Alexandra's head. 'You're going to stay with Kitty for a while and if you're good she'll buy you an ice cream.'

Alexandra looked up at Kitty. Kitty squeezed her daughter's hand, laid the other on Bet's arm. 'Thank you.'

'I'll see you in a couple of hours,' Bet said. She turned and walked away, her gait slow and graceful, swaying slightly.

Kitty and Alexandra walked along the promenade. It was a beautiful day, the light sharp so that it danced on the water.

'I like strawberry ice cream. What's your favourite flavour?'

Alexandra didn't say anything. She looked up at her, about to cry. 'I want my mummy,' she said.

Kitty felt the tears prick her eyes. A hollow feeling welled up inside her but she pushed it aside. A woman walked by with a small dog. 'Look, a sausage dog!' Alexandra broke free and ran towards it.

'Is it okay if she strokes him?' Kitty asked, bending down and giving the dog an encouraging rub on his head.

'Perfectly fine,' the woman said.

Kitty crouched down and took Alexandra's hand, drawing it close to the dog and running her hand over the dog's back. She thought Alexandra's hands looked just like Henry's and found herself imagining what she'd say to him if she took Alexandra home.

'Stroke him behind his ears, he'll like that,' the woman said.

'What's his name?' Alexandra asked.

'Bob,' the woman said.

Bob let Alexandra stroke him, looking up at her with soulful brown eyes.

Kitty saw the woman's gaze fall onto her ringless finger. They exchanged a brief knowing glance, at least Kitty felt it was knowing. She thought to explain but couldn't in front of Alexandra. 'Come on. Let the doggy have his walk, and we can have our ice cream.'

'How old is your daughter?' the woman asked.

'She's three,' Kitty said, noting the woman's brown polished brogues and the density of her stockings. She forced herself to smile. 'Wave to the nice doggy,' she said. 'Thank you so much, you've been very kind.'

The woman smiled, gave Bob a little tug on the lead. She would buy Alexandra a dog, she thought.

Alexandra was waving and then she looked up at Kitty. 'That woman thought you were my mummy.'

Kitty wanted to tell her, but she was caught unawares, not knowing where to start. She thought about Bet, remembering her rounded stomach, the plumpness of her flesh. Everything about her amorphous and as comfortable as a well-worn sofa. Kitty was angular with sharp edges.

'Can we go there?' Alexandra asked, pointing towards the beach. She tugged at Kitty's hand.

'Shall we have our ice cream first? We could go on a train if you like. You see, I don't have a towel so we can't go in the water, and it does look rather cold.'

Alexandra went on tugging, both hands pulling Kitty forward, exactly as she had done that day in church with Mr Abbott. She was surprisingly strong. Kitty slipped off her pumps and with stockinged feet trod tentatively across the pebbles. Alexandra hurried straight up to the water, jumping up and down, chasing the waves back and forth, laughing as the water foamed and slipped into the cracked surface. Kitty thought she'd better take off Alexandra's new shoes. She sat down, hugging her knees, and for a second she didn't recognise herself. She felt like any other young mother. She imagined her daughter older, at school, at university or maybe art college. The thought of Alexandra's future made Kitty tremble.

'Come with me,' Alexandra said.

'Okay, I will.'

Alexandra smiled that big smile of hers, mouth open. In that moment it felt to Kitty that Alexandra knew her, understood everything that had happened and had forgiven her. A simple cognition that offered meaning, a happy ending. The feeling spread across her chest, a warm pressure that pressed down on her sternum. She leaped up, leaving her bag and shoes, and ran towards the water, lifting her and swinging her around. 'Let's jump the waves, shall we?' She ran into the water with her stockinged feet, the water creeping up around her ankles, and jumped up and down while hugging her daughter until Alexandra was laughing, pointing at her feet.

'Your feet are wet,' she said.

Kitty nodded. 'Do you want a go?'

Alexandra frowned, two deep grooves forming at the top of her nose, as if the answer needed all of her concentration.

'Come on, then. Let's take your shoes and socks off.'

She put Alexandra down, undid her new sandals and slipped off her socks. Then she wrapped her cardigan around her waist so that she could take off her slacks and wriggle free of her tights. She was quick. Alexandra watched, occasionally putting her thumb into her mouth and gazing out to sea. She picked up a pebble and put it up to her nose to smell it.

'It smells of the sea doesn't it? Here. Let's see if we can find another one to keep.'

Kitty scouted around and picked up a round grey pebble and a piece of chalk. She drew a face on it, handing it to Alexandra, watching as her face cracked open. 'Here, you draw one.' She handed her a flat round stone and watched as her daughter ran the chalk along the surface of the stone, frowning.

'That's wonderful. Are you going to keep it, or can Mummy have it?'

Alexandra bit her lip. 'I want to do another one.'

While Alexandra was drawing, she picked up a shell, not the prettiest of shells but perfect and unbroken. She put it to her ear and heard the rumble of the sea behind her.

'Listen,' she said, putting it to Alexandra's ear.

Alexandra smiled and popped the shell in her dress pocket. 'Every time you want to hear the sea, just put it up to your ear.'

'I want to go there,' Alexandra said, pointing to the sea. They picked their way across the pebbles and stood at the water's edge. Alexandra crouched down, keen to touch the water with her hand, and as it rushed over their feet she looked up at her and laughed and fell onto her knees. Instantly, her dress was wet. At first she thought it was funny, but then her face crumpled and she began to cry. Kitty swooped her up, the action so natural it took her by surprise.

'Whoops-a-daisy!' Kitty said.

Alexandra didn't move but Kitty felt her body go rigid, slowly her lips puckered. 'I want my mummy!'

Kitty felt the wrench – a crack running through her. 'We'll have to buy you a new dress,' she said, then she remembered it was Sunday.

'I want my mummy.' Alexandra was crying hard now. A family stationed behind a windbreaker were all eating their sandwiches, staring.

'I want Mummy.'

'Mummy's coming in a minute.'

Kitty blinked back the tears, a burning fear rising up. 'Let's go and find Mummy, then,' she said. She took Alexandra back up to their spot on the beach and tried hard to dry the dress with her hanky. Alexandra was making sniffling noises and instinctively she picked her up and hugged her.

'Please don't cry, Alexandra,' she said. 'Let's go on the train and after that we'll get an ice cream. Would you like that?'

Alexandra nodded but her bottom lip stuck out. 'Mummy.'

'And then we'll find Mummy,' Kitty said.

She popped on Alexandra's socks and sandals, picked her up. She couldn't return her to Bet this wet. But she wasn't sure she *was* going to return her. She wasn't sure of anything at all.

'Come on, you. I think it's time for a ride on the train.'

She walked towards Volk's railway carrying Alexandra. All the while Alexandra's eyes scanned the landscape in search of Bet. Kitty felt her blood surge at the idea that she was not enough for her daughter, a sense of gratitude curdling against stale resentment. It wasn't Alexandra's fault.

They arrived just as the bright yellow and brown train was pulling in.

'Are we going on that one?'

'We certainly are, and when we get back, we're going to get that ice cream and have a little trip in my car. How does that sound?'

Alexandra nodded again. She seemed to have forgotten about Bet for now.

'Sixpence, luv.'

'There are two of us,' she said.

'The child's free,' the ticket collector said, catching sight of Alexandra's wet dress.

'An accident in the sea,' Kitty explained. 'Maybe the wind will dry it.'

'Needs a swimsuit.'

Kitty let Alexandra step up to the carriage. They walked to the back of the train. Kitty slipped her arm around Alexandra rubbing her arms to warm her. They waved to everyone and no one as the train took off. Alexandra was bouncing up and down, oblivious to her wet clothes now that something more exciting was happening. Kitty allowed herself to imagine taking her daughter to Beecham, feeding her boiled egg and soldiers, letting her run through the willow as she did as a child. A wash of calm entered, shifting something that had been raging inside for years.

FIFTY-FOUR

Bet looked at her watch for the fourth time in ten minutes. They'd sat down on a bench looking out to sea. The seagulls were hovering, their wing spans casting shadows across the street as they swooped and hovered, snapping at thrown food. Sammy had been distracted by a bag of whelks, which seemed to have had a nostalgic attraction more than a culinary one. He was licking his fingers, not a habit she was fond of, but she let it go. She was happy that half an hour had passed without mention of Alexandra and Kitty. The worry seemed to have passed on to her now the hour was approaching and Samuel had left off nagging. They'd agreed to meet at the same place they'd parted. The crowds were thinning. Soon families would be filling out the cafés eating fish and chips and drinking beer. The fluttering started up again.

'Feel this,' she said, remembering far too late that Samuel's fingers were covered in fishy slime. She pressed his hand down onto her floral frock. 'Can you feel it?'

'Not really,' he said.

Bet rolled her eyes. 'We'd better get back to the hotel.'

They stood up. Bet smoothed out her dress, dipping down to see if she smelt fishy. Sammy went off to dispose of the newspaper his whelks had been wrapped in.

'I'd imagine the little 'un is starving by now,' Sammy said on his return.

'She would have fed her, surely.'

'Well she's hardly a buxom wench.'

'Samuel, I don't know how you manage to get through life thinking about people the way you do.' Bet looped her handbag onto the crook of her arm and caught hold of him, feeling his muscles tense as if to take the weight of her.

'She won't be there,' he said.

*

Kitty helped Alexandra off the train, inhaling her little girl smell which filled her with memories of those first few days in the hospital. She looked at her watch. They'd been together over an hour already and yet it seemed like minutes. The dress had almost dried.

'Are we getting an ice cream now?'

Kitty crouched down, gave her a small peck. 'Yes, let's go.'

They walked along the promenade until they came to an ice cream parlour. She had half a mind to buy it and take Alexandra back onto the beach where they could cuddle up, but she could sense her daughter was uneasy.

'Do you need to go the loo, darling?'

Alexandra nodded. Kitty opened the door to the café and led her in.

'Shall we get our ice cream first?' she suggested.

Alexandra shook her head. 'I need a wee,' she said.

'Right,' Kitty said. 'Let me just put my cardigan on a chair and save us a table.'

Alexandra clung to her hand. 'Where is the loo?' Kitty asked a waitress who was buzzing around with trays of cups and sundaes.

'Downstairs, first door on the right.'

Kitty scooped Alexandra up, went to the back of the café and made her way down the stairs. The lino got gritty and smeared with dirt the further down she went.

'Down you go,' she said, letting Alexandra slide off her hip. Alexandra was waiting.

'Would you like me to help?' she asked.

Alexandra nodded, serious suddenly, her thumb working away inside her mouth. She supposed the business of going to the loo was serious for a three-year-old. She opened the door and wrestled with Alexandra's knickers. She remembered how her mother used to place paper on the seat, so she did the same. All the while Alexandra watched her, deep in concentration.

Finally, Kitty lifted her daughter up and placed her in position, politely turning around until the tinkling had finished. Kitty, bathed in a feeling of normality, could hear the clink and clatter of the kitchen, the far-off childish cries of pleasure upstairs in the café.

Upstairs Alexandra placed the stone with its smiley face on the table next to the shell.

'The stone is smiling at the shell,' she said.

She'd ordered chocolate ice cream, which meant that most of the time Kitty was armed with a paper serviette, trying to wipe her mouth clean. She would have happily spent the rest of her life mopping up after her child but a feeling of panic was raining down on her. The light was fading. She looked out at the promenade, at the families and couples strolling arm in arm.

'We need to get going, poppet,' she said. She wondered how Alexandra would react if she took her to the Morris. How long it would take her to forget Bet. *Mummy*.

The waitress came up with the bill, wiping the table

next to her with rigour. She turned round and picked up the change Kitty had left.

'She's a good little girl,' she said. 'A credit to you if you don't mind me saying.'

Kitty smiled politely while wiping the last traces of chocolate from Alexandra's mouth.

'Thank you,' Alexandra said, pushing the empty bowl of ice cream towards her.

'Aww, what a darling,' the waitress said.

'Thank you,' Kitty said, but a pain spread across her chest, stealing through her veins. *Alexandra was a credit to Bet.* She buttoned up Alexandra's cardigan, scooped her up into her arms and placed her neatly on her hip, remembering the day she'd escaped from the mother and baby home, the horror of that dreadful couple in the Rover arriving to take her with them, making her run.

She headed towards Kemptown. The Morris was parked on the left, third street up.

FIFTY-FIVE

Bet stopped Sammy just as he was about to go through the turnstile. She knew he'd make it all the more difficult for Kitty. The sea breeze had picked up and she could feel the damp wrap itself around her legs, her hands trembling with fear.

'Are you cold?' Sammy said, taking off his jacket.

'It's not that. I just think it would be easier if I did this on my own.'

'Easier for whom?' he said, wrapping the jacket around her shoulders.

'For everyone,' she said. 'I don't want Alexandra to pick up on anything.'

'I'll behave myself,' he said. 'You know I can when I put my mind to it.'

'Please,' she said.

'And what if she's not coming?'

Bet saw a telephone box just across the road. 'I'll telephone you,' she said.

Sam followed her gaze and said. 'By the time you get to that telephone box you could be halfway to the hotel in the opposite direction.'

'I'll find you,' she said, impatient, swept up by a feeling of foreboding. All the worry she'd put aside seemed to collect into one uncontrollable bout of dread. If she admitted this to Sammy she knew he'd erupt. She opened her handbag and took out their Instamatic.

'What you taking that for?'

'She'll not want to say goodbye, that's all. I thought if I offered to take her picture.'

He raised his eyes. 'That's if she's there at all. You can't argue with madness, Bet, and that girl is far from sane.' He wrung his hands, then stuffed them into his pockets. She felt a stab of anger.

'And if it were your daughter that got into trouble, would you say that then?'

Sammy dropped his head.

'I don't imagine Kitty wanted any of this.' They were standing by the turnstile. People had to dodge around them as they left the pier. She pulled Sammy to the side, the wind buffeting the window of the kiosk, her skirt, her hair. She could feel the stickiness of salt on her face. Sammy frowned.

'What if she doesn't come?'

'She will.'

'Then what? I can imagine us on holiday in Majorca or somewhere exotic and her being on the next table. It's not normal, is it? Leaving your baby on a doorstep, then turning up at church just to see her.'

'Because of Kitty, we have a daughter, and now we have another on the way. We should be grateful.'

'You're saying that now, but in a few minutes you'll see.'

He looked at her and there must have been something about her manner that changed his mood. He bent forward, gave her a peck on the cheek. 'I'll see you back at the hotel.'

'Don't panic if I'm not back straight away. I'm going to be gentle and kind.'

Sammy wandered off, pushing back his hair as the wind whipped it up, stooped against his own internal storm.

322

★

Kitty ran along the front. She hadn't realised they'd wandered so far towards Hove. She could feel Alexandra clinging to her neck. She felt heavy in her arms. 'Won't be long,' she said. Her lungs were battling for air, sweat had collected under her armpits, around her neck and under her blouse. She didn't want this to be the last day. She couldn't.

'Are you okay, Alexandra?' she asked as she bumped up and down on her hip.

'I want to go in the sea again,' Alexandra said.

'And you will, my love, you will.'

Kitty saw that she was still clutching the stone and the shell she'd given her. Down on the beach a father and son were jumping the waves. The mother and daughter were sitting on a picnic rug. Why couldn't Kitty just be normal?

As she looked out to sea she saw the low sun sparkling and the water blurred onto the horizon in the soft afternoon light. 'You are going to love life, Alexandra. I promise.'

She looped up towards the car in Kemptown, avoiding the pier by taking the back streets. The Morris was parked at the top of the hill. Kitty started to run, her heart pounding with the effort and fear. She remembered her mother's words: *Being a mother means putting yourself and your own needs second*. But we are all condemned to be ourselves, she thought. She sped past the rows of guest-houses with their blue and white awnings, and geranium-filled window boxes, the café she'd visited that morning, forgetting Alexandra wedged on her hip until her small voice asked:

'Is this the way to Mummy and Daddy's house?'

FIFTY-SIX

Bet was pacing around the spot where she'd last seen Alexandra with increasing vigour. The sea had grown dark and was crashing underneath her, curling around the pillars. The stones rumbled as they rolled back and forth. The wind had picked up and she felt the chill of it whip around her neck. She looked at her watch. Fear like a claw dragged at her insides. Fifteen minutes had passed and there was still no sign of them. Maybe Kitty was lost, she thought. It's easily done. But in her heart she knew this wasn't the case. Where would she start? She walked towards the helter skelter, breathless. The idea of Kitty taking her, stealing Alexandra back, was obvious to her now. Of course that's what she'd planned all along. What an idiot she'd been. First finding their address, then delivering the shoes to double-check she'd got it right. Where would she take her? Sammy said it, the girl wasn't right in the head. The man running the carousel was covering up the cars with green tarpaulin. Bet thought she would never see her daughter again. People like Kitty had money enough to run away. She turned back, headed towards the entrance. She was going to have to call Sammy.

Then she caught sight of Kitty running along the promenade, Alexandra bumping around on her hip, urgently pushing through the turnstile. Bet felt her knees buckle at the sight of them.

'Bet, Bet.'

Kitty put Alexandra down and Bet opened her arms and let Alexandra run into them.

'I am so sorry. We were further away than I thought and . . .'

Bet felt the tears track down her nose.

'I'm sorry,' Kitty said. 'We had a little accident. She got wet. Her clothes are still a little damp.'

'You're here now. That's what counts.'

Kitty's hair was a tangle, she was flushed and crying. Bet didn't expect to feel this much sorrow for the girl. She'd have happily skinned her alive a few minutes ago.

Alexandra was tugging at her sleeve. 'We've been into the sea, Mummy. And on a choo-choo train.' She looked down at her daughter and she appeared so contented she felt a wave of gratitude. Kitty had done the right thing.

'I thought you'd taken her,' she said.

'Yes, I thought you might think that.' She wiped her face with her sleeve. 'I almost did, but I thought about how much you loved her and everything you've done and, well . . .' Her face folded up. 'I had this moment, an epiphany if you like. I realised that I needed to put myself second.' Kitty dipped her head so that her slender neck seemed terribly long. 'I couldn't do it to either of you. It's not who I am, but for a while it was all I had, the dream of undoing everything.'

Alexandra jumped up and down beside them both, the sound of the sea and the pebbles scrabbling a comfort suddenly.

'We saw a dog. I want a doggy, Mummy.'

Bet was trying to piece together Kitty's confession. Alexandra, incapable of knowing how close she was to losing her, unfolded a clenched hand and showed her a stone with a smiling face drawn on it and her shell. 'I made you a present. It's for you, Mummy.'

Bet turned to see Kitty's pained face, a film of sweat shining across her cheeks. She reached up and squeezed her arm. 'Thank you,' she said.

Kitty nodded. 'I wondered if I might write . . .'

'I don't think . . .'

'I meant to you.' She looked out to sea, wiped her eyes. 'We've been through so much since that day in the tea shop.'

Bet hadn't expected to feel her heart ache for Kitty, but it did. 'I'm not much of a letter writer.'

'I just wanted to send you snippets, thoughts, snaps of my life. You might want to share them when she gets older but if you don't, I'll understand.'

'Well I don't suppose that will do any harm.' Bet thought: I suppose if you take a child in after finding her in a suitcase this is what you get. 'I brought a camera. I thought you might like a photo.' Alexandra was leaning against the railing, her head bent right over towards the sea. 'Alexandra, be careful!' she said. She turned to see Kitty staring at her.

'I'd love a photograph,' she said. 'I'll give you my address.'

Alexandra folded her hand into hers. Bet felt her swinging back and forth on one leg. She wasn't going to correct her, not at a time like this. 'Here, Ally. Go and stand next to . . .' she hesitated '. . . Kitty, and I'll take your picture.'

They posed, the two of them braced against the sea breeze, their hair parted and whipped by it. Bet noticed the tension in her daughter's face, the way she smiled with her mouth closed. It was as if she knew.

'Smile,' she said.

Kitty took Ally's hand and looked into the camera, an intensity burning that seemed aimed at Bet. Ally's smile was still stiff. Bet took the picture anyway.

'There you go,' Bet said. 'I'll send you a copy.'

Kitty nodded. Bet could sense her anxiety as Kitty's hand gripped Ally's shoulder.

'I'd like to send you some money, you know, to contribute.' Kitty was staring at Alexandra, her eyes glazed over.

'That won't be necessary.'

'I just . . .'

Bet held her hand up and shook her head. 'We're her parents and we'll take any responsibility that involves.'

Kitty's eyes welled up. They stood for a minute, the wind buffeting against them. She noticed then that they were the only people on that side of the pier. 'Let's stand over there,' she said, pointing to a sheltered spot. 'I've got to get going soon.' She took Alexandra's hand and they all walked to the other side of the pier where the wind was muted as if behind a closed door.

Kitty straightened up. 'Let me give you my address. If you need me, or should anything happen to any of you, please get in touch.' She took out a notebook, tore out a page and, tucking her hair behind her ear, scribbled out her address with a pencil. Alexandra had wandered off to climb on a bench. Kitty handed her the scrap of paper.

'I wish . . . I wish.'

'Hush now. There's no point in wishing for things we can't have. You need to get on with your life, Kitty. You made a promise, and now you've got to stick to it.'

'Yes, of course.' She finally faced Bet, her eyes speaking of the pain she was feeling.

Bet was beginning to feel that if she didn't go soon she'd be taking Kitty home with them. It hadn't occurred to her that she'd have to be the one to walk away.

She gestured to Alexandra to come to their side. 'Say thank you to Kitty, and give her a hug goodbye now, Alexandra.'

Kitty smiled, her lips twitching. 'I'm jolly grateful for everything, you know that don't you.'

Bet nodded and looked down at Alexandra who was waiting. Sammy's jacket was beginning to feel ridiculous hanging off her shoulders with no man to claim it.

Kitty crouched down. Bet noticed how her knees protruded out of her trousers like two halves of a cricket ball. Sammy was right, she was too thin.

'Bye-bye, Alexandra,' Kitty said. 'Thank you for a very special day.' Bet heard the crack of grief in her voice. Then Kitty whispered something into Alexandra's ear that Bet couldn't hear. Bet forced herself to turn away. Alexandra would probably forget, she thought, but for Kitty the memory would stick.

Alexandra looked into Kitty's eyes, then up towards Bet. 'Say thank you,' Bet said.

Kitty pulled Alexandra towards her, hugged her close for what seemed like an age, kissed the top of her head. Then she nodded to Bet and turned to leave.

Bet felt a wave of relief.

It was over.

FIFTY-SEVEN

Kitty ran to the Morris. She found herself thinking about Bet. If Bet was a colour, it would have to be a warm soft orange. A Tuscan burnt orange. Bet radiated a calm energy and Kitty felt glad that Alexandra had such a good person in her life. What colour would Kitty be? she wondered. Green like the sea, sometimes blue, sea green or grey. A mutable palette. She felt herself floating. Inevitably her mind wandered to Henry. She knew how to deal with the grief because she'd done it before but what was to become of them now? Too much had happened.

The Morris was doing its thing again, driving Kitty towards Beecham. She parked neatly to one side by the row of garages and thought about going through the kitchen garden and in through the back door, but she was a stranger now. She didn't get out immediately but looked at the place as a visitor would. It was, she realised, an extraordinary house. The grand proportions seemed to intrude into the landscape, its stone walls Gothic, the mullioned windows, clumsy. The years faded, and there she was, a young girl again, home to see her parents. She realised how she'd let Beecham stop in her mind, somehow believing that nothing would have changed and Saunders would arrive in her mother's old Bristol, but of course Saunders had retired and all Beecham had now was a daily. The Bristol had been sold and in its place a Rover was parked by the stables. A Rover not too dissimilar to the one that had been parked outside the mother and baby home on that fateful day.

Kitty made her way to the front door, ringing the bell, expecting a stranger to welcome her in. The door opened, but it wasn't a stranger, it was her father. She registered the shock on his face.

'Kitty, oh, Kitty.'

Kitty threw herself into his arms and sobbed. His cardigan smelt of tobacco and aftershave, of the library and paper speckled with mould, of everything she had known as a child. The familiarity took her further into her grief, swallowing her whole. His body felt thin and frail and suddenly the wound inside her spiralled open. She sobbed in her father's arms. He held her head like he used to when she was young, his hands rigid with tightened tendons as he stroked her hair. She could hear the dogs barking manically in the kitchen. She had come home.

'My sweet child,' he said. 'How Beecham has missed you.'

'I'm sorry, Daddy. I'm so sorry.'

'Shhh. There is no need.' Gently he placed his hands against her head and let her cry more. Kitty felt as if a great wall inside her was fracturing, bit by bloody bit.

FIFTY-EIGHT

Henry walked along the avenue following the white picket fences, lawns tumbling down into the sidewalk, post boxes punctuating each front garden. The sun was already high at eleven o'clock, the air filled with the hum of insects. The sound of lawnmowers and children playing, someone skating on the sidewalk, made Henry ache with nostalgia, and yet this place was a far cry from the home he remembered living in with his mother and father. Finally, he arrived at number 1079. A small weatherboard house painted an air-force blue. A bed of freshly dug earth was home to a row of heavily laden roses. An apple tree shivered in the breeze, its bright green leaves fresh and perky. He thought perhaps that he'd made a mistake as he walked up the brick-laid path that ribboned up towards a freshly painted white door. He could hear children playing out back and realised of course that they must be on their summer vacation. He rang the bell, heard a woman's voice shouting as a dog barked.

'Will you pipe down, Tolstoy.'

The front door swung open, and a pretty neat woman with short curls and a buttoned-up floral blouse smiled.

'What can I do for you, son?' she said.

'I'm looking for Charlie Roberts,' Henry said.

'So, you're Henry?' She smiled. Her eyes were hazel and warm, and he had the feeling that this woman was happy.

She turned and yelled at the dog again. 'Will you cut it out!' The dog barked and hopped about. Henry could see the animal's shadow through the frosted window of the kitchen door. 'Charlie! It's for you.' She turned back to Henry, put a finger to her mouth and winked. 'He's expecting you tomorrow.'

'Oh, I'm so sorry.'

The woman's face changed slightly, a quizzical frown forming, not unkind but curious. 'Don't be.'

'Charlie! You'd better come down.'

'I'll be right there in a minute.'

Henry recognised his father's voice, although it was less edgy than he remembered, but the deep bass tone, the soft Boston lilt was the same.

'You had better come through,' the woman said. 'I'm Norma by the way, we spoke on the telephone.'

She didn't hold out her hand, but instead beckoned him to follow her into the kitchen, pushing a black-and-white collie away, then grabbing his collar as he jumped up and down making a terrible racket. She guided the dog towards the back door, giving him a gentle push out into the garden. The dog seemed to propel himself onto the expanse of the back yard, and then Henry heard the screams of the kids again.

Norma turned back, offering him a curious look. 'Don't mind them, they're playing with the water fountain. I'll have them all traipsing through this kitchen later, including the dog, making muddy footprints. Gotta be honest, I'll be glad when vacation ends and it's barely started. Can I get you a drink?'

'Sure.' He was amazed how quickly he slipped back into a colloquial tone. How easy it was to lose the Campbell clarity of vowel and consonant in this woman's company.

'I've made some fresh lemonade, but we got some iced tea or a beer if you prefer.'

'A beer would be great,' he said. 'Though the lemonade sounds pretty cool as well.' He heard his father come down the stairs and walk towards the kitchen.

'Hello, son,' his father said. 'I was expecting you tomorrow.'

Henry turned to see Charlie Roberts standing behind him, his frame, his thick blade of salt-and-pepper hair mirroring his own. He recognised in that instant what he had always known: Charlie Roberts was his father and he'd missed him. Somewhere in the past fifteen or so years he'd lost sight of it. His mother had painted a picture so dark, but now he understood that it wasn't his father who was the drunk.

They hugged. Henry realised his father's hands were trembling. Charlie gestured to a kitchen chair, shaking his head, rubbing his chin. 'Gotta be honest, I thought I'd never see you again.' He took off his glasses, leaving a welt on the bridge of his nose.

They both sat down, the sound of the children, the dog, the water sprinkler in the background. Norma was crushing ice in a machine.

'I told him he'd track you down, but we didn't think he'd find you here in the States,' Norma said without looking at either of them. She was pouring the crushed ice into a pitcher. Henry could see the ease between this woman and his father, and understood that they were content and loved each other. But he could see the pain in his father's eyes and believed the pain had something to do with him.

Henry took the tall glass of beer Norma offered.

'Took me a while to find you,' Charlie said. 'I guess when I stopped looking it was easy. I knew it was you as soon as I read the article. It was your voice all grown.'

'I came here to do a Masters, got offered a job.'

'Looks like you did pretty well for yourself. Guess I have Dorothy to thank for that.' He took a swig of his beer. Henry wasn't ready to tell him about his mother just yet, nor did he want to speak of his daughter, although he guessed he already knew if he'd read the article.

'I wrote to you, back then I mean,' his father said. He was looking at Henry with wet eyes. Henry watched him swallow and was reminded of Howard's dogs when they were anxious. 'Guess your mother didn't pass the letters on.'

Henry took a breath. 'Mum died. She passed a few years back.' He watched as his father registered the news. Charlie laid both his palms on the table, shook his head again, then looked to his wife – Henry assumed Norma was his wife – for reassurance. Henry noticed his father's hands and thought how much they were like his own. Not just the shape, the long fingers, but the gestures, the way his little finger, his pinky, was bent.

'Well now, we're sorry to hear that,' Norma said and she rested a hand on Henry's shoulder. Henry understood fully that he wasn't a stranger to this woman, that his father had told her the story probably a thousand times. 'Why don't you take a seat? I think you and your dad have a lot of catching up to do. After that you're going to have to meet your brothers.' She put down the pitcher of lemonade. 'Just in case the beer doesn't quench your thirst.' Norma smiled and her eyes creased up. To Henry, they seemed full of light. 'I'm going to leave you two to it.' Norma went out into the back garden, immediately addressing the kids and the dog. 'I hope you're not making too much mess out here. Tolstoy, will you pipe down!'

Henry turned to his father. He was ready to tell him his story.

FIFTY-NINE

Kitty waited while her father went to fetch the dogs and followed him to the library. She was glad that he'd chosen that room and not the sitting room. There were bits of pottery about the place, and a few badly drawn sketches she'd done as a child. A paperweight she'd made her father while at school, and a photo of them all in the South of France before Henry joined the family. Alexandra would never see any of these things, the fabric of her past.

'I'll get you some tea or would you prefer something stronger?' he asked, walking towards the drinks trolley.

Kitty nodded. 'Is Saunders still in the cottage?'

'Of course.'

'Agnes as well?'

'Agnes still cooks for us, and Lillian comes up from the village every day.'

'Where's Mother?'

Her father looked at her, his eyes watering as his gaze dropped away. 'She's upstairs.'

He lifted the top off the decanter and poured them both a whisky. 'Hasn't moved from the bed for a few weeks now.' Howard's lips wobbled a little. 'She's close to dying, Kitty. That's why I wrote to you.' He handed her a glass, an inch of whisky in the bottom.

Kitty took off her cardigan and threw it across the chaise longue. Weeks had passed since she'd received his letter

335

and yet if felt like years. She looked out into the garden, at the stretch of lawn that was being mowed, the hum of the lawnmower just audible, the willow full and glorious. She had kissed Henry inside the cave of those branches. Beecham felt both odd and familiar, so much life had happened and yet here she was, her father's daughter. Her father's eyes spoke of a sorrow she understood.

'I want to apologise, Kitty,' he said.

'Don't, Pa, please don't say sorry.'

'I'm sorry for everything, Kitty. I didn't really understand how damaged your mother was by the affair I had with Dorothy. Before we go up and see her, there's something you should know.'

'You don't have to tell me, really you don't.'

'No, I must, because I think it will help you understand your mother's actions. I owe it to her, to both of you.'

Kitty nodded, feeling the weight of his words settle in her stomach before he'd even spoken. 'But, Dad, she lied. She told me Henry was seeing someone else. That hurt almost more than the knowledge that Henry could be my half-brother.'

'She was trying to protect you, Kitty. She believed that Henry was mine because Dorothy led us both to believe that was true. It was only speaking to Henry that made me realise that she may have done it in order to survive. I guess we'll never know. Your mother tried to do what was best for Henry, but she asked one thing: that my relationship with Dorothy remained a secret.'

'He's found his father, Daddy.'

'Well, unless we can shed some light on Dorothy's blood group, we'll never know. I know it's hard to understand but let me explain. You see, when Henry came into our lives, I didn't know who he was, but a year or so before then I'd bumped into his mother, Dorothy, in Brighton. I'd been there to have my watch repaired by a jeweller down in the Lanes and Dorothy happened to be in Lyons tea room. I was so shocked to see her sitting alone, I couldn't help walking over to say hello.'

As he spoke, his gaze was so direct that Kitty felt herself tense up.

'That was my first mistake.'

'I don't understand,' she said.

'You were eleven at the time and I don't know what I was thinking, but I was so glad to see her.'

Kitty watched as her father contemplated his next sentence. Beads of sweat glistened on his forehead. Instinctively she went to the window and threw it open. The smell of freshly cut grass filled the room. She could see the gardener out on the lawn pushing the mower across it, his body leaning forward. It was late for him to be working. She watched him labour in the soft evening light while her father spoke, knowing that her distraction would ease her father's confession.

'I started seeing her again. I don't know why, I suppose Dorothy was someone I couldn't resist and your mother and I . . .' He coughed. 'Well our relationship was not in good shape. Dorothy told me about leaving Charlie Roberts. God, there was something about that woman and I let my guard down.'

She turned to see why her father had stopped talking. He shook his head, his eyes wide open and for an instant she saw him as a man, not her father but a stranger who had lived a life she knew nothing about. He mopped his forehead with his handkerchief.

'Your mother was so difficult to please and Dorothy, well I guess she made me feel better about myself. It didn't last long. We spent the odd day together walking along the seafront, eating whelks, playing on the slot machines. I felt as if I was free for the first time in years. When she finally told me about a child, I was so taken aback by the fact she'd never mentioned it before that I didn't think to question it. She told me that was why she'd left Charlie. Of course I asked to meet my son, but she said it wasn't a good idea. Then, quite be chance, your mother found out about Dorothy and me – apparently a mutual friend had spotted us on West pier – so I was forced to end it. It was only when Henry came here for tea one day, we had a picnic out in the garden, and he told us all about how he'd come from America, that I slowly put two and two together, and so did your mother: Dorothy had moved to Steyning on purpose.'

Kitty remembered the first time she met Henry, the picnic in the garden. She'd bolted out of the French windows, running at full pelt and dropped with a thud onto the rug out of breath and sweaty. Clarissa's shoulders tensed up.

'How many times have I told you, Kitty, it's not lady-like to run?'

'But she's a child,' Howard said.

'Sit up, darling, and do try to eat sensibly,' Clarissa said as she pulled at Kitty's skirt to cover her knees.

Henry sat cross-legged on the tartan rug. Kitty watched her father's eyes settle on his scuffed shoes and bruised knees. The bees were feeding off the honeysuckle adding to the air of indolence.

Tom said, 'Henry lives in one of the cottages by the river.'

Kitty was irritated by how grown-up he sounded in the company of their parents.

338

'Recently moved here, have you?' Howard said. He closed his book and put it on the ground beside him, leaning forward as if to get a closer look at Henry's face.

'Yes, sir,' Henry said.

'Oh, do call him Howard,' Clarissa said.

Kitty looked from one to the other, observing her parents' naked curiosity.

'We were living in Boston but my mother wanted to come back home,' he said.

'In Boston?' Clarissa said, handing Henry a plate of sandwiches.

'Yep, my mother is English but my father's American.'

Henry didn't look at Kitty, he was clearly shy and she felt mildly irritated by his inability to acknowledge her.

'This is Henry,' Clarissa said. 'Tom's new friend.' There was a sharpness to her tone.

Finally, he said, 'Hello,' and bit into his sandwich.

'Hello,' Kitty said. She felt herself blush, knowing her cheeks were probably crimson.

'So, your father has work here?' Howard asked, accepting a cup and saucer that Saunders had given him. His hand shook so that the cup rattled a little.

'Don't worry, Saunders, we're quite able to help ourselves,' Clarissa said.

Henry turned to Tom's father. 'No, sir, my mother and I came back alone.'

A flicker of interest passed across Howard's face before he said, 'You're a brave boy, can't be easy coming back to England. One hears such stories of success coming from America.'

'Yes, sir,' Henry said. 'I've promised my father that one day I'll make him proud.' He smiled again. Kitty watched Tom shuffle around in his infectious confidence, but her father was frowning. 'What's your father's name?' he asked.

'Charlie Roberts.'

'And your mother?' Clarissa asked.

'Dorothy.' It was then Howard and Clarissa exchanged a knowing look. Kitty could sense a storm brewing inside her mother's head.

The lawnmower stopped just outside the window. She realised her father was still talking, so she went to close it.

'Of course it was clear Dorothy had deliberately chosen to be close to Beecham. The whole thing was a set-up.' He looked up at her, the shame visible in his eyes. 'By that time, Henry and Tom had become friends. But, when Dorothy realised I wasn't going to leave your mother, she became frustrated. She accused me of using her, but it wasn't like that. I suppose she felt rejected. We humans often act from some unrecognisable dark place we don't understand. I was lost and so was she. Some part of me never stopped loving her. But it was simply too late.'

'Mum told me about you and Dorothy, but she never mentioned that you were seeing her when Henry came into our lives,' Kitty said, wrenching free from the memory of her mother that day in the studio when she'd painted that thick red splotch of paint in protest.

'She probably didn't tell you, because she didn't want *you* to lose the idea of a perfect father. Your mother worked hard to keep up appearances. For whatever reason it was important to her that the world saw us as perfect.'

'So, when I saw you and Dorothy in the garden, what were you arguing about?'

Howard ran his hands over his face. 'I had no idea you'd witnessed that.'

'I've never been able to shift the image of you both that day. The way you looked at each other. It felt wrong.'

'She wanted me to leave your mother, and I wasn't able to do that. I'd hurt your mother enough, and I couldn't bear to leave any of you.'

Kitty sighed. She would never forget the sight of Alexandra as she waved goodbye. She felt the tears slip down her cheek.

'So, you see when you got pregnant with Henry's child it was the worst thing that could have happened to your mother. She believed he was my son and I think in some way she couldn't bear the idea of our past infecting your life. Weird thing is she was determined to do the right thing by him.' He took out his handkerchief and patted his brow. 'It's all my fault.' Her father was standing with his hands hanging limply by his side, his jowls loose with age.

'Dorothy was broken by gossip,' he said. 'I've lived with that knowledge for years. You see, the first time around I chose your mother because my father insisted, but there was something about Dorothy, that smile. She could've ended the war with it. When she came back into my life it was like a breath of fresh air. She made me feel so alive . . .' He walked to the window, brushing away a cobweb that had formed.

'We all make mistakes, Kitty. I've spent years regretting not standing up to my father, and your mother has spent years regretting her actions towards you. She's going to die soon. It would be good if you could let her go peacefully.'

'You can't possibly know the pain I've suffered,' Kitty said.

'All parents suffer their children's woes.'

'Irony is that Henry believes he's found his father,' she said.

'Has he? Are you sure?'

'He seems pretty certain.'

'I take it he's told you about the blood test?'

'Mum told me about the blood test.' Kitty felt an ache grow inside her chest. 'It was inconclusive.'

'Yes, we needed to know Dorothy's blood group, which of course is impossible now that she's dead.' He bowed his head. 'I think in some ways I wanted Henry to be my son, but if Charlie *is* his father, then you have my blessing. I, of all people, know how important it is to be with the person you love.'

'It's too late for that.'

'I made a mistake, Kitty. And there's always a price.'

'Why did I have to the pay the price?'

'We all did,' he said. 'In some way.'

'In what way has Tom paid?'

'He lost a sister when he needed her most.'

'That wasn't my fault.'

'No, but it was your choice.' Kitty drank a bit of the whisky, trying to digest the conversation. She wondered what Alexandra would be doing now, whether Bet would read her a story, put her smiling stone in pride of place.

'I went to see her today,' she said. 'My baby, I mean, well she's three now. Her name is Alexandra. I've been in touch with the mother.'

Her father looked at her, his eyes watery and unsure. 'Is that a good idea, Kitty?'

'Don't worry, it was the last time.' And then she began to cry. 'She really is the most beautiful little girl. So full of life.'

'Just like you.'

'And Dorothy, perhaps?'

'Your mother was joyful once. Life is hard for everyone, Kitty.' He went and sat next to her on the chaise longue, putting his heavy arms around her shoulders. 'I know you won't believe it now, but you will heal.'

They sat like that, the two of them, the evening sun pooling into the room. Kitty sensed the possibility of something fresh and new.

'Shall we go up?'

Kitty nodded.

'It's almost supper time so there's a chance she's awake. She eats upstairs these days. Agnes usually makes soup.' He drank his whisky. 'I'm beginning to love that first drink better than any other,' he said.

Kitty saw her father's pain, and felt the sharp jab of her own. She would never forget the way her daughter waved goodbye, as if to a stranger.

SIXTY

Henry couldn't believe how easy it was to talk with his father. They went to the beach for a walk while Norma made lunch, on Norma's insistence. He realised how unaccustomed he was to this laid-back way of being. His father was never much of a talker, but Henry found walking beside his dad relaxed him. He took long strides, and always seemed to have his hands in his pockets unless he was throwing stones, which he was doing now, crouching low, his feet spread wide, skimming them across the surface.

'You remember when I taught you to do this.'

'Sure, I was hopeless at it.'

'Here,' his father said. 'You need to flick your wrist and use your finger to spin it so that it jumps.'

Henry picked up a stone. The beach was sandy, with long tufts of marram sticking out between the dunes, but there were a few pebbles closer to the shore. He showed his father the stone, remembering now how his father used to inspect them.

His father's face broke open into a smile. 'So you *do* remember.'

Henry crouched down, turned his body to the side, his father's words coming back to him. How old would he have been? Six or seven. It must have been just before they came back to England. He sent it off and it spun and danced across the sea.

'I think you've been practising.' His father laughed, patting him on the back. Henry thought for the first time in a while about his future. The fact that he'd found his father changed everything.

'So tell me about this girl,' his father said. 'And you have a daughter, which means I have a grandchild.'

Henry didn't want to discuss a child he might never meet. He'd put that part aside, but he knew he'd have to face it at some point.

'Kitty's beautiful, full of life, sometimes a little quirky but she has something, you know?' he said.

'Sure do.' His father laughed. 'Is she kind?'

Henry wondered if he was thinking about Norma, or maybe his mother. 'She *was* free as a bird until . . .' He sighed, this was why he was here after all. He looked into his father's eyes and saw concern. 'She got pregnant.' His father's face was serious, as if attuned to every sentiment Henry felt. 'She is kind, it's just she had to give our daughter away.'

'Well I kinda guessed something bad had happened from your article.'

Henry looked out at the sea, at the Atlantic waves rolling into the shore, the swell more menacing this side of the Atlantic. He turned to face his father, as steadily as he could. 'She thinks I'm her half-brother. Her father had an affair with Mum before I was born.'

His father screwed his face up in consternation. 'Oh, yes. I remember it well. I gave her an ultimatum. But there is no doubt in my mind that you're my child.'

'Well, Mum told Kitty's father that *he* was my father, not you. I suspect she did it to extract money out of him.'

His father shook his head. 'That's typical of your mother, I'm afraid. If only she'd have answered my letters. I said I was able to send her money. That I didn't bear a grudge.'

Henry nodded. 'So obviously her parents are none too happy.' Henry thought about Clarissa. He'd been angry about so many things but she'd made sure there was a roof over his head when it mattered. It was as if the act of finding his father allowed the anger to dissipate.

'I think Mum saw it as a way to care for me, give me the best.' He looked up at his father who was an inch taller than he was. 'I don't want you to think ill of her.'

'Well, you can't blame her for wanting the best for you, but that's a pretty big lie, son.'

'Thing is, Kit believes it's true and I need a blood test to prove you're my father and I'm not her half-brother, but it's not even that simple.'

His father picked up a stone that was round and flat and stained with sea salt. He crouched down and sent the thing spinning across the water, jumping eight times or more. Henry lost count. 'The war did things to people, son,' he said. 'A lot of people survived but they forgot how to live. Your mother loved the war, it meant she could work, and she was a good-time girl, that was for sure. Popular as well.'

'Norma seems lovely,' Henry said.

'Oh sure, she's steady, a good woman, which is exactly what I need.'

Henry looked out to sea, the roar of the waves was soothing and he felt himself break open. 'Will you do a blood test?' he asked. He wasn't asking for himself, he was asking for Kitty and he hoped his father could see that.

'Sure, I can do that.' Charlie nodded. Henry could not be sure if he was offended or not, but after a minute he pressed his hand to his chest. 'But I know you're my son. I know it right here.'

Henry found it difficult to look at him. He felt it too, but it was hard sometimes to feel the same as

346

someone, and anyway it wasn't necessarily going to make a difference.

He blinked and looked at the sky. 'Problem is, we need to know Mum's blood group as well.'

His father stopped scouring the beach and looked up. 'Oh, that's easy. She's O rhesus negative. I remember because it caused complications when she was pregnant with you. Think I even kept the paperwork.'

And just like that his father solved the biggest mystery of Henry's life. He could prove Howard was not his father.

SIXTY-ONE

Kitty climbed the stairs, the familiar smell of wood polish and summer flora filling her with nostalgia. She felt her stomach tighten as her father lumbered past her and opened the door to their bedroom. She held back, instinctively knowing that her father would need time to explain Kitty's arrival. She waited by the window and looked out at the willow, the lake, the tennis court which hadn't been used in years. Her childhood was out there like a ghost.

And then her father was by her side. 'Your mother is ready,' he said. 'The nurse has just changed her sheets.'

Kitty turned and followed him. Instead of the anger she'd felt for so many years, she felt overwhelmed with a sense of loss: for her daughter, for a time when she thought her life would be filled with promise, and for the blind hope that had plagued her the past few years. But now she was crossing an unknown threshold. She took a deep breath.

The bedroom was cool and in darkness, just a crack of light divided the room. A nurse was tucking her mother into freshly laundered sheets. She turned as they walked in, gathering up the laundry.

'She's due her painkillers in half an hour,' she said. 'I'll be back then.'

Clarissa was lying on her back, her skin yellowed with jaundice, her cheekbones rising up from her face like polished stones. Her lips were pale and dry. Howard walked

348

to the bedside and dipped a sponge into water, wetting her lips, letting the liquid trickle into Clarissa's mouth. Kitty felt the wrench of regret as she took her mother's hand. Her father was right, there was no time left for hatred or anger.

'Kitty is here, Clary,' her father said.

Her mother frowned but didn't open her eyes. 'It's the morphine,' her father said. 'She has good and bad moments.' Her father got up, drew back the curtains a little, letting a patch of dusk colour the carpet. He went to the chest of drawers and pulled open the top right-hand drawer. 'She asked me to give you this, should you not arrive in time.' He handed her a big brown album. Kitty, realising it was heavy, stood up and held it with both hands. She sat down on a chair beside her mother's bed. The stillness in the bedroom was interrupted by a cat fight in the garden.

Clarissa's eyes opened, milky yellow and unfocused. She turned her head towards Kitty and smiled, a slow shift that changed the shape of her face from oval to round. She lifted her hand, her arthritic fingers stretched out. Kitty took them.

'Thank you,' Clarissa said, and then closed her eyes again.

'I'll make us a pot of tea.'

Her father took small steps as he made his way downstairs. Kitty was left with her mother, and the pain inside she'd felt since leaving Alexandra seemed to spread as she listened to the rasp of her mother's breath and the birds outside, probably at war with the cat.

With her other hand she turned the pages. The album was filled with pictures of family lunches. Tom's children running around in the garden with the dogs, Anne pregnant. An Easter egg hunt down by the lake. The Christmases she'd missed. At the back were clippings her mother had collected of Kitty's recent art show, critics appraisals and a catalogue. Kitty kept turning the pages, seeing how her absence had been tracked. She was surprised by one of her mother alone by an easel, smiling at the camera, paint brush in her hands. There was a photograph of Alexandra that Bet must have sent. The letter slipped out at the end along with a photograph of Alexandra.

She looked at her mother, who nodded. Speaking slowly, she explained. 'I got in touch with Bet. Read it, darling. It was easier for me to write those words then, than speak them now.'

Kitty nodded. 'I will,' she said.

'Please read it now,' her mother said.

My Dear Kitty,

I know how angry you have been but look at what you have achieved. You have so much talent. I wanted the best for you but these last three years I can see that wasn't my right. We live our lives. We make mistakes. I have lived with regret. Love is love, however it is felt. It is messy, tangled up by our own needs and fears. How it is given is not always how we would want to give it. I was filled with a fear that didn't belong to you or your daughter and I am sorry. I was filled with spite at your father's rejection and the actions of a woman you barely knew. When I asked your father why he chose Dorothy, he told me he had fallen for her smile. Funnily enough, it was when Henry came into our lives that I lost my own.

I am deeply sorry for not supporting you. I am sorry that you've felt anger for all these years. I am sorry that I lost you and you lost your daughter. I am sorry that I shall never meet her.

Be happy my dearest child. I am your mother. Nothing can change that.

Love, Ma x

Kitty sobbed quietly and stroked Clarissa's hand, watching a tear roll down her mother's temple.

'Thank you,' Kitty said.

'I love you,' her mother said, the words barely formed, a whisper.

'I know,' Kitty answered. And in that moment she did know. She knew love wasn't always perfect. Kitty held her mother's hand and watched as the blotches on her palm spread.

SIXTY-TWO

August

Henry realised how much time had passed and how much he'd changed as soon as he arrived at Beecham to find several expensive cars parked in the driveway. The polished gloss of money meant nothing to him any more. He didn't need to ring the bell. The front door was ajar. The murmur of hushed voices became apparent as soon as he walked into the hallway. Saunders arrived with his usual dignity, a nod of the head acknowledging the years that had passed since they last saw each other. Henry was shocked to see that he'd grown old these past few years.

'Would you like me to take your coat, Mr Roberts?'

'I'm fine, I'll leave my case here seeing as I don't know what room I'm staying in.'

'I believe you have the main guest room, Mr Roberts. I'll see to it.' Saunders offered him a knowing smile.

Henry walked down the hallway, struck by the sense of occasion. He felt Clarissa's absence despite the crowd of people gathered in the sitting room. The room was a fug of chatter, the clink of glasses, the hum of mourning. He walked in feeling invisible, and then he saw Kitty next to Howard, petite and vulnerable. She looked up and smiled, a real smile, free of inhibition. This was the mother of his child, a child he'd probably never meet.

'Henry.' She broke free and strode towards him, her arms spread open before falling into an embrace. She didn't appear to notice everyone watching, probably startled by the inappropriate nature of her greeting. 'You came.'

'Of course.' He kissed the top of her head.

'I thought you wouldn't make it.'

'I sent you a telegram.' He took her hand. 'Tom asked me to speak.'

'I didn't receive anything.' He felt the lightness of her touch, their fingers entwined until she pulled away.

'I sent it to the Kensington address.' Henry had sent it from the office before leaving for the airport.

'I've been here, with my family.'

He seemed unable to say anything, words felt utterly inadequate. He acknowledged Howard. Howard dipped his head slowly, raised his hand. A feeling of gratitude surprised Henry. These people had cared for him in their messy way. Kitty led him towards her father, and just then Tom turned to embrace him, his hand patting Henry on the back in that old school chum manner he'd never lose. Tom's face bore the signs of worry and responsibility, but it suited him.

'I am so glad you could come,' he said.

'How could I not?' Because of Clarissa he had become a Campbell after all, and he'd been luckier than most. 'You asked me to speak,' he said. 'I wondered if you wanted to cast your eyes over this.' He pulled out the pages he had tucked into his jacket pocket. Tom looked down at the fingered pages that Henry had scrawled out while on the plane.

'No, I trust you,' he said.

Anne, an infant in her arms, their third child, gave him a peck on the cheek. 'You've made Tom's day,' she whispered.

'I am so sorry,' Henry said when he eventually arrived at Howard's side. Howard nodded.

'So am I,' he said. 'She was fond of you, you know. None of this was your fault.'

Saunders cut his way through the huddle of mourners and whispered something in Tom's ear.

'It's time, everyone.'

'Stay by my side,' Kitty said. 'Please.' She looped her arm around Henry's and they walked down the panelled hallway together, the smell of lavender wafting up from the garden.

★

Kitty had wept during the service, Georgie by her side, but the tears had felt honest and she was glad of them. After the funeral, while everyone gathered for the wake in the drawing room with the French windows opening out onto the garden, the striped lawn, the smell of rosemary and lavender and sweet honeysuckle, Henry and Kitty walked down to the boat house. Kitty couldn't quite believe that after three years apart, after all that had happened, they still shared that ability to read each other's mind, communicate without words. They made their way down to the end of the jetty in step, and sat down, their bodies brushing against each other. They sat like that for a while, feet dangling off the end, their silence a blessing.

The lake was as it always was, alive with insects, dragonflies gliding across it, occasionally cracking the dust-covered surface. The lilies were in bloom, the roses fully blown. Kitty longed to strip herself down and dive into the water. She wanted to be alive again.

'It's quite extraordinary isn't it, how life is so persistent even in the face of death? It seems almost rude,' she said.

'I couldn't quite believe how many people were there,' he said. 'That church was empty when my mother was buried.'

'Mother was a member of every committee from here to the Isle of Wight, it's hardly a measure of success. She was a member of the Women's Institute, for heaven's sake. The church was full of people I didn't even know.'

'Some people can go through life and touch so many people's lives, and others can get to the end of their life only having destroyed everything they touched.'

'Your mother did what she could, Henry. I understand her better than anyone. She was human, she was a mother struggling to give you the best. She protected you with lies, as my mother did.'

Henry frowned, brought his hands up to his face. 'She made so many mistakes.'

Kitty thought how elegant his hands were, his long fingers, the span of them. She had always loved his hands, it was his gift to a daughter he'd never met. She prised one free and held it. She was ready.

'I had a child,' she said. 'A daughter, our daughter. Her name is Alexandra.' She felt the release of honesty, and it was only when she'd spoken their child's name that she could look at him. His eyes reached into hers, and she felt for the first time that their love was tangible and real.

'I know,' he said. 'Tom told me, but please don't be angry with him. Because of that I wrote an article about what is was to have a child I didn't know, and what it was to want desperately to find my father. Because of that article my father found me.' He looked away, shook his head, and she was surprised that she didn't feel angry with Tom. She didn't feel angry with anyone.

355

'She *is* beautiful, and well cared for. I will tell you the story, but for now, let's just sit here.' She turned and pointed to the boat house. 'This is where she was conceived.'

'It makes me sad to know I will never know her,' he said.

'She will know of you,' she said, 'one day.'

The sound of summer surrounded them, a dog barking, the murmur of the mourners and the occasional outbreak of laughter, the buzz of insects.

'Tell me what happened,' he said.

She gripped his hand tightly, willing herself to stay composed.

'My mother convinced me of so many things: that you were seeing someone else, that by telling you I would force you into a marriage you didn't want and finally that there was a possibility we were brother and sister. Because I was frightened and ashamed, I let her words carve *our* future, and *our daughter's* future. She even went as far as finding our daughter a suitable couple, people who the mother and baby home approved of. But when it came to the moment of handing her over I couldn't do it. I wanted to know that she was with the right kind of people. So I left her on the doorstep of a woman I'd met once, Henry.'

'Who?'

'A woman called Bet. You see, she'd lost her child and it seemed right somehow. She was warm and comforting. Everything the Campbells are not.' She dipped her head, took a breath. 'They kept her, but I kept going back to check she was okay because I couldn't let our daughter go. That's how far from reason I strayed. It was only when I came back here that I realised that my mother was full of fear and I'd allowed her fear to infect my life. She believed you were my brother and that wasn't her fault.'

She looked up to see that Henry was crying, probably because she couldn't. They were passing grief between them, this mantle of love and life they had no idea what to do with.

'Now, forgiveness is all we have,' she said.

'Is that what *you* did, forgive your mother?'

'I had nothing left, Henry. There was nowhere else to go other than acceptance. As I watched my mother fade away, I realised that it wasn't just that I didn't want to lose our daughter, it was that I couldn't accept the pain that loss entailed. Confronted by my mother's death, I had nowhere to hide. By facing the pain, I felt suddenly free, if that makes sense. And that was how I was able to forgive and accept.' Henry slid his other hand across her lap and cupped them both in his. Kitty thought about Alexandra, how one day she would have to ask her for forgiveness for giving her up. They sat watching the water, relishing this moment by the boat house where it all began.

'And the child, is she happy?'

Kitty broke free, thought for a minute, remembering Bet waiting for them both at the bottom of the helter skelter, scooping up Alexandra into a warm embrace. 'Yes, yes, she is.' She picked at a tuft of grass, hiding her tears from him.

He dug into his pocket, wrenching out a sheet of paper. 'I have the results of a blood test here.' He flattened out the sheet with his hand. 'It seems my father and I share the same blood type, B. Your father is AB, but my mother is O rhesus negative, and that means that my father would have had to be a B or an A.'

'I see,' she said, although she didn't quite understand. 'It sounds extremely complicated. What does it mean?'

'It means Charlie Roberts is my father, and Howard is your father and definitely not mine.' She hadn't expected this.

'Does my father know?'

'I'm about to tell him. Kit, I knew he wasn't my father.' He stabbed the piece of paper with his index finger. 'I just knew and this is the proof.' He folded up the paper, tucked it into his jacket pocket. 'We could get our daughter back, Kit.'

She looked at Henry. He was so familiar to her, and yet she felt as if she couldn't reach him suddenly.

'No,' she said. 'That would not be the right thing to do, not now, not ever. She needs stability, and besides, it would break Bet's heart and our daughter's heart as well.'

She watched him process the thought of his daughter, that lock of hair that refused to stay in place. She reached out and touched it. His eyes met hers.

'There is no one else, Kit. There never will be,' he said.

'You say that now, but . . .'

'No, I know there will never be anybody like you.'

Kitty turned and blinked the tears away.

'Come to America with me,' he said. 'We could start again.'

Kitty looked down into her lap. Her black dress was covered in dust. She could hear the mourners talking, the purr of their voices floating towards her. She had left her father and Tom to it. 'We had better get back,' she said. She got up, brushed herself down.

'When is your flight?'

'Thursday,' he said.

'But that's in two days.'

'I know. It was that or not come at all.'

Henry stood up, his hands wedged into his pockets. She noticed the creases around his mouth. He walked towards the boat house. Kitty followed, knowing now that people would be missing her, feeling the need to conform, perhaps for the first time in her life. The door to the boat house was open. Henry snatched her hand, stepped inside into the dusty interior that smelt of wood and varnish. The memory of that night Alexandra was conceived came back to her unbidden, or perhaps it was bidden by Henry.

He pulled her towards him, held her face in his hands. She tried to look away but his eyes demanded her attention. Then all the years of unspoken feeling filled the space, their desire unleashed, clashing against the memory of that one night and the loss of their child. When he kissed her she felt as if something inside her snapped.

'I have wanted to do that from the minute I saw you,' he said. 'I will always love you, Kit, you need to know that.'

Her heart was beating fast. Something was unravelling deep inside her. She wasn't ready for more tears and yet there they were. She led them both out of the boat house and they walked towards the others waving as Tom gestured for them to hurry.

SIXTY-THREE

Henry sat beside Tom two days later, tapping his fingers on the armrest, anxious about the time and, of course, Kitty. Tom cut through the traffic with a sense of urgency. Marble Arch was a horror show, people cutting in front of them, hurtling around the monument as if it were a race track. London seemed hot and humid, Hyde Park appeared burnt, the grass parched and brittle. Henry thought about his daughter who was somewhere out there in the world, cared for by strangers. Kitty had shown him a photograph of her with Alexandra on the pier, but it was hard for him to fully embrace her as his daughter – she was a stranger to him. Besides, how could he reconcile himself to the joy and the pain her birth had caused?

'I hope you come back soon. Seems a pity the children won't get to see much of their uncle,' Tom said. 'They are your niece and nephews, of a kind,' he said, 'even if it is no longer official.'

'I know,' Henry said. 'And I will make a point of honouring my role.' He wondered if Tom's promise to go out and see him would ever come to anything. With the cost of four extra air tickets to consider, it seemed unlikely.

'You'll be Uncle Henry,' Tom said, smiling. Henry knew that Tom was attempting to keep things jolly but he wasn't in the mood to pretend that everything was okay.

'I keep thinking about this child,' Henry said.

'I know. I know. Is that why you're tense?' Tom said. He turned to face him, just as a car cut in front on them.

'Watch out!' Henry said.

Tom swerved and zipped down past the palace, not even bothering to indicate.

'It's Kitty, isn't it?'

Henry was quietly impressed by Tom's intuition. 'Shouldn't you have taken that turning?' he asked.

'Don't try and change the subject.'

'She hasn't said yes, and she hasn't said no. I spoke to her last night and she said that if she decided to come, she'd see me at the airport. Does that mean she's booked a flight?'

'Oh, I'm so glad to hear my sister is showing no signs of turning into a considerate human being.'

Henry laughed. 'Only you, as her brother, have the right to sarcasm.'

★

Kitty had packed everything up into a trunk and had given Georgie instructions regarding the removal company, along with a key. She and Alan were due any minute and Kitty had one thing left to do. She sat down at her kitchen table and pulled out the Basildon Bond pad and her mother's fountain pen.

Dear Bet,

I thought I should let you know that I am about to leave for New York. I'm not sure how long I will be. It could be months, or years. It rather depends. Please give Alexandra a hug, tell her that I am going in part for her, for all of you. I want to leave you all in peace and I

*think the distance will help. Please tell her that I am
going to be with her father, it turns out we're not related
after all, which I had thought to be true at one point.
Please tell her also that she was born out of love. There
is so much I want to say but I won't.*

*I have enclosed several addresses: my childhood home,
which I believe you already know, my gallery and my
best friend, Georgie, should anything happen.*

Thank you, for everything.
With love,

Kitty Campbell

Epilogue

Mother's Day, 2019

Ally took the letter her mother passed to her and opened it, smoothing it out and looking at her hands as if they were new hands that had just been gifted to her by a father she never knew. All those years wondering why her brother had inherited features and some gestures from his parents and she hadn't. Her hands were nothing like her parents' hands and now she understood why. She remembered how her cousins had joked about her being delivered by a stork that was drunk. Had they known? There were so many questions that needed answering.

She read the letter again: *please tell her that she was born out of love*. A feeling of peace swept over her, followed by a well of sadness.

She had never felt so confused.

The paper was yellowed and the ink faded, but Kitty's handwriting was what struck her most: it was just like her own, slanting slightly forward with looped letters and long-tailed 'y's. A woman she couldn't remember, her mother, loved her and missed her. Ally had never felt so bereft, so disorientated and lost.

The crowds had thinned and the light had faded to a soft dusky pink. She could see her reflection in the window, and her mother, her dear mother, sturdy and reliable, who had fought hard for her, sitting opposite. Outside the Thames was an inky ribbon of darkness.

She wondered what would happen next.

Her mother handed her another photograph of Kitty Campbell and a man she assumed was her father. He was tall, with thick dark hair and dark eyes. He had one hand around Kitty's waist and the other hung limply at his side. Hands with long fingers like her own. Kitty was dressed in a short bridal gown, a veil sticking out stiffly from an ornately dressed bun on top of her head. They were both smiling, but she could see her mother was hesitant. These were her parents and she felt something crack inside her. Grief for their absence from her life. She couldn't imagine how Kitty felt having walked away from her child. She thought of the many women across the world forced to do the same. The blunt pain she felt was familiar, a pain she'd carried and not fully understood.

There was still no sign of the children, Rob must have stopped off for a bite to eat, she thought. Her mother reached for her hand.

'Will you forgive me?' she said. Her voice was shaky.

'For what?'

'For leaving it so long?'

'Mum, you were scared, and you didn't want anything to change. Forgiveness is a given. I just feel so utterly blown apart and I'm sorry, because that's no reflection on my love for you. I just don't know who I am any more. I don't think I ever did.'

'Well, you're a wife and a mother to two exceptionally brave children for a start. And you're our daughter, and Kitty and Henry's love child as well. They never forgot you.'

Ally ached with the idea of these two strangers knowing she was out there in the world without them. 'I do want to meet Kitty, and I want to meet Henry too.'

Her mother's lips puckered. 'Oh, Ally, Henry died a few months ago. Not long after your father went, actually.'

Ally felt a stab of sadness she didn't quite understand. 'Oh, I see.' She poured them both a glass of water. Her mother took her glass and swallowed it down.

'I was thirsty,' she said, and then her mouth wobbled as she went to speak. 'Did you really feel the odd one out?'

'Oh, I've been going on about feeling the odd one out for years. Antony and I are so different if you think about it. Rob even said he wondered if Antony was adopted because we look nothing like each other. I said it was probably me and we laughed. Can you believe that?'

Her mother dipped her head. 'If it weren't for this exhibition, I might have avoided telling you again, and it's not fair on you, or on Kitty either. She's waited long enough.'

'Does Antony know?'

'No, he doesn't, and it's up to you if you want to tell him.'

Ally's phone pinged. *Had to stop off for food. On way home now. Rx.* She loved the way he always signed it R, when it couldn't possibly be anyone else. Why do we love people's flaws? she wondered. 'I *would* like to meet Kitty,' she said again.

Bet nodded. 'I'm glad,' she said and picked up her phone, stabbing the keys with arthritic fingers. She had always been proud of her lack of fear around technology and as she sat opposite Ally, frowning and puckering her lips, Ally felt a deep wave of love. This was her mother and she was proud.

Ally leaned forward and touched her mother's wrist. 'Happy Mother's Day, Mum, and thank you.'

Kitty sat on the four-poster bed in the hotel room wondering why the walls were covered in green fabric. She understood that somehow this was to give the hotel a feeling of opulence but to her it was simply anachronistic. Her phone pinged. A lifeline to the world outside. She'd expected it to be one of her sons but it was a message from Bet.

She wants to meet you. Call me tomorrow, Bet x.

Kitty called Georgie. 'She's agreed to see me,' she said.

'What, not even a hello?'

'Hello,' Kitty said.

'Darling, that's wonderful, I'm so happy for you. Really I am.'

'You don't sound happy,' Kitty said.

There was a moment's silence on the other end of the phone. Kitty imagined her friend sitting in her cottage in Wales. That sweet little front room that was littered with artefacts, stones found on the beach, bits of bark, anything that Georgie could steal from nature and use for inspiration.

'I just don't want you to build your hopes up, that's all.'

'It's not hope this time,' Kitty said. 'It's belief.'

'Good.'

Kitty could hear Georgie rubbing at some piece of wood, smoothing it down as she spoke. 'What are you doing, you're making an awful racket?'

'Sorry, I'm finishing this piece for you to take back.'

'I hope it doesn't weigh a ton, you know how the airlines are these days.' Georgie's dogs had started to bark. She tried not to be irritated. Right now she needed Georgie all to herself.

'Be quiet will you!' Georgie screamed. 'Kitty.'

'What is it?' Kitty asked, an anxious feeling bubbling up, making her want to raid the mini bar.

'Just don't expect her to love you straight away, that's all.'

Kitty knew that Georgie was right. That she had no right to expect anything of her daughter other than curiosity. Georgie had promised to come and stay in London for a couple of days and suddenly Kitty wanted her to come right now. 'You're still coming to the show in Cork Street, aren't you?'

'I told you, yes. Apart from anything else, Alan and I want to meet your daughter,' Georgie said.

'Do you think she'll come?'

'Yes. Besides, how else am I going to give this present to you?'

Kitty was reminded of her wedding day at the registry office in Brooklyn on 5th May 1967. Georgie and Alan had flown over from England. Georgie had carried her sculpture by hand, holding it on her lap all the way.

Henry had brought a friend along from the *New York Times*, his father, Norma, his father's wife, and his two brothers, who fought the whole day long. Her own father was living in Kenya by that time but he sent them both his blessing. Tom and Anne made their excuses – a child with chicken pox – but privately Kitty had been glad to have a Campbell-free wedding. She bought a cream dress with lace sleeves and a stand-up collar. She had her hair pinned up with flowers tucked into the bun, a short veil and satin shoes.

As the registrar pronounced them man and wife, Henry squeezed her hand, brought it up to his lips and kissed her wedding ring.

'I have loved you always,' he said. 'And will do so forever.'

And he had.

They had twin boys in March 1973. They were ten years younger than Alexandra, both married, now with children of their own. She so wanted Ally to meet them so that Kitty's life was no longer divided into two halves: before and after Ally was born.

★

Bet heard the telephone ringing and frowned. She was exhausted from her day with Ally at the Hayward Gallery and had woken up late. She'd just settled down to last week's accounts. Her finger was blackened with the ink that had leaked from her pen. It hadn't been a good morning. She looked down and admired her new camel trousers, checking to see that the ink hadn't left any trace. When Samuel had died she'd been shocked by how well he'd prepared for her future. She'd known he was a risk taker, but she hadn't really understood his capacity to prepare for the worst. She'd presumed she was in charge of the safety nets, but no, Samuel had covered that area of their life as well.

The phone continued ringing. She thought she would leave it, but its persistent peal made her wonder if it might be important. Anyone sane would have given up by now, and then she remembered Kitty. She'd allowed herself to forget.

'Hello.'

'Bet, is that you?'

Bet recognised Kitty's voice instantly. She'd heard it on Radio Four only weeks before, the way the words glided out of her mouth as if each were covered in soap. When she finally heard that Kitty had become a well-known painter, Bet had wondered why she'd never mentioned this in her letters. But the vulnerability in her voice was unmistakable. It was the same voice as the girl on the pier, just older. She remembered a few days after that day in Brighton finding Alexandra in their hotel bedroom with a shell held up to her ear.

'The sea,' she'd said. She'd carried that shell around for days afterwards, then it almost got forgotten in the hotel bathroom but Bet had picked it up and given it to Ally along with the letters and the photographs.

'Is that you, Kitty?' Bet asked, feeling braver as the seconds passed.

Bet had thought many times of all the things she would say to Kitty, but now she was speechless. For so many years now they had only written to each other.

Bet looked in the mirror and flicked her fringe to the side, remembering the painting with the red splotch tearing in a sea of blue.

'So, is she okay?' Kitty asked.

'Yes, she took it well,' Bet said and quite unexpectedly she cried. 'It's good to hear from you, Kitty.'

*

Kitty had waited for over sixty years to hear her daughter's voice again, but the two days she'd had to wait before she could see her went more slowly than she thought possible. She sat in the café on the Southbank wishing she'd suggested somewhere more salubrious than an all-day coffee shop. Hell, she didn't know London well enough. The smell of pastries was making her feel nauseous. A group of young boys dressed in suits huddled over coffee and their phones, scoffing down their chocolate croissants, all talking with their mouths full. She picked up her newspaper. The *Guardian*. She wondered if her daughter would mind if she was reading when she arrived. A newspaper is too cumbersome, she thought. She picked out her book instead. She'd bought it two blocks down from their apartment in New York in a second-hand bookstore, but the density of the language felt inappropriate. She'd worn her grey trouser suit. She had an identical suit in red but red felt wrong somehow. An impudent red, she thought. The tea was already cold when she sipped it. She ordered a coffee instead. That day came back to her. All those years pushing the memory away, turning her back on it until she had become her own defence, but now she embraced the memory as she would her child.

She'd fed Alexandra one last time in the Morris, wrapped her tightly in one of Anne's shawls, placing her in Tom's suitcase, a pile of napkins around her and the hospital blanket. Alexandra had looked at her with such trust that it broke her now to think of it. She had left her on the steps of Bet's house, the suitcase open, watched Alexandra's eyes flicker and close. She ran her fingertips across her fine web of hair, her jaw clenched as she knocked. Then that moment, that split second when she wanted to grab her back. She watched from the shadows as Bet opened the door, still tempted to show herself and beg forgiveness, but Bet dipped down to pick Alexandra up and Kitty ran.

★

Ally trotted down the steps onto the Southbank, strode towards the café. She walked in the shadows, nervous still but unable to slow herself down. This was the moment she'd formed in her mind over the last few days: heartbreaking, a moment of release, forgiveness.

370

Forgiveness, her mother had said, is part of love. But how could Alexandra love this woman? She could only admire her from a distance. Opening the door five minutes before they were due to meet, she didn't expect to see Kitty waiting. Kitty Campbell was petite and poised. An elegant old woman dressed in a grey suit with white hair pinned into a French pleat. Alexandra took a minute to watch, the clatter of tea cups and the steam of the coffee machine around her. She was surprised by the clash of sadness, of rage, of love that ran through her. Up until this moment all she'd felt was a mixture of acceptance and anticipation. But this small tense woman, coiled tight, was the same person who had left her on a doorstep, the same woman who had jumped the waves in Brighton. How on earth had she managed to walk away? Alexandra heard her mother's words: *she had very little choice.* But there would always be a hard knot inside Ally which no amount of reasoning could unravel. And yet she wanted to know Kitty, understand her, make sense of the years of knowing something was missing.

Kitty looked up from her book, turned and after a second, waved.

Alexandra moved towards her.

ACKNOWLEDGEMENTS

I have always believed that a novel is written by more than one person and in my case this is definitely true. I would like to thank my agent Rowan Lawton, who believed in me when I didn't, and whose brilliant editorial eye brought this novel up to scratch. Also to my editor, Harriet Bourton, who shared her expertise with understated generosity. Both of you have taught me so much. To the many people who have kept me sane along the way: my dearest friend Saskia Sarginson for her unwavering support and sharp understanding of the human condition, without whom I would never have finished this novel; Alex, who became chief cook in our busy household; Emma Haynes with her eye for detail; Frances Merivale, who is a wizard when it comes to plot issues; Oliver James, who was born holding a blue pencil; Fiona Mitchell, who read this novel at first draft stage; M. John Harrison, who was a brilliant mentor to me in the early years; Kara Gnodde, who allowed me to write in her home; and Tim and Ken, who hosted many writers' retreats. And finally to my writers group: Dan, Eleanor, Frances, Jacquie, Jayne, Jon, Karen, Samuel and Tim.

Credits

Sara James and Orion Fiction would like to thank everyone at Orion who worked on the publication of *Mothering Sunday* in the UK.

Editorial
Harriet Bourton
Olivia Barber

Copy editor
Francine Brody

Proof reader
Jane Howard

Contracts
Anne Goddard
Paul Bulos
Jake Alderson

Design
Rabab Adams
Joanna Ridley
Nick May

Editorial Management
Charlie Panayiotou
Jane Hughes

Finance
Jasdip Nandra
Afeera Ahmed
Elizabeth Beaumont
Sue Baker

Audio
Paul Stark
Amber Bates

Production
Ruth Sharvell

Marketing
Brittany Sankey

Publicity

Alainna Hadjigeorgiou

Sales

Jen Wilson
Esther Waters
Victoria Laws
Rachael Hum
Ellie Kyrke-Smith
Frances Doyle
Georgina Cutler

Operations

Jo Jacobs
Sharon Willis
Lisa Pryde
Lucy Brem